VEIL of MIST

VEIL of MIST

ARCHIVES OF THE WARDEN
Book Four

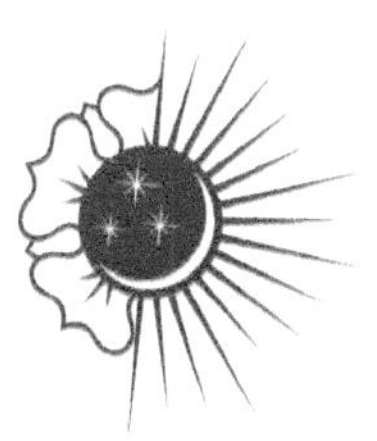

V. K. DIXON

xenia house press

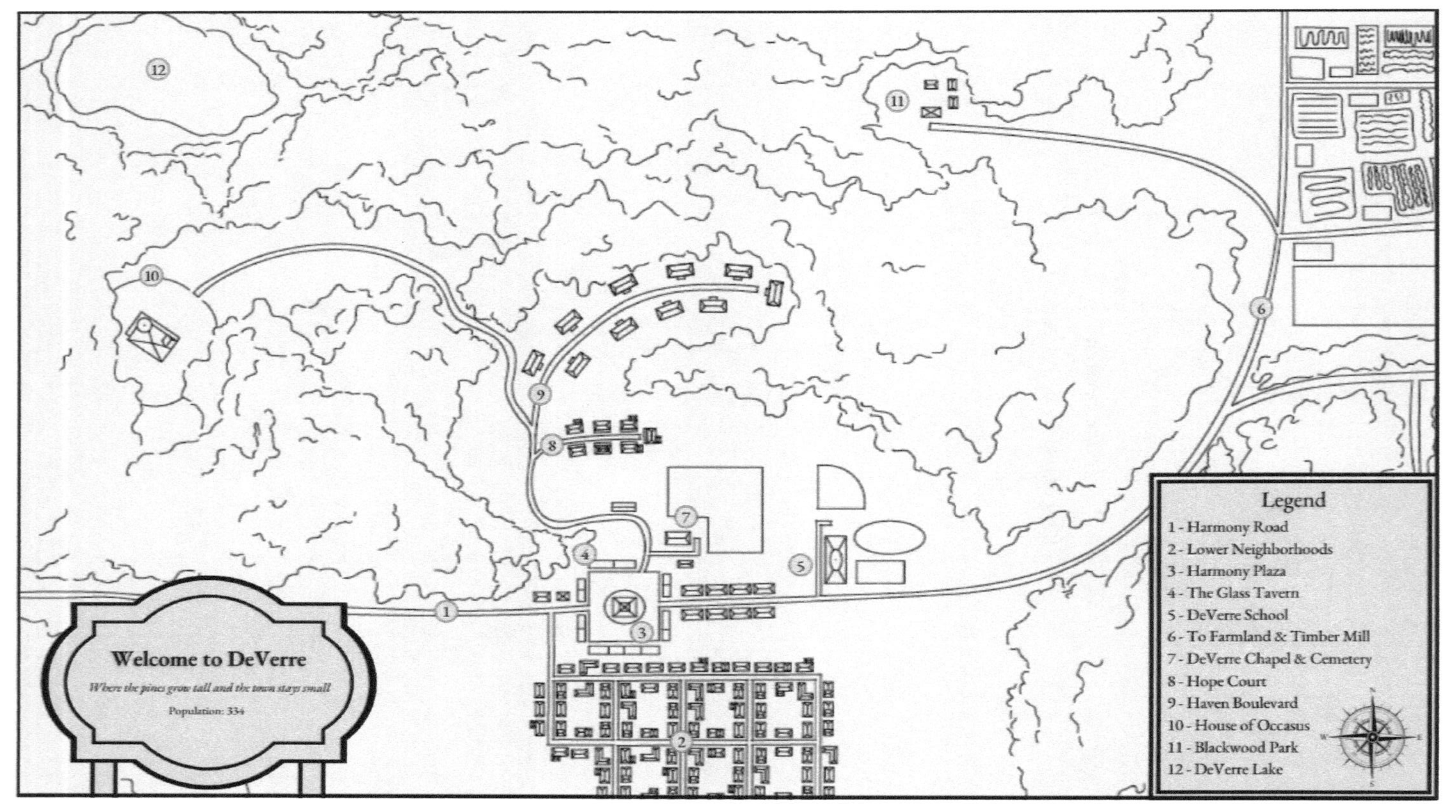

Welcome to DeVerre
Where the pines grow tall and the town stays small
Population: 334
Legend
1 - Harmony Road
2 - Lower Neighborhoods
3 - Harmony Plaza
4 - The Glass Tavern
5 - DeVerre School
6 - To Farmland & Timber Mill
7 - DeVerre Chapel & Cemetery
8 - Hope Court
9 - Haven Boulevard
10 - House of Occasus
11 - Blackwood Park
12 - DeVerre Lake

Table of Contents

Eight years ago . . .

In the small town of Porthaven, Maine, Cait Lewan lived with the stain of her father's rumored curse. After her parents' murders, she and her sisters were brought to Porthaven and placed under protective custody, though young Cait never knew from whom or what they were being protected.

Living as a social outcast, seventeen-year-old Cait feared the rumors that plagued her family history. Tales of witches and demons had besmirched her beloved father's reputation, and now, one of his daughters was said to be the heir to his curse. Worse, Cait was convinced that she was the one the demon chose, haunted as she was by dreams of beasts and a creature that stalked her.

Desmond Simon was the Varon heir and the golden child of Porthaven High. Popular, intelligent, and destined for greatness, he didn't want any of it. Burdened by the weight of responsibility, Desmond acted out, pretending to be rebellious and irreverent when in truth, all he wanted was to live up to the demanding expectations put in place for him. But Desmond had a secret: He was in love with the Lewan girl.

Cultivating a hidden and forbidden friendship, Cait and Desmond would do anything for each other. Even if that included letting go of their dreams of being together.

But when beasts of the spirit world started randomly appearing out of the Veil in Porthaven, Desmond discovered that the rumored Lewan family curse was not as idle of gossip as he thought. He and his father, William, the town mayor and leader of the Warden, learned that the Veil was damaged and producing these beasts on its own—a seemingly impossible feat.

As a member of the Warden, Desmond had always known more about Cait's parents' untimely demise than he let on since, after all, it was a result of their ties to the spirit world.

Cait's father, Owen, was no witch, and he hadn't sold his soul to a demon. He was a Vessel, a Wielder of great power tied to a spirit-being— a creature of unknown power and origin that the Warden was desperate to control—called the Wolf. Porthaven itself had been built to house another Vessel in the Faulk family and their spirit-being, the Leviathan. Upon the instruction of the Raven, Corva—another spirit-being whose prophecies are infallible—the Lewan daughters were brought to Porthaven not for their protection but for the protection of the new Vessel: whichever daughter the Wolf chose.

Worried that Cait's family "curse" might impact her, Desmond worked to find the truth behind the damaged Veil. He uncovered another prophecy from Corva, one his father had hidden from him his entire life. He discovered that the Warden knew of the danger to Cait's father's life and hadn't done anything to stop it. Even more troubling, the prophecy itself put Cait in potential danger, stating, "Our success shall come only at her great sacrifice."

But when Cait's dreams took a turn for the worse with the appearance of a raven who harkened Desmond's death, Desmond realized the truth: Cait was the Wolf's new Vessel.

Desperate to save her from this fate, Desmond returned to the Veil, determined to fix it. Before he could enact his plan, Cait appeared on the Veil's island seemingly out of thin air, just before twelve beasts emerged from the Veil. While Desmond tried to use his powers to send the beasts back into the spirit world, it was Cait who, wielding for the first time in her life, managed to control them, returning them to the ether and sealing the Veil herself. Then she collapsed.

When Desmond returned Cait to her home, she dreamed a new dream. One with the raven, the damaged Veil, and a strange, redheaded woman . . .

Upon an unexpected inheritance, brothers and co-authors Peter and Spencer Collins moved to the small town of DeVerre, Washington, to accept the grand estate of their estranged great-aunt, Diane Larkin, and pursue their lifelong dream of being full-time authors. Along with their inheritance of a new house, two dogs, and the townspeople's suspicions, they found themselves drawn into the mysterious past of their great-aunt and the reason for her move to DeVerre over thirty years ago.

Through the town librarian, Ava Bernard, the brothers learned that the home they'd inherited from Diane—the House of Occasus—was once owned by the principal founding family of DeVerre: the Varons. The old Varon estate was rumored to hold a vault that held the town's greatest secrets. She explained to them that it was for this reason that the townspeople didn't like Diane and remained wary of the brothers.

In their early exploration of the town's history and Diane's decision to make DeVerre her home, the news of a string of animal attacks reached them. Peter became suspicious of the attacks, though Spencer tried to ignore them altogether.

With the help of Diane's closest friend, Cassandra Clement—who, to their surprise, was a young and attractive woman their own age—the brothers discovered that they were not biological Collins as they believed. Their ancestors originated from DeVerre. Diane and her brother, Phillip, the brothers' grandfather, had been born in DeVerre and adopted by the Collins family on less than legal terms. Cassandra taught them about Diane's search for the parents she'd lost and introduced them to the spirit world that the two women had discovered together. A world filled with ghosts, phantoms, and beasts.

One such phantom was Gerard Alarie, whom Cassandra had tethered to their home in exchange for his knowledge about the history of DeVerre.

Together, the trio sought out the truth of the brothers' past and the secrets held in the town. Their pursuit of answers led them to Owen Bernard, a Wielder of the spirit world and agent of the Warden sent to

DeVerre to ensure its safety. Owen taught them about the Warden—an organization dedicated to protecting the spirit world from the machinations of the Druids—and about the Veil hidden within DeVerre—a space where the line between the spirit world and physical world was thinnest.

As a team of four, Peter, Spencer, Cassandra, and Owen discovered the presence of Druids within the town, working to take over the Veil. Their investigation led them to the discovery that Cassandra's cousin, Debbie Mercier, was one of these Druids intent on taking control of the Veil and that the cult had orchestrated the "animal" attacks.

When Debbie attacked the brothers, Cassandra came to their rescue, shattering Debbie's soul with an arc of the spirit world's essence.

In the wake of their battle, Peter, Spencer, and Cassandra worked to figure out their next move. They knew the Druids wouldn't take lightly the damage inflicted on Debbie. But they also knew they were in too deep to back out. They needed to find the truth behind their ancestry and keep the Druids from claiming control of the spirit world.

With Owen's continued help, they worked to find the vault hidden in their home and to uncover the identity of the Druids. They also continued their research on the Warden, the Druids, and the spirit world, hoping to find any information that might give them an edge in protecting the town. While Owen continued to explain more of the Warden's history, he told them of a Warden town—Porthaven, Maine—regarded as a cautionary tale due to a devastating incident eight years prior.

Through weeks of trial and error and a near-death run-in with the Druids, they finally found Occasus's vault and the secrets they were so desperate to uncover. The brothers learned that they were Varons. Their great-grandparents had secretly worked to bring down the Druids, which led to the sacrifice of their lives. They also learned the names of the Druids within DeVerre, arming them with the knowledge they needed to take the cult down and reclaim their rightful inheritance as protectors of the spirit world.

But before they could enact their plan and rid the town of the Druids, the cultists attacked their home, twenty against four. Only through a feat of extreme, unknown power did Cassandra drive the Druids back, saving their lives. Now, the team faces the remaining threat of Druids in their town and the desperate need to earn the townspeople's trust.

However, before they could convince the town of anything, Peter stumbled upon a meeting between Gerard Alarie and Alexander Frossard—the town doctor recently discovered to be the Druid leader. Unable to get away in time, Alexander took Peter captive, leaving Spencer unaware of his brother's plight.

Now, we return to DeVerre, where the brothers must find their way back to each other as reality and prophecy collide . . .

PROLOGUE

Three months ago . . .

Gerard knew what he would find when he walked into the living room an hour ago. He was unprepared for the specifics, but that had been intentional. They'd left him out of the planning, giving him everything he needed to tell the truth when Cassandra inevitably asked.

"Stay out of the house," the Frossard kid had told him over the phone. *"Go to the lake or visit your wife's grave or do whatever it is you phantoms like to do. Just be out of the house that morning."*

Gerard never liked working with Connor Frossard. Not that there was much love lost on either side of the arrangement. It was evident from the start that the Frossard brat didn't like him either. Whether it was due to the family snobbery passed down through the generations or if it had to do with his elevated sense of "morality," Gerard got the distinct impression that Connor thought of him as a lesser man, as though he were petty in his pursuit of vengeance.

Working with Alexander was far superior. Though the father carried the usual pretension of the Frossard bloodline, at least he didn't act like that self-righteous prig of a son he'd raised. Whether he appreciated Gerard's quest or not, Alexander treated him with respect.

However, contact with Alexander was rare, a necessary precaution. The odds of Diane or Cassandra asking questions about Connor weren't high. Especially since he was out of town for medical school. It caused regular frustrations for all parties, going through a middleman. But it would be worth it in the end.

They would give him Franklin, and he'd exact his vengeance.

At the price of Diane Larkin's life.

It was not a cheap cost, no, but ultimately worth paying.

He'd taken Connor's advice; in the bright light of noonday, he'd stood in DeVerre's cemetery. Gerard couldn't feel the summer sun on his skin as he stared down at his wife's grave marker. Nor could he appreciate the gentle breeze that cooled the air. As a phantom, he no longer felt anything external; the senses of taste, smell, and touch were pointless when you were dead.

However, he could feel the rawness in his throat, the nails biting into his palms, and even the heat rising in his face. But anything outside of himself? That was intangible to a dead man.

Unfortunately, the lack of a heartbeat was a minor inconvenience to the organ equated with emotion.

Anger, love, rage, sorrow—Gerard still felt those. And more than anything, he felt lonely.

Staring at the small gravestone, Gerard's fists hung at his sides. Whoever had engraved his wife's name had done so with care. *"In Loving Memory, Kristina Roux-Alarie,"* the headstone read. Sixty-six years of weathering aged the once shiny, light marble. A small gouge from hail or some other natural damage marred the left corner. No flowers or tokens of memory graced the plaque.

His eyes drifted down. Beneath Kristina's name, lay another engraving. One that held Gerard's gaze far longer: *"Baby Alarie, unborn."*

Yes, Gerard could still feel emotion.

He could feel pain—the same pain that had lingered in his chest for nearly seventy years. It was that pain that drove him to walk back into Occasus this afternoon and the same emotion that kept him playacting when Diane complained of stomach cramps over the next hour. It was that pain that made him prepare tea to soothe her nausea when she began to vomit convulsively, knowing it wouldn't do any good.

They hadn't told him how they intended to kill her. Another precaution. But it became clear to him within the first ten minutes of his return—it was poison.

Gerard didn't let himself linger on the thought. He didn't search out the source of the poison or the proof of it. The less evidence—the less information he could offer Cassandra—the easier it would be for him to remain free of suspicion.

As Diane's breathing grew worse, she moved to lie on the couch. Gerard was of little help. That was one of the conditions of being a phantom: He couldn't touch living beings. He couldn't hold her hand or pat her back. The one comfort he could offer the woman was the cool, damp cloths he applied to her forehead. He was as useless—no, more useless than those dogs that followed the woman around like shadows.

It hurt to watch. A different kind of pain than the death of Kristina and their child. But pain all the same.

Four years ago, when Cassandra made Gerard a phantom, he never would have considered betraying her or Diane. Cassandra's offer to help gave Gerard the chance he'd all but despaired of. Together, they would gather proof of Franklin's betrayal, and then he would exact his revenge. Franklin had taken his child from him; Gerard would take Franklin's lineage as well.

Shortly after, it became clear to Gerard that Cassandra would never agree to such a request. No matter what she'd promised when they first struck their bargain, she wouldn't kill someone she thought was innocent.

Gerard should have broken the deal immediately. But it was that loneliness—that damned sense of isolation that came with being dead, being wholly separated from the world—that kept him a phantom.

Watching the world, hearing it but never being able to take part in it, always being kept separate and alone—truly, miserably, devastatingly alone—it was too horrible to go back to.

His weakness kept him working with Cassandra and Diane for all those years. The fear of returning to that solitude. Of becoming nothing and no one once again.

He should have ended it. He should have ignored the pain. But he was too weak.

And then the Frossard boy showed up.

Gerard didn't know how they'd found out about him. But when Cassandra and Diane were out one morning, Connor arrived. He stood on the porch and spoke aloud. *"We know you're here. We know she tethered you. And we know that whatever she's agreed to give you, we can offer more."*

And he'd been right.

Cassandra had offered him proof—a menial sense of justice with no real restitution exacted from Franklin.

The Druids offered Gerard something he never could have imagined.

They offered him Franklin in the flesh.

"That's what you want? Revenge?" Connor had asked, his perfect blue stare scanning Gerard. The curl of the boy's lips revealed his disgust. *"Fine. We can give you that. But we'll give you something better than Franklin's grandchildren."*

"Can you?" Gerard asked with wary reserve.

"Yeah." Connor scowled as though the admittance tasted foul on his tongue. *"Yeah, 'cause we can give you Franklin."*

Gerard narrowed his eyes. *"He's dead."*

The pretentious brat had the nerve to shrug. *"We can fix that."*

Even now Gerard could feel the way his hands had trembled at the thought. *"We can fix that,"* the boy had said, as though it were some mundane task to raise the dead.

"We can fix that."

As though the problem of death was no problem at all.

The words rang in Gerard's head for weeks before he met with the kid again.

"We can fix that."

They could fix the little problem of Franklin being dead. The inevitable question that followed was: Could they reverse the deaths of Gerard's wife and child?

"No," Connor had insisted. *"They aren't ghosts."*

"What do you mean?" Gerard had demanded.

"In order to bring someone back, they have to be a ghost," he'd explained. *"It's a similar process to tethering a phantom. But it's more involved and . . . It really shouldn't be done at all. But we will. Do it, I mean. My dad is willing to bring your brother and you both back to life; then, you can kill him yourself."*

Months passed, but the flame that promise had sparked in Gerard still burned like an inferno.

Now, bright, golden light flowed through the windows of Occasus, the afternoon sun radiant. It tinged everything butter yellow, saturated and rich. A beautiful day for a morbid end.

Diane lay on the red damask couch, her head propped up by one of the woven pillows. Anguis and Nex sat with their long snouts resting on the edge. She'd lost the strength to run her fingers through their wiry fur. Her white hair stuck to her pallid temples, the wrinkles of her aged skin far deeper than usual. Her breath came out in ragged, halting puffs.

"Gerard," she whispered, the singular word splintered.

He took a seat on the coffee table, chin tucked. Guilt clawed at his chest despite the static heart inside his dead body. "I'm here, Di," he murmured. It was a pitiful offering, but it was all he had left. He wouldn't abandon her. He wouldn't cower from what he'd done.

"Would you . . ." She licked her lips, chapped and brittle from her hours of sickness. "Call . . . Cassandra for . . . for me? I want her . . . to know—"

Her words were cut off by a violent cough that turned into a gag.

Gerard snarled inwardly. He'd agreed to her death, but he hadn't agreed to this torture. Whatever poison they'd given her, it was cruel.

Unable to aid in any way, Gerard waited for Diane to lay back once more, her focus entirely on breathing through the pain.

"I have to tell you something, Di," he murmured, gaze locked on her agonized expression. This was his penance, he decided, watching the choice he'd made—watching his friend die.

Her eyes, usually so blue and bright, turned to him, cloudy with tears of agony.

Gerard held that awful gaze. "When I was alive, I knew your mother," he told her. "And I knew you."

A gasp cut through the jagged breathing. "Why didn't . . . you tell me . . . before?"

"If I gave you everything that first day, you wouldn't have needed me. I couldn't have lied to Cassandra, but as she let you do the asking, it was never a problem. But I am very sorry, Diane. I wish it didn't have to be this way."

"What way?" she breathed.

"You're dying." He glanced at the clock. They'd not given him an exact timeline, but they'd told him when he could return. "I imagine you'll be dead shortly. But you deserve the truth first. I knew you and your mother. She was murdered by her own father and brothers, all because she married the wrong man."

A single tear broke from the corner of Diane's eyes. It streaked across her pale temple and into her hairline like a shooting star. There for a mere second, then gone forever. "Why?" she asked, voice broken from pain, both physical and emotional. "How do you—?"

Gerard leaned forward, urgency in his voice. "You're running out of time, Diane. Let me finish my story."

She blinked, and another tear raced across her skin. She looked so very much like her mother, even now in her old age. Sharp, intelligent eyes. Narrow, oval-shaped face. Expressive, distinctive features.

"I didn't know at first," he promised. "I didn't even realize who you were until they told me. But when I asked, they gave me the truth. It was part of the deal. I wouldn't betray you without giving you this."

It was a pitiful recompense but a redemption of a sort Gerard liked to think.

"Your mother was Seraphine Frossard," he told her. "She married Michael Varon, and they tried to take down her family. Why, I'm not sure. Something to do with the spirit world. But clearly, her family wasn't supportive. So they killed Seraphine and Michael, and they sent you and your brother away."

The tears were flowing openly now. Diane didn't say a word, only held his stare.

"They don't have my allegiance," Gerard said. "Whoever they are, whatever they want, I don't care. But they can do what neither you nor Cassandra can. They can give me *true* justice."

"Whoever . . . killed your wife . . . is dead."

"For now," Gerard confirmed. "But they can fix that."

Diane's breathing grew rapid. It sounded like ripping paper. "Cassandra?"

"She'll live. It's part of the deal."

There was a jagged sigh of relief. Then her eyes locked on his again. "My mother?"

"Seraphine."

"She . . . wanted me?"

The tearing pain of guilt ripped up his chest and into his throat. "Yes, Diane, she did."

"My father?"

"Michael wanted you too. But they were like me—too focused on justice to let life get in the way. And it got them killed, same as me."

Diane's eyes fluttered. She was fighting to hold on, he knew. Fighting for all she was worth. But it wouldn't last. Not long.

"I'm glad you know now, Diane," he whispered. "Even if it was for a moment. You deserved to know."

Her chest rose and fell in a slow, painful-looking intake and exhale.

Another breath, slower still.

A breath in.

A breath out.

And her body stilled.

Gerard stared at her, the dogs whimpering. "My apologies, boys," he murmured, reaching out just to be sure.

With a gentle, hesitant touch, Gerard slipped his fingers under the still-warm hand of Diane Larkin. But instead of passing through, he felt the first brush of flesh against his own in sixty-six years.

"She's gone."

CHAPTER ONE

Spencer

"**D**id you get my scarf from the hook inside?"

Spencer looked over at Peter. He and his brother were both dressed in puffy coats, thick gloves, and beanie hats. Whereas Cassandra, standing at Spencer's side, wore only her moto jacket and a knitted black scarf looped around her neck.

Spencer scanned his memories of that morning. "I didn't think you were wearing a scarf," he said.

"It's freakin' cold out here, man," Peter countered. "Of course, I had a scarf."

Cassandra smirked. "Says the guy who walked outside without a coat on fifteen minutes ago."

Peter tossed her a frown. "I was in a rush."

"Well, go get it then," Spencer said as they rounded the corner toward the front of the chapel. Only the Jeep remained in the parking lot, its dark green mimicking the pines hidden under the heavy snowfall.

Peter motioned to the snow-filled parking lot. "I can't get in. Everyone's gone."

"The church is never locked," Spencer said.

"Oh. Really?" With a shrug, Peter broke away. "Be right back, then."

"We'll be in the Jeep," Spencer called.

"Cool," Peter said over his shoulder. "See you in a sec."

As his brother headed for the large wooden doors of DeVerre Chapel, Spencer turned back to Cassandra. The chilly winter breeze brushed wisps of her wavy dark hair around her cheeks, turning a soft pink in the cold. In her all-black ensemble, she was a shadow amongst the snow that covered DeVerre. And, as his eyes met hers, Spencer found his head beginning to grow fuzzy at the warmth that glowed back at him from the hazel depths of her direct stare.

Spencer was beginning to recognize that look of Cassandra's. He didn't see it often—the sparkle of affection that lit up the flecks of jade within. But he found with amazement that it was increasingly in her gaze when she turned his way.

Weak in the knees and hesitant to speak, Spencer gestured for Cassandra to lead the way to the Jeep. Their boots crunched across the lot. She started for the back passenger door—her usual seat—but Spencer found himself talking before he even realized why. "You should sit up front," he said, surprised that his voice came out steady.

Cassandra eyed him. "Pete's not gonna be that long."

Spencer opened his door. "He can sit in the back."

With humored apprehension, Cassandra moved for the front.

Spencer started the Jeep, immediately turning on the heat to defrost the windshield. Hot air hissed out of the ventilation. He shivered, rubbing his gloved hands together. He'd thought he could manage the Washingtonian winters with little problem. But the climate was far more frigid and permeating than the weather of their old home in Virginia.

Fighting off an onslaught of subsequent shivers, Spencer passed Cassandra a shy grin to fill the silence stretching between them. A little snort of laughter came from her. She crossed her arms lightly, relaxing back into the Jeep's tan cloth seat. "You know," she began, one of her sharply arched eyebrows lifting as she appraised him. "That was an especially thoughtful thing you did back there."

Spencer furrowed his brow, and Cassandra tipped her chin toward the graveyard behind the chapel. "Oh," he said, unable to help his smile's growth.

Upon his suggestion, they'd visited Seraphine Frossard-Varon's grave—their newly-discovered great-grandmother. There, he'd given Cassandra a tiny picture frame, a drawing of baby Diane inside, that he'd found in the vault of their home. He'd offered it as a token to honor Diane's mother's memory. Tears of mingling appreciation and joy had sprung to Cassandra's eyes as she set the little frame on the stone in remembrance.

"Yeah, I mean, I—I just thought it was the right thing to do," he said.

"Mm," Cassandra murmured, scanning him as though she knew his intentions weren't that innocent.

And while Spencer's original idea to visit their great-grandparents' resting places *had* been that innocent, finding that drawing of baby Diane on Michael Varon's desk gave him the additional consideration of how much Cassandra would like it. Then he'd thought about how appreciative she'd be when he showed it to her. The plan to take it to Seraphine's grave was heavily influenced by how happy it would make Cassandra.

Spencer stared out the windshield to hide his scheming thoughts. The ice receded under the torrent of heat blasting against the glass, slowly dissolving the fractal spines of frost that laced across its surface. He scanned the white-washed chapel exterior and the dark wooden doors, anticipating Peter's exit.

"I know you didn't know her," Cassandra said, her raspy voice softer than usual, "but Diane would have been proud of you. Of both of you."

Drawn back to hold her dark gaze, Spencer felt his throat dry up. "Thanks," he said. "I wish we could have met her."

"Me too," she muttered, a regretful smile on her lips.

"I've been wondering, though: Do you think there's any chance that Diane is out there? You know, as a ghost."

"No," Cassandra replied immediately.

"You're sure?" Though she'd sounded confident, Spencer couldn't help but press the idea. "If she was . . . I just—I wish we could tell her. About her parents."

"She knows."

Spencer blinked at her in shock. "What?"

Cassandra gave him a pointed look. "If she's gone—which I'm sure she is—then she's in Heaven, and she knows. She'd know everything now."

"Right." Spencer turned to look at the backs of his gloved hands. "I guess . . . I guess that's good."

She set her hand on his forearm, giving it a gentle squeeze. "I wish she could have been here too."

Spencer's eyes were locked on her fingers, thumb now brushing against his coat sleeve. Her touch worked through the many layers of his clothing to his skin. Holding his breath, he raised his eyes to meet hers. There it was again—that soft and nearly affectionate sparkle. The one that made him grateful he was sitting down.

Clearing his throat, Spencer managed to scrape out, "I wonder what's taking Pete so long." The weight of Cassandra's hand resting on his arm caused his chest to strain with anticipation.

"That's a good question," she murmured, leaning forward in her seat.

Spencer could have sworn that her chin angled in his direction, and the blood drained from his face.

The instinct of flight kicked in. "We should check on him," he said, the words tumbling out as he fumbled for the keys, moving from her touch. He twisted the keys free, only to realize he should have left the Jeep running. But it was too late now.

Refusing to look back at Cassandra—unsure of what reaction he might find in her expression—Spencer pushed open the Jeep's door, leaping out into the snow. The biting air tingled against his nose and cheeks, a relief from the stifling warmth that had crawled up his chest, around his collar, and onto his neck. He trudged through the snow toward the chapel, sure that his entire face had turned red.

What had just happened? Spencer wasn't highly versed in romantic relationships or even in the early stages of encouraging flirtation, but either his overactive imagination was playing tricks on him, or Cassandra had just implicitly invited him to kiss her.

Immediate regret pressed against Spencer's ribcage. He should have kissed her. He'd wanted to for long enough. And he wasn't sure he'd have the courage to do it even *if* she offered again.

But then, what if he'd read the situation wrong? Cassandra was naturally a more physically affectionate person. She sat and stood close to him and Peter, brushing their arms, giving them friendly pats of encouragement on their backs, or even a slap on their chest when they were overly annoying. Touch was far more platonic for Cassandra than either of them.

No, Spencer had made the right decision by getting out of there. He couldn't trust himself to read Cassandra on a good day. It was a joke, thinking that he could correctly interpret her in the haze of his . . . well, whatever this feeling of attachment and desire was that filled his chest.

Spencer reached for the cold, snow-coated handle of the chapel door. Cassandra stepped to his side as he pulled it open, and they entered the dark building. He frowned as he took in the room.

Shadows clung to the corners of the chapel, the arched windows emitting the dimmest light of the cloudy day. The entryway, where he'd expected to find Peter, was empty, and there was no movement amongst the wooden pews farther ahead. The sanctuary was completely still, returned to its peaceful state after the service.

"Pete?" he called.

He waited, sure his brother would pop his head of wild brown hair around the corner, his signature grin on his lips.

There was no movement. And Peter didn't respond.

Turning to his left, Spencer moved for the reverend's office, the door ajar. He pushed it open, thinking that Peter must have taken it upon himself to rummage about for information. But Peter wasn't there either. The office was as empty and untouched as the rest of the chapel.

Frowning, Spencer turned back to Cassandra. "Did you see Pete walk out?" he asked.

Cassandra stood at the office's threshold, lips parted and eyebrows pulled together in confusion as she scanned the room. But she didn't answer.

"Cass," Spencer prompted, and her eyes flashed to his face.

"Sorry, I—I thought. . . ." She shook her head, a shadow crossing her expression. "No, I didn't see him."

The chill of dread beaded at the base of Spencer's skull, causing him to shiver as it trickled down his spine and across his scalp. "Pete?" he called again, moving back to the sanctuary.

The chapel wasn't large. Aside from the reverend's office, the sound booth, and the bathrooms, there was nowhere to hide. Spencer glanced into the production alcove where Owen usually ran the sound and PowerPoint for the services. The computer screen was blank and the soundboard buttons unlit. No Peter. He checked the bathrooms, but Peter wasn't there either.

"Pete," Spencer said his brother's name as a demand now. He heard his tone getting thicker—almost angry. It sounded desperate to his own ears.

Yet Spencer didn't feel desperate. He felt annoyed. His jaw was clenched, and he glared at every inch of the church. The dark corners mocked his resolve, reminding him of the beasts that the Druids had summoned in Occasus last night. His imagination taunted him with suggestions of shadowy creatures flitting from pew to pew, sneaking up to attack.

Spencer yanked the beanie off his head. "Peter, if you're playing some stupid game, I swear to God, I'll kill you," he almost yelled.

"Spencer—" Cassandra's voice cut through his anger and drew him to look back at her.

In the shadows of the snowy day and the dark building, Cassandra's sharp features appeared even more striking—like chiseled marble, he thought. She stood with her arms hanging limply as her dark eyes flickered from his face to the room and back. She looked haunted and nervous, like the memories of the demons they'd fought the night before plagued her the same as Spencer.

"Where's my brother?" Spencer found himself demanding, though he knew she didn't have the answer.

Cassandra's mouth worked open and closed a handful of times before she found a reply. "He could be with Anna," she offered.

"He didn't leave."

"Maybe he did." She took a cautious step in his direction. "Maybe we just didn't see him."

"Cass," Spencer said her name as though it were a curse.

Her eyes lost their previous uncertainty and gazed intently at him, a new determination to the set of her mouth. "I'm calling Anna," she said, not waiting for his approval as she pulled her phone out of her pocket.

Spencer shook his head. "He would have told us."

Cassandra ignored him, holding the phone up to her ear. "Hey, Anna, I—uh, I just wanted to check . . . have you heard from Peter? Or seen him in the last, um . . . ten minutes?" There was a short pause before Cassandra pursed her lips. "No, uh—no, everything's . . ." She stopped, then met Spencer's eyes.

"We can't find Peter," she said.

Whatever else Cassandra said to Anna after that, Spencer didn't hear. A roaring filled his ears, her words repeating over and over.

They couldn't find Peter.

The coolness of fear spread, covering Spencer's skin in gooseflesh. His hands began to tremble, and he turned to clasp the pew beside him in a white-knuckled grip.

They couldn't find Peter.

Breathing grew difficult. His chest constricted, and his mind began to cloud. The thought that he might pass out surfaced. But he had one last resort before he would lose himself completely.

Spencer dug in his coat pocket. His hands shook so badly that it took him twice the amount of time it should have to pull out his phone, find Peter's number, and dial it. The low rumble of a dial tone trilled in his ear. Once . . . twice . . . so many times that Spencer lost count.

His brother's voice came through in its playful, throaty tone: "This is Peter. If you've reached this message, it means that I either don't care to answer right now or that I'm otherwise indisposed." A light chuckle accompanied his voice. "Leave a message at the tone, and I'll probably get back to you." *Beep.*

Several seconds of silence stretched as Spencer glared at the cross at the back of the sanctuary. He worked to steady his breathing, then said into the phone, "Peter." His voice came out flat and heavy. "If you don't give me a call back right now . . . I'm going to assume you're dead. Do you understand that? If I don't hear from you, then I have no other choice, okay? And if you're dead. . . ."

Stinging tears came to the corners of Spencer's eyes, blurring his vision as he glared at the wooden cross. His insides felt as though they'd been carved out, his body left empty and purposeless. Because if Peter was dead, he wanted to be dead too.

"Call me," Spencer demanded one last time, then hung up. He kept the phone in his hand with a futile hope that it might ring. He needed it to vibrate and flash Peter's face on the caller ID.

Steeling himself, Spencer continued to glare at the cross. *He's not allowed to be dead,* he told it. *Do you understand? You can't have him yet.*

A hand landed on Spencer's arm. He jumped, whipping around to find Cassandra there. She backed away, hand still raised from where she'd touched him. Her lips were parted in worry, her eyes watching him like he was a predator disturbed from its slumber.

"Spencer," she whispered, her velvety voice attempting to soothe him. He determined not to let it. "I called Tom."

The name of the marshal caused Spencer to furrow his brow. "Why?"

"Because we need him," she replied as though it should be obvious.

Spencer slipped his phone back into his pocket. It wasn't going to ring. "What is he gonna do?" he asked, the deadpan tone of his voice striking him as far too dispassionate for the circumstance.

Cassandra glared, confused by this version of him. "He's gonna help us find Peter."

"Yeah? How?" Spencer demanded. "There's nothing here, in case you haven't noticed. This place is empty. What is he going to find that we haven't?"

Mouth still ajar, Cassandra stared at him in incredulous silence.

But Spencer didn't care if she thought he was being unreasonable. His brother had disappeared—his greatest fear was finally coming to life; he was allowed to be irrational.

Turning away from her, Spencer scanned the chapel with a sweep of his eyes. The shadows taunted him but remained unmoving. Snow clung to the ironwork of the windows, a chill seeping into the sanctuary from their thin panes. And the hollowness of Spencer's body only seemed to increase as his own words sank in: DeVerre Chapel was empty.

Spencer frowned. "There's nothing here," he murmured, stepping away from the pew. He drifted to the coat hooks that lined the back wall. They were as empty as the rest of the church. No winter garments had been left behind in the wake of the cold morning.

Not even Peter's scarf.

Spencer gaped at the empty hooks. "He's not dead," he whispered, reassuring himself.

"What?" Cassandra said.

Spencer turned back to her, a barely palpable hint of hope spreading through his gut. "Peter's scarf isn't here," he explained. "And neither is his body. If a Druid killed him, they would have left him here, right? To send one of their messages. But he's not here. And there's no sign of a struggle either. There's *nothing* here."

Cassandra stared at the room around them, understanding coming to her too. "They took him," she concluded.

Spencer asked the only question he had left. "But why?"

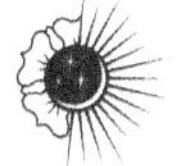

CHAPTER TWO

Owen

A twinge of pain shot through Owen's neck, waking him. His eyes were heavy, and his mouth was dry as he slowly came to consciousness. Confusion hit him first. Why was it so bright? Why did his pillow smell like dogs and dust? And why wasn't Ava beside him?

Then his memory returned.

He wasn't in his home. He was in Occasus, staying with the Collins brothers and Cassandra Clement. They'd offered him the spare bedroom at the back of the house because Ava . . .

The thought brought Owen back to full consciousness.

Ava.

Owen jolted upright. He stared around Occasus's living room. Through the large windows, he caught sight of the pale gray sky. Snow drifted lethargically to the ground, a thick layer already blanketing the white earth.

Owen removed the throw blanket someone had draped over his body in his sleep. The house was silent as he scanned the living room. He sat on one of the two red couches that flanked the cold fireplace. Books were scattered across the coffee table—novels and nonfiction alike—in a haphazard fashion. A couple had fallen on the floor, their binding open and pages ruffled.

Through the French doors that always stood open, he checked the office. Built-in bookshelves, the partner desk, and another barren fireplace. But no Spencer.

Owen swung his legs over the side of the couch. "Peter?" he called. Standing, he looked at the clock on the mantel. It was late enough that both brothers *and* Cassandra should be up.

"Spencer?"

No reply.

"Cassandra?"

Owen moved through the office to the dining room. But Cassandra wasn't seated at the far end, nose in her Bible as was her routine in the morning. In fact, the table sat askew, a couple of chairs toppled. The sideboard was pulled away from the wall, and one of its lamps had been shattered across the wooden floor.

A small seed of panic rose in Owen's stomach. What had happened last night? They'd been fighting the Druids for . . . God only knew how long, he realized. Despite all his training through the years, he'd never been prepared for *that*.

Memories of beasts lunging for them, slicing the air with their horrifying claws, and snapping with their gargantuan maws bled into the back of his mind. Shadows and fear. Druids and death.

A singular memory leaped to the forefront, and Owen's hands flew to his gut.

The attack had come from behind—a wendigo, stabbing with its huge, razor-sharp claws into his back and straight through his stomach.

Making short work of the buttons on his torn shirt, Owen pressed a hand against the flesh there. No marks, no damage, no sign that the wendigo had struck him at all. But he could feel it—like the wound had branded him internally.

Rebuttoning his shirt, Owen moved through the bottom floor of Occasus. He'd been healed somehow. The wendigo's attack preceded his final memory of the night: hitting the gravel as he blacked out. So how had he gotten back into Occasus? Who had healed him? It must have been either the brothers or Cassandra. He hadn't taught them healing yet, but they must have figured it out. How had they survived?

Likely, the trio had gone up to the vault, but he didn't feel much like running up three flights of stairs when his head still spun from the haze of his recovery.

"Gerard?" Owen called, hoping the phantom would deign to offer assistance.

The phantom didn't appear.

Owen sighed, moving for the front staircase. He'd have to check for himself. Even if they weren't in the vault—

The thought crashed to a halt as Owen remembered something even more important.

Ava had been up there, waiting with Anna.

His wife was in the vault.

His wife, the woman carrying his child.

A blend of joy and irritation pricked Owen's heart. She'd kept it from him for three months. And even knowing it, she'd thrown him out and refused to take him back.

Owen set his foot on the first step when a sudden *thump* from outside caught his attention. He paused, hand on the banister, gaze flying to the front window next to the coat closet.

Out on the snow-covered lawn of Occasus, a white van loitered. Three men stood at the back of the vehicle. Owen recognized them immediately: Marshal Tom Garnier, his deputy, Hunter Durand, and the mortician, Gabe Chapelle.

Another *thump* resounded as Gabe shut the second door on the back of the van.

As the men spoke, Owen scanned the grounds of Occasus. Where they had fought for their lives hours ago, now pure white blanketed the grass and gravel drive. Anguis and Nex pranced through the powder, nipping playfully at one another as though it was the greatest day of their lives. And there, in front of the house, only five cars remained: Owen's sedan, Cassandra's truck, the two police cars, and the mortician's van.

The missing Jeep wasn't the only vehicle that caught his notice. Ava's hatchback was gone as well.

So they weren't in the vault.

Owen moved for the front door. He had to remind himself to unlock it, not used to the city precautions still ingrained in the brothers. The cold winter air puffed into the foyer, reminding him to grab his jacket from the closet before stepping onto the porch. His breath came out in a fog. The far corner of the porch rail was splintered, and the swing to his right hung from only one chain.

Gabe's white van had already begun its retreat back toward DeVerre's center. Both Tom and Hunter turned, spotting Owen. The deputy tossed a wave before getting in his cruiser and departing.

"Morning," Tom called, nearing the porch. Snowflakes sprinkled the shoulders of his thick brown coat. "You look alive."

Owen felt his brow lift. "Was that in question?"

"Not really," the marshal admitted. "When Ava left this morning, I knew there was no danger of that."

His stomach twisted at the thought of his wife. "Where are they?"

"At church."

The statement struck Owen as ridiculous. "Why?"

"I told them to go," Tom explained. "Time's coming that we tell everyone the truth. And it's best for the people of DeVerre to see them as the good guys."

The understanding did little to ease his discomfort. "The service should be over."

"They should be back anytime," Tom confirmed.

Both men looked through the gates of Occasus as though expecting the Jeep to come cresting over the small hill the estate sat on. Owen knew that Ava wouldn't be with them. It was Anna's birthday. She would go home and prepare for the party she'd been planning the last several weeks. Even if a party sounded absurd to the rest of the world after last night, Ava wouldn't let anything stand in the way of celebrating her sister.

Tom turned back to Owen. "Listen, I want to stay, but I've got a lot on my plate," the marshal said with a heavy sigh. "I'll try to come back this evening. Then maybe we can figure out our next step. But for now, I've got fourteen dead Druids, and Robert's still missing."

"Actually," Owen began, "I have some information about that."

If Tom was surprised to hear this admission, he didn't show it. He stood impassively, his shoulders relaxed, and his head cocked lazily to the side. "Do you?"

"You suspected?" Owen noted.

"The Collins brothers aren't very good at lying," Tom remarked. A half-grin tugged at the side of his mouth. "When I spoke with Spencer two days ago, I could hear it in his voice—there was something he wasn't telling me."

"And you didn't confront him about it?"

"I had no reason to."

"It's your job," Owen replied indignantly. He couldn't understand why the people around him were so accepting of morally gray choices.

Tom didn't take offense at the charge. "True," he said. "But it's also my job to protect this town. And as I'm convinced that you all are the best means of doing that, I'm willing to accept some ignorance in matters that should be kept strictly off the record."

"So, you don't care to know that Robert was a Druid?" Owen asked.

"And that he was killed by his own people? Or that they dropped him off—"

Tom held up a hand. "Stop, Owen," he ordered. "If I know the truth, then I have to *do* something about it."

Owen stared back at him, incredulous. "You're seriously going to let a man's murder go unanswered?"

"Not at all. If the man was murdered by the Druids, then the crime will get its answer once we put an end to them."

"That seems like a loophole."

"Sometimes you need loopholes."

"I don't like being an accomplice," Owen said.

Something like cynicism twisted Tom's expression. "It's a bit late for that," he said. "For all of us."

Owen raised his chin, appraising the marshal.

"Whatever happens," Tom continued, "whether or not we save this town, we're all going to have to do some things that we never would have considered weeks ago. But it's what must be done. Fourteen people died last night—that's a truth we can't escape. How many of them did you kill?"

An inexplicable guilt filled Owen. "None of them," he admitted.

Tom's brown eyes grew hard. "What?"

"I didn't kill any of them," he said, noting for himself the exception of Rene Mercier's death. He'd seen Cassandra shatter her soul, leaving her to live as a hollow shell of herself. Unwilling to allow someone to survive in that state, he'd killed her body. Something between a mercy killing and a simple release of the woman's spirit.

"You mean to tell me," the marshal stepped up to the bottom of the porch stairs, a tremor of fury in his voice, "that you let those brothers and that young woman kill fourteen people while you stood by and did nothing?"

"I kept the beasts at bay."

"You let them kill," Tom spat, "but you wouldn't do it yourself?"

Owen heard the accusation. He accepted the weight of it. "Yes."

He knew it was wrong. Just by fighting beside them, he was as involved as anyone. But when he came face to face with the men and women that he'd lived with for the past decade, the people he attended church with, the parents whose children he taught in the school . . . He couldn't do it.

He couldn't take their lives.

And he feared what that choice would cost him in the end.

A sharp trill cut through the air, and they both jumped. Tom swore under his breath, pulling his cell from his coat pocket. His brow furrowed as he stared at the caller ID. His dark eyes flickered to Owen's face as he lifted the phone to his ear. "Hello?" There was hardly a second's pause before he exclaimed, "What?"

The call lasted thirty seconds with evident rapid-fire explanation on the other side of the line. Tom kept affirming the caller, assuring that he would be there immediately. There was no doubt the two were speaking over one another.

Tom hung up, a haunted look in his eyes. "That was Cassandra," he explained. "Peter's missing."

Owen's heart sank. "Missing?"

"He—I don't know. He went into the church by himself after service, and when Spencer and Cassandra went to find him, he just . . . wasn't there."

Panic lanced through Owen's chest. "Did they see anything? Do they have any idea—?"

"No." Tom cut him off, backing away from the porch. "I have to go. They're still at the church, and I promised them I'd help. Anna and Ava are already on their way. Are you coming too?"

Owen took one step forward to join but froze. What would be the point in all of them congregating within the church to search for Peter? What good could Owen do there? With the marshal, Spencer—who would undoubtedly go to the ends of the Earth for his brother—and the three women there to do the work, Owen would just be another body, another voice, cluttering up the process.

"I'll stay here," Owen said, waving Tom off as the marshal reached his car. "If you find anything or need anything, call me. But for now, I'll be more useful here."

Tom didn't hesitate. He slipped into his cruiser and took off across the snowy gravel drive away from Occasus.

Owen lingered on the porch, letting the cold seep into his bones.

This was dangerous territory. The Druids were getting more aggressive. More threatening.

But it was a good sign, wasn't it? It meant they were getting close. It meant the Druids were getting desperate.

Turning on his heel, Owen reentered Occasus. He resumed his original path to the vault, retrieving his phone from his pocket. He'd promised to make this call days ago. He knew it was necessary then but hadn't been able to bring himself to *do* it yet.

As he turned the corner to the second flight of stairs, Owen put the phone to his ear. The *whir* of the ring grated in his ear only twice before the call connected, and the man on the other end answered.

"Well, if it isn't the professor," the deep voice rang through, loud and clear, blended with the background noise of children.

Owen's gut twisted. That was the exact reason he'd put off this call. But that nickname, "Professor," reset his focus. Peter had called Owen that not two weeks ago.

If they were going to save Peter—if they were going to save DeVerre—they needed this man.

"Hey, Silas," Owen greeted, "hope I'm not interrupting."

"No, the girls just had swim practice today," Silas replied. "I've got the pleasure of watching from the sidelines. Do you have any idea how hilarious it is watching five and seven-year-olds attempt the backstroke?"

"Can't say that I do," he said. The cheering and joyful cries in the background accompanied a mental picture of the scene. He could practically see Silas sitting on the bleachers while his two daughters—Ellie and Tara—splashed about in a pool with their peers.

Silas chuckled. "How's life, man?"

"Life is . . ." Owen grimaced, walking through the hall on the third floor to the spare room. "Actually, that's why I'm calling."

"Really?" Silas quipped. "It's not to catch up? I'm hurt."

The jibe held no bite or disappointment. Silas and Owen had been friends since high school. Silas was four years older than Owen, and he'd become somewhat of a mentor in the early days. As they got older, they became close. And though phone calls were infrequent, they kept up regularly through emails and social media.

"Yeah, well, I think you'll find this particular request intriguing," Owen said.

"Oh, yeah? What've you got for me?"

Setting his hand on the latch of the vault, Owen opened the door. "I've found some family of yours in DeVerre," he explained. "And they need your help."

CHAPTER THREE

Cassandra

Cassandra couldn't shake the prickle of familiarity that clung to her mind. From the moment they'd walked into the chapel, a dull thrum filled her head like an alert, tingling at the base of her neck. She tried to ignore it in exchange for paying attention to their search. But it lingered, and she couldn't figure out what it was or where it came from.

When Anna and Ava had arrived, they'd done a full, secondary search of DeVerre Chapel. While they knew they wouldn't find Peter suddenly standing in one of the rooms, they wondered if there was a hidden room or vault on the premises. Spencer spent the entire time in the reverend's office, shuffling through every object on the desk, bookshelves, and cabinets.

Tom wore a look of concern when he walked in to find Spencer in the middle of his search. Cassandra figured the marshal was worried about obtaining a warrant. Instead of saying anything, he left Spencer to his devices and turned to help the women in a third scan of the building.

Now, they were back in the foyer, Spencer leaning against the office doorframe. Tension held his shoulders taut despite the frightening indifference his expression displayed. Cassandra could feel his anger from across the room. It was a low, roiling thing. Thick in the air and prone to exploding. She feared what would happen when it finally reached its critical mass.

Anna and Ava stood close together. The younger Lambert sister wore a nervous frown, nibbling on her bottom lip. Ava's ever-stoic demeanor hadn't changed. Tom wore his concern on his sleeve. His thick eyebrows hung heavily over his deep-set gaze, his fingers constantly running over his mustache.

The marshal's eyes darted to Spencer before speaking to Cassandra. "You're sure he didn't just go off on his own? To pursue a lead or something?" he asked.

Though it was a course of action that Peter would take, it held no ring of truth.

While Cassandra shook her head, Spencer glared at him. "He's not answering his phone," he said sharply. "He came back inside to get his scarf, and within five minutes, he disappeared without a trace."

Tom scanned the empty coat hooks in thought.

"How could he just vanish?" Anna asked. In her robin's egg-blue coat, she looked like a beacon of brightness in the dark chapel.

Ava turned to Tom. "Did Owen say anything before you left?" she asked. "About disappearances connected with the spirit world?"

"No," Tom said apologetically. "He didn't say much, actually, and I didn't think to ask."

"What if," Anna offered, a weak, hopeful tilt to her tone, "Peter wasn't taken? Maybe he just discovered another vault or something."

Cassandra watched Spencer as he shifted from foot to foot, hands fisted at his sides. He'd unzipped his coat, his denim jacket peeking out from beneath. His shaggy brown hair clumped together from how often he'd run his fingers through it. It was a behavioral tic she'd relegated to Peter. But in his panic, Spencer had adopted his brother's habit.

Cassandra swallowed past the dryness in her throat. "Should we do another search, specifically looking for a vault?"

"We couldn't find it," Spencer murmured. "Even if there is one here, Peter wouldn't have found it either."

"Why not?" Tom asked.

"Vaults can only be seen by their owners until the owner invites someone inside," Spencer explained. "Peter wouldn't have stumbled upon one randomly. He would have had to be invited in."

Tom brushed his mustache in thought again. "Sam would own the chapel's vault. We could talk to him."

"He wouldn't necessarily be the owner," Ava countered. "The township of DeVerre owns the chapel grounds, not the Chapelles. I don't know if property ownership plays a role in the creation of a vault, but technically, any resident of DeVerre *could* have created a vault on the church property."

"Maybe even a Varon?" Cassandra offered.

"Not possible," Spencer cut in, fingers tapping an erratic rhythm on his thigh. "Peter would have shown up by now if he'd found another vault we owned. And since he hasn't, it's clear someone took him. But Tom had the right idea. We need to talk to Sam."

Tom nodded in agreement, then his brow furrowed. "Wait . . . why? If we don't believe there's a vault here, why would Sam know anything?"

"Peter came back in here, and now he's gone," Spencer said, almost like he was accusing Tom of being an accomplice. "Even if Sam wasn't here when Peter was taken, he'll likely know who was."

Tom hesitated. Sam was his best friend. Of course, he would want to keep him out of the suspect pool. But Spencer was right. There was a chance that—involved or not—Sam would have information.

Ava didn't share the marshal's reservations. "It couldn't hurt to pay him a visit."

"Sam's not—" Tom sucked in an irritated breath before starting again. "He *can't* be involved in this. He would no more take your brother than he would attack his daughter and Brendan with a hellhound."

The debate for the reverend's innocence had merit.

And it sparked a thought in Cassandra's mind. "Why *was* his daughter and Brendan attacked?" she asked.

They all remained silent as the question lingered.

"Has no one asked that?" she pressed. "If Sam isn't a Druid—which admittedly seems unlikely," she added when Tom opened his mouth to object, "then how *is* he involved? Because it has to be in some manner. Otherwise, why attack his daughter?"

"The hellhound killed Brendan," Spencer reminded her. "It would have been after him."

Cassandra conceded the point. "Still . . . it makes you wonder."

Spencer gave her a nod, though he didn't meet her gaze. A detail that didn't escape Cassandra's notice.

This was what she feared. From the moment they'd discovered Peter's absence, worry had climbed up from her gut, along her ribcage, and lodged in her throat. What if Spencer blamed her? She'd already fought this battle once, this concern that the brothers saw her as the source of their troubles. After all, she'd brought the spirit world into their lives. They'd insisted that the spirit world had found them itself in the form of a hellhound intent on ending their lives. But Cassandra could feel the immediate distance between her and Spencer now. His withdrawal could easily be explained as his fear for his brother. Or it could be that he was realizing just how much trouble agreeing to help her had brought them.

"We all agree, then?" Ava asked, disrupting Cassandra's anxious thoughts. "We pay Sam a visit and see what he knows?"

Though Tom still looked dubious, he nodded. "It's our best lead at this point."

"Good," Spencer said, then trekked past the marshal without waiting for the rest of them to follow as he shoved through the chapel doors.

The snow fell relentlessly, as though it was trying to cover the whole of DeVerre and its secrets with it. Cassandra hurried to keep up with

Spencer while Tom got in his cruiser, and the Lambert sisters returned to their vehicle. Spencer didn't look back or spare her a glance as they walked to the Jeep. Nor did he say a word as they got in, his sharp gaze focused on each task. Putting the key in the ignition, turning it over, buckling his seat belt, and habitually checking his mirrors. The stereo crooned to life, picking up where the CD had left off earlier.

Spencer slammed the dial, silencing the radio. Then he pulled out of the parking lot behind Tom's cruiser to follow him to the Chapelle house. Cassandra considered trying to talk to him to apologize for everything. For the shock of Peter's absence, for the fear they both felt, for her role in it all.

But she knew this version of Spencer. This still, silent determination of his meant one thing: He'd shut down. Not because he couldn't function. Not because his fear had finally gotten the better of him. No, this was not a stagnation. This was a warning sign. A clear message to warn the world to stay out of his way. A sign that his anger had reached a trigger point, and he was about to explode.

Following the brown and white police car the short distance up the road, they turned right onto Hope Court. It shouldn't have surprised Cassandra, she supposed, that Sam lived on the same street as Tom and the Bernard/Lambert family. This quaint cul-de-sac was the oldest neighborhood in DeVerre. Until the past fifty or so years, the small neighborhood was the prime residence of the founding families. Excepting the Varons, of course. They'd always lived at the top of Whitehill Way, in the house now named Occasus by its unknowing heir, Diane Varon-Collins-Larkin.

Parking at the end of the cul-de-sac, Cassandra turned to take in what she now realized was the Chapelle residence. Like the other houses, it was small, quaint, and old. Its porch held a white railing and mismatched furniture. The light blue exterior had faded in the weather of the Pacific Northwest, giving it a distinctly lived-in, comforting feel. Snow covered the rooftops in blankets of white, the bushes out front already weighted down in the first fall of encroaching winter. Two vehicles sat in the driveway, the SUV slightly less snow-laden than the sedan to its right.

The *click* of Spencer's seat belt unlatching spurred Cassandra into action. They climbed out of the Jeep, joining Tom at the mailbox by the Chapelle family driveway, waiting for Ava and Anna to cross the lawn.

Cassandra glanced at Spencer. His back was rigid and his gaze sharp, the steady silence of his rage undisturbed. But she caught the almost imperceptible shake of his hands as he slipped them into his coat pockets.

Her heart lurched. She wanted to reach out and pull him into a hug. She wanted to promise him that it would be okay. That they would find Peter and he'd never lose his brother again.

Instead, she crossed her arms against the cold and the desire to comfort him.

The quintet walked up the snowy path to the Chapelle's porch. Their footsteps crunched through the snow, the crisp scent stinging Cassandra's nose. An icy breeze nipped at her ears as it whipped up her dark waves.

Uncomfortable in the tense silence, Cassandra turned to Anna, walking at her side. "I didn't realize you lived next door to Sam," she said, keeping her voice low as though to speak at all was sacrilege.

Anna passed her a soft smile. She should look cheery in her bright, puffy coat, her curly hair drifting around her face like a cloud. But even her smile couldn't hide the way her eyes darted around as if hoping Peter would appear and exclaim it was all an elaborate prank. "All my life," she said. "I even used to babysit Juliet. The Chapelles have lived in this house and the Raynes in that one," she motioned to each building in turn, "since the founding of DeVerre."

Cassandra nodded, not sure what else to say.

Their boots clattered against the warped and weathered floorboards of the porch. A frostbitten, autumnal sign hung from the door that read, *"Give thanks to the Lord for he is good, for his steadfast love endures forever."* No doubt a Thanksgiving decoration for the holiday, two weeks away. It reminded Cassandra of her parents' home in Spokane, and she tried not to tense at its innocent presence.

"I think I should take the lead on this," Tom said, his dark stare intent on Spencer. "Sam trusts me, but if we want answers, it'd be best to keep him accommodating."

Spencer gave a tight nod.

Standing next to Anna at the back, Cassandra swallowed down her nervousness as Tom knocked. Through the door, two muted voices reverberated from the interior of the house. Light and familial in tone. Happy. Unconcerned. At peace.

Spencer shifted in front of Cassandra, the already strained tension in his shoulders somehow finding a way to tighten. Her fingers twitched, begging her to touch his back and soothe the rage coursing through him.

The aged, white door opened with a gentle creak of the hinges. Samuel Chapelle stood on the other side, dressed in jeans and a seminary alumni sweatshirt. The scent of apples and cinnamon drifted out of the home.

Seeing his friend first, the reverend gave a ready grin. "Tom," he greeted, clearly surprised though not unhappy at his arrival. "What are—?"

Sam's words died the second he took in the rest of the group, hovering like a dark shadow. The corner of his smile slipped as his ginger eyebrows pulled together. "What's going on?" he asked, tone falling flat.

"I hate to intrude on your time with Mel and Juliet, but . . ." Tom glanced over his shoulder at the group he'd brought with him. Then he gave his friend a serious, if apologetic, look. "We have some questions for you."

"Questions?" Sam repeated, his blue gaze sweeping over Ava, Spencer, Anna, and Cassandra. He turned back to Tom, his friendliness waning. "What is this about, Tom?"

Tom looked slightly abashed as he said, "This is an official visit, Sam. Could we please come inside?"

An instant expression of shock and frustration washed over Sam's face. "An official visit? With them?"

"Sam, please."

The simple, weighted request hit the reverend with the same surprise it met Cassandra. Tom wasn't just asking—he was pleading like he feared that his friend would refuse them. Or, more likely, she thought, that he was involved.

The irritation on Sam's face died, and he took a step back. Then he moved out of the way, gesturing to the entry hall. "Come on in," he said.

"Thank you," Tom muttered, stepping onto the faded rug of the hall.

Slowly, the five of them entered, stomping the snow from their shoes. Sam opened the coat closet, already full to bursting, and took care of their winter wear for them. Cassandra handed over her scarf and leather jacket. Spencer elected to keep his denim jacket on, his snow-damp hair hanging limply against his forehead.

Drifting farther inside to free up space in the entryway, Cassandra took in the rest of the Chapelles' home. A welcoming open floorplan awaited them, filled with cozy, well-worn furniture. Renovated at some point in the last decade, the house was modern while still holding some original charm. Nothing was ostentatious or grand. Certainly not as pretentious as Debbie and Mike's almost sterile, suburban mansion on Haven Boulevard.

Light flooded in from the windows all along the back of the house. Sam's wife, Melanie, and his daughter, Juliet, sat at the dining table, mid-meal. With the women's dark features and richly tanned complexions, they looked little like their patriarch. Middle-aged and motherly, Melanie had always been kind to Cassandra, though she never went out of her way to befriend her. Today was no exception.

However, Juliet Chapelle stared directly at Cassandra, her deep brown eyes wide.

"Make yourselves at home," Sam said, gesturing to the living room.

A massive, comfortable-looking gray sectional sofa filled the space, two large chairs flanking it. The fireplace roared with warmth, and autumnal decor ensconced the mantel, featuring a garland of red and yellow leaves, tiny woodland creatures, and a wooden carving of a cross.

While Anna and Ava didn't hesitate to sit on the far side of the sofa, Cassandra lingered at Spencer's side, and Tom cleared his throat. The marshal dropped his voice, leaning closer to his friend. "This is . . . sensitive, Sam," he warned with a pointed look toward the reverend's wife and daughter.

Sam's brow furrowed. "Sensitive enough that my family can't hear?"

"I suppose that's up to you," Tom admitted.

The reverend's light gaze flickered from Spencer and Cassandra to Ava on the sofa. Understanding dawned in his expression. He turned sharply to his wife. "Mel," he called, a plain signal in the utterance of her name.

Melanie Chapelle raised a rounded eyebrow, her expression indecipherable even as her steady gaze posed a clear question to her husband.

Sam held up a placating hand. "I'll explain everything to you later," he promised. Then his eyes flickered to their daughter.

Drawing back her shoulders, Melanie nodded. She set her fork on her plate and rose. "Jules," she said, her voice sure and serene. "Let's take our meal upstairs." Sam and his wife were a team; that much was clear. A unified front that would protect their daughter at all costs.

Juliet looked infuriated, her hands curling into fists on the table. "Mom, you can't be serious. This has to be about—"

Another tip of Melanie's dark brow silenced the teen.

Setting her jaw, Juliet glared back at her mother, then at her father. She gathered her plate, sulking as she followed her mother's directive. But when she passed Cassandra and Spencer on the way to the stairs, she scanned them as if desperate for whatever information she could soak up in these last few moments in their presence.

It didn't surprise Cassandra. The seventeen-year-old had witnessed her boyfriend's death at the hands of a hellhound only a month ago. If her lack of appearance at social functions hadn't been proof enough, her haunted gaze and slouched shoulders made it clear that she was still mourning.

But her willingness to defy her parents made another thing clear: She wanted answers.

Regretful that she couldn't offer the girl the truth she sought, Cassandra gave her an apologetic smile. Juliet's expression pinched with surprise at the gesture. Her dark eyes flashed to the Lambert sisters on the sofa. Then she followed her mother up the staircase.

Tom and Sam took the chairs on opposite ends of the room, leaving Cassandra and Spencer to join the sisters on the sofa. Its plush length offered an abundance of room, and it didn't escape Cassandra that Spencer chose to sit with plenty of space between them.

The crackling of the fireplace filled the room as Sam let out a long sigh. "Speak your piece," he said directly to Tom.

Even in the distance between them, Cassandra could feel Spencer bristle. His knee began to bounce as he fidgeted, the anxiety finding its way out. "Where's my brother?" he demanded before any of them could speak.

Tom shot him a look that said, "I thought we agreed that *I* would lead."

But Sam's shock trumped Tom's frustration. "Your—your brother is missing?" the reverend asked.

One of Spencer's thick eyebrows rose in confirmation and a hint of accusation. "The last place he was seen was entering the chapel."

Sam began to shake his head in immediate denial. "I don't know anything about that. I was here with my family."

The alibi didn't soothe Spencer's conviction, but Tom jumped in before he could say another word. "We aren't here to accuse you, Sam," he assured. "We just wondered if you might know who else was in the chapel after the service. Around eleven or noon."

"No," Sam promised emphatically. "I leave the chapel open for anyone to use at any time for prayer or reflection. I have no idea who might have stayed." He turned back to Spencer, concern lighting up his face. "You're sure he's missing?"

Spencer opened his mouth, but Tom cut him off with a glare. "It seems that way," the marshal said, then went on to explain their discovery and search at the chapel. "We believe he was taken."

Running a shaky hand over his rust-colored beard, Sam looked like he was racking his brain for answers. "I—I don't know, I'm sorry," he said with such emotion that it was impossible to question his sincerity. "I wish I had something to tell you, but—I have no way of knowing who might have been there. No one asks about using the church. They know I leave it open."

Ava finally spoke up, holding Anna's hand comfortingly. "Is there a vault in the chapel?"

Cassandra flinched, surprised at her blunt question. But she supposed there was no reason to mince words at this point. They needed answers, and they had little to lose. Might as well be upfront.

The perplexed expression on Sam's face deepened the early stages of crow's feet around his eyes. "Well, I have a safe in my office if that's what you mean." His mouth twitched in concern. "Why? Was something stolen?"

Tom and Ava shared a long look. Cassandra knew they were gauging how quickly to reveal the truth. All of them were. Anna met Cassandra's stare, almost pleading with her.

Turning back to the reverend, Cassandra chose to handle the issue. She'd done this before, explaining the spirit world to Peter and Spencer a month ago. Granted, she hadn't known everything then. In fact, she'd had several details incorrect at the time. Owen would have been the ideal candidate for the job, but he wasn't here, and it fell to her as the most experienced Wielder in their midst.

Holding Samuel Chapelle's worried gaze, Cassandra adopted the confident demeanor she always offered people—the one that said she wasn't fazed by them or their reality. "Nearly twenty-five years ago," she began, "your father told my parents to take me away from DeVerre. You disapproved. Why?"

Sam frowned, his confusion growing by the second. "I, uh—" He looked to Tom, who offered no more help than a shrug.

With a sigh, Sam pinched the bridge of his nose. He shrunk down into his seat. "It seemed wrong to me," he muttered. "Taking a child from their home because of—because of things beyond their control."

Cassandra offered a dry grin. "Ghosts, you mean?"

Sam eyed her, dubious. "If you'd like to call them that."

"What else would you call them?" Spencer demanded.

Cassandra gently tapped his arm—not as a warning but merely an assurance that she knew what she was doing. She held the reverend's stare. "You didn't share your father's concerns about my ability to see ghosts?" she pressed.

"Seeing—" Sam cleared his throat and began again. "Seeing ghosts isn't an altogether unique situation in DeVerre."

A cool, superior sense of knowing drew Cassandra to sit upright. Her entire life, she'd suspected that the Chapelles were involved in the spirit world—that they knew more than they were willing to say. And finally, she had confirmation.

Ava let out a huff, giving voice to Cassandra's internal satisfaction. "You know, for a reverend," the librarian said, her dark eyes shining with irritation, "you sure are an adept liar."

Anger lit Sam's tense expression. "I am not a liar," he said.

"But you are a Druid," Spencer accused.

"A Dru—what?" The notable shake to Sam's voice wasn't from fear or guilt; it was from bald-faced shock. "What are you talking about?"

Tom sent them a scathing look. "Would you all let me take care of this?" he growled. Then he turned back to Sam. "Listen, I know you're aware of the spirit world."

Another flare of shock in Sam's eyes.

"Yes, I know about it too," Tom admitted. "I've known my whole life. The Garniers didn't listen when the town made the pact to erase it. Not when we knew it could become a weapon to destroy our home."

Sam worked his jaw back and forth. "You've known this whole time?"

Tom's heavy eyebrows lifted in challenge. "Apparently, so have you."

Sam sighed. "Yes," he muttered. Then he turned to Ava and Cassandra. "I never lied. I told you both that you should forget about what you thought you knew and leave well enough alone."

"The problem is," Cassandra returned, "it isn't 'well.'"

"It is, though," Sam insisted. "DeVerre agreed to end its connection to the—the . . . the spirit world." The words came out choked, but the reverend hurried on. "For the past century, it's been left dormant. And DeVerre has been safe because of it."

"Tell that to your daughter," Ava charged.

Sam shot up in his seat. "Excuse me?"

Tom broke in again, attempting to mediate. "Juliet and Brendan were attacked by a beast, Sam," he explained.

Sam's hands began to shake as he shifted in his seat. His eyes grew distant, drifting to the far side of the room in thought. "It's happening again," he murmured.

Spencer's knee stopped bouncing, exchanging a look of shock with Cassandra. "Again?" she prompted.

Sam shook his head, back to rubbing his beard. "This wasn't supposed to happen," he said. His eyes shot to the marshal. "You know that."

Tom frowned. "I do?"

"Yes," he insisted. "This was—that was the point of it all."

"The point of what?" Cassandra asked.

"The point of ending it," he exclaimed. "Our great-grandparents knew that in order to protect DeVerre, we had to remove all connection to the spirit world. We had to stop messing with things we didn't understand. So, we ended it. And it was supposed to fix the problem."

"Exactly what problem did they think they were solving?" Ava asked.

"The attacks," Sam whispered like it might bring the spirit world upon them now. "The deaths."

The group took a collective breath of surprise.

Spencer's face lit with a sudden awareness, like he'd connected dots that Cassandra hadn't even known were there. "The graves," he muttered.

"What graves?" Cassandra asked.

His icy blue stare met hers for only a second before turning to the reverend. "In the cemetery, there are seven Chapelle graves," he said. "I noticed them when you showed me the Varons' last week, but didn't get a good look. When we went through today, I noticed them again. All seven Chapelles died on the same day in February of 1915."

Sam nodded, answering the unasked question within Spencer's words. "No one knew how it happened," he said. "But one night, beasts of the spirit world broke free of the Veil. They came and wiped out the whole of the Chapelle family. Every single man, woman, and child. Except for my great-grandfather, Jean."

Cassandra set a hand to her mouth, taking in what the story might mean for their cause.

"Only the Chapelles?" Ava asked.

"Yes," Sam confirmed.

"That sounds awfully coincidental."

Cassandra shook her head with a clarity that none of the rest had. "Beasts can't just break through the Veil," she said.

This earned looks of confusion from Tom, Sam, Anna, and Ava.

"They have to be summoned," she said.

Understanding dawned on them all.

"It was intentional?" Anna asked, her gentle voice shaken.

"It was murder," Tom said.

Cassandra nodded. "Beasts are summoned with a purpose," she explained. "Whoever summons them gives them a direct task. Once the task is completed, the beast is released back into the spirit world."

"Which is why you can't find your 'wolf,'" Spencer added.

Tom gritted his teeth, fury seeping out of him. But it was Sam who spoke. "That's not what I was told."

"Told about what?" Ava asked.

"The attacks," he said. "They weren't intentional. It was because the Varons were negligent. They weren't keeping the Veil in check, and it allowed the beasts to slip through."

Spencer tensed in loyalty to his newfound family, but Cassandra answered before he could. "That's not how it works," she said. The book on beasts from the vault had been plain: The creatures *had* to be summoned into the physical world by a Wielder. They couldn't break free of their own volition.

"It was the Druids," Spencer said, coming to the same conclusion as Cassandra. "They intentionally released the beasts and had them murder the Chapelles, all so they could blame the Varons and get control of the town."

Sam frowned. "That's not—"

"Of course, that wasn't what you were told," Spencer interrupted. "They lied, don't you get that? They wanted to control the Veil, and they needed the Varons out of the way to do that. So, they lied to the entire town, tricking them into believing that the Varons were at fault. That was the point of it all. That's always been their goal. Get rid of the Varons; get control of the Veil."

Although Sam didn't look entirely convinced, a glimmer of fear lit his eyes. "Then they succeeded?"

Spencer's smirk held no humor within it. "Not quite."

Sure that now wasn't the time to go into the Varon blood that ran through the Collins brothers' veins, Cassandra took back control of the conversation. "Do you understand what we're telling you, Sam?" she asked. "Whatever you were told about the spirit world, you've been lied to. I don't know whether it was by your parents, Alexander Frossard, or whomever else you happen to be close to. But they intentionally told you false information to keep you on their side. On the Druids' side."

Shaking his head with renewed confusion, Sam leaned forward. "I don't understand," he insisted. "You keep talking about Druids, but—are you saying that—that we have a *cult* here in DeVerre?" He looked to Tom with those last few words. It was clearly a request directed to his closest friend, the only person he trusted in this room.

With a resigned sigh, Tom returned his friend's stare. "Yes," he confirmed. "There is a cult of Druids within DeVerre. I—well, I knew about the spirit world my whole life, but until a week ago . . . I didn't realize about the Druids."

Sam's gaze flickered to Spencer and Cassandra. "And you learned about it from them?"

"I did."

"You *trust* them?"

"I do."

With a shaking hand, Sam resumed manhandling his beard. "I—I don't—this . . . My father told me that the spirit world had to be contained. That it required supervision—suppression." His eyes lifted to Cassandra. "Was that a lie too?"

Unsure how to answer that, Cassandra adjusted in her seat. "I'm unaware of any need to *suppress* the spirit world," she said. "Like I said, the beasts have to be summoned. They can't get out on their own."

"Then why would someone need to control it?" he asked, his desperation making it clear that he wanted to understand. He wanted to know why he'd been lied to, why he'd been manipulated.

"The need for control is less about protecting the town and more about ruling it," she explained.

"Ruling it?" Sam sounded aghast.

"The Druids want control of the Veil. We aren't entirely certain why, but we know that's their ultimate goal. A goal for which they've been murdering to achieve."

Sam's gaze shot to the staircase. His next word was a hollow whisper. "Brendan?"

Cassandra nodded apologetically. "Debbie was summoning hellhounds—beasts to murder citizens of DeVerre who were linked to Wielders."

A steady stream of emotions passed through Sam's expression as he worked through her words. "Debbie Mercier? Your cousin?"

"Yes."

"She was a Druid?"

"Yes."

The fury reignited in Sam's face. "She was the one who murdered Brendan?"

Cassandra could see that he didn't need confirmation this time. He was irate.

"How—how did you find out?" he asked.

"She tried to kill Peter and Spencer," she said, not quite ready to go into the full details. "But she's not alone, Sam. She was just the one summoning the hounds. There are others still trying to take control of the Veil."

"Who took my brother," Spencer said.

"I don't see how I can help you with that," Sam said, his sorrow blatant. "I wish I could, but I don't know who the Druids are."

"We do," Tom said. "In the Varon estate, Mr. Collins and his brother found a . . . It's called a vault. And in that vault, they found a journal written by Michael Varon."

Sam looked from Tom to Spencer and back. "Michael kept a journal? Does it . . . does it give any indication as to why he went mad?"

"He didn't go mad," Spencer said. "The Druids murdered him."

Sam raised his chin, evidently intrigued.

"Do you know about Seraphine Frossard?" Ava asked.

The reverend glanced at Spencer, surely remembering the name from when he'd asked about the woman's grave earlier that morning. "No," he replied.

"She was the illegitimate daughter of Lloyd Frossard," Ava explained.

Sam seemed surprised by this. "The Frossards—they're not the sort to have affairs," he defended. "Do you have proof she was his child?"

"My grandfather did," Ava informed him. "He chronicled her relation in his personal records of DeVerre."

"What does she have to do with Michael?"

"They were working to stop the Druids," Spencer inserted. "Michael and Seraphine fell in love and married secretly."

"There would be records of their marriage. Records that don't exist." Sam said it almost like a question, glancing at Ava for confirmation.

"Only his father, Matthew, knew of their marriage," Spencer said.

"But there would have had to be an officiant."

"Matthew officiated."

"Was he ordained?"

"The semantics of their marriage isn't of consequence," Ava interrupted. "The journal states that Michael Varon married Seraphine Frossard and that they had two children together before her father murdered both of them and Matthew Varon, then covered up the children's parentage, sending them away from DeVerre."

"Her father? Lloyd?" Sam's tone suggested he wasn't convinced.

"The leader of the Druids," Spencer said.

Now Sam looked downright baffled. "The Frossards—no, the Frossards aren't Druids," he said with a nervous chuckle. "Alexander is one of the most devoted members of our congregation. He's a dear friend—to both me and Tom."

"And he's the present leader of the Druids," Spencer said, voice flat. "Likely the one who gave the kill order for Brendan."

Sam's gaze flew to Tom, begging him to contradict it.

Tom said nothing.

"No," Sam muttered. "Alex—Alex wouldn't do that."

"We have proof that the Frossards are the leaders of the Druids, Sam," Tom said apologetically. "And while we don't have direct evidence of Alex's involvement yet, there is little doubt in my mind. Especially after last night."

"Last night? What happened last night?"

Tom turned to Spencer and Cassandra, inviting them to explain.

Giving Spencer a nod, Cassandra turned the conversation over to him. "It's your story to tell," she whispered. "And he's your brother."

Spencer's expression drew taut, a weight of responsibility drawing his features into a hard, determined expression. Then he turned back to Samuel Chapelle and told him everything that had happened over the last month and a half of their time in DeVerre.

CHAPTER FOUR

Spencer

Spencer felt depleted. Hollow. Empty of all emotion.

After spending hours explaining everything to Sam, the reverend fumed with anger. It infuriated him that he'd been tricked—manipulated by the man he had once considered a mentor. He'd trusted Alexander with his life, yet the man had called for an attack on Sam's daughter and the beloved young man he had once hoped to call his son.

An anger that mimicked the powerful surge rushing through Spencer's veins.

However, the reverend was of no more help in finding Peter than he was in giving them answers about the Druids. And despite the catharsis of telling their story, Spencer felt helpless in the wake of the conversation.

He couldn't believe it—Peter was missing, and there was no way to find him, no lead to follow.

When Spencer asked Tom for their next step, the marshal just sighed. "First, I have to inform the families of the fourteen Druids that their loved ones are gone. If I don't—well, soon they'll be coming for more than just my job."

Though Spencer understood the need for the task, he couldn't help his irritation. "What about Peter?"

"There's nothing we can do right now," Tom said, somewhere between apology and frustration. "Let me take care of last night's disaster. We'll figure out your brother's situation tomorrow."

"Isn't Peter's *situation* obvious?" Anna spoke up, surprising them all. She'd remained so quiet during the conversation with Sam that Spencer had almost forgotten her presence. But now her brown eyes were filled with agitation. "Alex took him. And we have to save him."

Tom scratched his brow. "We have no reason to suspect—"

"Of course we do," she said, a glimmer of wetness in her gaze. "He's the leader of the Druids. He was clearly looking for some chance to hurt Peter and Spencer, and he found it."

"We have no proof," Tom returned, his tone direct and firm. "We can't go charging into the Frossard home accusing him of abduction."

"You were planning to charge into his house to accuse him of murder last night," Cassandra reminded him.

Tom leveled her with a bored stare. "And then you killed fourteen of his cult members," he said. "We had the chance to accuse him without fear of the town's disapproval last night. But with the . . . current state of things," he continued hesitantly, "we have to be careful. The Frossards are beloved. If we hope to have a chance of bringing them to justice, we need substantial evidence of their crimes."

"We have evidence," Spencer said. "Michael Varon's journal."

"That implicates Lloyd as their leader. Not Alex."

"But he's Lloyd's—"

"That doesn't matter," Tom interrupted. "We have no direct proof that Alex is involved with the Druids in any way. We may be able to prove their existence in the '40s, but we can't prove it now."

"But we can prove that Peter and Spencer are Varons," Cassandra said. "Won't that count for something?"

Sam nodded, expression lightening as if an idea struck him. "That will stand for a great deal." He turned to Spencer. "If you can prove your lineage, the whole of the Frossard family will be called into question. If for no other reason than that it will reveal Seraphine's identity and Lloyd's lies."

"That's—" Tom paused, the thought sinking in. He pursed his lips in consideration. "That's not a bad idea."

"We can call a town council," Sam suggested, something akin to excitement in his voice. "If we get the leadership of the town on our side, the rest of the citizens will follow."

"In case you've forgotten," Ava said, "Alexander is *on* the council."

"So is my mother," Sam said. "And if I lend my voice, I know she'll listen. As will the rest of the town."

The group fell silent, but Spencer heard the unspoken truth ringing in the back of his head. The rest of the town would listen, so long as they weren't Druids.

But it was their best shot. Their *only* shot. If they could convince the mayor and council—Alexander Frossard aside—then their chances of convincing the town increased exponentially.

Cassandra shifted at Spencer's side. "It's worth a shot, right?" she asked.

Spencer didn't know what to say, so he turned to Tom.

The marshal was dubious. "It's a start."

The problem foremost in Spencer's mind remained unsolved. "And what about finding Peter?"

Tom leveled a fatherly stare at Spencer. "If the Druids have him, the best place to start is bringing them down. There was no trace at the chapel. And we can't go house to house searching for him *until* we get the town on our side. Give it until the meeting tomorrow. Once we've secured the town's support, we'll find Peter. First thing."

The promise—albeit sincere—didn't feel like enough. Not to Spencer. Not when his hands wouldn't stop trembling. Not when his heart kept pounding its furious rhythm beneath his ever-tightening ribcage.

The pressure building inside Spencer's chest over the last couple of weeks had become an almost constant companion to him. He'd grown used to the ball of fear pressing against his ribs. It felt like an uncomfortable but manageable sort of tumor that plagued him.

But this shaking? This sense that his whole body was spiraling out of control? Spencer couldn't handle it.

He couldn't handle being without his brother.

But it was the only option he had.

No matter how much he itched to go to Alexander Frossard's home, arcs of the spirit world blazing, demanding Peter's return, he couldn't. He had to wait. He had to be patient. And it was killing him.

Now, weary and vacant from their meeting, Spencer drove back to Occasus with Cassandra, utter silence between them. The Jeep ground the snow and ice beneath its tires—freshly switched over to all-weather by Aaron Lambert. The engine roared as the heater blasted, drying out the interior and adding to the feeling of fire in Spencer's throat. He hadn't intended for the silence between him and Cassandra. Nor did he like it. He simply couldn't bring himself to speak. What was there to say? That he was angry? Should he admit to her how his brain kept fantasizing about all the ways he'd kill Alexander if he hurt Peter?

His hands trembled, so he gripped the wheel until his knuckles turned white.

No, he couldn't speak. Not when he had to fight so hard to keep a hold on his sanity. He couldn't even bear to have the CD playing in the background. The second it had started earlier, he'd panicked. The music reminded him too much of their dad, of what Spencer had already lost.

He couldn't lose Peter too.

The purple and orange of twilight painted the pines with an eerie glow. The snow had stopped, but the dark shades of the sky distorted the once-beautiful scenery into a haunting landscape. One that taunted Spencer's imagination. Ghosts and beasts lay in those trees, creeping specters summoned by Druids to kill him and Cassandra. He could see them with his mind's eye as though they were real and waiting.

His pulse raced and he sped up the winding road faster than he should. Cassandra didn't say a word. She didn't even flinch as he whipped through the gates of Occasus, slamming to a halt before flinging the gear into park, ripping the keys from the ignition, and barreling out of the Jeep as though a hellhound were on his heels.

Spencer could hear his boots pounding against the porch with aggression. He put his key in the door before realizing it was already unlocked. As he let the door swing open, his panic roared like a hurricane in his ears.

The world went still as he scanned the foyer, blood pumping louder and louder.

"What—?"

"Shh," Spencer hissed as Cassandra stepped up behind him. He held out his hand to stop her. "The door was unlocked," he whispered.

Cassandra froze, following his gaze. He could hear her breathing hitch with equal fear.

The scrape of claws on wood tore into the silence, and they both jumped. An arc of bronze light surged into Spencer's hand, his power sending a tingle across his skin. But Cassandra grabbed his wrist, halting him as Anguis and Nex bounded around the corner from the office. The dogs rushed down the hall straight for them, joyous at their arrival.

Cassandra sighed, stepping around Spencer to greet the dogs.

But Spencer's heart continued to hammer against his chest. Someone could be inside the house, waiting for them. A beast could still lurk in the shadows.

"Cass," he began, but the creak of the stairs cut him off.

He whipped toward it, stepping through the door to block Cassandra from the attacker.

Owen appeared, mouth open to greet them, which quickly shut when he caught sight of the arc flowing around Spencer's hand. Panic lit his dark blue gaze, and he immediately scanned the foyer. "What happened?" he asked, voice low with concern.

Cassandra sighed, setting her hand on Spencer's arm. "Did you happen to leave the door unlocked?" she asked Owen.

"Oh." Owen glanced at the front door, brow furrowed. "I guess I did."

"That's what I figured," Cassandra murmured, a small grin coming to her lips.

Spencer didn't share in her wry humor. He fought to quell the anger and fear within him as he said, "I'd appreciate it if you locked it in the future."

"Sorry," Owen said. "I'm not used to it anymore."

Sure that small-town living would never lessen his paranoia, Spencer only nodded in response before he turned to shut the door. The lock turned with a resounding *snap*.

Spencer moved to the coat closet. He hung up his coat and denim jacket, then turned to Cassandra, holding his hand out for her things. The dogs sat on each side of her as she quickly shrugged off her jacket.

"I take it you didn't have much luck?" Owen asked cautiously.

Spencer bit back a sharp retort. *Obviously,* they hadn't had luck. If they had, Peter would be there.

"Not exactly," Cassandra said. "We did speak with Sam, though."

"Really?" Owen descended the rest of the stairs to stand with them in the foyer. "What did he have to say?"

Spencer shut the closet door, moving around both of them for the back of Occasus. He shut out whatever response Cassandra gave as he headed down the hall, flicking on every light as he moved toward the kitchen. The lower floor of Occasus was filled with a golden glow from the incandescent bulbs as the sun sank below the horizon. It was a minimal comfort—light in the presence of encroaching darkness. But it also revealed what remained from the beasts' attacks last night.

Though there was little lasting damage, the marks of their fight showed in the furniture knocked out of their homes. Scrapes marred the walls and ceilings, though it seemed superficial at worst. Something that could easily be covered up by a layer of paint or a patch of wallpaper. The dining table sat askew, its chairs toppled onto the Turkish rug.

They'd planned to clean up today. Peter had suggested it. Go to church, then return to right all the misplaced furnishings and scattered knickknacks. Then they'd figure out their next step.

Spencer averted his gaze from the broken vintage lamp that had fallen from the dining room sideboard. He remembered the hydra pushing through the dark, yawning hole that was the entrance to the kitchen, proceeding to bump into that sideboard, knocking free the decor so intentionally placed on its surface. He hoped the lamp hadn't been a family heirloom.

Feeling around the wall for the light switch, Spencer's willpower faltered, his imagination convincing him that if he didn't turn the light on fast enough, then a wendigo would wrap its razor-sharp claws around his wrist and yank him into the darkness to devour him whole.

The *snap* of the switch brought immediate relief to Spencer's imagination. Light filled the kitchen, assuring him that no beasts waited in the dark. It was only him, standing there and staring into the room, now marked with more signs of a struggle. The barstools sat at odd angles beneath the island, and the paintings hung off-center. A chip marred the granite countertop from one of Tom's stray bullets.

But the light couldn't ease his thoughts.

Fears warping his reality, Spencer hurried across to the fridge. His boots *thumped* out an erratic rhythm, reminding him how unstable he was. His hand shook as he opened the refrigerator door and pulled out ingredients without thought. He was on autopilot. Some strange form of self-preservation reminded him that he hadn't eaten all day. Breakfast hadn't sounded right after waking from the horrifying fight for their lives, and Peter was taken before they could have lunch. While Spencer couldn't stomach the idea of eating anything, he knew Peter would be appalled if he didn't.

Peter had always taken care of him in those ways. Spencer was prone to forgetting simple things like meals when he was working or writing. His brother ensured he didn't waste away.

As Spencer dug the last object out of the fridge, he heard Owen and Cassandra enter the kitchen, the skitter of the dogs' claws clicking along. They kept their voices respectfully low as they entered the kitchen, clearly not wanting to bother Spencer but feeling they needed to speak with him.

Grabbing a plate from the cabinet, Spencer turned around to begin making himself a sandwich. He glanced at the pair for a split second, disinterested in the wrap-up Cassandra gave Owen. Nex ambled around the island, nudging Spencer's leg with his nose. But he couldn't bring himself to bend down and pet the dog.

He took his first bite of the sandwich when Cassandra finished her overview, and Owen began to tell them about his day. He'd spent it in the vault. Spencer understood why Owen hadn't joined the search party. He didn't blame him for it either. There'd already been too many people involved in today's panic.

"I think I found some books that might be helpful," Owen said, piquing only the slightest bit of Spencer's interest. "There are three that cover the Warden and its early days. Histories of the organization itself. I've never seen them before, but when I scanned them, there were discussions on the different fights against the Druids over the centuries."

"Really?" Cassandra adjusted one of the stools back in place and took a seat. "Did it specify how they defeated them?"

"I'm not sure," he said. "Like I said, I just did a scan. I was trying to find as much that could help us as possible."

Cassandra nodded, her dark waves grazing her back with the motion. "You said three books, right?"

"Yes."

"Why don't we each take one?" she suggested. "They may give us the exact information we need."

Spencer swallowed his bite, setting the sandwich on his plate. "No," he said.

Owen and Cassandra looked at him in surprise.

"We need to focus on the essays," he said. "If the Druids stole them, then they're the priority."

Cassandra's shoulders slumped. "I can't read Old English like that," she said.

"But I can."

"Then I guess you and I will read the books, Owen."

Spencer shook his head. "I'll need your help on the essays. I can translate, but you helped Diane with the research previously. It might spark something in your memory as I read."

"Okay," she agreed reluctantly.

Spencer's brow lowered. Cassandra didn't want to work with him on the essays. She'd been excited about them only a handful of days before. So excited that she hugged him. Which he knew wasn't an entirely shocking reaction. Her friendly physical affection was expected at this point. But it did make her hesitance now notably strange.

"I'll start on those books, then," Owen said. "It might take longer, but I think you're right, Spencer. Elijah's essays need to take precedent."

Cassandra's brows pinched together. "Don't you have to go back to work tomorrow?" she asked.

Brushing a hand through the air, Owen dismissed the thought. "When I called out last week, they informed me that they'd hired their replacement, so they wouldn't need me anyway."

"Oh." She hesitated, licking her lips before she spoke again. "Do you think . . . will Ava go back to work?"

"Yes," he said.

"That's too bad," Cassandra said. "We could use her help."

"Oh, I wouldn't worry about that," he said. "She's got enough in the Rayne family records that she'll have plenty to keep her occupied *and* get us the information we need."

While Cassandra considered this, Spencer polished off the last of his sandwich. As neither of them had taken the opportunity presented by the dinner supplies, he began putting them away. He tossed Nex and Anguis each a piece of lunchmeat, then washed his hands.

When he turned back around, Owen and Cassandra were watching him silently. He crossed his arms and leaned against the counter's edge, waiting for the thoughts he could see clouding Cassandra's gaze.

Turning back to Owen, Cassandra said, "Gerard could help you with those books."

Owen furrowed his brow. "Where is Gerard? I haven't seen him all day."

Cassandra motioned toward the front of the house. "He's in the living room," she said with a flippant grin. "Sulking."

The phantom chose that moment to make his appearance. "I don't sulk," Gerard grumbled.

"Sure," Cassandra said placatingly. "Would you be willing to help Owen with those books?"

With an unnecessarily long sigh, Gerard threw his gaze to the ceiling. "I suppose," he said. "I'm not sure what good studying them is going to do you, though. Research has never saved anyone's life."

Spencer eyed Gerard, catching how the phantom didn't once look his way. Not that the phantom paid much attention to him in general. He and Peter had never gotten along with the dead man. But Gerard wasn't usually so . . . distant perhaps was the best term. Almost as though he was intentionally putting up a front of disinterest toward Spencer.

"This research could," Cassandra said, then turned back to Owen. "Do you think Anna would be willing to read the third book when she's not working?"

"Probably," Owen said.

"Great." Cassandra stood then, passing a surreptitious glance to Spencer. It had been subtle but not enough for him to miss it. And it tipped him off that, for some reason, Cassandra was wary of him.

With a deep breath, Cassandra swept a more confident gaze around the men in the kitchen. "It's been a long day, and I have a feeling tomorrow's not going to be much better," she said, moving away from the counter. Anguis followed at her side. "I'm going to bed."

"You haven't eaten anything," Spencer said. He wasn't sure why he felt the need to remind her. Maybe it was simply because it was what Peter would have done.

A bemused smile pulled at her lips. "I'm not hungry," she said, then left.

Spencer stared at the staircase well after her dark form had disappeared. Something was wrong. Something that he thought should be obvious to him. Yet, with the present fuzzy state of his brain, he couldn't quite bring himself to puzzle through it.

Turning back, Spencer found both Owen and Gerard staring at him with a look akin to worry.

A hollow chuckle escaped Spencer. "I'm not going to go off the rails," he said. "So you can stop looking at me like I'm a basket case."

"I'm sorry, Spencer," Owen said, his calm voice unnaturally affected with emotion. "We'll find him."

Spencer could only bring himself to nod.

"What was that book you wanted me to read?" Gerard asked Owen, keeping the room from falling into silence once more.

Owen gestured to the ceiling. "It's in the vault," he said. "I can show it to you if you want to get started on it."

"I don't sleep, so I may as well do something with my night," the phantom said.

The two men were making their way to the door when Spencer called, "Gerard."

Both men turned, but with one glance at Spencer, Owen stepped out, leaving them to talk.

Spencer walked around the island while the phantom lingered by the doorway. Gerard stood several inches taller, but Spencer was used to looking up to people. He'd only minded being short during high school when all his peers shot past him. But as he grew older, he realized that height meant little in the real world. And there was something about the knowledge that people tended to underestimate you when you didn't tower over them that gave him a sense of confidence.

"What is it?" Gerard asked, his dark gaze scanning him with a bored glint.

And he still didn't meet Spencer's eyes.

"Aren't you curious where Peter is?" Spencer asked.

Gerard didn't even blink. "I overheard everything I needed to hear."

"You haven't given me your condolences."

Gerard's lips twitched beneath his beard. "When your brother is dead, I'll offer my sympathy."

"Mm." Spencer tucked his hands into the pockets of his jeans. "Thanks."

The phantom's eyes did meet his then. "For what?"

"Well, first," Spencer said, "for not treating me like I'm about to lose it."

"Don't be ridiculous," Gerard muttered. "You're not that weak."

"Maybe you could explain that to everyone else for me," he said. "Because they're all watching their words—ignoring the obvious as though I won't be able to handle my brother's abduction. Like I'll crack under the pressure of it."

Gerard rolled his shoulders. "No, I don't think this will break you. I imagine you're just biding your time. Preparing for the moment when you take matters into your own hands. Just like I did."

Spencer raised his brow, interested in the morsel of backstory that Gerard had revealed. But even if the phantom was right, he didn't want to give his plans away. And he had something else to say.

"The second reason I'm thanking you," he said, "is because of all the people in this world . . . I know you'll look out for Cassandra like I would."

Gerard narrowed his eyes. "Like you would?"

Realizing how that might have come across, Spencer shifted his footing. "Not—not like that." He cleared his throat and started again. "You'll keep her alive. No matter what. And . . . I'm grateful to you for that because . . ."

In the silence that stretched off Spencer's unsaid words, Gerard lifted his chin. A knowing grin pressed his lips together. "Because if it comes down to it," he finished for him, "you'll burn this town to the ground to find your brother."

Spencer held his stare.

"And damn whoever gets in your way."

Spencer blinked.

"Even Cassandra."

The pressure of Nex's body resting against the side of Spencer's leg felt like a two-ton weight as he spoke. "I'm going to find Peter," he said, voice low and thick. "No matter what it takes. But knowing that you'll protect Cassandra should the worst happen . . . *that's* what I'm thanking you for."

The sly glimmer of understanding in Gerard's eyes confirmed exactly what Spencer hoped for. "Oh, don't worry, kid," the phantom promised. "I won't let anything happen to my tether."

CHAPTER FIVE

Anna

It was the worst birthday she'd ever had. Not that she should be thinking about herself at a time like this. Peter was missing, and there was nothing she could do.

Sitting at the kitchen table with her siblings and Haley, Anna's mind wasn't on the celebration. She stared blankly at the cards in her hand. This wasn't the time to play card games. They should be out looking for Peter. Yet, Tom was right before, they couldn't do anything.

Anna had never felt so helpless, both last night and today. When Ava announced her pregnancy in the vault, Anna stood there in so much shock she hadn't even managed a proper goodbye to Owen, Peter, or anyone else. The following hour and a half, Anna had spent in trembling silence, trying to figure out what to feel. She was afraid—she knew that. But she was also angry.

Her entire life, she'd been so close to the Frossards. They'd been a second family to her. Ever since that fateful day in kindergarten when

Krista Guillaume had stolen Anna's coloring book from under her hands, and five-year-old Connor stepped forward.

Of course, Anna knew who he was the moment she saw him. She'd seen him so many times around town—at church, school, downtown, and even the library. He was the Frossard son. Everyone knew him. And the moment he'd approached their table, she'd frozen in awe.

His blond hair glowed like sunlight as he tapped Krista on the shoulder. It was such an adult thing to do that the tears welling in young Anna's eyes stalled completely. Her gaze darted between the boy and the girl before her.

"I don't think that's yours," Connor told Krista.

Pink crayon hovering over the flowers outlined on the page, Krista's jaw dropped. She knew Connor too. "Uh, I—I just wanted—"

"Give it back."

Her strawberry-blonde pigtails whipped back and forth as she looked around, desperately searching for salvation from the command. When she saw the teacher was busy helping the other children with crafts on the far side of the room, she pursed her lips in determination. She turned back to Connor with the most superior expression a kindergartner could muster. "We're supposed to share," she said.

Crossing his arms in a decidedly mature manner for a child, Connor wasn't impressed. "Did you *ask* if you could share?"

Krista's guilt displayed itself across her pudgy, youthful face.

Connor held out a hand, expectant.

Cheeks ablaze, Krista thrust the coloring book at Connor, tossed the crayon on the table, and shuffled away. If Anna hadn't been so shocked, she might have giggled at the girl's abashment.

With wide-eyed wonder, Anna watched as her rescuer turned. Blue eyes like the sky met hers as Connor proffered the coloring book with a smile. "I think this belongs to you," he said.

Anna couldn't be sure, but she thought her whole face had washed over with a blush. She took the book back, carefully resting it on the table.

As the coloring book didn't *technically* belong to her but rather to the school, she couldn't determine if his statement was correct. But she *had* elected to color while the rest of the children surrounded the teacher to make paper-mache. She hated how the sticky glue substance felt on her fingers for hours after the art was finished.

"Thank you," Anna whispered with a tiny sniffle.

Picking up a crayon, Anna turned back to the wagon she'd been coloring before Krista stole the book from her. She expected that Connor would go off to join the other children with their paper-mache. He'd seemed excited about the activity when the teacher had announced it only minutes ago. But he remained in her peripheral, watching as she made a single stroke on the page.

Unable to proceed with him watching, Anna took a cautious look over her shoulder at him.

He smiled again, then pointed to the page. "I like that you chose blue," he said, his boyish lisp contrasting his mature observation. He settled his hands on his hips as though surveying a particularly impressive work of art. "Most kids color wagons red. But that's what everyone does, you know? I like that you chose something different."

Anna gaped at him.

He just continued to smile.

Blinking a few times, unsure why he was still standing there, Anna tried to figure out what he wanted. Most kids ignored her. Not because she was the odd one out or out of rejection, but simply because she preferred it that way. Anna liked fading into the background. She enjoyed being quiet, coloring in the corner while the rest of the children screamed and pushed and wrestled and made messes.

Yet there he stood, patient and observant and far too old for his age. And suddenly, Anna didn't want him to join the other kids.

Scooting the coloring book across the table, Anna held his attentive gaze. "Would you like to color with me?" she asked meekly.

Immediately, Connor nodded, blond wisps of hair flopping onto his forehead. He dropped down at her side, graciously taking the opposite side of the coloring book without complaint. He was the perfect coloring buddy, Anna had found. Left-handed, his elbow never bumped into her or interrupted her progress, working on either side of the book. He never stole or fought for the crayons but asked to borrow them when she was done. He drew with gentle, steady strokes rather than tearing up the page with his enthusiasm. He even managed to stay inside the lines for the most part, a great recommendation, in her opinion.

But best of all, he'd been silent. Not once did he start to chatter mindlessly or pester her with questions. He just dipped his head and colored, like her.

And from that day forward, they'd been inseparable.

Anna didn't know when she'd fallen in love with him. Sometimes, she thought it had been that first day. Then she reasoned that a five-year-old didn't know what romantic love was.

And yet, her entire life, Anna had known that Connor Frossard was the most perfect man she could find. Tenderhearted, strong, and patient. He could always tell what she was feeling and just what she needed, be it a hug or a conversation or simply sitting in silence and coloring, like they had as kids. She hadn't known a day without him until he went off to college.

Connor was the only person other than Ava with whom Anna had ever shared her art. Because she knew she could trust him. She knew that he would never push her or suggest how she might try something new or even mention his personal opinions on them. No, Connor never talked about Anna's art with her; he let her talk to *him* about her art. He would sit there and listen and smile and laugh as she told him all about the process and the mistakes she made. And then he would tell her, "This one is my favorite."

"You said that about the last one," Anna would reply.

Connor would nod, rest his arm around her shoulders, and let out a long sigh as he stared at the piece as though it were hanging in the Louvre.

"They're all my favorite, Banana. Picking one over the others would be like picking what I like best about you. And that's impossible."

Yes, Anna was angry. Because those memories—that warmth and joy that had spread through her limbs when Connor held her close and made her feel like the only person in the world—reminded her that she'd been lied to her entire life.

The Frossards led the Druids. They were murderers and liars, and they were trying to take over DeVerre. They were trying to tear the Veil, whatever that meant.

And they'd taken Peter.

Anna drew her thumb along the ridges of the playing cards in her hand. This wasn't just the worst birthday she'd ever had—it was the worst year. Connor's engagement, Ava kicking Owen out, nearly dying at the hands of that horrifying beast. And now, this.

"It's your turn," Haley reminded Anna, her voice soft and hesitant.

"Sorry," Anna muttered, half-heartedly drawing a card from the deck.

After dinner, presents, cake, and a short video call with their parents in Canada, Ava had insisted they end the night with a round of rummy, per Lambert family tradition. Though Anna wanted to fight the ridiculous idea, she knew there was no winning against her sister. And really, being surrounded by family was preferable to being alone. Sitting in her room, trying and failing to paint, sketch, or even read a book, would be torturous.

Though Anna preferred the role of ready-servant over being the center of attention, the presence of her siblings—including Owen and Haley—always soothed her. The urge to be the cheerful, compassionate, understanding friend wasn't as strong. She could just be herself: quiet, thoughtful, and creative. Her family's presence made her feel that way . . .

Her family, and Connor.

"All right," Aaron said, giving the bridge of his glasses a shove up his nose. "I've had enough of this. Would you two mind explaining just what happened last night?"

They'd already told Aaron and Haley about Peter's mysterious disappearance—which was the reason Spencer, Cassandra, and Owen weren't joining them. But Ava had refused to say anything more on the principle that it was Anna's birthday, and they shouldn't talk about that stuff on *her* day. Despite the fact that Anna didn't feel like celebrating.

"Huh-uh," Ava said. "We're not discussing that. It's your turn."

"Look," Aaron slammed a random card on the discard pile, "while you and Anna got front-row seats these last few days, I've been kept in the dark. Our town is in danger—our *lives* are in danger."

Haley brushed her fingers against the back of Aaron's hand demurely before going to select a card from the deck. Whether it was in encouragement or to calm him down, Anna wasn't entirely sure.

Aaron spared his girlfriend a glance. "There are Druids trying to kill our friends," he said, his voice calmer, if still insistent. "And possibly even us now. I'd like to know who they are and how to stop them."

Ava's jaw just tightened.

So Anna spoke up. "The Frossards are the Druids," she said, eyes locked on her cards. She stared at the vibrant red of the hearts. Then tossed the queen onto the discard pile. "And we stop them by finding Peter and telling the rest of the town the truth."

Ava frowned but didn't speak. Haley and Aaron stared at Anna. She knew her tone had been flat—far less forgiving and friendly than anyone would expect from her. But she also knew it wasn't her anger that worried them.

It was her connection to the ones who were threatening their lives.

"People aren't going to believe that easily," Haley said.

"They're not going to have a choice," Anna said. "There's going to be a town council tomorrow, and Spencer, Cassandra, Ava, Tom, and Sam are going to tell them everything. Then the rest of the town will have to choose a side."

Aaron nodded, determination in his dark eyes. "Then we better be ready to help people pick the right side."

Ava reached for the draw pile. "People will choose whatever side most closely aligns with their loved ones," she said flatly. Most people might perceive her tone as indifference or arrogance. Anna knew it was fear. "If they have Druidic family members, it won't matter what logic you use—they'll side with them."

"Do we know any Druids?" Haley asked, her bright blue eyes wide. "Aside from the Frossards, I mean."

"Probably," Anna said. "But we aren't sure who they are yet."

Haley's pink lips turned down. "I hope it's no one we're close to," she whispered.

As Anna opened her mouth to warn her not to get her hopes up, they all jolted in their seats as a rapid knock came on the front door.

Aaron jumped up but stayed waiting at the table. "Were we expecting someone else?" he asked, his voice low.

"No," Ava said.

"That's what I thought," Aaron mumbled. Then he moved. "Stay here."

"Aaron," their older sister warned, but he waved her off.

Anna watched as Aaron moved from the kitchen, his hand going to the back of his waistband, shifting the hem of his shirt. She fought off a gasp of surprise as his fingers curled around the handle of a handgun. She'd known he had one, along with his permit, but he'd never regularly carried it.

The three women shared a look.

From her vantage at the table, Anna could see the front door. In the small house, it was a short walk from the kitchen to the living room. She watched as Aaron approached the door, one hand still on the holstered gun as he reached for the handle.

Were they being too paranoid, Anna wondered. Perhaps it was one of her friends coming by to say happy birthday. Or maybe some of the neighbors.

But with Peter taken and the Druids out there, could they risk it?

The door opened, and Aaron drew his head back in surprise. Then he stepped out of the way. A girl stood there, her navy coat hanging open over her jeans and t-shirt. Anna instantly recognized the rich olive complexion and dark hair.

Rising from her seat, Anna hurried forward, drawing Juliet Chapelle's gaze. Seeing Anna, she took an involuntary step into the house. "I have to talk to you," the teen said.

Anna motioned for the girl to come the rest of the way in, and Aaron shut the door behind her. "What is it?" Anna asked.

Juliet glanced nervously around the Lambert siblings and Haley. If Juliet was here—if she had something she needed to say—Anna had no doubts that it involved their conversation with her father.

Setting a gentle hand on the girl's arm, Anna angled closer. "Would you like to talk in private?"

After a second's hesitation, Juliet shook her head. "No, that's—that's fine," she said. "Could we maybe sit down though?"

"Of course."

Once Anna, Juliet, and Ava had taken the couch—Aaron and Haley on the loveseat—the girl turned back to her. "I wanted to tell you earlier," Juliet began, wringing her hands in her lap. "But my parents—well, they still think I'm—that I'm broken by Brendan's death. And maybe I am, but . . ."

The haunted look in Juliet's dark brown stare told Anna it wasn't just fear that she felt.

Hardening her jaw, Juliet straightened her shoulders. "I'm tired of being sad and scared," she said, her voice tense with emotion and perhaps both of those feelings. But also with anger. "I know something more is going on. And I want to help."

Anna exchanged a quick look with her sister. It wasn't surprising, she supposed. Juliet had experienced trauma that few people ever would. She'd seen her boyfriend killed by a hellhound. For her to assume that something more was involved seemed only natural.

But still, Anna wasn't sure what the girl thought she could do. "Help in what way?" she asked.

"It wasn't a wolf that killed Brendan," Juliet said. None of them balked at the claim. And she caught it.

Her eyes brightened, hope lifting her countenance. She'd been saying this all along—and it was clear that this was the first time she'd ever been believed.

Juliet's demeanor bore up with this newfound support. "I know it was a beast," she said, surprising them. "And I know it's connected to the spirit world."

It was Ava who spoke. "How do you know about this?"

Juliet shrugged as though it should be obvious. "My Uncle Gabe told me."

Anna tried not to let the shock show on her face. Gabe Chapelle knew about the spirit world too? What was the mortician's role in all this?

Setting her hand on Juliet's, Anna leaned forward. "Tell us everything."

CHAPTER SIX

Peter

Peter could have sworn he heard the dogs barking. He began to raise his head to tell them to be quiet when he realized the thrumming, angry sound was coming from between his ears. In the next second, he became acutely aware of the ache spreading from his head across his temples and down his neck.

Grimacing against the pain, Peter lifted a hand to rub his forehead. "Ow," he grumbled, moving to sit up. Why was he lying on the floor anyway? And what room in Occasus had a concrete slab?

"Good evening," a man said, his rich voice calm.

Peter whipped around, head spinning and vision spotting. He grunted as the room around him came into focus, and the voice's owner became clear. The memories flooded back. The church. The voices. The revelation.

Gerard was a traitor, working with the Druids.

And Peter was the only one who knew.

Narrowing his gaze—not yet free of those obnoxious floaters—Peter glared at his captor.

Alexander Frossard sat on the far side of the room in an antique brown chair beside a fireplace. The sophistication of the scene mimicked a painting of a dapper gentleman presiding in his study. Now in a sweater and jeans, Alexander looked like a smarmy Ivy League alumni, his perfect blond hair and superior jawline an insult to every other human in existence.

But after taking in the leader of the Druids, Peter's eyes shifted to the rest of the space, realizing for the first time that he really was a captive. While Alexander sat by the roaring fire—a massive mahogany hearth and built-in shelves surrounding it filled with hundreds of books and decorative boxes—that part of the room was on the other side of the steel beams that kept Peter locked in a narrow, concrete room. His bedroom in Norfolk had been bigger than this.

"Seriously?" Peter said, motioning to the bars in front of him. "You guys have a *dungeon* in your home? How Bond villain of you."

Closing the book in his lap, Alexander grinned lazily at Peter. "Villainy is perspective, Mr. Collins," he said. "And this is my personal study. That little room you inhabit," he tossed a finger in Peter's direction, "is as recent as your presence in our home."

Frowning, Peter considered that. He'd become acquainted with dozens of fantastic ideas over the past month and a half since their move to DeVerre. The ability to create something where there was nothing before being the freshest discovery of them all.

Rising from his place on the floor, Peter scanned Alexander thoughtfully. The man watched as he stepped up to the bars, slipping his arms through to rest on the crossbeam. He felt like a cowboy, locked in a good, old-fashioned jail cell. But Peter couldn't find anything cool about being locked inside it. "We're not on the natural plane, are we?" he said.

Alexander arched a golden eyebrow. "You Varons aren't the only ones with tricks up your sleeves."

A jolt of shock ran through Peter's chest. He straightened his shoulders. "You know?"

Alexander's laugh was full and friendly. If Peter hadn't been his captive, he might've found the sound contagious. "I've known since before you were born, son," he said. His eyes twinkled an eerie, yellow-tinged blue in the firelight. "Diane and Phillip disappeared from the rest of DeVerre's eyes, but we never stopped watching them. Just as we've watched you and your brother."

Fear trickled from Peter's skull down his spine. "How'd you manage that level of creepy?" he asked, voice tight in his throat.

"We have friends everywhere, Mr. Collins."

"It's Varon," Peter replied on instinct.

Alexander let out a small huff, relaxing in his seat. He didn't deign to respond but returned to his reading.

Scanning the room once more, Peter took in what Alexander had revealed to be his study. It reminded him of the vault in Occasus, though this had a distinctly sinister vibe. Outside the cell, mahogany slats stretched across the floors, covered by a large rug—a woven pattern depicting a lush, emerald green and dark brown tree. Bookshelves filled all the walls. The fireplace sat on Peter's right, two wingback chairs— including the one Alexander rested in—before its hearth.

A grand desk sat on the far side of the room, its chair empty. The wooden face of the desk bore intricate etching featuring another opulent tree with leaves and vines twining through a Celtic knot design. A stained glass lamp like something out of the late 1800s rested on its top, glowing amber and gold. The desktop bore neat stacks of books, a tray of papers, and organizational apparatuses, giving it a clean, efficient appearance.

This *was* Alexander's office, where he conducted his business and planned his schemes.

"Why keep me here?" Peter asked incredulously. "Aren't you worried I'll learn your secrets?"

Alexander's smile was dry. "Oh, I'm sure you'll pick up a thing here or there."

"And that doesn't bother you?"

The lack of response told Peter all he needed to know.

Alexander wasn't bothered because getting out of this cell was impossible. At least, getting out alive was.

"You intend to kill me," Peter surmised. The thought should have scared him, he knew. He should be trembling with the realization. And yet . . . he only felt irritation.

"Most likely," Alexander said simply. He flipped a page.

"Why keep me at all, then?"

"I'm not wasteful, Mr. Collins," he said, eyes locked on his book. "I have use for you a bit longer."

Peter thought to ask what that use was, but the flatness of Alexander's tone paired with the smug grin on his lips made it clear that the man was enjoying his control of the situation too much to give away all his secrets.

No, Peter would be stuck here, unsure of his future until he was either dead or being exploited in whatever manner the Druid leader deemed useful. Likely, as a weapon or a hostage—something to hurt his brother and Cassandra.

The silence stretched, and Peter's throat tightened. He had to get out of here. He couldn't let this man use him against his brother or their friends.

Flexing his hand, Peter wondered if he could catch Alexander unaware. What if he sent an arc at him? The Druid leader was focused on that book in his lap. He turned another page, the movement languid as his eyes drifted to the top lines. Could he end the Druid leader's life now and save the town? Even if Peter wound up dying in the process, it would be worth it, right?

The abrupt resurgence of Alexander's smooth voice caused Peter to jump. "If you're planning my assassination, Mr. Collins," he said, "I'd recommend you desist."

Peter worked to calm his racing pulse. "Oh, yeah? You think I'm not capable of it?"

"You misunderstand me," he said. "I certainly believe in your capabilities. They simply aren't relevant."

"What does that mean?"

Alexander's gaze lifted from the page to meet Peter's. "Try it," he said, tone bored.

The invitation rankled. Peter knew it was a trick, an attempt to show him just how powerless he was against the Druid. And yet he couldn't help the urge to give in, to show Alexander Frossard that he underestimated him, that the blood of the Varons he so flippantly shrugged off ran through Peter with far more power than the Druid leader could ever imagine.

Wielding the spirit world was a matter of will, Peter had learned. A simple use of intention and action. A strange revelation when, just a week ago, he couldn't so much as see a ghost, let alone wield an arc.

But when the time had come—when Peter had faced down a Druid and a hydra in The Glass Tavern, Anna's life in his hands—he'd felt the sudden and resounding knowledge radiating through him. He'd felt the tremor of power tingling over his skin, and, without thought, he'd thrown forward an arc of golden light that saved them both.

Fighting the Druids at Occasus had required nothing different. He willed the power forth, and it responded. He told it what he wanted, and it listened.

Now, as Peter willed that tremor to resurface and flicked his wrist, expecting an arc to burst forth, nothing happened.

Alexander's derisive huff rang through the study as Peter studied his hand in disappointment.

A flash of shimmering black slammed into Peter, blasting him back. Still looped through the bars, his arm caught, yanking painfully as he dropped to the ground with the force of Alexander's arc.

Peter's body spasmed, flaring with pain from the arc only seconds before he collided with the floor. Unable to control his movements, his head smacked against the concrete. Pain seared into his skull as he sprawled out on his back, vision going black and spotty. His muscles screamed and ached as his pulse thudded at his temple, a warm trickle of liquid seeping out.

The paralysis of the Druid's arc didn't even allow Peter to blink away the fuzziness of his vision. He was locked in place, his body numb and his lungs burning. He thought his back might be arching from the contraction of his muscles, but he couldn't be sure. His senses blurred between absolute pain and subconscious reaction.

Motes of flashing light swam in Peter's vision. Everything was a haze before his eyes, either from the damage his head suffered or from tears in his eyes—he wasn't sure which. But he was sure that the dark figure nearing the bars of his cage was Alexander Frossard.

The shadows darkened around Peter as the spots dwindled, his gaze still obscured. Was that from a descent into unconsciousness? Or was the Druid summoning beasts?

Resting a hand on the bars, Alexander crouched to his level. The blazing firelight caught in his golden hair.

Peter wanted to get up—to charge those bars, reach through, grab hold of Alexander Frossard's throat, and squeeze until every last gasp of air escaped the man. His body began to shake, tingling with the resurgence of feeling he knew wouldn't come in time. Alexander wasn't a fool. He wouldn't approach the cell unless he *knew* Peter posed no threat.

With the strike of the arc still surging through his veins, Peter had to lay there, powerless against anyone or anything.

Alexander's perfect face came into focus as Peter's vision grew sharper, though the edges remained a blur. The Druid's expression was impassive as his piercing blue eyes studied his prostrate captive. "No, Mr. Collins, I have no intention of killing you right away," he said. "Not while you present me with much-needed leverage."

Peter shuddered. Was it because of the pain or because of the fear caused by the knowledge that he *could* be used against his brother?

A tiny quirk of Alexander's lips said he found Peter's predicament amusing. "That said," he added, voice taking on a dark timbre, "I will relish the opportunity to break you in the meantime."

Dread leaked out with the stream of blood that now coated the side of Peter's face. The shadows around him lengthened, and he swore he saw movement within them.

"Welcome to my home," Alexander Frossard said, stepping away from the cell. "I hope you enjoy your stay."

CHAPTER SEVEN

Owen

Anna and Aaron arrived at Occasus bright and early with the news. Gabriel Chapelle knew of the spirit world, beasts, and the Veil. And he'd taught his niece, Juliet, all about it.

A fact that Juliet's father, the reverend, wasn't aware of.

"Juliet is convinced that the hellhound was sent after her," Anna explained, recounting the conversation as they all stood in the kitchen, cups of coffee in hand. "She said that she and Brendan were out at Blackwood Park. They liked to walk the trails together and forage to see if they could find anything special. They had a collection, apparently."

The sweet innocence of the teens' romance struck Owen. Being an "old" married man, he often reminisced on his early relationship with Ava. A little over twelve years ago, they'd met at college in their shared Biblical history class. Ava was a freshman; he was a junior. She was the youngest student in the class, only earning her way into the advanced course by testing out of the requirements. Her accomplishment was one of the many things that recommended her to him at the outset.

Walking through the forest to collect small memories together wasn't so far from their early dates. And it pulled at his chest, drawing on the guilt and separation he felt from his wife all the more.

"They were out there that morning," Anna continued, "walking the same trails they always followed. And they'd separated a bit. Brendan stopped to study some animal tracks while Juliet wandered ahead—within sight—to check out a patch of flowers still holding on in the cold. That's when she heard a growl. Juliet said she froze, thinking it had to be the wolf everyone was talking about. She assumed those were the animal prints that Brendan had found.

"She knew she should warn Brendan, but she was concerned that calling out would draw the wolf's attention," she said. "So she stood there, unsure what to do. The beast stepped into sight then, and Juliet couldn't help it—she screamed, and the hellhound charged."

Anna paused, a glimmer of compassion in her eyes. She shook her head, curly wisps floating around her face. "It went right for her. And Juliet was sure she was going to die. But then . . . then Brendan was there. He dove in front of her, his hands raised. Juliet said she thought it was strange—how he held his hands out. Less like he was trying to stop the beast and more like . . . more like he was trying to *do* something."

Owen could well imagine what she meant. It wasn't an attempt to halt movement—it was an attempt to control the beast. "Did it work?" he asked.

"Yes. But too late."

They all knew the end of the story, but even Owen felt the tug to hear it all the same.

"As Brendan jumped in front of Juliet," Anna concluded, "the hellhound hit him instead. It drove him to the ground, even as Brendan kept fighting. He finally grabbed hold of the hellhound, and then . . . it was gone. Juliet said it turned into smoke the second he got a firm enough hold."

"Brendan was a Wielder?" Cassandra said in shock.

Owen sighed. "And apparently, he knew how to control beasts."

"But you said the hellhound went for Juliet," Spencer said.

Anna nodded. "Brendan's death was a mistake. He saved Juliet's life, but his wounds were fatal. He didn't even make it until the ambulance arrived."

"He knew what it was," Spencer said. "Brendan knew that it was a hellhound sent to kill his girlfriend, and he sacrificed himself."

"Sounds like we need to have a conversation with his parents," Owen concluded. He'd known Brendan. He'd taught him several times during the past several years working as a substitute at DeVerre's school. Considering how small the school was, they managed on a skeleton staff. They regularly called on Owen to help out.

When the announcement of Brendan Descoteaux's death hit DeVerre, Owen hadn't been immune to the mourning. The kid had been a model citizen. He had a heart of gold, a diligence for learning, and a clear devotion to his friends and family. To see a life like that cut down before he even reached his prime was devastating, no matter how distant the relationship might have been.

"Do we know his death was a mistake?" Cassandra asked.

Anna nodded. "It was obvious to Juliet that it only attacked Brendan because he got in the way. And Gabe has told her enough that, after the shock of it all, she figured out where it came from."

"Which," Aaron interjected, "is why we need to talk with Gabe. Being the town mortician is creepy enough. But teaching his niece about the spirit world? That makes him the ideal candidate for investigation, right?"

"Yes, but that will have to wait," Cassandra said.

"Why?"

"We're meeting with the town council this morning," Spencer said.

Anna pulled in a frustrated breath. "Right," she murmured. Then her dark eyes locked with Owen's. "Are you going too?"

"I intended to," he said. "But I'm beginning to question if that's the best use of my time."

Spencer's brow furrowed. "You're our only Warden member. Well . . . former member."

"I *am* a Warden member," Owen corrected. "I just don't work for them anymore."

"Either way, your information could be crucial."

"Could it?"

They all stared at him silently. Because what could they say? Owen knew there was little good he could do in that meeting. DeVerre was no longer a Warden town. Even Tom and Sam didn't know about the organization. Whatever Warden information or support Owen might provide would have little bearing on the conversations inside that meeting.

And like the search for Peter, he would only be another voice in the crowd of all the others.

"We don't have the luxury of time," Owen said. It was perhaps the most frustrating fact of their lives at the moment. For an entire decade, Owen had lived in DeVerre, looking for the very information he now had access to. Ten whole years in which he could have been studying these texts locked within the vault. Ten years when he could have been preparing.

And now he had no time.

Bearing up under his decision, Owen motioned to Spencer and Cassandra. "You two go to the meeting with Tom, Sam, and Ava. Take the journal and all other information that might help prove your case. *Make* them listen to you."

Owen then gestured to his siblings-in-law. "We'll talk to Gabe and hopefully come back with far more information—far more hope—than we had this morning."

"You really think Gabe can help us?" Cassandra asked doubtfully.

"The better question is," Spencer said, "do we think Gabe can be trusted?"

"We trust his brother," Owen said. "And at this point, we don't have much choice—of whom to trust or where we seek information."

"But what if it's a waste of time?" Spencer asked. "You could continue your research. Or try to find Peter."

Owen met Cassandra's hesitant gaze. They all knew finding Peter was a long shot. Whether or not Alexander Frossard orchestrated his capture, there was little to be done until they found proof or got the town on their side.

A likelihood Owen couldn't help feeling dubious of.

He'd refrained from sharing his skepticism last night. It was clear in the way Cassandra walked on eggshells around Spencer and by the young man's dark mood that any revelation of doubt would not be wise. Owen wasn't blind; something was going on between the pair. And if even she felt the need to watch her tongue—to watch her every move, it seemed— then Owen wasn't about to push the matter.

And he had to admit, there *was* a chance of the meeting's success. Marginal as it might be.

Between Sam, Tom, and Ava, they might manage to convince the mayor and council members. What the fallout of such a meeting would be, Owen didn't know.

Part of him feared letting them go without him. What if Alexander responded with violence once backed into a corner? With Ava there, could Owen risk it? With the lives of his wife and child on the line, he questioned if he was brave enough to leave their fate in anyone's hands but his own.

But that was the very reason Owen decided against joining them. He wouldn't cling to control. He knew there was no such thing. Faith meant trust—it meant relying on others as well as himself. And he knew that if it came to a fight, Spencer and Cassandra would be more than capable of keeping his wife safe.

And in the meantime, Owen could be helpful elsewhere.

"This is the best chance we've got," Owen said. "And who knows—Gabe might be able to give us something that helps us find Peter. He could know something about the Frossards and the other Druids that we don't."

"From what Juliet said," Aaron added, a hint of cynicism in his tone, "I wouldn't put anything past him."

Though Spencer and Cassandra hesitated, they both agreed to the plan. They would head for the council meeting while Owen and the Lamberts visited Gabe Chapelle. Any additional allies could change the course of everything. And while they waited on the result of the town council meeting, they would prepare for what came next.

Opening the door of his sedan, Owen watched the Jeep drive past the gates of Occasus. He said a quick, internal prayer for the meeting they were headed to. Then he slipped into the driver's seat. Aaron had picked up Anna on his motorcycle, so they piled into Owen's car for the short drive.

Owen glanced at Aaron in the rearview mirror. "Haley didn't want to come?" he asked.

He knew that Aaron would never have kept Haley in the dark or told her to stay home. He also knew that Haley wasn't the sort to shy away from difficult situations. She was lighthearted, girly, and quirky, but she was also fierce, bold, and loyal. And she was an excellent fit for the Lambert/Bernard family.

Owen still wasn't sure why, after five years of dating, Aaron hadn't asked the woman to marry him yet.

"She's got work," Aaron said. "She'll join us this evening, though."

"At which point," Anna added with disappointment in her tone, "I'll have to go back to work."

After the attack at The Glass Tavern, Haley had covered all of Anna's shifts, helping her recover from the traumatic event. Now that Anna had cleared her head enough, it was time for her to rejoin society outside of Occasus.

And Owen thought that was for the best. Though she might not know it, Anna was somewhat of a pillar of DeVerre's community. People trusted her due to her relationship with the Frossards, her friendships within the church, and her willingness to help with every holiday event the town hosted. To have Anna standing on their side was as potentially beneficial as having Sam and Tom's support.

They drove through the forest-lined road of Whitehill Way, the pines heavy and the macadam packed with snow. The morning sun shimmered on the blanket of crystalline white that covered the earth. This was always Owen's favorite time of year. Growing up in Canada—an even colder climate than Washington—he savored the late autumn renewal. No matter how many times he saw it, something about the frigid snowfall invigorated his senses.

Whitehill Way veered onto Trinity Lane, winding past the two northern neighborhoods of DeVerre. Though his heart pricked as they passed his and Ava's home, he didn't let himself so much as glance down that cul-de-sac, remembering the last moment he'd spent there.

Taking the turn just before DeVerre Chapel, Owen pulled the sedan into the parking lot of DeVerre Funeral Home. The whole lot was covered in snow, and the white van was parked by the front door. Despite the extra workload after the Druids' attack on Occasus, Gabe was still working alone. There was seldom a need for more than one mortician. Up until the past few months, deaths had been limited to the natural course of life.

Stalactite-like icicles hung from the funeral home's eaves and porch overhang. The ashen brick and solemn gray door lent an air of somber eeriness to the building. Owen's mind echoed Aaron's earlier sentiment that Gabe Chapelle's lifestyle lent itself to a certain degree of darkness.

Owen held the door so that Anna and Aaron could enter before him. They stepped into the foyer, a compact reception area. To their right lay the receiving room, a place for gathering family and friends to sit before entering the viewing area beyond the door at the back of the room. Owen hadn't been within the funeral home since his move to DeVerre. Any funeral services he'd attended took place at the chapel. This small building was only used for the care of the body, and its dark and dreary atmosphere seemed to soak up all the emotions from the few mourners who entered its walls.

Yes, Owen's mind resounded, a decidedly eerie place.

In the foyer, a spindly reception desk waited. The deserted space bore only one notice of welcome. A sign rested on the desk's surface: "Working in the back. Ring the bell _ONCE_. I'll get to you when I can."

Owen grinned at the sign as he tapped the silver bell. Gabe's infamous personality matched his career path. While his older brother was the kindhearted reverend, the mortician was the gruff cynic of the family. He undoubtedly found his gloomy job perfectly mundane and his dark surroundings invitingly serene. The citizens often lamented how such a disparity could exist between brothers.

The bell's chime vibrated through the foyer for a handful of seconds. Owen and the Lambert siblings stood in the following silence. A hum pressed in on Owen's ears, the rustle of Aaron's habitual shifting from foot to foot the only sound for several minutes.

"Do you think we ought to ring it again?" Anna asked, her voice a whisper.

"No," Owen said, pointing to the sign. "I have a feeling that wouldn't make the best start."

Anna sighed as she tucked her hands into her coat pockets.

Even Owen began to tap his foot as they waited for the dark wood door behind the desk to open. Several minutes later, Gabriel Chapelle stepped through, dressed for business, the sleeves of his dress shirt rolled up. Hair more auburn than the copper of his brother's, there was still a notable red tinge under the dim recessed lights. His sharp blue eyes took the trio in with a steady sweep, his dark eyebrows lifting in interest. "I was wondering when someone was gonna show up," he said. "Gotta admit, I was expecting the brothers."

Aaron and Anna both looked at Owen.

Taking the hint, Owen stepped forward. "They had other business this morning," he said.

Gabe's nod said this wasn't news. It wouldn't surprise Owen to hear that the whole town knew of the council meeting.

"How can I help you?" the mortician asked.

"I believe we might have some things to discuss," Owen said.

Gabe grunted, a healthy dose of skepticism clear in his grin. "What makes you think we have anything to discuss?"

"Your niece suggested we talk to you."

The smallest flicker of surprise crossed Gabe's face. "Juliet sent you?"

"Yes."

"Hm." Gabe's gaze flickered to Anna. "Well, I suppose there may be some information that we could exchange."

Owen frowned. "Exchange?"

"I have questions too."

"But," Anna said, "Juliet said you knew about the—"

"We were told you could help us," Owen interrupted before she could give away information they might not be ready to share. He didn't like how reluctant Gabe was. Though he supposed it might be wise in a town like DeVerre, where enemies could be lurking around every corner, it seemed that Gabe should trust them based on his niece's recommendation.

"Help, sure," Gabe said. His eyes narrowed. "But first, I need to know what help you're looking for."

Owen paused, considering. His heart beat at an erratic rhythm, fearful that he might put his wife's family in more danger than he could protect them from. But something in Gabe's steady stare—calculating as it might be—spoke more honestly than anyone in DeVerre ever did.

He wanted answers just as badly as they did.

Owen nodded to Anna, prompting her to ask her previous question.

Anna took a deep breath. "You know about the spirit world?"

"I do," Gabe said.

"What do you know?" Aaron asked.

"Not as much as I'd like. What do you know?"

"A great deal more, I'd imagine," Owen said.

His thick eyebrows lifted. "Information you'd be willing to share?"

Owen nodded. "Once you give us some idea of what you know."

The hum of silence pressed back into the foyer, and Owen cursed the secretive nature of DeVerre for the thousandth time since his move there. Even when you offered the truth, the townspeople doubted you. And Owen suspected that it was the Warden's fault. All their secrecy and fear bled into their towns, creating an atmosphere of half-truths and ostracism.

Holding the mortician's distrustful, scrutinous gaze with an open and sincere one, Owen hoped the man would see that they could be trusted. Truly, genuinely trusted.

After a long, drawn-in breath, Gabe sighed. He gestured to the sitting area, its wood-paneled walls and dark emerald couches morbidly welcoming their presence. "Why don't you have a seat?"

CHAPTER EIGHT

Cassandra

The meeting room met every one of Cassandra's menial expectations. She'd had no reason to enter the town hall before today. The small white-washed, moss-covered brick building served as the government headquarters. Its bell tower only rang on holidays anymore but gave the edifice a quaint appearance, particularly amongst the snow. Only the police station, library, and school had any other connection to the governing force of the town. And as Cassandra had little use for any of those services in the past four years, she'd not so much as looked at the hall for longer than a passing glance.

But now she stood inside its walls, at the end of a long, bulky wooden table with Spencer, Ava, Tom, and Sam by her side.

Stock art lined the bland cream walls of the meeting room, and simple furnishings were spread throughout the room. Cassandra could practically smell the mustiness of the '90s on the worn-down carpet. The council had agreed to update the businesses of DeVerre over the past decade, but the government building had yet to receive special attention. Even the chairs surrounding the council table bore dated leather seats and backs.

At the head of the table sat the town mayor, Fred Guillaume. His salt-and-pepper hair reminded Cassandra of her father. But the similarities ended there. Tall and trim, Fred looked like a pine sapling that had shot six feet into the air and forgotten to grow any branches. His business suit hung too loosely around his shoulders, giving the distinct impression of a kid playing dress up. Even with his sharp nose and heavy brows, no one would ever consider the mayor to be imposing.

As Cassandra scanned the rest of the table, she realized that was likely the exact reason Fred wound up with the job twenty years ago—he wasn't a threat to anyone.

Then she realized they'd made a huge mistake by requesting this meeting.

The town council stared back at their group, clustered at the foot of the table. The five council members sat poised in their seats, expressions ranging from serene to wary, interested to bored. They waited to hear from their marshal, reverend, librarian, newcomer, and resident outcast. Alexander Frossard sat amongst them, angled toward the group, a pensive look on his face as though he had no clue what might be coming.

The instant they walked into the room, Cassandra felt Spencer tense. Not that he hadn't already been tense. With the way his hollow and distant gaze settled on random spots of nothingness, she wondered if he had gotten any sleep or sat up in terror the whole night. He walked with a rigid back and stiff neck, his hands regularly fisting and unfisting at his sides.

But seeing Alexander Frossard sent a whole new tension into Spencer's frame. His jaw went taut, a vein pulsing in his neck. Cassandra caught the slightest tremor in his hands before he pressed them against his sides.

Cassandra had cautiously placed herself on the side of the table closer to Alexander to act as a surreptitious boundary between them. She didn't think Spencer would be foolish enough to attack the man, but the increase in his labored breathing and cutting glares put her on edge.

However, it wasn't Alexander's presence that worried her most.

The identities of the three other council members were of far greater concern. Tony MacDonald, Alan Sauveterre, and Leonard Guillaume—a distant cousin of Fred's. All three members of known Druidic families. All with loved ones lost on the grounds of Occasus two nights ago.

Only the single female council member's presence inspired any confidence. Elizabeth Chapelle—Sam's mother—gave her son a pleasant smile when he'd entered. Her strawberry-blonde hair had turned almost golden-white with age, the wrinkles on her face an ever-present reminder of her joyous demeanor. Universally liked, the woman was quick with wise and gentle words. And though Cassandra had never been on the receiving end of the woman's attentions since her return to DeVerre, she'd witnessed her kindness enough to know the lack of relationship between them came from the distance Cassandra created—not from Elizabeth.

But would one ally be enough?

Then again, was she their only hope?

Cassandra herself was proof that being related to a family with Druidic ties wasn't evidence enough to condemn a person. None of the men—Tony, Alan, Leonard, or Fred—were confirmed Druids. Any of them could be innocent. Even if they did know something, they might be like Sam—duped by those they considered closest to them.

She prayed that was the case.

"Good morning, all," Fred greeted from his seat. His wide mouth seemed to hold a perpetual amused grin. Though today, it also bore a somber tilt, likely from the news of a lost family member.

After making a round of introductions, the mayor began the meeting. "We were requested to gather today at the behest of Marshal Garnier and Reverend Chapelle. Obviously, we needed to meet anyway, what with

Saturday night's horrific events." He cast a not-so-subtle suspicious glance at Spencer and Cassandra. "But it seems they have some information to offer with regard to that."

The council members nodded at the mayor's words, then turned to the group with expectant stares. It was Alexander who spoke.

"We'd appreciate any light you can shed on the situation, Sam and Tom." He said it so genuinely—so perfectly—that Cassandra might have believed it. If only Peter hadn't gone missing.

Tom worked his jaw back and forth as Sam glared openly. "Oh," the reverend said, "I'd be *happy* to shed some light, Alex."

The whole council drew back at his cutting tone. Elizabeth's bright eyes flickered between her son and the town doctor. A look of surprise drew Alexander's face into a frown.

Ava stepped in front of the men. Her small stature didn't seem so miniscule when she lifted her chin and met each council member's eyes. "As per the *obvious* nature of this meeting," she mocked the mayor's words, though with a gentle tone that made the barb sound unoffensive, "the most important thing for the council and Mr. Mayor to know is that those who lost their lives on the grounds of Occasus Saturday night went to the estate intending to kill the Collins brothers and Miss Clement."

An immediate rush of shock and appall passed through the council and mayor. They exchanged worried glances and muttered dismay at the suggestion.

"Why would any DeVerrean do that?" Alan demanded, his black hair shining in the light that streamed through the windows on the far side of the room.

Tom rested a hand on his hefty belt. "Probably because they were told to."

"By whom?" Elizabeth asked, genuine concern lacing her tone. "Who would do something like that?"

"And what would be the point?" Tony added. His brutish, square face reminded Cassandra of a bulldog. "They're kids. Sure, we don't care for them squirming their way into our town. But we have no reason to want them dead. We aren't *that* opposed to outsiders."

"They must have gone to talk with them," Leonard said with a dismissive glance toward Ava.

"Fourteen people?" Sam demanded. "A delegation of fourteen DeVerreans went to *talk* with three others?"

Elizabeth rested a finger against her cheek as she considered her son's words. "I must admit, I find that strange as well. I'm not even sure why they would need to talk with them in the first place. Talk about what?"

"The kid's standing right there, Lizzy," Tony said with a thrust of his hand in Spencer's direction. "Why not ask him ourselves?"

Tom scowled. "The man's twenty-six, MacDonald."

Cassandra couldn't help but smirk at Tom's defensive reply. But then, this was Spencer. It was Peter who the marshal once had a problem with.

Tugging a hand from his pocket, Spencer stepped forward, an envelope clutched in his grasp. "This is why they came," he said, showing the council the crinkled letter.

As confusion plastered across all their faces, only Alexander had the wherewithal to respond. He leaned forward in his seat, holding out a hand. "May I?" he asked.

Blinking at the Druid leader, Spencer didn't move. Cassandra could hear that he'd stopped breathing as well. She imagined that his anger locked him in place, fighting the urge to charge around her and demand the location of his brother.

Then he sucked in a breath and passed the letter to Alexander.

"Thank you," Alexander said with a gracious nod. His eyes scanned the paper, the room silent as Elizabeth angled to read over his shoulder.

A deep frown creased Alexander's otherwise perfect face. "This is . . . disconcerting," he said.

Tony gestured for the letter, and it was passed across the table. Alan and Leonard read along while Alexander informed Fred of the letter's contents.

Alexander turned back to Spencer. "There's no postage on the envelope. When and how did you receive this letter?" he asked.

Spencer's jaw flexed, his shoulder brushing Cassandra's as he shifted from foot to foot. The deliverer of that letter had been the dead body of Robert MacDonald, the Druid who had attacked Peter and Anna at The Glass Tavern—both Fred's nephew-in-law and a distant cousin to Tony. The man whom the town still assumed was *missing* since they'd covered up his death by having Gerard dump the body into the lake.

"It showed up on our porch," Spencer said prudently.

Alan looked up from the letter with a look of consternation. "It says three days," he noted.

Leonard pointed to the paper still in Tony's grasp. "Yes, it specifically says they would arrive Sunday morning. Yet this massacre took place on Saturday night."

Ava crossed her arms. "This is what bothers you?" she said. "A timeline inconsistency? How about you take issue with the fact that a *cult* has infiltrated your town, Leonard."

Tony gave his own aggressive huff. "What proof do we have that there's a cult?"

"I'd say that letter in your hand is a pretty good start," Tom said.

"This isn't proof of anything," Tony said, brandishing the letter before tossing it to the table with a careless flick of his wrist. "It's typed, there's no address, and nothing to link it to anyone besides the Collins brothers. And they're writers, right? Who's to say they didn't print it off themselves?"

"And what?" Sam's caustic question set a charge through the air. "Conspire to lure fourteen DeVerreans to their home so they could kill them? How would they even begin to do that?"

"How are any of us to know?" Tony spat back. "Maybe they wrote it after our friends and family showed up and they massacred them. We don't know what these boys are capable of."

"However," Alan said sharply, "we are *all* aware of Miss Clement's questionable past. Maybe she put them up to it."

Cassandra couldn't help her scoff, but it was Spencer who spoke up. "She's your family, jackass."

Alan blanched at Spencer's retort, withdrawing into his seat as though it had been a physical blow.

Lifting a placating hand, Alexander looked to his fellow councilman. "We are not in the business of making accusations, Alan."

"No," Tony said, his black eyes glimmering as he gave a pointed nod to Tom. "That's supposed to be *his* job."

"You got a problem with how I do my job, MacDonald?" Tom demanded.

"We've all got a problem with how you do your job, Garnier," the brute growled back. "It's hard not to take issue when our family and friends keep dying under *your* watch."

"Let's not get into a pissing contest," Ava muttered to Tom, halting his ready reply. Then she turned back to the council and mayor.

"We were there," she announced. "When Toni, Casey, and Alyssa Frossard, Clayton, Tasha, Kevin, and Elsie Dumont, Louis, Neil, and Dawn Alarie, Emily Guillaume, Jordan MacDonald, Sarah Sauveterre, and Rene Mercier showed up at Occasus along with six other unidentified men and women—" Ava pulled in a breath as the members of the council dipped their head at the names of their lost family.

Without giving them long to dwell, Ava continued. "Tom, my sister, my husband, and I were all there. Owen and Tom *saw* those twenty individuals attack Peter, Spencer, and Cassandra. Their response was self-defense and nothing more."

"Twenty individuals," Tony grumbled, "for three people? You expect us to believe that?"

"Why would we lie?" Ava asked.

"This is our family," Alan yelled, his voice breaking with emotion.

He thrust a hand at the letter on the table, genuine tears in his eyes. "My *wife* was not a cultist!"

Cassandra swallowed past the guilt burning in her throat. She didn't know if she'd been the one who killed Sarah Sauveterre or if it had been Spencer or Peter. But she did know that, like everything else, she'd played her role in the woman's death.

Elizabeth reached across the table to rest her hand on Alan's, whispering words of comfort.

"Dawn was my daughter," Tony said, fury in his glare. "You wanna tell me she had it out for these kids too?"

"My family was involved too," Cassandra said. "Rene and I grew up together. Trust me, it wasn't exactly a pleasant surprise when she tried to kill me."

"This doesn't make any sense," Alexander said, his voice even and soothing. "Perhaps there's something to what you say, but . . . these accusations you're laying against our families . . . it's hard to accept."

His gaze was so steady, so convincing—it was almost laughable.

And before she realized it, Cassandra did laugh.

The room froze at the sound, and Cassandra could have sworn a smug glint flickered through Alexander's eyes.

Seeing that she'd made a mistake, Cassandra shook her head. There was no going back now. Holding the steady stare of Alexander Frossard, she gave him a humorless smile. "You're a really good actor," she said. "But you made a surprisingly stupid mistake."

"I'm sorry," Alexander said, bewilderment drawing his blond brows together. "I'm not sure what you're talking about, Miss Clement."

"I bet everyone at this table is a Druid," she said. "Except for Mrs. Chapelle, perhaps. I'd imagine she's as in the dark as her son was until a day ago."

While the council all responded with expressions of bafflement, playacting or not, Sam stepped up to the table. "You lied to me, Alex," he said, voice taut with rage.

Alexander adopted a pained expression. "Sam, I—"

"Shut up!" Sam slammed his fist against the tabletop. "*You* killed Brendan! It was your call, and *you* killed him!"

"Sam, I would never!"

Cassandra jumped in before the man could get in another lie. "Brendan wasn't even the intended target," she said. "The hellhound was sent after Juliet."

Sam blanched, red dots of fury sprinkling his cheeks. "What?"

"She told Anna last night," Cassandra said. "She didn't tell you because she thought you wouldn't believe her when she told you it was a beast from the spirit world. But the hellhound was sent for her. It only killed Brendan because he sacrificed himself to save her and send the beast away."

A hush fell over the room as Sam began to shake.

"Miss Clement," Alexander's voice—steady and sure—cut through like a blade, "these accusations you're making are truly obscene. You all come in here talking about cults, and . . . beasts, and murder as though this were some sort of horrifying fairy tale. Our families are grieving. We have all lost someone dear to us. And you have the audacity to accuse us of . . . being cultists?"

"We have proof that you're cultists," Spencer said, a dull edge to his tone.

"You already offered your proof, kid," Tony growled.

Spencer held out a hand to Cassandra. She'd already begun digging in her messenger bag, heavy with their evidence. She handed him the journal first, slowly gathering the rest as he pleaded their case.

"You all may have wondered why Diane moved here nearly forty years ago," he said with slow intentionality as he shuffled through the pages of the journal. "Turns out she came here to find her mother."

"Her mother?" Elizabeth asked.

"Diane and her brother—my grandfather—Phillip, were adopted by the Collins family in December of 1940," Spencer explained. "Honestly, that should have been a dead giveaway. Because something else remarkable happened in DeVerre, December of 1940.”

Elizabeth’s mouth dropped open as the truth resonated. The rest of the council, along with the mayor, remained impassive at this revelation.

Spencer held up the journal, open to the page of their evidence. “This is the journal of Michael Varon,” he said. “My brother and I found it in a hidden vault within Occasus, thanks to Ava’s help.”

Ava gave him a little nod.

“In an entry from October of 1940, Michael wrote, *‘It is the truest joy to know I now have a son as well as a daughter. Our sunshine, Diane, and our new ray of light, Phillip.’*” Spencer looked up from the journal. “There is ample evidence within this journal of Diane and Phillip being the legitimate children of Michael Varon and Seraphine Frossard after their secret marriage in 1937. The couple was working together to bring down the Druids within DeVerre—led by Seraphine’s father, Lloyd Frossard.”

A small, humorless chuckle came from Alexander. “Well, that’s where you have your information confused, son,” he said. “Seraphine was the daughter of a distant cousin.”

“My great-grandfather, Vernon Rayne, has evidence to the contrary,” Ava said, tossing a folder onto the table next to the letter. “Go ahead, keep them. I have copies.”

The council members and the mayor exchanged surprised and concerned glances as Elizabeth lifted a hand to her mouth in shock at all the news coming to light.

Alexander merely sighed. “All right, maybe Seraphine was my grandfather’s daughter. That’s not what I was told, but I can tell you for a fact she never had any relationship with Michael Varon.” He said the name like it tasted foul on his tongue.

“Then why did your great-uncle, Lee Frossard, escort Diane and Phillip to the Collins family in Norfolk?” Spencer asked, showing the photo from Diane’s corkboard.

"Because they were Seraphine's children," Alexander admitted. "The poor girl was taken advantage of, and my grandfather was gracious enough to help her care for the children."

Spencer huffed. "So you'll claim us as your blood, but you won't acknowledge that we're part Varon as well?"

"We all know that Michael Varon was a psychopath," Alexander said, his tone hard for the first time. "Whatever he wrote in that journal of his—*if* he wrote that journal at all—was clearly the ravings of a madman."

"*If?*" Spencer demanded. "Do you think my brother and I took the time to write this too?"

"You are authors, aren't you?"

The journal hit the table with a *crack*, causing Cassandra and several of the other members in the room to jump. "Where is he?" The question rumbled out of Spencer as he placed his hands on either side of the book.

Alexander's handsome face pulled together in the perfect imitation of confusion. "I don't understand," he said. "What are you talking about?"

"Yesterday morning at approximately 11:30 a.m.," Tom said, "Peter Collins went missing at DeVerre Chapel."

Elizabeth gasped, and Fred blinked rapidly with shock, but the rest of them showed no response to this news.

"Sam?" Elizabeth swung to face her son, alarm growing across her face. "What is going on here?"

Sam shook his head, his eyes darting toward Alexander swiftly, a look of cold resignation darkening his features. His reply was a low undertone, directed toward his mother only. "We'll talk later."

Alexander turned to his fellow council members. "I think I've had about enough of this," he said, then began to stand, the three other councilmen following his lead. "Whatever it is that you are attempting to accuse me and my family of, Mr. Collins, let me be plain: I had nothing to do with your brother's disappearance or the deaths you two and Miss Clement dealt two nights ago. I'd ask that you refrain from smearing my name in this town, or else I'll be contacting my lawyer to pursue defamation against all three of you."

Elizabeth gaped up at Alexander but seemed at a loss for words. It was so clear; he'd stacked the council in his favor. No matter what they tried to do, they would never get the support of the town officials. And even Elizabeth Chapelle's voice wouldn't be enough to get the rest of the town on their side.

Alexander turned to Fred. "Mr. Mayor—"

Fred looked up at the Druid leader, mouth ajar in stunned confusion.

"I'd like to call this meeting to a close," Alexander said. "With your permission, of course."

"What—Alex, no, I—" Elizabeth began to protest, but Fred cut across her.

"Yes," he murmured, sounding as baffled as he looked. "Yes, of course, Alex, whatever you think is best. This truly is—I don't fully understand how you came up with such a horrific story, young man," the mayor bumbled, turning to Spencer. "The Frossards are the backbone of this town. Your allegations are absolutely absurd."

"Fredrick!" Elizabeth scolded.

Her reprimand went unheard as the other four councilmen and the mayor moved to leave.

Cassandra didn't know what to do. She could hear Sam and Tom beginning to protest, then muttering back and forth with Ava when they realized they could do nothing to stop the meeting from ending, unresolved as it was.

But Cassandra's eyes were locked on Spencer, his hands still pressed firmly against the table as he glared at Alexander Frossard. The Druid leader walked with his head held high, not so much as glancing at the young man he'd dismissed with such callous disregard.

Fury practically leaped off Spencer like waves of heat from flames. His breathing was steady, and his body was still, but the fire burned in the air around him. And as Alexander moved to pass Spencer, he whispered the one thing that would unleash that rage.

"You Varons always were easy to kill."

It happened in the blink of an eye.

Spencer's hand shot out to take hold of Alexander's arm. Then he yanked, twisting the Druid around in front of him.

Alexander's face slammed into the table with a resounding *thud*.

A cry of alarm from Elizabeth pierced the air as Spencer bellowed, "Where's my brother, you bastard?"

The councilmen sprang forward to defend their leader as Tom and Sam blocked them. They yelled at each other, two against three, all with righteous indignation. The mayor looked absolutely perplexed as to what he should do. Ava watched everything with a cunning eye, her hand resting on her stomach, subconsciously protecting her child.

Cassandra could only focus on Spencer. Her heart hammered in her chest, somewhere between awe and horror at his bravery and violence. She didn't know whether she should stop him or let him bring the man to the brink of his life.

However, Alexander—the entire top half of his body pressed firmly against the table—remained silent, the smallest fraction of a smile on his lips.

A spike of dread pierced through Cassandra's chest. "No," she whispered.

With no reply from Alexander and a hand on his collar, Spencer hauled the man up to slam him back down on the table. There was a sharp *crack* as the doctor's head hit the table once more. "Where is he!" Spencer demanded.

But Alexander didn't respond.

And Cassandra knew this was just what the Druid wanted.

"Spencer," she called.

His blue eyes flashed to her face, the anger within them burning hot.

Cassandra wanted to go to him, to take hold of his hand and draw him away from the Druid. But she knew this was not the time to compel him through touch. He was too deep in his fury for her to douse the flame without getting burned herself.

So she stood her ground, holding his gaze. "This isn't the way," she said.

The room had quieted as she challenged him. They were all watching, waiting to see if he'd listen. Or if he'd return to his rage.

Spencer's throat bobbed as he swallowed, still holding Alexander against the table.

Cassandra gave a gentle shake of her head. "Not like this," she whispered.

"He has Peter," he said as though she'd forgotten.

"I know," she promised. "But *this* won't get him back."

Alexander stupidly—or perhaps intentionally—spoke up. "I don't know what happened to your brother," he said.

Spencer snarled. "I don't believe you for a second," he spat. Then he shoved him against the table, releasing him. "But as I'll need you to return him to me, it won't do to kill you yet."

The threat lingered as Spencer backed away, and Alexander slowly pushed himself off the table. A bright red line split the man's forehead, and he dabbed at it, hissing at the touch. His fingers came away bloody.

Alexander sighed as he inspected them. "I'd advise you to seek help for anger management," he muttered.

Enraged, Tony shoved at Tom's shoulder, then thrust a finger in Spencer's direction. "Arrest him!" he commanded.

Cassandra could see the conflict within Tom, his dark eyes flashing between Alexander and Spencer. He knew what his job required of him here: He *should* arrest Spencer for assault. No matter how much he didn't want to.

Alexander held up a hand, stalling any justice from being served. "I won't press charges," he said. "The boy is clearly distraught, and I won't hold his misplaced anger against him."

A collective relief washed through the room even as the tension remained.

But Alexander wasn't done. "I would, however, like to put forth a request for the probation of Marshal Garnier."

Shouts of disbelief and denial came from their friends and Elizabeth. Cassandra couldn't bring herself to do anything. Not while she continued to watch Spencer carefully. He made a slow retreat from Alexander, his hands clenched at his side. He was still fuming, still burning. And she feared what would happen if she didn't get him out of there.

Alexander continued, directing his words to the mayor and council members. "It's very clear that our marshal's judgment has been impaired," he said, then turned to the marshal. "I'm not sure what's going on with you, Tom, but—really? You're siding with these boys rather than the people you've known your entire life?"

A thick scoff broke out of Tom. "You're losing this town, Alex," he said. "Fire me if you like. But the Varons have returned, and we Garniers will always side with the *true* leaders of DeVerre."

"Leaders?" Alexander shook his head in disappointment. He glanced dubiously at Spencer. "You want a leader like that?"

The pregnant pause echoed through the room as Tom gave no response.

Alexander turned to Fred. "Shall we vote on the matter?"

Cassandra didn't wait any longer. She hurried forward to gather the journal and papers from the desk, shoving them into her bag. She didn't care to hear the sham of a vote. Alexander had the council in his pocket. They all knew what the outcome would be.

Grabbing Spencer's arm, Cassandra gave only one tug before he moved with her, Ava at their side as they barreled out of the room.

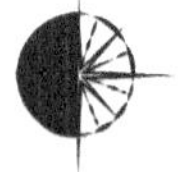

CHAPTER NINE

Spencer

The blistering fall air burned Spencer's face as they broke out of the town hall. Cassandra remained at his side, her hand hovering near his arm as though she was worried he'd bolt back inside to take down Alexander for real. And after his display in the meeting room, he supposed it was a valid concern.

But the anger that roared to life in Spencer then had burned up all its fuel. Now, the shaking had returned. Coiling, pulsing, and pressing through his limbs.

Ava followed closely behind them, muttering about the farcical meeting. They hurried across the lawn, the thick snow crunching under their feet. The late morning sunlight reflected blindingly off all the snow that covered the earth, road, sidewalk, and buildings. It even obscured the plaza plaque.

Spencer wondered if the women could see the way his body trembled. He could never tell if the spasms were internal or external. Was it all in his head? Most things were. Maybe they had no idea that he was on the brink of a panic attack.

When was the last time he'd had one? Spencer couldn't remember. Peter always did such a good job of noticing when he was on the verge and distracting him before it could happen.

Crossing the street from the circular town center toward the library, Spencer's eyes fell on the Jeep. Their dad's Jeep. His hand twitched uncontrollably as he dug the keys out of his pocket.

That was the last time he'd had a real panic attack, he realized. In the months after their dad died, they'd become somewhat regular in Spencer's life. But Peter had helped him get them under control before their mom could take it seriously and suggest therapy. For years, they'd all but disappeared, and Spencer hadn't even considered that they might make a resurgence.

The very last time he'd ever lost control had been when he'd gotten behind the wheel of their mom's minivan for the first time. After teaching Peter how to drive two years prior, their mom had relinquished teaching Spencer to him. And as the brothers sat in the driveway, fifteen-year-old Spencer in the driver's seat, the moment had finally come for him to put the car in drive.

"I can't," Spencer had muttered, staring at the road beyond their driveway.

"Sure, you can," seventeen-year-old Peter had promised. "We've gone through everything. Blinkers, lights, park, reverse, mirrors, all of it. Now, you just gotta put it to practice."

Spencer could only blink.

"You've got this, Spence."

"I can't," he repeated.

"Why not?"

"Because."

"That's not a real answer," Peter said, a thread of humor in his voice.

Spencer shook his head. "I can't."

"Look, Spence—" His brother heaved a sigh. "We've been working on this for hours. We're just going around the block."

But Spencer's hands were clammy, and his chest was tight, and his imagination was warning him of all the ways he could screw up and get them both killed. And he'd freaked out.

"I can't do it, Peter!" he yelled, going to unhook his seat belt. He fumbled with the button, his trembling fingers feeling thick and heavy as he grappled with the buckle. "What if I forget something? What if I don't hit the brakes fast enough? Or—or the blinker stops working? Someone could run into us. Shit!"

It was the first time Spencer had ever used profanity. He'd always held his tongue in the past, determined to be the perfect son. But his hands were shaking, and he couldn't get the buckle to unclasp, and he was starting to struggle to breathe. He yanked away from the buckle to press a hand to his chest, where pain began to radiate. It felt like a monster inside his ribcage, growing too large and attempting to force its way out.

"Spence!" Peter jerked forward, seeing his distress. He managed to get the seat belt unhooked in one press. Then he grabbed his brother's arm. "What is it? That's a stupid question. I know what's happening. Uhhhhhh . . . Hey, you—you don't have to drive, okay? If you wanna stay home all the time and—I dunno, be a hermit or whatever, it's no big deal."

Listening to his brother ramble, Spencer worked to gain control of his breathing. His heartbeat thrummed in his skull, but Peter's chatter gave him a center. A reminder that his brother was there and that no matter what, as long as he had Peter, everything would turn out just fine.

"Yeah," Peter continued. "We can work out a system, you and me. I'll be, like, the face of our writing duo, and you'll be the eccentric recluse that everyone talks about. They'll start questioning if you're even real, and it'll be great! We can make it a whole marketing piece. You know, the mystery dudes who've got a mystery of their own."

As Spencer's breathing slowed, Peter slugged his arm. "I can see it now—" He drew a hand through the air, mimicking a headline. " *'Does Spencer Collins Even Exist?'*"

The ridiculousness of Peter's comment had pulled a singular, disbelieving laugh out of Spencer. And that was all it took. Because Peter was there. And Spencer would always be safe so long as Peter was there.

But Peter wasn't there anymore.

Tearing the keys from his pocket, Spencer fought against the uptick in his breathing. He could feel the pressure again—that monster pushing against his ribcage, desperate to get out. The keys jingled as they dangled from his shaking fingers.

Behind him, Ava and Cassandra discussed something, voices low and serious. He thought it had to do with changing their plans and finding some other way to convince people.

A conversation that didn't matter right now.

"Here," Spencer said, interrupting as he shoved his hand toward Cassandra.

Looking down at the keys swaying between them, Cassandra came to a halt in the middle of the street. "Wha—what?" she asked.

"I don't think I should drive," Spencer said.

At his tight words, Cassandra glanced at Ava, then turned back and cautiously reached for the keys. "You're sure?" she asked.

Spencer forced himself to nod. Ever since his mother had signed the title over to him on his sixteenth birthday, he'd never willingly let anyone drive the Jeep but Peter.

And somehow, Cassandra seemed to understand this unspoken truth as she reluctantly—almost reverently—took the keys from him now.

Spencer gave Ava a quick goodbye and hurried to the other side of the Jeep. He could hear the women exchanging a longer farewell—Ava stating that while she had to work at the library, she would come to Occasus in the evening to do whatever she could to help.

He climbed into the passenger seat, unsure if the cold or his fear caused his shoulders to tremble with a shiver. Stupidly, he'd forgotten his coat that morning. He ran a thumb along the hem of his denim jacket. It didn't keep him warm enough in the Washington fall. But he'd been living in a daze since yesterday morning.

The driver's door creaked open, and Cassandra leaped behind the wheel. Spencer worked to swallow down the tightness settling into his throat. He kept his eyes on the frost that spiderwebbed from the corner of the windshield.

Without a word, Cassandra started the Jeep. She checked the mirrors and seat but didn't need to make any adjustments—she and Spencer were the same height, after all. The stereo remained off, only the growl of the Jeep's engine and the hiss of the heater filling the space between them.

Spencer thought he saw Cassandra scanning him out of his peripheral, but he didn't turn. And he didn't try to pretend that he was okay. He was too busy trying not to scream.

His chest grew tighter, the monster inside pushing harder.

As Cassandra steered them back toward Occasus, Spencer refused to look at the town hall, instead keeping his eyes angled to the right at the edge of the snow banked against the sidewalks. The plaza gave way to open space, with only the chapel and firehouse in immediate sight. The funeral home—tucked behind the chapel—peeked through as they veered with the road.

A fleeting curiosity over Owen, Anna, and Aaron's meeting passed through Spencer's mind. He hoped they were still gone from the house. He wasn't entirely certain he could talk with them. No matter how important the information might be.

Spencer's breath caught in his throat. He wasn't sure why. It was just getting harder to breathe.

Raising a hand to scrub over his face, he forced himself to take a long, controlled breath. He leaned his head against the headrest, closing his eyes.

He could hear Cassandra shifting in her seat. She was probably wondering if she should do something. He felt bad for her. There was no way she could know how to help. No way she *could* help. No one ever could. Only Peter.

Spencer sat up straight. He couldn't think about it. That would make it worse.

But as they turned onto Whitehill, he saw Haven Boulevard to his right: the neighborhood occupied by Alexander Frossard and his Druids. The blackened remains of the Mercier house loomed within sight of the road, surrounded by pristine white mansions. The house that Spencer had burned down. The one that Peter had almost died in.

Spencer's hand pressed against his chest. His jaw strained from how hard he'd been clenching it. And he couldn't get his lungs to fill with more than a short burst of air.

On either side of the road, the shadows of the pine trees hung like wraiths in his vision. They swayed threateningly in the wind. Was that a flash of movement he spotted? Had Alexander dispatched a hellhound after them again?

Spencer blinked. No, there was nothing but trees and snow and empty brush.

An early winter was in full swing. Any predators within the woods would be hibernating, right? But beasts didn't hibernate. They came with one purpose, one focus until the job was done.

Was that how Alexander had gotten Peter? Had he sent a beast to retrieve him? That didn't make much sense, though. Peter was a Wielder—a Sage. He'd brought down beasts easily only two nights ago.

Two nights ago.

The memories hit Spencer like a blow to the back of the head. Wendigos, hydras, hellhounds, scylla, and beasts he had no name for yet. Darkness and terror. Blood and pain. Chaos and death. So much death.

The monster swelled inside Spencer's chest, causing him to grimace.

"Spencer?" Cassandra's voice brushed lightly across his consciousness.

His imagination pressed in. Dark shapes lined the trees out in the woods. But when he looked, they were gone.

Spencer blinked rapidly, the snow blinding him with its brightness. There was nothing out there.

"Spencer, are you—"

"Pull over."

"What?"

Spencer hadn't realized he'd said it until Cassandra responded. Nor had he realized how much he needed it.

"Pull over," he repeated.

"We're almost home," she offered. He didn't like how nervous, how worried her voice sounded. "Can you—"

"Cassandra." He tried to keep his tone calm, but it came out clipped. "Pull. Over."

"I don't—"

"Just do it."

The Jeep swerved cautiously over the road. Despite Cassandra's control, Spencer's head swam. He could imagine the Jeep tumbling over onto its side, rolling and crashing into a tree. He could see Cassandra hanging upside down, only held in place by her seat belt, as blood coated her temple, matting her hair to her cheek.

It wasn't real, Spencer reminded himself. His imagination was getting the better of him.

Before Cassandra could put the Jeep in park, Spencer slammed the release of his seat belt and yanked open the door. He heard her call his name as he shoved his way out of the vehicle, but he didn't stop. He couldn't stop. His chest hurt. His body shook. His head spun.

Where was Peter?

That was a stupid question. Spencer knew where Peter was.

Peter was gone.

"Oh, God," Spencer gasped, his breath coming out in a puff of air.

Stumbling through the trees, Spencer didn't know where he was going. He just knew he needed to move. He needed to get away. Maybe if he walked far enough, he could escape the terror that was ripping its way through his ribcage—slamming against his chest.

Cassandra followed. He knew that by the sound of footsteps that echoed his and the occasional whisper of his name—a plea for him to let her help.

She couldn't help.

Peter was gone.

Spencer came to a halt. He pressed his fingers into his scalp against the roaring that now lived there—the repetitive reminder of that single, horrifying truth: Peter was gone.

"No," Spencer muttered under his breath. "No, no, no, no."

He couldn't do this. Not again. The last time he'd lost someone, he'd had Peter. If he lost his brother . . . ?

"I can't," Spencer heard himself say.

The sound of footsteps went silent behind him. "Can't do what?" Cassandra asked softly.

Turning around, Spencer found her standing several paces back, maintaining a distance from him like one would from a wild animal. Intrigued but afraid.

"I can't," he repeated. "I—I can't live without him."

Compassion and pain tore across Cassandra's expression. She stepped closer, easing the slightest tension in Spencer's muscles. "We'll find him," she promised. "Whatever we have to do, we'll find him."

Spencer shook his head. "What if he's—"

"He's not," she said before he could even suggest it. "He's worth more alive."

"You don't know that."

She took another step.

The monster in his chest eased back.

Her intense stare commanded him to listen to her words. "They know," she said, "just like I do, what you'd do to save him. It would be foolish of them to do anything *but* keep him alive. They need him."

The logic was there, but Spencer's mind conjured dozens of scenarios that might change the facts. Accidents happen all the time. What if Peter fought them? What if he died in the process? Even if he didn't, being leverage was almost worse. What if they forced Spencer to betray Cassandra to get his brother back? Could he do that? Could he trade Cassandra's life for Peter's? He didn't like how hard that was to decide.

"I can't do this again," Spencer said, staring up at the towering pines around them. "I can't lose someone else."

The snow glittered in the hazy beams of sunlight streaking through the pine trees. His dad would have loved it here. The woods, the house, the people. David Collins would have loved every minute of life in DeVerre.

This should have been their home, after all. They were DeVerrean. They were Varons. This was their home, and it was where they belonged.

Yet here Spencer stood in this frozen forest, his every nightmare coming true.

"I can't do it," he whispered to the air. "I'm not brave enough to be alone."

He watched his words coil into a fog as they breathed out of him. They evaporated into the cold sky as though he'd never said them at all.

"You're not alone, Spencer." Cassandra's tone was rough and insistent.

He met her gaze, her sharp eyebrows pulled together, low over her intense stare. She looked almost in pain as she took one step closer. A chill spread across his skin at that fierce look.

Cassandra shifted from foot to foot, the snow and pine needles crunching beneath her. The sharp, earthy scent of the trees grew harsher as soft beams of sunlight broke through to catch in her hazel eyes. They lit up like jewels, glittering and variegated. She opened her mouth to speak again, her words so soft that the wind almost couldn't carry them over the five feet that separated them.

"I'm here."

Her rich, raspy voice hit Spencer like a jolt of electricity. Cassandra was here. She had *chosen* to be here with him, and he didn't have to be alone. His breath hitched, his heart stuttered, and his brain lost control. But this was nothing like the feeling of panic.

This was absolute insanity.

Before he could regain his sense of reason, Spencer crossed the two long strides between them. He saw her flinch at his sudden approach just as his hands took hold of her face and pulled her close to meet his lips with hers. Instantly, Cassandra's hands flew up to grip his arms. He tensed, thinking that she'd push him away. Instead, she leaned in, returning his kiss.

Heat rose at the base of Spencer's skull, spreading to warm his whole body. The fear was gone, the monster in his chest docile at the stunning truth that Cassandra Clement was *here*.

He brushed the pad of his thumb across her cheek, feeling the elegant hollow of her high cheekbones. She felt so small under his touch. So delicate, like vintage lace curtains that had seen too much sunlight. And yet she held onto him with such strength. Her fingers pressed into his biceps as though she couldn't even begin to consider letting go.

Spencer lost himself in kissing her. He forgot everything but her. All his thoughts were zeroed in, thinking only of the way her silky, dark brown hair tangled around the ends of his fingers. Her sharp, graceful nose brushed against his. Her skin radiated warmth into his palms. And her breath mingled with his as they lingered within these kisses far longer than he'd expected.

Heart pounding against his chest, Spencer forced himself to pull back. It felt like trying to pull apart the world's two strongest magnets. His head swam in her nearness, trying to convince him that he should go back for more.

Spencer rested his forehead on Cassandra's, unable to manage much more self-control than that. Nothing else had changed. Their heavy breathing still twisted between them as they held onto one another with firm grips, his hands on either side of her face while hers held firm to his arms.

A sudden surge of panic tore through Spencer's veins. He'd just kissed Cassandra—without any real confirmation that she wanted him to. His throat went dry, and a tremor went through his hands. The hands that still held onto her.

Spencer released her, opening his eyes to face whatever she might say. But her grip on his arms didn't let him pull back farther than a handful of inches. And the look on her face wasn't at all what he'd expected.

An amused grin lifted Cassandra's lips. Her dark eyes locked with his, staring back and forth between them as though struggling to figure out what he'd meant by kissing her.

"Cass, I—" The words died before he knew what he meant to say.

In one swift movement, Cassandra released him and rested a hand against her mouth as she let out a thin laugh. "That was surprising," she muttered.

Spencer considered apologizing, but he didn't think he wanted to.

She smirked at him. "Can't say it wasn't enjoyable though."

A nervous laugh eked out of Spencer. He ran a hand through his hair as he backed away from her. "Ah, it, um . . . it wasn't—I mean, it was surprising to me too."

Cassandra reached across to tap his chest with the back of her hand. "Well, I didn't mind, so don't be weird about it, all right?"

Unsure whether that was her way of accepting his interest or if she was letting him down easy, Spencer cleared his throat. "All right, but . . ."

"But, what?"

He eyed her for a split second before dropping his gaze, too uncomfortable to be so honest while looking at her. "What if it happens again?"

A few seconds of pause drew Spencer to glance back up at her, needing to figure out what she was thinking. There was an odd blend of curiosity and humor in her grin. "You having a panic attack? Or you kissing me because of it?"

Though he wouldn't say he'd kissed her *because* of the panic attack—it'd been more due to the awe he felt at knowing she cared about him too—he didn't bother to correct her.

"Either," he said. "Both."

She crossed her arms, causing her leather jacket to pucker around her scarf. "Well, how about this," she said. "If you have another panic attack, I give you permission to kiss me if it'll stop it. And in the meantime, I'll consider myself one lucky girl."

Spencer didn't quite know how to take that. She hadn't exactly accepted him. But then, she hadn't rejected him either. He thought maybe he should ask for clarification. It would be a mistake to assume that she wanted a relationship when she didn't, just as it would be a mistake to assume she didn't when she did.

Fumbling to find a way to address the topic, Spencer ran a hand over his mouth. Then he realized that he'd just kissed Cassandra with that mouth, and it sent a whole flurry of other thoughts soaring through his head.

"Come on—" Cassandra's voice broke through his wildly churning thoughts. She tapped his arm as she angled back toward the footsteps that had led them here. "We ought to get home."

Spencer frowned. "I don't want to go home," he muttered.

She turned around, a single brow raised in question.

"I don't like being there when Peter's. . . ."

Cassandra raised her chin in understanding. "Where do you want to go, then?"

Holding her steady, confident stare, Spencer suddenly felt everything click into place. Whatever Cassandra felt—whatever she wanted out of their relationship—he knew what he wanted. He knew what she meant to him. And if the Druids were ever foolish enough to try to get him to betray Cassandra for the release of his brother . . . well, they'd find themselves with far more than fourteen cultists lost.

Spencer pulled in a deep, clear breath of frigid air. It burned his lungs, but he smiled because he *could* breathe.

"I want to find my brother," Spencer said at last.

Cassandra waited, her steady gaze expectant.

He sighed then. "And I think that means we *have* to go home."

CHAPTER TEN

Peter

Peter was running.

The frozen woods chilled him to the bone, the moonlight glinting off the icicles and snow that hung from the boughs of trees. Darkness surrounded him, obsidian black variegated with glittering silver stars and a full moon. Fog filtered through the pines, clinging to the air and shrouding the forest in mystery.

Sprinting around another tree, Peter glanced behind him once. He knew running would do no good. The rumble and rush of pursuing beasts droned through the night. They were gaining. And he wasn't fast enough to outrun them.

But he had to run.

The puff of Peter's breath turned to mist in the air. He had to keep running. If he could make it to Occasus, he would be fine. If he could get to Spencer, everything would be okay.

Shadows filtered through the fog all around him—the beasts catching up.

Peter pushed harder.

He didn't fully understand *how* he'd gotten free of Alexander's prison. It'd been far too easy to slip out of the cage, sneak out of the Frossard vault, and into the forest beyond. Far, far too easy.

Peter worried that he'd done exactly what Alexander wanted. Maybe Alexander wanted him to get free for this exact reason—to send the beasts after him, torturing him with the hope of freedom, with the return to Spencer, and then take it away.

But Peter would take the chance. Whatever game the Druid was playing, he'd play it. And he would get back to his brother.

A sharp jerk on his foot caused Peter's heart to jolt, and he plummeted. He hit the ground hard, pain exploding into his body from the sharp rocks and twigs of the forest floor. He whipped around, expecting a beast to hover over him, ready to strike. But all he found twisted around his foot was a protruding root, snow freshly shaken loose from his collision.

Pushing off the ground, Peter could feel the bloody cuts on his hands and the skinned knee that poked through a hole ripped in his jeans. He didn't care. He couldn't care. The shadows of the beasts flashed around him in the moonlight, their growls and chitters echoing in the still woods.

He had to move. He had to get up. He had to keep running. He had to get to Occasus.

The *whoosh* and whisper of beasts chasing him pressed in on all sides, melding with the pounding of his heart. Peter's feet fumbled and slipped over the icy earth. The air burned in his lungs. Pushing against trees to remain steady, his hands stinging from their cuts, he charged on.

A faint glow appeared through the forest ahead of him. The porch of Occasus. Only a short run farther, and he'd be home. He could make it.

Calves stinging from the extended sprint, Peter's lungs shuddered in his chest. He really needed to start working out with Spencer. When he got back, when he was free, that would be first on the agenda.

Peter broke through the tree line and out onto the road. The moon beamed overhead, casting over the world an eerie, white halo. The gates of Occasus hung open before him, their wrought iron twisting into the Varon crest. Fog drifted through the coiling pattern of the heavy, black behemoths. It was the most welcoming sight he'd ever seen.

The porch light of Occasus cast amber into the darkness—a steady glow of hope.

Peter bolted for the door.

The growls and hisses of the beasts grew louder, the rustle of their chase now a reverberating thud. Their nearness pressed in on Peter's awareness, alerting him that the beasts weren't just closing behind him. They were surrounding him.

From the grounds of Occasus, beasts sprang from the shadows and the fog, hulking, twisting, charging. There were beasts of varying sizes with tendrils, claws, horns, beaks, and scales. They rumbled, howled, hissed, and snapped. Neon-yellow eyes glinted in the moonlight. Haunting, horrifying gazes all zeroed in on Peter as he ran.

He picked up his pace, legs screaming at him to stop. But he couldn't. Not when he was so close.

Movement drew Peter's attention to the front window of Occasus. His heart leaped with joy. Then it plummeted.

In the living room, he could see Spencer. His brother sat in one of the wingback chairs, visible in the turret's rounded edge, head in his hands. He looked so broken, so lost, so alone. And Peter knew it was his fault.

But Spencer wasn't alone.

The movement—the thing that had gained Peter's attention—was a man walking.

Not a man.

A phantom.

Gerard stepped up behind Spencer, shoulders back and chin held high. He looked out and saw Peter running for his life. But instead of alerting Spencer, the phantom smiled.

Peter clamped his jaw tight, anger searing through him.

He had to get in there. He had to reveal the traitor for what he was.

Gerard turned away, a gun suddenly in his hand.

Panic bubbled up and out of Peter. "Spencer!" he yelled in desperation.

The phantom raised the weapon, aiming it at the back of Spencer's head.

Peter ordered his legs to move faster. He was so close. So terribly, wonderfully close. The stairs were only ten feet away. He was going to make it. He *would* make it. He would get back and save his brother.

A tentacle snapped around his ankle, ripping his foot from under him. With a cry of alarm, Peter dropped. He hit the gravel drive, pain pulsing into him from the sharp pebbles.

The scylla's tentacle began to drag him back, and Peter fought to scramble to his feet. But the viscous *slurp* of another tentacle sliced through the air and hit him with a slap, sucking and tearing at his skin through the fabric of his sleeve.

"No," Peter panted, struggling against the beasts even as their limbs wrapped tighter and tighter around him. He scrambled against the gravel, twisting and turning and writhing with all his might to rip free of their hold.

Nothing worked.

Peter closed his eyes, screaming in anger. He had to break free. He was so close. He had to get to Spencer.

Drawing on all his will, Peter screwed up his face in concentration, summoning forth an arc.

No golden light erupted. No tremor of power rose across his skin. No spark of power filled his fingertips.

Then he heard the gunshot.

"Spencer!"

A sharp gasp burst out of Peter as the razor-like claws of a wendigo embedded in his chest. He hardly felt it, their sharpness dulling the initial puncture. Then searing pain flared across his skin as the wendigo ripped down, tearing flesh, muscle, and tendon.

The shadows of a hundred beasts crashed down upon Peter. Tearing, slashing, sucking, wrenching, and rending—all of them pulling him apart, limb from limb, flesh from bone. Pain tore his throat as Peter realized he was screaming. He didn't even know when he'd started. But his vocal cords tore, and his voice broke as he thrashed against the beasts, screaming his brother's name over and over and over.

~

"Spencer!"

Peter gasped himself awake, his throat raw as he jerked up, heart hammering in his chest. His brother's name came out clipped, his voice breaking like a teen's as he heaved for breath.

The startling dichotomy of feeling unbearable pain one second and then being whole and well the next struck Peter as he sat there on the concrete floor of his prison cell. He looked down at his body, sure that he'd find blood and gore and skin peeling from muscle. But he was fine. No cuts, no wounds, no blood. Nothing.

Running a hand over his intact Henley, Peter's muscles shook from the relief of waking and finding himself out of that nightmare and safe in the cage of the Frossards' vault.

A relief that was short-lived when he realized he was still here, in the cage of Alexander's design.

And there, in the corner of his prison, in the dark recesses of the shadows, neon eyes watched him.

Backing farther into the cell bars, Peter couldn't tell what kind of beast Alexander had watching him. Cassandra hadn't had time to educate them on all the different species. They knew of hydras, wendigos, scylla, and hellhounds—he knew them better than he ever wanted to. Whatever this beast was, he didn't care to find out.

A flutter of movement from the beast and a *clack* taunted him as the creature's beady eyes blinked sideways.

Whatever this beast was, it didn't mind watching, waiting. It was patient. And it was adamant in its study of him.

Letting out a long breath, Peter held the thing's gaze. "You come here often?"

The thing blinked again.

"Yeah, me neither."

Settling back against the bars, Peter scrunched into the farthest corner from the beast. This position let him keep one eye on the creature and the other on the study at all times. Unless he fell asleep, of course. And there wasn't much to do but fall asleep.

Peter wished he could stay awake. He didn't know how long he'd been stuck in this prison. Time kind of got away from you when you were stuck with only a beast for company. But in the past however long, he'd drifted in and out of consciousness, falling into restless, terrifying sleep plagued with nightmares and beasts and pain and death.

For the first time, Peter wondered if he was getting a glimpse of what Spencer experienced. Was this why his brother had always hated going to bed as a kid? Were his nightmares this awful? He couldn't imagine that they were. No one could survive this sort of terror every night, could they?

Curling his shoulders, Peter scanned the small cell for the hundredth time. Bare concrete walls and ceiling matched the floor with no furnishings and no light source beyond what the study provided beyond his bars. Dingy and utterly inhospitable. At least there was a tiny alcove with a toilet.

"I'd give it a one-star rating," Peter said to the beast. "Could've at least provided a toothbrush."

But he'd been divested of more than he'd been granted. They'd taken his coat and scarf, leaving him only with the flannel, Henley, jeans, and boots he'd been wearing to church, however many days ago that Sunday morning had been. His phone had been in his coat pocket, so they had that too. He didn't even have his notebook with him. All he could do to pass the time was sleep, talk to the beast, or examine the study.

None of which was particularly entertaining.

Sighing, Peter motioned to the office behind him. "So, what? You his eyes and ears while he's gone?" he asked the beast.

A flutter, a blink.

"Mm." Peter turned to the room beyond his cell but kept a wary eye on the creature. "What's it like working for the bad guy? Does he pay well? You get benefits or something?"

A clack—Peter decided it sounded like a rather large beak.

He gave the corner a bemused glance. "Dental, eh? That's pretty nice."

The thing gave a throaty, rather menacing croon.

"Ah, yeah, I suppose a bird wouldn't need a dentist, huh?"

The fire still roared, its heat soothing against the cold of the concrete, but the shadows it cast on the room were menacing with the threat of beasts. The room remained empty each time he woke from his nightmares. He didn't know where Alexander had lurked off to, but with the man gone, he had a better opportunity to investigate his surroundings.

Peter had, of course, attempted to break out of the cell. He'd tried jimmying the lock any way he could. It was an old-fashioned kind of lock, requiring a skeleton key. Why Alexander had chosen that design, he didn't know. But he'd broken every aglet of his shoelaces, twisting and turning them into the tiny hole. They'd taken his belt—which he supposed was a smart move—so he'd run out of options pretty quickly.

Now, he settled for learning whatever he could while trapped in the Frossard workspace. It was rather stupid of them, he thought, letting him stay where their leader did his work. Though Peter guessed they didn't expect him to get free.

That was another stupid mistake.

Even if he died trying, Peter would find his way back to his brother.

Scanning the bookshelves another time, Peter tried to get a read on the titles nearest him. The shelves covered most of the walls. An obnoxiously agreeable design, in his opinion. In fact, the whole room was rather agreeable. It reminded him of a British gentlemen's lounge in the 1800s with its wood paneling, leather chairs, rich rugs, and luxurious designs. He could practically smell the cigars and whiskey. Sans his cell, he liked it.

The books were even more frustrating. Most of the ones nearest him were novels. Mystery, suspense, and adventure novels. The stuff he'd actually read. He'd even attempted to reach his arm through the far end to grab a book off the shelf, but the beast had scratched its claws—wherever it hid them—against the concrete and fluttered as it drew near. So Peter had stopped. He hadn't gotten that close anyway.

As the desk sat on the opposite side of the room, Peter had no luck gathering information from it. Besides, its well-organized surface didn't hold much to begin with.

Peter supposed that was why Alexander didn't mind keeping him in here. There was no chance for him to glean any insight.

"So I've been thinking," Peter said, turning back to the beast. "This is a long shot, but hear me out, okay? What if we formed an alliance?"

Its neon eyes blinked with that weird sideways shutter.

Peter fought the urge to grimace. "You help me out of here, and you get to see something outside of this cage, huh? It's a big world out there. Seeing as how he summoned you in here, I'm imagining you haven't seen anything else, right?"

Another blink.

"What'd'ya say? You wanna start an uprising?"

A guttural twitter.

"Right, well," Peter sighed, "you can't blame a guy for trying."

The click of a latch startled Peter, and he whipped his head around to see the study door open.

Alexander Frossard walked in, shoulders back, dressed like he was going to the country club. The slacks and button up fit him so well that Peter assumed he got them custom-tailored. But his typically perfect face was marred by a long, sharp slit across his forehead. Butterfly bandages held the wound closed, which was obviously received and cleaned recently.

Cell to his ear, Alexander ignored his prisoner while he entered. "That's too late. We need you here before the summoning."

Peter raised his brow. The summoning of what?

The man walked to his desk. "I've told them you'll start tomorrow." He paused, listening. "I don't care if you had plans. Cancel them."

Another pause and his expression eased. "Excellent. I'll see you at the vigil," he said, then ended the call. His controlled movements— pulling out his chair, sitting down, and shifting through his papers—said he was in no rush to acknowledge Peter. Instead, he picked up a pen and began to take notes.

Discovering an urge to annoy the man, Peter said, "Have a back-alley brawl, doc?"

Alexander didn't even flinch.

Peter decided to see how far his patience went.

"The clinic closed today?" he asked.

No response.

"Or did you lose all of your clients?"

A flutter sounded behind Peter, but when he looked back at the beast, it showed no signs of aggression.

Turning back to the Druid, Peter tried a new tactic. "You know, with all this time to think," he began, "I've had a bit of a revelation."

Alexander flipped another page and turned to the computer next to him.

Still sitting on the floor, Peter slipped an arm through the bars to rest on the lower crossbeam. "Technically," he said, "you're my cousin. Or half-cousin twice removed, or something like that."

There was no reply from the beast or the man.

"That makes us family," he continued. "After all, I'm just as much Frossard as I am Varon. And from what I've been told, Frossards value blood over anything. This leads me to the conclusion that no matter what my brother and I do, you aren't gonna kill us."

That brought the twitch of a smug smile to Alexander's lips before he forced his expression back into indifference.

Assured that the man *was* listening, Peter shrugged. "Though I suppose you did kill Seraphine." His eyes followed the angles of the tree etched into the desk. "Not you personally, of course, but your family. Yet you didn't kill her kids. I'm all ears if you'd care to share more."

Alexander flipped another page.

Peter smirked. "Guess not."

The click of the keyboard reminded Peter of his brother. His eyes drifted up to the cut on Alexander's forehead. It split halfway down from his hairline, still fresh enough to shine in the warm lamplight.

"Where'd you get that injury?"

A tightening of Alexander's jaw.

"It was Spence, wasn't it?"

The typing stopped for only a fraction of a second, confirming his suspicion.

Peter chuckled under his breath. "I've never been prouder."

No verbal reply from Alexander, though the doctor fought down another twitch of his mouth.

Peter wondered if it was a grimace or a grin.

"Did you check yourself for a concussion?" Peter taunted. "Spence can hit harder than you'd expect. Did you know he can knock people out with a single punch? He's kind of badass like that. I'd hate for you to have a seizure or something from untended head trauma."

With a heavy sigh, Alexander finally looked at Peter. His smooth, square jaw was set firmly. "You are quite obnoxious."

Peter leaned his head against the concrete wall, a grin on his lips. "I get that a lot," he said. "You could move me if you'd like. This place is neat and all, but it's not very entertaining."

"That's the point," Alexander said, returning to his work.

Watching the man, Peter wondered if there would ever come a moment when the Druid leader's work provided beneficial information.

Maybe if he paid enough attention, he could glean some snippet, some hint at what the Druids had planned. Or, at the very least, what their mood was.

At the moment, it appeared to be very calm.

"What're you working on?" Peter asked.

Reaching up, Alexander pinched the bridge of his nose. "Mr. Collins," he said. "I do believe I mentioned that you were of more use to me alive. I'm now beginning to find your value greatly diminishing."

Peter paused. Was it irritation alone that brought this threat? Or had something happened? In either case, he needed more information. "Any way I can increase my value?"

Alexander's piercing blue gaze cut into him. "Be quiet."

"Mm." Peter drew his arm back through the bars. "I'm not very good at that."

"Learn," Alexander ordered.

Then he turned back to his work.

Peter followed the order begrudgingly, but he continued to watch the Druid. Alexander started to run his fingers through his blond hair, grimacing as the action tugged at the cut on his forehead. A bead of blood welled in the corner.

The wound was still fragile then. Not deep enough to need stitches but bad enough that it reopened easily. Peter wondered how Spencer had managed it.

Frowning, Peter drew his knees up as he leaned against the concrete wall. A bigger, more terrifying question was *why* Spencer had done it. Had there been a fight? Was his brother okay? What about Cassandra? Had she been there? He hoped so. If Cassandra was with Spencer, then his brother would be fine. As long as she was still alive. . . .

Peter's throat went dry. He wouldn't go down that line of thought. He couldn't.

The beast in the corner fluttered again, drawing his attention. Its eyes glowed with violence, but it remained hidden.

"What kind of beast are you?" he whispered to the creature.

It blinked.

"I've guessed that you're birdlike," he said, trying to keep his voice quiet enough not to let Alexander hear. "But I don't think Cass ever mentioned bird-beasts. I'm sure there's some name for you in that book of hers, but do you have a name for yourself?"

A double blink this time.

Peter blinked back, surprised. Was it trying to communicate with him?

"Is that a yes?"

A double blink.

His heart sped up. Could he be making a connection with this creature? Was that possible? Could he convince it to help him escape after all?

Alexander's voice broke through the study, causing Peter to startle. "The valravn are highly intelligent creatures," he said in a bored, distant tone. "They like to play with their prey, proving they have the greater mind. I'd not recommend attempting to befriend one. They'll most assuredly betray your confidence, crack open your skull, and eat your brain."

Wincing, Peter glanced back at the beast. "Valravn, huh?" he muttered. "Sounds birdlike, all right."

"Quite."

"You know why they're all animal-based?" he asked, eyes still on the beast.

"They are not *based* on anything in our world, Mr. Collins," he said, a hard edge to his voice. "They are creatures of undefined origin and design. We can only describe them with the knowledge and concepts that we have on this side of reality. If anything, birds are valravn-like."

"So you believe that valravn came before birds?" Peter asked, turning back to the doctor.

"I believe," Alexander's words were sharp, "that this world will never be fully complete until we make it complete. What is on this side is a shade of what is on the other. And if people like your Warden friend would open their eyes, they would see that we have settled for a false version of reality. A half version."

Peter narrowed his eyes at this information. Alexander knew about Owen and the Warden. "You think the Warden is in the wrong then?"

What a stupid question. Of course, the Druid thought the Warden was in the wrong. They'd been fighting for centuries.

Alexander smiled—a terrible, confident, crafty smile. "I think they're blind," he said. "And I'd like to open their eyes."

A shudder raced through Peter as that cold, calculating gaze held his. "How?"

The chuckle that slipped through Alexander was echoed by the valravn's croon in the corner, its trill sending a cold dread into Peter's chest.

"I should have thought it was obvious, Mr. Collins," the doctor said, hands clasped together on the desk before him. "I intend to release the spirit world upon them. Then they will see."

He said it with such certainty and with a stronger conviction than Peter had felt about anything in his entire life.

"They'll see," Alexander repeated. "And they'll either serve with us or die."

Peter flinched as the valravn rumbled out a violent sound of approval. He didn't ask any more questions. He didn't think he wanted the answers.

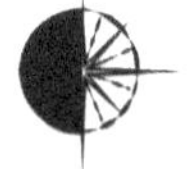

CHAPTER ELEVEN

Spencer

During the rather silent drive back to Occasus, Spencer struggled not to glance at Cassandra every two seconds until he finally resolved to get over it. Whatever was happening between them, at least it was happening now. Despite his past reluctance to pursue a romance—with her or any other woman—somehow, he felt ready for it. Of course, things were awkward between them, as they always were during the start of a relationship, but he refused to let it faze him or her. They could work out the details later when they had less pressing issues to resolve.

Like the recovery of Peter.

Feeling far more in control, Spencer had resumed his place behind the wheel, even turning the stereo back on. The classic rock reminded him of what he was fighting for. He supposed he had Cassandra to thank for that. Somehow, she'd managed to settle the chaos of his mind long enough for him to return to reality. He decided he ought to find a way to thank her beyond simple words. He wasn't sure how yet.

The snow and gravel drive rumbled beneath the tires as Spencer pulled up to Occasus. Only Cassandra's vintage red truck and Aaron's motorcycle waited for them, which meant that Owen and the Lamberts were still at their meeting with Gabe.

Nex and Anguis met them at the door with wagging tails. Spencer took extra time to scratch each of them behind the ear. Both dogs pressed into his affection as though absolving him for ignoring them since Peter's disappearance. His chest was still tight, but he could breathe easily as he brushed his hand over their wiry fur.

"So," Gerard said, popping into view as Cassandra hung up her jacket, "what happened?"

With his attention still on the dogs, Spencer gave a quick rundown of the meeting, conveniently leaving out the part of his panic attack and the rest of their time in the woods. His mind caught on the recent memory of their kiss, though. He couldn't keep himself from glancing at Cassandra as she leaned against the stair railing.

When Spencer finished his recounting, Gerard only had one question. "What now?"

"I guess," Cassandra said with a sigh, "we wait for Owen, Anna, and Aaron. If their meeting is still going, then Gabe must have a good amount of information. We wait, learn what they learned, get their advice, and decide our next step then."

"That's not what I meant," Gerard grumbled.

"What did you mean?" Spencer asked, rising to remove his jacket.

"You attacked their leader," he said, his irritation clear. "You've played your entire hand. What do you think you can gain by staying here? There's no fighting them. They've already won."

"They haven't," Cassandra said. "If they'd won, we wouldn't still be here. They need something from the vault. As long as we can keep them from it, they *can't* win."

"Besides," Spencer added, shutting the coat closet, "they took Peter. Obviously, they're hoping to trade him for what they need."

"Then why haven't they contacted you?" Gerard asked. "If your brother is a hostage, where's the ransom demand?"

That was a question that Spencer had intentionally ignored asking himself.

"Your brother is dead, kid," Gerard said. "I'm sorry, but the sooner you accept that, the better off you'll be."

Spencer wanted to yell at the phantom—to fight him and the logic he presented. But he couldn't speak. Not as the shaking rippled through his hands and his tongue turned to lead.

The gentle brush of Cassandra's finger against his arm sent a spiral of tingles across his skin. "Peter's alive," she said, her hazel eyes locked with his. Her surety impressed itself on him, wrapping around his tension like a blanket and soothing his concern. "Whatever their plans, the Druids know that he's worth more to them alive."

"He's a Varon," Gerard said. "He's their biggest threat. If they don't kill him, they deserve to lose."

Cassandra shot the phantom an annoyed glare. "They deserve to lose either way."

Gerard dropped it.

She turned back to Spencer. "I think we should work on the essays while we wait for the others. We may as well use every opportunity we have."

Thankful for the chance to do something of consequence, Spencer nodded and followed Cassandra to the office. The large window on the far side of the room let in a gentle wash of cheery light, the pine trees in the yard creating silhouettes along the floor and desk. Spencer's laptop and story notes for *Wenzel & Frankly* splayed across the desktop. His heart did a little jolt at the reminder of his brother. But he squashed it as Cassandra dropped her messenger bag onto the desk and began to dig out the folder of Elijah Lawrence's essays.

Spencer pulled a chair in from the dining room, setting it next to his desk chair. Cassandra gave it a cursory glance, and her lips twitched up at the corner, but she continued to organize the essays without comment. Instead, she instructed him on where to find Diane's concordances of Old English and Latin on the floor-to-ceiling bookshelves surrounding the fireplace on their right.

They were exactly where she directed. "I'm surprised you knew where to find them," he said, bemused. She'd made it clear she had no interest in developing her linguistic skills.

Cassandra barely glanced at him. "I organized them."

"You did?"

She grinned even as she sorted through the essays. "Diane and Liam weren't big on orderliness," she said, slipping a paperclip onto a group of papers. "I finally got so fed up with the mess that I begged Diane to let me organize everything."

"I didn't take you for a neat freak," Spencer said as he joined her at the desk, amused by the idea.

She tossed him a sidelong smirk. "There's a difference between being a 'neat freak' and being annoyed by clutter. Besides, every good library has a method to its madness."

Spencer set the concordances on the desk. He scanned the essays as she grouped another handful together. There were eleven in total, all multiple double-sided pages in length. "Where do we start?"

"Well—" She shuffled through the final papers, clipping them together, then setting them to the side to pick up one of the thicker stacks. "This is the essay that talks about the Great Wolf. Do you remember me telling you about that?"

A memory sparked in the back of Spencer's mind of standing in the office with Cassandra and Peter nearly a month ago. They'd gone through the draft of Diane's second book—the one she'd left to Cassandra that was supposed to contain Elijah's essays. "Yeah, you said the Great Wolf was an Irishman, right?"

"Yes, well—no, I don't know," she said, turning toward him. She gestured with the essay in her hand. "Diane and I *assumed* it was a man. But . . . I was thinking about what Owen told us—about the Warden and its founding. And while I don't remember the passage exactly, I do remember that the Great Wolf was released in Amesbury, England."

Spencer frowned, knowing that the location was familiar but unable to place it.

Cassandra arched her brow, prompting him as she clarified, "The home of Stonehenge."

The connection came immediately. "Stonehenge was a Veil."

"A Veil that the Druids tore in 1567. Only a handful of years before Elijah wrote these essays."

Spencer rubbed his hands together, eyes going to the essays. "Do you think . . . well, what do you think that means?"

"I don't know," she admitted, exasperation thinning her voice. Desperation caused her expression to tighten, bringing a rather cute scrunch to her nose. "But if this has anything to do with a Veil being opened, I think it's our best bet."

Nudging the desk chair closer, Spencer motioned for Cassandra to sit down. "Then let's get started."

~

Spencer had forgotten just how miserable translation was. He'd also forgotten the headache that accompanied it. The antiquated language swam circles in his brain. It shouldn't be so hard to read something their language was built on. Yet this language felt wholly foreign to him. After all, he'd studied Latin in college, not Old English. And while there were similarities, the distinctions were irritatingly difficult to separate.

An hour into their studies, Spencer rubbed his temple. They'd made it through the first of seven pages. This was going to take forever.

Spencer was immensely grateful that Owen, Anna, and Aaron chose that moment to return. Under Cassandra's insistence, they took it as a lunch break, clustering around the kitchen island as they ate.

"What did you learn?" Spencer asked, hoping for a better report than their meeting. Guilt clawed at him for screwing that one up so royally.

Anna and Aaron both turned to Owen, handing the lead over to him. "Well," he said with a sigh, "it seems we have more allies in DeVerre than we thought."

Hope sprang into Spencer's chest. "Really?"

"Apparently. Gabe said that he leads a small group of men and women who—like Tom and Sam—know about the spirit world. To a certain extent, at least."

"That's great!"

Owen held up his hand, stalling Spencer's optimism. "The trouble we may face," he said, "is that most of them want to *destroy* the spirit world. And that isn't exactly compatible with our goals."

"Why do they want to destroy it?" Cassandra asked.

"The Chapelle massacre in 1915 left its impact on the people of DeVerre," Owen said. "I'm guessing that was the point. There's a lingering distrust for all things relating to the spirit world. And I don't see that changing anytime soon."

Spencer tried to process this news. "So . . . what does that mean for us? Will they help us fight the Druids?"

As Owen considered his answer, Aaron gave a firm nod. "Gabe said they would," he assured.

But that brought a grimace to Owen's face. "In theory," he said. "If nothing else, they'll stand with us against the Druids. And yes, Gabe did say they would help us. The problem may come when they want to see an end to the spirit world while we attempt to protect it."

"You think they'd turn on us?" Cassandra asked.

"Maybe." Owen shrugged. "But this is a regular debate in Warden towns—the correct handling of the spirit world. With Varons on our side,

I think we'll find a lot more leniency and support, no matter our stance. But that doesn't change the fact that they have their own thoughts on the subject and may balk at our efforts."

Spencer frowned, taking it all in. "Will they still care about a Varon's opinion when the town stopped trusting them a century ago?"

"Did they truly lose the town's trust?" Owen asked. "It doesn't look that way to me. Tom, Sam, and Gabe certainly don't seem bothered by your ancestry. In fact, they all seem quite grateful for it."

"And Ava supports it too," Anna said. "She's actually kind of excited about it."

Though Spencer appreciated the sentiment, he couldn't help but remember their meeting with the mayor and council. "But will the rest of the town feel the same?" he asked. "Numbers matter. And right now, we've got four out of three hundred."

Owen raised his brow in consideration. "You have a point," he admitted. "I suppose it all depends on how many Druids make up the population."

"Seems like it's a pretty good percent," Spencer said, thinking about the council. He ran a hand over his face, realizing they needed to share their morning activities as well. "Look, we've got a bit of a problem."

Over the next several minutes, Spencer and Cassandra relayed the meeting with the council. He intentionally skipped over the part where he slammed Alexander Frossard's head into the table—twice—and he was grateful that Cassandra didn't find it necessary to bring it up either. Though it might be pertinent, possibly even valuable information to share, he knew the look that Owen would give him. And he didn't care to be scolded for his brash reaction.

"Alexander stacked the council," Spencer concluded. "We won't be receiving any support from them. He's even got the mayor on his side."

"I don't think Fred is a Druid, though," Cassandra said. "He's just . . . kind of gullible."

Aaron let out a grunt that said he wasn't surprised.

"What about Elizabeth?" Owen asked. "You said she acted bothered by your story."

Cassandra nodded. "She's definitely not on their side. Alexander's actions completely appalled her. She even tried to stop him from shutting down the meeting."

"Do you think that means she'll side with us?"

"It wouldn't surprise me if she talked with Sam about that very thing after we left. Whether or not she'll help us. . . ."

Owen crossed his arms, lunch forgotten. "I'd imagine with both of her sons on our side, she'll readily support our cause."

"What is our cause?" Aaron suddenly asked. "I know I'm new to all of this, but . . . it seems like something I should know, you know? What's our goal? Beyond getting rid of the Druids."

"Our goal," Owen said, "is to protect the Veil."

"The lake, right?"

"Right. The Veil is a location where the space between the physical world and the spirit world is thinnest. It's a tangible passage between the two. The Druids want to tear the Veil, releasing the spirit world into the physical. Stopping them is the first step to keeping it safe."

"What's the second step?"

"Bringing the Warden back to DeVerre," Owen said matter-of-factly.

Spencer furrowed his brow. "I thought you said the Warden had enough problems."

"They do," he said. "But a town with a Veil to protect will draw plenty of aid."

"So why wouldn't they help us fight now?"

Owen held up a hand to halt Spencer's argument. "I'm already working on that."

The cryptic answer didn't satisfy much, but Spencer could see in the serious glimmer of Owen's dark blue gaze that he wouldn't be giving them any more information. "Okay . . . so, what now? Did Gabe have a plan?"

Owen nodded. "He wants to meet," he said, "to introduce his people to us. That way, we can all determine our next steps together."

"When?"

"Tomorrow evening. He wants to do it before the chapel's vigil on Wednesday to be sure his people know the truth."

"What vigil?" Spencer asked.

"To honor the lives lost Saturday night."

"Gia's organizing it," Anna said bitterly. She picked at her plate, eyes downcast as she added, "She asked me to help."

"Are you going to?" Cassandra asked.

"I don't think I have much of a choice. It's a good opportunity to keep an eye on the Frossards, right? Besides, if Gia asked, then they still think I'm on their side."

"Or they're trying to keep an eye on *you*," Spencer said.

"I'm with Spencer," Aaron said. "I don't think you should do it."

"What am I gonna say, Aaron?" she asked. "'Sorry, I'm not interested in helping to respect the dead'?"

"They were Druids. We don't have to honor their deaths."

"*All* lives are sacred," Owen said. "Druid or not."

Aaron's jaw stiffened, but he let the subject go.

Owen turned to Anna. "Be careful," he said. "But help Gia. They've known of your relationship with Peter and Spencer for longer than this last week. They may try to capitalize on it, but even that could be to our advantage. She may say or do something that gives you some information we didn't have before, even if it's simply through trying to get you on their side."

Anna nodded, her shoulders drawing back with determination.

Addressing Spencer and Cassandra once more, Owen gave them an apologetic expression. "I don't think you two should attend the vigil, though," he warned.

"Because the town blames us?" Spencer said.

"For the moment," he said. "Once we talk with Gabe and his people, we'll have a stronger chance of changing that opinion."

With a sigh, Spencer shook his head, remembering the farce that was the town council meeting. "Will they even believe us? The Druids have painted us as murderers. No one is going to listen."

"Some will," Owen said. "And the rest . . ."

"I'm going to work on that," Anna said. "I have a lot of friends. So does Haley. And we'll do whatever we have to do to convince them to listen."

"What if they don't?" Cassandra asked, her voice sounding slightly hollow.

Owen shrugged. "Then our best bet is keeping the Druids from tearing the Veil."

"And what about finding Peter?" she asked.

Spencer gave her an appreciative glance. He hadn't wanted to ask it; he didn't want to appear selfish in the face of all these important issues. But the question was plaguing him. While they were focused on stopping the Druids, who would save his brother?

"If the Druids do indeed have him," Owen said, "then they're holding him *somewhere*. Anna, maybe you and Haley can ask around—subtly— and see if anyone has any ideas?"

"Sure," she said, nodding emphatically.

"What can I do?" Aaron asked, a determination in his tone that Spencer recognized. It was the same sound that sometimes came through in Peter's voice. The demand to be regarded, to be heard, to be given a purpose.

Knowing just what their friend needed, Spencer drew back his shoulders. "Help us here, when you're able," he said. "We have a million questions that we still need answers to, and thousands of books that might hold them. And when you *can't* be here, be our eyes around the town."

Spencer met Anna's gaze, including her in his next charge. "You two still have to live your lives. People need to see you and trust you as they always have. And when you have the chance, tell them what's really going on. We're going to need all the support we can get."

Anna and Aaron Lambert nodded, accepting their roles in this strange new quest—their individual roles in the salvation of DeVerre.

"I don't think any of us should be alone either," Cassandra said. "It's too dangerous. We can't risk anyone else going missing or being attacked."

They all nodded in agreement.

Looking around the kitchen, Spencer felt the ache of Peter's absence. There was a hole in their group. A link that had been removed. But they couldn't fall apart; not if they wanted to save him.

Spencer glanced at the woman standing next to him. Yes, there was a hole where his brother belonged. But in his search for Peter, he was thankful to have Cassandra Clement at his side.

CHAPTER TWELVE

Anna

Anna did her best to remain calm. Back to work in the tavern, she listened and watched as she went from table to table. With no connection to the spirit world, there wasn't much she could do to save DeVerre. Yet, however small a part she could play, she would be of use.

After their meeting at Occasus, Aaron took Anna to work, remaining with her while Haley went with Ava to spend the evening researching in the vault. It wasn't abnormal for Aaron to spend his evenings in the tavern with either Anna or Haley; thus, no one would find his lingering presence strange. He sat at the bar, eating or messing around on his phone when Anna was busy with work.

Still, Anna struggled to keep her head on straight as she returned to the routine of waiting on tables and manning the bar. Waitressing had always been an easy, enjoyable job. The owner, Evelyn, managed The Glass Tavern with an understanding, hands-off approach. She trusted her employees to get the job done, having known most of them since childhood. There was always one waiter and one chef per shift. Only on busy days was a second waiter needed, and Evelyn allowed her staff freedom to run their shifts as they saw fit.

During her slowest shifts, Anna would sketch behind the bar. The hours sometimes stretched between customers, allowing her to fill page after page, book after book, with drawings over the past nine years. Even with Aaron's company, this was one of those nights. While a handful of parties had come and gone, only one table remained now—Danielle MacDonald and some of her cousins.

Glancing up from her sketchbook, Anna surveyed the table. The five of them sat talking with somber moods. They'd all had family members die in the fight at Occasus.

"Who are you looking at?" Aaron asked, keeping his voice low.

Anna dipped her head back down. "Just checking to see if Dani's table needed anything," she said.

"Then why did your jaw do that twitch thing it does when you're agitated?"

She frowned at her brother. "It did not."

His glasses reflected the pendant lights as he raised his brow.

"I wondered if Danielle or her cousins might be . . ." Anna's gaze flicked to the table, then she mouthed, "Druids."

Aaron set his phone down. "And your conclusion?"

"I don't think they are."

"You sure?"

"I've been listening carefully, and though they're all understandably upset, nothing they've said or done has suggested that they're . . . You know."

"They'd be smarter than that, though, right?" Aaron suggested. "The Druids have kept their presence a secret for over a century. Anyone in the town could be one of them. Even the people we trust the most."

Knowing that truth intimately, Anna looked up at Danielle. "I hope not."

Anna had already lost her best friend—Connor. Aside from Haley,

Danielle was the closest friend she had left. Five years ago, Danielle had returned from college in Spokane and joined Anna's Bible study shortly after. She was gentle-spoken and clever, offering her opinions thoughtfully, advising wisely, and laughing easily. Over time, Anna and she began to confide in one another, their friendship growing strong and comforting. To imagine Danielle as a Druid broke her heart.

But then, imagining *any* DeVerrean as a Druid hurt.

Anna shaded the tendril in her drawing. She reminded herself that the subject was a vining plant—not the beast that had attacked her the last time she stood in the tavern. The Glass Tavern looked the same as it ever had—dark green and wood-paneled walls, brown leather booths, and multi-colored liquor bottles behind the bar. The mellow jazz trilled over the stereo system serenely, and the lights glowed with their comforting yellow beams.

Anna couldn't help expecting the music to crackle and fall silent as the lights flickered out just as they had a week ago.

She gripped the charcoal pencil tighter, the shading growing heavy on the page. It had taken all her strength to walk into the tavern to start her shift. Everything in her wanted to bolt. She wanted to run home and refuse to return to reality. How could she when *reality* wasn't real? Not anymore.

Everything had changed that night. When Peter had joined her in the tavern—when he'd lied to her, then brought a Druid and a beast back into the building with him.

Anna felt so stupid, so duped. Not just by him but by everyone. By Connor and his parents. By Owen. Even her sister had known about the spirit world. Now she had to wonder if the only people who hadn't lied to her were Aaron and Haley. Were all her friends Druids? Did they all know? Was she so easily led that she missed the cult that lived under her nose?

Yes, she was.

The lines of her drawing grew thick; the shading turned menacing. What a fool she was, living her whole life believing that DeVerre was a quaint, idyllic town. She'd loved it here. While her friends chose to go to college, she stayed after high school. She didn't want to grow up. Some grand career in the city held no appeal for her. Everything she cared about was here in DeVerre—her parents, her siblings, her friends—why would she ever want to leave this beautiful, happy town?

But it was all a lie, a fantastic story she'd worked up for herself. While she pretended that everything in DeVerre was a fairytale, it was all a horror story run by an evil cult of Druids.

Everything she'd believed in was a lie.

DeVerre. Connor. Life.

"You okay, Nana?" Aaron's deep voice cut into her thoughts, and she immediately flinched at the nickname.

As kids, Aaron started calling her Anna-Banana, which was shortened to Banana—the name Connor adopted over the years. Eventually, Aaron shortened it even further to Nana, but that didn't change the fact that it reminded her of all the years the three of them— her, Connor, and Aaron—had spent together. Years where they'd grown inseparable.

Years in which Anna came to trust Connor more than anyone else, only to discover he was the best liar of them all.

Nodding a bit too vigorously, Anna met Aaron's concerned gaze. "Fine," she muttered.

"Tell that to your sketchbook."

Looking down, Anna found the tendril was almost completely black with the shading she'd pressed into the page. She sighed, tossing the pencil to the side in exchange for her eraser. It wouldn't fix the mistake. She'd applied too much pressure, marring the page. But she could lighten the overall effect.

Aaron played with his empty drink tumbler. "Wanna talk about it?" he asked.

"What is there to talk about?" Anna replied. "Everything we knew is wrong. There's no point in rehashing what we can't change."

"That's not what I'm referring to."

Anna frowned.

Aaron held her stare steadily. "He was my friend too."

That caused Anna's whole body to tense. "I don't want to talk about him," she said sharply. "*Ever* again."

He swirled the last dregs of ice in his glass. "Okay." He paused, then added, "What about Peter? You wanna talk about him?"

Averting her gaze, Anna focused on erasing the heavy shading. "What is there to talk about?"

"You two were getting kind of close."

"Don't say it like that."

"Like what?"

Anna chewed on the inside of her lip. "Like he's gone."

A long beat of silence passed between them before Aaron muttered, "He is gone, Nana. Even if it's just until we find him."

When she didn't reply, he reached across the bar and took her hand, stopping her frantic erasing. "I don't want to see you get hurt by another guy," he said, dark gaze worried. "Whether or not it's intentional on his part."

Heart squeezing, Anna didn't know what to say. How could she tell Aaron it wasn't like that between her and Peter? She liked him—a lot. He was cute, funny, and loyal. But he wasn't . . .

Anna's first instinct after discovering Peter's lie—after he'd brought that beast to her—had been anger. It terrified her, that horrifying creature. But it enraged her more. How dare he lie to her face and then endanger her life? How dare he upend her perfect little life?

Then, in the solitude of the next morning, Anna realized that she should be grateful to Peter. His lie, albeit a lie, was well-intentioned. He'd meant to protect her. He'd meant to let her go on living in her blissful ignorance, keeping her out of the dangerous reality of DeVerre. And it wasn't fair of her to be angry with him over a lie.

Because she'd lied to him too.

Every time Anna thought back to that night, she felt ashamed. Not because of her tears or her fearful reaction to the beast. Nor because she'd pressed him about Ava, forcing him to lie to her in the first place. No, she was ashamed because she'd used him.

Holding Aaron's gaze, Anna knew the truth she was too mortified to share. This shame, this guilt—it had begun to grow over the past several weeks. She hadn't recognized it at first. She'd thought it was merely the awkward exchanges between her and Peter, making her thoughts a jumble and their relationship complicated. But after his disappearance, Anna realized what a fool she'd been.

It struck her as she'd lain awake last night. Her fear for Peter and her anger at his disappearance all revolved around one thing. Dread and shame welled within her as she finally admitted that unforgivable truth to herself: She'd only shown Peter her sketchbook and begun to flirt with him because she wanted to prove to herself that she was over Connor.

She was using him to forget her ex. She was attempting to rebound. And Peter didn't deserve that.

No, Aaron didn't need to worry about Peter hurting Anna.

He should be worried about Anna hurting Peter.

The wave of Danielle's hand got Anna's attention. Aaron sighed and pulled back. "Take care of 'em," he said, hopping down from his barstool. "I've gotta use the restroom anyway before we go."

Anna nodded and shoved away her reproachful thoughts as they parted. She walked across the tavern to approach her final table of the night. "Can I get you guys something else?" she asked.

"Just our checks," Danielle said, a sorrow-tempered smile on her face.

Anna cashed them out and returned to her sketchbook only to realize that Danielle wasn't leaving with the rest of her family. The bell chimed above the front door as they exited, and Danielle took the barstool across from Anna.

"Hey," Danielle began, her usually warm voice a trifle airy. "Could I talk to you for a second?"

Worry branched through Anna's chest. She shut her sketchbook beneath the bar counter, out of sight. "Sure. What's up?"

"Well, I—" Danielle shifted in her chair. "I know this is probably weird, but . . . have you talked to Spencer recently?"

"Spencer? Uh, yeah, I saw him earlier today."

"So, he's—he's okay?"

Anna hoped that her surprise didn't show on her face. Did Danielle know about Peter? Could she help them find him? She was a MacDonald, and they were close with the Frossards. Maybe she'd heard something.

Cautiously, Anna decided to find out. "Yeah, I mean, he's doing about as well as can be expected, I guess. Why do you ask?"

Danielle's warm tan skin turned rosy as she blushed. "Oh, uh, it's just—we were kind of . . . talking—"

Anna couldn't help her internal jolt of disappointment.

"But I haven't heard from him in several days. And after everything that's happened—with what everyone is saying, I'm just . . . I'm kind of scared for him."

Understanding dawned on Anna. Guilt shamed her for having thought her friend could knowingly associate with Druids.

Anna squeezed Danielle's hands, which rested on the bar top. "He's fine, Dani," she promised. "And I'm sure he'd appreciate you asking."

Danielle muttered "thanks" even as she continued to wring her hands.

Pressing her lips together, Anna couldn't quell her curiosity. "Are you . . . I don't mean to pry, so if you're not comfortable telling me, it's fine. But when you say *talking*, do you mean . . . ?"

The woman's blush deepened. "To tell the truth, I'm not sure. Like, I really thought he was interested. But if you're right and he's okay—which is good, I'm not saying it wouldn't be—but if he is, then why hasn't he texted me?"

Anna didn't know if she should tell Danielle that she doubted Spencer's interest. Peter was positive that Spencer and Cassandra were well on their way to a relationship. And Anna had to admit that she saw it too.

Leaning forward, Danielle kept her voice low. "Anna, can you tell me . . ." She paused and took a deep breath. "I know you haven't known them for long; I'm just hearing a lot of really weird things around town. But you've been friends with Spencer and his brother for weeks now, and you seem to know them well. So, can you tell me . . . can you tell me what's going on?"

Absentmindedly playing with the cover of her sketchbook, Anna tried not to let her emotions show in her expression. "What's going on with what?"

"With everything," Danielle said. "Uncle Tony is insisting that Spencer, Peter, and their friend had something to do with Dawn's . . . with what happened Saturday night. He came into the diner today, ranting to Aunt Jo about—gosh, I don't even know what he was saying. But I heard him mention 'that Collins boy'—and maybe he meant Peter, but either way, he said that he attacked Alex and—"

"He attacked Alex?" Anna gasped.

"That's what he said," Danielle said, then shook her head. "Why would either of them do that though? It doesn't make any sense."

Out of her peripheral, Anna saw Aaron returning from the bathroom. She worried that his arrival would shut down the conversation with Danielle. But her thoughts were so jumbled she couldn't wave him off fast enough.

If Danielle was telling the truth, Spencer had conveniently left out that tidbit in his summary of the council meeting. Cassandra hadn't corrected him, but would she? Cassandra had admitted to liking Spencer a few days ago. Would she cover for him like that?

It didn't matter. Whether Spencer had attacked Alexander or not, he surely had a justifiable reason. And this was a chance for Anna to be of some use.

Danielle might not be quite as influential in the social spheres of DeVerre as Anna, but she was a MacDonald. Her voice on their side would carry weight. People would listen, especially if she stood against her family, exposing them for who they truly were.

When Aaron took the seat next to Danielle, the young woman shrunk a bit, offering him a hesitant greeting. Anna didn't let her have a second to retract her question. "Listen, Dani, I know this sounds strange, but I need you to trust me."

Danielle's eyebrows pulled together, wary.

Aaron eyed them with equal concern, but Anna gave him a firm nod. He caught her meaning and tipped his chin up. "'Bout time we start telling people," he muttered.

Danielle looked even more confused. "Telling people about what?" she asked.

"Things aren't what they seem in DeVerre," Anna said. "Whatever Tony has told you, whatever anyone in your family has said, you can't believe them."

"Anna—"

"No, listen to me—the Frossards are liars. And anyone who trusts *them* can't be trusted either."

Danielle's nose scrunched. "I don't understand, Anna. I thought you were friends with—"

"I thought so too," she interrupted. "I thought I was best friends with Connor, and then he turned out to be a class-A jerk. I thought that Alex and Gia cared about me like a daughter. But now I know that was all an act. They don't care about me; they don't care about anyone. They're liars and murderers."

Danielle's jaw dropped in horror.

"Things are changing in DeVerre, Dani," she said. "The truth is coming out, and you're going to have to pick a side. Everyone will."

"A—a side? Between what?"

"Between good and evil," Anna said.

CHAPTER THIRTEEN

Cassandra

After hours and hours of translating Elijah Lawrence's essay, Cassandra left Spencer to his own devices late that night. They'd made it through three pages, picking up speed as she'd helped him develop a key to simplify the process, making her grateful for the research skills she'd picked up as a theology major in college.

Gerard grumbled that their efforts were useless—"What good is theological mumbo-jumbo going to do you?"—but they'd ignored him. And for their efforts, they were rewarded with a startling passage.

" *'The Wolf,'* " Spencer said, reading the translation, " *'was unknown to us, locked away in the depth of shadow and mist, a cage to which only the Seekers hold the key. His residence within is indeterminate, the history of his existence ancient beyond our imaginings as his power draws upon fathomless depths. Whelan, through his trickery and deceit, convinced us to look away from the Wolf and his vassals, Children of Smoke and Dust, teaching the Prophets the responsibility of Protection over Intellect.'* "

"So, they *were* betrayed?" Cassandra surmised, tapping her pen on the concordance she held in her lap. When she and Diane had worked through the texts, they'd found evidence to suggest as much. But with all her newfound knowledge of the spirit world and the Druids, everything made far more sense.

Spencer scratched his eyebrow in thought. "Seems that way. Whelan . . . Is he the Irishman you mentioned? The one with the grandson?"

"Saulf," Cassandra said, remembering the grandson's name. "I believe so. Saulf isn't mentioned in this essay, but we assumed that because his name means 'sea wolf,' he was the Wolf referenced."

"But he was Whelan's grandson," Spencer said. "And the Wolf was released in . . ." He checked the essay dates. "1567."

"When the Warden was formed."

Spencer's brow furrowed. "Hang on—" he looked toward the front door, "isn't Occasus's number 1567?"

"Yeah," Cassandra said in awe. "Yeah, it is."

"Which, I guess, isn't that surprising," he said. "The Varons were committed members of the Warden. It makes sense that they'd honor the creation of the group in their home's address."

Cassandra wondered what else in DeVerre had been founded off the Warden. Everything pointed back to the organization. The problem was, she hadn't yet decided if they were truly the good guys. After all, they promoted secrets and skepticism just as much as the residents of DeVerre.

Spencer looked up at the ceiling in thought. Owen, Ava, Gerard, and Haley were all in the vault, working through the vast texts within the library. Spencer needed the quiet to manage the translation, so they stayed in the office on the main floor.

"Owen said that the Warden was founded in response to the Veil being torn at Stonehenge, right?" he said.

"Yeah, I think so," she said, trying to remember their conversation at the lake two weeks ago.

"So that means that this event," he gestured to the pages, "the Release of the Great Wolf, coincided with the tearing of the Veil."

Cassandra rested her elbow on the arm of her chair, propping her chin on her hand as she looked at the essay. The age of the originals showed through on the scanned copies the Irish reverend had sent to Spencer. Their edges were crackled and wrinkled, and lines of faded ink bled from a quill pen. The words of a man who lived 600 years ago, immortalized on printer paper. And every word felt like it held some key to who she and Spencer were today.

"Do you think they were the same event?" Spencer asked.

"I don't know," she said. "But if the Wolf is Saulf, then . . . what does that mean?"

"*Can* the Wolf be Saulf?"

"What do you mean?"

"The Irishman, Whalen, was in Amesbury, releasing the Wolf in 1567. If the Wolf and his *grandson* were the same person, then . . . Whalen would have had to be in his sixties or seventies, right?"

"Maybe," Cassandra said, pursing her lips in thought. "But people married younger in the 1500s, didn't they? I mean, they didn't exactly have long life expectancies."

Spencer ran a hand through his hair, ruffling up the bits that fell onto his forehead. "I mean, most men were around my age or a little older, and women generally were in their late teens or early twenties."

Amused at his immediate presentation of the facts, Cassandra smirked at him.

He blinked at her amused inspection. "What? I studied classic British literature in college, and their culture impacted the text, so I had to study that too."

"Which led you to study their love lives?"

"British literature is almost exclusively romance," he said. "That or tragedy. Sometimes they're the same thing."

"You were a nerd in college, weren't you?"

A small, embarrassed grin pulled at his lips. "I was an academic," he corrected, his ice-blue gaze meeting hers. "If that makes me nerdy, then fine. But all my time spent in the library gave me the skills to translate these essays, so I'd be thankful for it if I were you."

Cassandra found the bashful confidence of his defense adorable. And she suddenly realized that, with her chin resting on her hand and his head turned toward hers, their faces were precariously close together.

Carefully, she drew back. "We're getting off-topic," she said. "You think Saulf can't be the Wolf because he was too young at the time?"

"If he was even born at all," Spencer said. He didn't notice her discomfort or the distance she'd intentionally placed between them, turning back to the pages with renewed focus. "It seems likely that Whalen was releasing someone completely separate from his grandson. If Whalen was strong enough to lead that sort of charge, then he was almost certainly young himself. Men of any amount of age weren't exactly virile back then."

"Wow," Cassandra murmured, amused by this version of writer and black belt Spencer Collins. "You really are an academic."

He gave her an annoyed though amused frown as she continued, "So Whalen's grandson wasn't the Wolf. Does Elijah give any indication who was?"

Spencer scanned the lines. "Not yet," he said with a sigh. "But there are four pages left in the essay, so he still might. And since he likes to use a lot of symbolism, there's a chance that we won't even recognize the reference until after we've read some of his other essays in conjunction with this one."

The thought of enduring another six hours of work only to make it through three more pages made Cassandra's brain swim. "In that case," she said, rolling the desk chair back. "I'm going to bed. I've had as much Old English as I can take in one day."

Spencer tossed her a distracted smile. "All right, have a good night," he said, turning back to the essay.

"You're staying up?" she asked.

He shrugged. "I want to get a bit more done."

"It's almost midnight, Spence." She nudged his shoulder. "You should get some sleep."

"I'll finish up soon," he promised. "I just want to finish this page."

"Okay." She backed away slowly, Anguis padding along at her side. "Well, I'll see you in the morning."

Spencer lifted his gaze from the essays, a strange look in his eyes as he smiled at her. "Goodnight, Cassie."

The way he said her name like that—*Cassie*, like it was some sweet, gentle thing—always confused Cassandra. She'd never cared what people called her: Cassandra, Cass, Cassie. Her brother, Isaac, even jokingly called her Andy sometimes, stating she was too much of a tomboy to have such a girly name. Names were names, and they didn't mean much to her.

But the way Spencer said her nickname, *Cassie,* was completely different. Even from how he said Cass or Cassandra.

And it baffled her.

Realizing she was still staring at him, Cassandra muttered "g'night" before spinning on her heel and hurrying out of the room. Anguis plodded along, happily unaware of her cringy behavior. What was wrong with her?

Well, Cassandra thought, she knew what was wrong with her. Spencer had kissed her. And that put their relationship in a strangely undefined place. Something not quite platonic but not romantic either. After all, a kiss wasn't a declaration of love. This kiss least of all.

It had been spurred by a moment of panic—a desperation not to feel alone. She understood that need. She'd felt alone most of her life.

For someone like Spencer, someone so used to having his brother always beside him, being apart from Peter would be strange enough. Having him taken captive would be terrifying. Understandably, he panicked. His fear got the better of him, and he did something impulsive to stave off that fear.

Cassandra didn't mind. If he needed to feel that someone was there, she was happy to be that person for him. Whether it was helping him translate essays, supporting his ideas, or letting him kiss her.

Flinching at the thought, Cassandra pushed into her bedroom. Could she handle that? Being kissed by Spencer with no promise of anything serious? Could she even consider it appropriate? Of course, she'd been kissed by her ex-boyfriend, Jake, a handful of times ten years ago. But this was different.

This wasn't her boyfriend. And unlike those times with Jake, she'd kissed Spencer back—her friend who happened to have a panic attack and who kissed her because he was desperate for distraction. Could she justify that? Could she allow it, even if it had been a pulse-altering, senses-buzzing, mind-stilling series of kisses? How could she not?

Leaning against her closed door, Cassandra met Anguis's steady stare. He sat in the middle of the room, a knowing look in those amber eyes.

Cassandra scowled. "Don't look at me like that. It's not my fault he's good at kissing."

Anguis blinked judgmentally.

"Shut up," she said, then went to splash cold water on her face.

~

Gray clouds mottled the morning sky, an ominous start to the day. Cassandra dressed quickly, pulling on her uniform of all-black sweater, jeans, and boots. She swept on her typical, simple makeup, spritzed herself with the perfume on Diane's dresser—wrapping herself in the woman's scent like a hug—and gathered her devotional supplies.

Since the chaos of Saturday night, Cassandra now realized that she hadn't picked up her Bible in the past two days. With all they had on their plates, it was understandable. But she wouldn't let another day get past her without starting it right.

Stepping out into the hall, Cassandra glanced down its length. Peter's door hung open, unoccupied. Her heart gave a little wriggle in her chest.

The hollow shadows cast throughout the room reminded her how empty the house felt without his presence.

Ducking her head, Cassandra snuck past Spencer's closed door, to the back staircase. Anguis sped past her, his nails clicking cheerily on the wood. She followed him into the kitchen, patting his head just before he slipped out the pet door into the yard.

Cassandra turned on the coffee machine, brewing the first pot of the day. The scent of grounds warmed her as she scooped them into the filter. The gurgling water followed her out the kitchen door as she went to set her things at the back of the dining room table.

Stepping out of the kitchen, Cassandra glanced into the office. The overcast morning gave the room an enchantingly haunted appearance, still and empty as it was. The cold hearth of the fireplace, the rows of books, and the thick rug held memories of years with Diane. On the partner desk, the litter of writers filled the surface: stacks of books and papers, a jar of pens and highlighters, a long empty mug resting on top of the concordances next to Spencer's open laptop and the glowing desk lamp.

With a frown, Cassandra tilted her head. Then she saw Nex lying on the floor, his alert ears flickering at her arrival. The dog opened its eyes, his tail giving a muted *thump* against the rug.

Cassandra turned back to the desk, realizing the office wasn't as empty as she'd thought.

Hidden by all the detritus, Cassandra had missed Spencer, his arms resting on the desk, his head resting on his arms. His dark brown waves stuck out, mussed around his peaceful face. The soft puff of his breathing whispered through his parted lips.

Cassandra quietly set her Bible and supplies on the dining room table. She cautiously stepped into the office, not wanting to startle him. "Spencer," she whispered, but he didn't stir.

Nearing the desk, she got a better view. He wore the same long-sleeved thermal tee, dark blue jeans, and boots as yesterday. With almost his whole torso lying on the desktop, Cassandra didn't think anyone would ever solve the mystery of how he'd not fallen out of his chair in his sleep, perched on its edge like that.

She suppressed her laugh, moving to stand at his side. The heavy shadows made his facial hair appear thicker than usual. She wondered if he was dreaming, his dark eyelashes utterly still upon his round cheeks. "Spencer," she said, catching the smallest twitch of his expression at her voice.

Ever so carefully, Cassandra set her hand on his shoulder to wake him gently, whispering his name once more.

Spencer jerked up, practically sending the chair sailing back. His eyes were wide and his breath ragged as his gaze worked to focus. He stared at her in a stupor, mouth ajar.

Nex had raised his head at the sudden movement but yawned now and laid his head back down.

Biting her lip, Cassandra tried not to smile. "I take it you slept here?" she said, making sure to keep her tone light as he woke.

"Oh, uh—" Spencer looked at the desk, swallowed, and rubbed his eyes. "Yeah, I guess I did."

Dark circles and shadows hollowed out the contours of his face. For the first time, she wondered if he'd been sleeping at all the last two nights. From her understanding, he struggled to sleep as it was. Being without Peter surely made his nights even harder.

Cassandra brushed back some of the dark hair matted to his forehead. She'd only meant to keep it quick and lighthearted, but she found her fingers continuing to run through the ends of the waves that turned up into curls, soft against her touch. His hair was one of his more attractive qualities, she thought. And in the short time she'd known him, it had grown down to brush the tips of his eyebrows. If he didn't get it cut, it'd cover his ears soon.

The sudden realization of what she was doing—playing with his hair—hit Cassandra as she noticed Spencer staring at her, frozen as though he was unsure what was happening.

Pulling back immediately, Cassandra tucked her hand behind her back. Her face heated as she passed him a dry grin. "Sorry," she muttered, unable to meet his gaze.

"No, it's. . . ." Spencer trailed off, still staring at her.

Cassandra's eyes dropped to the rug. Whatever he'd meant by kissing her, what he *hadn't* done was ask her to start treating him like her boyfriend. Nor had he invited her to run her fingers through his hair.

Spencer cleared his throat and stood, bringing them within inches of each other. Cassandra slipped around the side of the desk, giving him a wry grin to make it clear she'd meant nothing by her touch. He eyed her for a handful of seconds before rubbing the back of his neck as he stretched.

"I, uh—I guess we should get some stuff done?" he said.

Cassandra continued to back away. "I was going to read my Bible," she said. Why did it suddenly feel so difficult to have a normal conversation?

"Oh." Spencer's gaze followed her direction. "That's a good idea."

"Thanks." Cassandra wanted to roll her eyes at herself.

"Well, um—I think I should, uh. . . ." Spencer motioned to the ceiling.

It took longer for Cassandra to gather his meaning than it should have. He needed to freshen up, having slept in his clothes. "Right," she said, then backed fully out of the office and his path.

Spencer hesitated, mouth open like he was trying to figure out what to say.

"Take your time," she said. "I'll be busy for the next while anyway."

"Cassie, I—"

"Spencer," she interrupted, too embarrassed to address the matter. "Go on. We've got lots to do today."

Spencer nodded and moved for the back staircase, Nex on his heels.

Heaving a huge sigh, Cassandra settled into her seat. She immediately opened her Bible, refusing to be mortified by the exchange.

Rejecting the dozens of embarrassed thoughts that tried to resurge, Cassandra worked twice as hard as usual to get through her devotional time. She had to reread most passages two or three times to come up with anything vaguely resembling comprehension. She barely highlighted or made any notes. Eventually, she gave up.

Spencer returned nearly an hour later, coffee mug in hand. The ends of his hair remained damp from his shower, the waves dipping into his eyes. Freshly dressed in black jeans and a long-sleeved tee—its steely blue obnoxiously suited to complement his eyes—he tipped his head toward the office.

"I'm, uh—I'm gonna get back to it on the next pages," he said awkwardly. "Feel free to join whenever. No rush, though. Take as much time as you need."

Cassandra capped her pen and smirked. "You know, Spencer," she said. "I do believe I told you not to be weird yesterday."

A flash of something—was it embarrassment or horror?—played across his face. "I'm not being weird," he said. "I just—I'm not really sure what 'normal' is anymore." He paused, then added, "Between us."

Cassandra closed her notebook. "Normal would start with not acting like things have changed. We're the same people we were two days ago. So, act the same as you did two days ago."

"Two days ago, I was on the verge of a nervous breakdown," he said.

"And yesterday, you *did* have a nervous breakdown."

Spencer raised his brow. "And then, I kissed you."

A nervous laugh slipped out of her. "Well, if you feel like you're going to panic again, tell me. I want to help in whatever way I can. But in the meantime, could you *not* act like you're afraid of me?"

"I'm not afraid of you," Spencer muttered, though he took a step back as she stood.

"Can you look me in the eyes when you say that?"

His blue eyes flew up to hers with a determination that surprised her.

"I'm not afraid of you, Cassandra," he said. "I just haven't quite figured this out yet."

She thought to ask what there was to figure out when the stairs creaked.

They turned to see Owen arriving via the kitchen, looking professional as ever in his slacks and casual button up. Thankfully, he didn't regard them with any knowing or uncomfortable stare, so she assumed he hadn't heard their conversation.

"Good morning," he said. "Glad to see you're both awake. I had an idea."

"What's up?" Cassandra asked.

Owen smoothed the hem of his shirt. "It's time I trained you both."

"Trained us?" Spencer asked excitedly. "Like, to be Wielders?"

"You're already Wielders," Owen said. "I'm going to train you on how to use your powers as a Sage properly, both by wielding arcs and accessing the spirit world in general. I'd also like to teach you the various factors involved in being a Wielder."

"What kind of factors?" Cassandra asked, somewhere between interested and nervous. She knew Owen was far more cautious with his powers than she. And he viewed her level of power as concerning. It seemed strange that he'd want to teach her how to develop it.

"We'll get to that later. First things first," he settled his gaze on her, confirming her thoughts, "I'm going to teach you to wield an arc without shattering a soul."

The statement rippled through Cassandra's chest. She knew it wasn't meant as an accusation, but it certainly felt like one. "It isn't like I *want* to do it," she said. "But we don't always have the luxury of letting people live."

"That's not what I'm suggesting," Owen said. "But if you're going to bring someone down, you should learn to kill them. Not leave them a hollow shell of a human."

Guilt surged through her.

Spencer's jaw tensed, his gaze flickering between Owen and her as though trying to decide whether he should come to her aid or allow their friend to explain himself.

Cassandra drew her shoulders back. "I didn't realize there was an option," she said.

"You didn't notice that neither Spencer nor Peter left any of those Druids in a catatonic state?" Owen asked.

"I didn't notice much that night."

"Every Druid left the next morning was dead," Spencer said. "I saw what happened to Debbie, and none of them looked like that."

Cassandra frowned. "I did the same thing to Rene, though. I felt it—just like with Debbie."

"I killed her," Owen said regretfully. "During the fight, you didn't take down any Druids. Peter and Spencer did that. While we were fighting, I took care to be sure that Rene actually died."

"What do you mean?" she asked.

There was a compassionate tilt in Owen's expression as he explained. "Shattering a soul is the worst possible end. It is a living death. The body and the spirit live on, but the soul—the mind, will, and emotions of a person—are gone. There's no coming back from it. It's the fate every Wielder fears. The Warden never condones it, not in any case. Death is a mercy from that sort of existence."

Shivers broke along Cassandra's skin. She'd done that. She'd enacted the most unimaginable punishment twice. No wonder it hurt so much. No wonder the guilt and pain lived on in her heart, clinging to the recesses of her mind like an ever-present monster, reminding her what she was capable of.

Spencer shifted uncomfortably, his gaze alight with something she couldn't quite read.

"This is my fault," Owen said. "I should have taught you sooner, but . . . well, I'm not exactly the most qualified, so I put it off."

"What makes you less qualified than someone else?" Spencer asked, an edge in his voice.

"My power is strong but shallow," Owen said.

"What does that mean?"

"A Wielder's powers are directly proportional to their faith as well as to their will," he explained. "I have the faith. I don't have the will. My powers can feel my hesitation—my lack of desire to use them. So they sometimes fail me or fall short in effect."

"Why don't you have the desire to use them?" Spencer asked.

"I'm a scholar," Owen said with a shrug. "I prefer the study to the practice."

Gesturing to the front door, he continued, "Why don't we go outside? I'll teach you how to feel the essence of the spirit world around you. Then we'll draw on it, *slowly*, and I'll teach you how to imbue it with the appropriate will for each purpose."

While Cassandra knew she should accept whatever Owen could teach them with gratitude, she couldn't help feeling condemned for her poor control over her powers. She'd dealt unimaginable damage to Debbie and Rene—her own family—by accident. What other harm could her powers wreak?

After stopping in the foyer to bundle up—Cassandra putting on a real coat this time—they stepped out onto the porch of Occasus. A light flurry of snowflakes danced through the air, settling on the vehicles in the drive. Another layer of snow blanketed the earth last night. It capped the brick and wrought iron fence, clinging to the Varon family crest at the top of the gate. Anguis and Nex ran through the yard, barking as they played in the snow.

Following Owen through the yard, he led them toward a small grove of trees. "I know it's cold, but it's safer to practice out here," he said. "We can use the trees as targets."

"I thought arcs couldn't harm the physical," Spencer said.

"They can't harm it, but they still have an effect," he explained. "An arc can connect with the atoms of any substance, amplifying the electrical current running through them."

Spencer's eyes grew wide. "The lightbulb," he said.

Cassandra and Owen both stared at him in confusion.

"Uh—" He shifted awkwardly, then motioned toward the gates of Occasus. "When we were fighting Debbie—" He looked to Cassandra now. "One of your arcs hit a lamp. While every other light in the room went out, that one kept flickering. It's what gave me the idea to break it, hoping it would start the fire."

With a lift of her chin, understanding came to Cassandra. "So, arcs can create a spike in electricity?"

"If they're powerful enough," Owen said.

"That's handy."

"And," Spencer added, "a good reason *not* to practice inside Occasus."

Owen motioned for them to stand back from the trees. White flecks of snow dotted his blond hair and the shoulders of his light brown coat. "Let's get started," he said, adopting a professorial tone. "As I said, we'll start by getting a feel for the essence of the spirit world around us. Learning to experience it and feel it at all times is key to quickly and effectively tapping into its power. If you don't have this connection, you can easily lose it in the chaos of the moment. You need to *know* what the spirit world feels like so that you can access it when the time comes."

Spencer removed his hands from his coat pockets. "How do we do that?" he asked.

"By resting," Owen said. "By being still."

Spencer blinked, and Cassandra pressed her lips together around a dry smile. Of all people, Spencer Collins was not one for rest. Different from Peter, he didn't care for the stimulus of constantly hopping from one activity to the next, but she knew perfectly well that his brain was always alive, seeking some form of distraction. When things got too stagnant for him, he went on walks or to the gym. People might assume him to be a homebody, but in reality, he was a wild storm of activity contained in human form.

But to be fair, Cassandra wasn't a big fan of being still herself. She hated being alone with her thoughts. She'd much rather have the distraction of a good book or a conversation to being "at rest."

Owen took in their mutual wariness with a keen eye. "It's hard to begin, but you'll get the hang of it quickly," he assured. "The first step is to quiet your mind."

Spencer sighed, and Cassandra didn't feel any more optimistic.

"Everyone has their own method of stilling their mind," Owen said. "Some people like to close their eyes, creating a mental image to hold their focus. I find that more difficult, my thoughts tending to jump from one idea to the next. Looking at the world around me, seeing it for everything it is and everything it could be is what centers me. It keeps my mind from wandering. If you find that too much to focus on, just pick one object. Study it, hone in on it, and let your mind still as you ponder it."

Cassandra doubted that any of those suggestions would work for her. Her mind tended to turn in on itself brutally when it was still. She didn't see the world around her; she saw herself. And she didn't like herself very much.

"Once you've quieted your mind, the next step is to listen," Owen said. "You can hear it, the spirit world. It's this . . ."

His words trailed off, his dark blue gaze drifting to the sky, to the gates, to the fence, to the dogs, to the grass, to the world all around them as he gathered his thoughts. "This sound beyond all other sounds," he said reverently. "It's a pulse separate from everything else—above everything else. You don't hear it until you do, and then it's always there."

The concept sailed straight over Cassandra's head. A sound beyond sound? Separate and above? Unheard until heard? Owen was almost as confusing as Elijah Lawrence's essays.

"So," Spencer said, drawing out the word. "We get quiet, pick something to focus on, and listen?"

"To start," Owen said. "Once you hear it, I'll lead you in the next step."

"What if we don't hear it?" Cassandra asked, certain the odds of that were higher.

Owen shrugged. "You might not," he said. "Which is why we'll start slow. Try to focus, quiet your thoughts, and listen for the sound beyond sound."

With their instructions before them, Cassandra and Spencer shared one last look before beginning their practice. She decided to try Owen's method first. The idea of closing her eyes and letting her inner thoughts rule wasn't appealing. So, she'd scan the world around her, looking for her center.

A shiver worked its way up her spine, her toes cold in the snow. Cassandra shrugged it off, surveying the ground of Occasus. Normally, she loved the property: the emerald pines and grass, the glowing sunlight, and the grand mansion. But under the clouded dull-gray sky, white sheets of snow, and drooping foliage, the somber atmosphere filled her with leaden disappointment. When had it become so sorrowful?

Cassandra abandoned her scan to try the approach of selecting one focus: Anguis. His coppery-brown fur stuck out against the white of the landscape, his nose down as he sniffed the earth, making tracks in the snow. The dog made her smile, reminding her of the first time she'd met him. Diane had purchased the dogs after her husband, Liam, had passed. They'd still been puppies when Cassandra first visited Occasus. She could remember Anguis's awkward lumbering through the house. He'd been harder to train than Nex, always headstrong and full of spunk. But the minute Cassandra met the dog, he'd bounded to her side and never left.

The thoughts were a bittersweet memory. The image of Anguis's floppy puppy ears flashed in her mind as she saw the full-grown dog in the yard before her. Those early years of his life were the only seasons of Cassandra's where she truly felt welcome and wanted. The only period of time she hadn't felt like a mistake. At least, that's how she felt whenever she was with Diane.

But when she returned to the Merciers' for the night or went to Spokane to visit family, the feelings of isolation would resurface. Feelings that were renewed with the arrival of Druids and her rising powers.

Cassandra bit back those thoughts. This was why she didn't like being alone, giving her thoughts room to develop. She didn't need to remember the trauma that made up her life. Pain was pain. Everyone lived with it, so why dwell on it? Sitting in your thoughts served nothing and no one. Just move on and let it go.

"I—" Spencer's hushed voice cut through her thoughts. She turned, seeing his eyes open and focusing on some small point in the distance. "I hear it," he whispered.

Disappointment flooded Cassandra as Owen gently praised Spencer's success. "Hold on to it," Owen said. "Listen to it and feel its vibration, its presence surrounding you."

Spencer nodded, hands clasped before him habitually as he stared off into space.

Owen's dark blue gaze shifted to Cassandra, hopeful.

With a tiny shake of her head, Cassandra had nothing to offer. She felt no draw of internal quiet. All she heard was the noise of the earth gone to rest in late autumn. Nothing.

Suddenly, there *was* a sound.

Cassandra furrowed her brow, listening. She could hear the faintest hum, almost a purr or a whir.

"Do you—" Owen began, then paused, his gaze going beyond her shoulder toward the gate of Occasus. He heard it too. And it was coming nearer.

Cassandra turned, drawing Spencer out of his focus. "What is it?" he asked.

"I don't—oh." Cassandra sighed, understanding dawning on her as the sound's origin clicked into place. A silver SUV pulled through the gates.

"Is that Aaron and Haley?" he asked. "He said they'd be coming by today."

"It's not Aaron," Owen said, then motioned for them to follow. "Come on, I have someone to introduce you to."

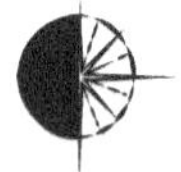

CHAPTER FOURTEEN

Spencer

The SUV pulled up to the front of Occasus. Nex and Anguis bounded over to join them at the foot of the porch. A man sat inside the vehicle, but its tinted windows obscured his details. The shiny lacquer and streamlined body of the SUV looked positively futuristic next to the Jeep and truck.

The rumble of the engine cut off, and Owen stepped forward. "Well now, Professor," the man laughed as he stepped out of the vehicle, "you've got yourself a fancy pad here." His black-brown hair and dark coat contrasted starkly against the gray and white world around them. His suntanned face bore a large smile, strong jawline, and the hint of a "five-o-clock" shadow.

Owen and the man clasped hands and exchanged a quick embrace. "It's not my place," Owen said with an unusually full smile. "Let me introduce you to my friends."

Spencer and Cassandra watched with interest as the man approached.

He was tall with sharp yet full features. His dark hair seemed drawn to falling across his forehead, and he had deep-set, piercing blue eyes.

"Spencer, Cassandra," Owen gestured to the man, "this is my old friend, Silas Varon."

Instantly, Spencer's shoulders drew back.

"Silas," Owen continued, "this is Cassandra Clement and Spencer Collins."

"Nice to meet you both," Silas said, holding out his hand.

Spencer accepted the handshake, though words felt impossible. "You, uh—you too."

As Cassandra took her turn at greeting Silas, Owen spoke again. "Spencer and his brother are the ones I told you about."

"I assumed as much," Silas said, then turned to Spencer. He lifted a finger to motion between his and Spencer's faces. "You've got the nose."

"What?" Spencer asked.

"The Varon nose," Silas said. "It's very distinct. And obnoxiously *cute*, as my wife likes to say."

Cassandra sniggered beside Spencer as he continued to gape at the man.

"Why don't we go inside?" Owen suggested.

At the word "inside," the dogs hurtled up the porch to the door, and Spencer forced himself to get a grip. "Right, yeah." He moved out of the way, motioning for Silas and Owen to go up before him. "Come on in."

Silas hesitated, eyes flickering to Cassandra. "Ladies first," he said.

Wry grin in place, Cassandra slipped past Spencer, their shoulders brushing in the process. The men filed in behind her, entering Occasus's foyer to shed their coats. Cassandra offered Silas a drink, which he declined. "I got a coffee on the way from Spokane," he said.

"You live in Spokane?" Spencer asked.

"No. I just flew in this morning."

"Oh."

"Owen called me," Silas explained. "Said he'd met some family of mine and that they could use my help."

Turning to Owen, a feeling of overwhelming gratitude welled up in Spencer. "Your friend from Harmony?" he said.

Owen dipped his head. "We went to school together."

"I'm a bit older than the professor, but he's wise beyond his years, so I like to keep him around," Silas said with a dry expression. "When he told me about your situation here, I knew I had to come. I don't live in Harmony anymore, but I called some family there too."

"More Varons are coming?" Spencer asked hopefully.

"Uh, no," Silas said, a flat yet apologetic tilt to his voice. "They're not . . . they're a bit busy at the moment. But I'm here. And, believe it or not, that'll probably be all you need."

Cassandra arched an eyebrow in amusement. "One Varon against an unknown amount of Druids?" she asked.

"*Three* Varons, ma'am," he said. "As soon as we find this kid's brother."

"Varons are that powerful, huh?"

Spencer knew Cassandra wasn't as skeptical as she sounded, merely intrigued. She'd seen how powerful he and Peter had become with no training. He still didn't know what to make of it himself.

Silas shrugged. "Yeah."

"Huh." Cassandra's eyes kept flickering from Silas to Spencer and back.

Spencer scratched the back of his head. "Did you want to have a seat?" he asked.

Joining the dogs in the living room, they made themselves comfortable. Silas and Owen exchanged pleasantries about travel, family, and life while Cassandra and Spencer sat on the opposite couch. Silas had two daughters, now lived in Montana, and evidently knew everything about Owen's life—with the exception of recent events.

"How's Ava?" Silas asked.

"She's doing well," Owen said, though his voice was strained.

"At the library still?"

"Of course."

Silas grinned. "Of course," he muttered, turning to Spencer and Cassandra. "Every Warden town is the same."

"How so?" Spencer found his knee bouncing but didn't care to stop the nervous twitch.

"Oh, you know." Silas waved a hand through the air in dismissal. "The jobs get passed down from family member to family member. We're highly traditional. And I know my share of Raynes. Scholars, all of them. Probably the reason Owen wound up here in the first place."

"It was inevitable," Owen admitted.

Silas grinned. "He's got a type."

Cassandra chuckled under her breath, but Spencer struggled to smile. This man was a Varon. They were family. And he knew things about their ancestry that could shed so much light on their past.

"You are from Harmony, though?" Spencer asked.

"Born and raised there," Silas said. "But I moved to Gold Mountain about a decade ago."

"Why?"

A shadow passed across his expression, bright eyes dimming for a fraction of a second. Then that confident grin returned. "Work."

Spencer thought he recognized that hesitation. "Warden work?" he asked.

"There isn't much other kind for us Varons."

"So Gold Mountain is a Warden town too?"

"It is."

"Is it like DeVerre?" Spencer asked.

"In what way?"

"Does it have a Veil?"

Silas glanced at Owen, a sly tilt coming to his lips. "Is he always this persistent?"

"Usually," Owen said.

"The Collins brothers are what you'd call 'inquisitive,'" Cassandra said, crossing her legs demurely.

Wanting an answer, Spencer prompted Silas again. "Does it?"

With a bored shrug, Silas replied, "It does now."

That immediately brought a dozen new questions to Spencer's mind.

But before he could ask one of them, Silas continued, "Listen, as much as I'd love to swap stories with you, that isn't why I came here," he said, leaning forward in his seat. "I'm here to help you stop the Druids. We can't have them open this Veil. And it would behoove us all to regain control of the town as well."

"Warden control?" Spencer asked. "Or Varon control?"

Silas smirked. "They're often one and the same."

"Pete and I aren't interested in running a town."

"You may not have a choice." Compassion filled Silas's tone like he understood the weight of what he was suggesting but saw no way around the truth of it. "Responsibility sort of gets thrust upon our family, whether we asked for it or not. And you may have to accept far more than just the responsibility of running a town in the end."

"Our family," Spencer repeated, the sentiment heavy. "Why us? What did the Varons do to . . . earn this fate?"

"Blame it on Gabriel Varon," Silas said, then moved on, glossing over the fact that Spencer had no idea who or what he was talking about. "Whether or not this ends with you and your brother in charge doesn't matter. There's more at stake here than simple bad guys looking to play king in a tiny town. They're trying to release the spirit world. They're trying to gain *final* control over it."

"What does that mean?" Cassandra asked.

Silas glanced at Owen. "That's classified information," he said.

Spencer glowered at the man in disbelief while Cassandra let out a scoff. "Seriously?" she said. "We're fighting for our lives, and you're going to redact information?"

"Hey," Silas raised his hands in surrender, "I'd love to tell you the details. The fact of the matter is, I don't know myself."

"But you're a Varon," Spencer said. "I thought we were the—the head of the Warden or something."

"Oh." Silas laughed as though that was the most ridiculous thing he'd ever heard. "No. The Varons may be the most *powerful* family, but we aren't in charge. Not by a long shot. In fact, most of the leadership isn't our biggest fan."

Spencer and Cassandra shared a look. "Why not?" he asked.

Silas opened his mouth, froze, and then looked at Owen. "Do you know?"

Owen let a small huff slip out of him. "If you don't, then I certainly don't."

Silas turned back to Spencer. "Best guess?" He shrugged. "They don't like the fact that we're this powerful. But there's a chance it goes deeper than that. They've held this grudge for a while, though. Longer than I've been alive."

Spencer didn't know what part to focus on: the fact that they were so powerful, that Silas had no clue why the leadership disliked them, or that they held a grudge in the first place.

"Do you know who the leaders of the Warden are?" Cassandra asked.

"I know one of them," Silas said.

"And they are?"

His lips turned up in the corner. "Another classified detail."

Cassandra turned to Owen. "And these are the 'good guys'?"

"Can I call you Cassandra?" Silas asked abruptly.

"Huh?"

Silas gestured to her. "I don't know what to call you," he said. "Do you like to be called Cassandra? Do you have a nickname? Would you rather I call you Miss Clement?"

Her mouth hung open for a second before she regained her composure. "Cassandra is fine."

"Great," Silas said, then began to explain. "Cassandra, the Warden keeps things secret because it is vital to their survival. And sometimes it's because they're stupid. But most of the time, it's because they're working very hard to keep our organization safe and afloat."

Silas motioned between Owen and himself. "I know more than Owen, and Owen knows more than the majority of Harmony," he said. "What information is granted is based upon a few factors. Most importantly, your classification as a Wielder. Being a Sage, as Owen is, puts him at the top of the organization. However, as a Sage *and* a Varon, with dozens of generations of ancestors within the Warden, I'm provided with even more information. It's a hierarchy of trust, a burden of knowledge that you are only granted when you've *proven* the ability to carry its weight."

"And being a Varon automatically proves that you can carry it?" Spencer asked.

Silas gave him an amused expression. "Seems ridiculous, doesn't it? But believe it or not, there's only ever been one Varon who 'broke bad,' and he was only part Varon. We're a rare breed."

"Then why doesn't the leadership like us?"

"Again, I don't know."

Spencer's knee continued to bounce as he processed through all the information. What did it matter? How did it help? Silas had said it himself: He'd come here to help them retrieve Peter, defeat the Druids, and regain control over the town. Facts which prompted another question.

"How long are you here for?" Spencer asked.

"However long it takes, I guess."

"Hopefully, just a few days," Owen said. "I'm . . . optimistic that with your help, we can wrap things up far more easily. And then, if you'd be willing," he turned to Spencer, "I'd imagine a few days of training would be appreciated."

A sudden spring of hope welled up in Spencer. This was a Varon sitting in front of him. The first he'd ever met. The only family member they knew from their grandfather's true ancestry.

"Yeah," Spencer said, thrilled at the prospect. "Yeah, it would be—it'd be amazing. Whatever you could teach us. Both about our powers and about our family. We know so little about the Varons or their time in DeVerre. The only information we do have is a journal from Michael Varon."

"Well, I'd be happy to help in whatever way I can," Silas said. "Being a Varon isn't easy, I'll tell you that. And if I can make it easier, then sure, I'll help. But I'll be honest with you, I'm not sure I'll be able to tell you much about your family."

That confused Spencer. "But . . . you are our family, right?"

"Oh, we are *distantly* related, kid," Silas said with a little chuckle. "Like, *generations* of distance. We're probably fourth cousins twenty times removed or something. So while, yes, we are family, this isn't some Varon reunion where we bond over our mutual relations. You wouldn't know a single name I gave you, and quite frankly, I only know about your line because your however-many-times-great-great-whatever was chosen to carry on the inheritance."

Spencer furrowed his brow. "Inheritance?"

Silas grimaced. "That's—well, we can talk about that later. For now, the best thing to focus on is you all getting me caught up on what exactly is happening here in DeVerre," he said. "Who's their leader? Do you have specific members' names already? What plans do you have in place? Do you know when they're planning to make *their* move?"

"That's gonna take a while," Spencer said.

Silas gave him a crooked smile, and somehow Spencer recognized it as the same one he and Peter had inherited from their dad. "Then it's a good thing I took the red-eye."

~

Hours later, Spencer, Cassandra, and Owen had related the story of the last month and a half to Silas. They told him about Diane and her suspicious death, the hellhound attacks, Elijah Lawrence's missing and recovered essays, the fight with Debbie, Cassandra's history and abnormal jumps of skill, the fight with the Druids three nights ago, and Peter's disappearance the next day. And then, they'd introduced him to Gerard.

"You tethered a phantom?" Silas asked Cassandra, his voice laced with disbelief.

She shrugged, a slight wash of red tingeing her temples. "Diane found the information in one of Elijah's essays," she said. "Gerard has been incredibly helpful."

"He has," Spencer said. "Though he's also been a hassle."

Gerard grinned. "I'm hurt that I haven't won you over yet."

Eyes narrowed, Silas studied Gerard. "You were murdered?" he asked.

"I was."

"By a beast?"

Gerard frowned. "I don't know how."

"You didn't see what killed you?"

"No."

Silas nodded as though that was confirmation. "It was a beast."

"How do you know?" Cassandra asked, gaze flashing from the phantom to the Varon.

"He has no injuries," he explained. "Ghosts—and therefore, phantoms—always display their forms at the time of death. However, when the death is inflicted by spirit world means, the physical damage sort of gets lost in translation. So the ghost or phantom shows no sign of injury."

"He could have been suffocated or poisoned," Spencer suggested.

"Suffocation would still leave signs," Cassandra said.

"Something attacked me," Gerard confirmed.

Silas turned back to Cassandra. "In the future, I'd advise you not to tether ghosts," he said. "The dead are dead for a reason. The longer they have a link to the physical, the harder it is for them to move on."

"Why would it be possible to tether them if we shouldn't?" she asked.

"I don't know," he admitted. "I just know that the act of tethering is far more serious than we realize. As it is, I'd like to get a look at these essays of Elijah's. The Lawrences are incredibly protective of their family's articles, so I've only seen snippets of his works."

Spencer got stuck on the mention of the Warden founder's family. "The Lawrences are still around?"

"Oh, yes," Silas said. "They're still quite impactful."

"Are they the Warden leader you know?"

Silas's smile was confirmation despite his silence.

"Interesting," Spencer muttered.

"With all the information you've given me," Silas continued, moving on from the rabbit trail, "it seems we need to meet with this man, Gabe Chapelle. We can't know what's going on in DeVerre until we've talked with him. Nor can we make any real decisions until we get his information. From there, we can figure out what to do."

Spencer pulled in a deep breath. "And what about finding Peter?" he asked.

Silas held his intent stare. "We can't go off half-cocked. We need to gather all our facts, make sure we know what we're up against, and then we'll save him. I promise. I'll help you find your brother."

Though Spencer didn't want to wait another day, not even another second, to find Peter, he knew that Silas was right. And despite his fear, having another Varon to help them gave him hope for the first time in forty-eight hours.

"All right," Spencer said. "Let's get to work, shall we?"

CHAPTER FIFTEEN

Peter

"I never realized how numb your butt could get from sitting on concrete for fifty years," Peter said to the valravn.

The beast blinked.

"I know, I know." He waved his hand. "It can't have been fifty years. I'd have hair down to my waist if it'd been that long."

He ran a hand through his greasy hair, realizing it was longer than he usually let it grow. Soon, it'd be like Spencer's, falling onto his forehead in messy waves. But this wasn't the result of years. Nor even weeks of imprisonment. This was simply due to their move to DeVerre. Roughly a month and a half ago, they'd left behind Virginia to come to this small Washington town with the hopes of following their dreams.

What a mistake it had been.

But Peter was reasonably convinced by his inspection of himself that he had been here little more than a few days, maybe a week at the most. Alexander and the valravn were the only beings he'd seen since his imprisonment. The Druid brought him intermittent, menial meals, but little else gave him any sense of time. He wished he wore a watch.

The inability to tell time wreaked havoc on his internal clock. Peter did whatever he could to stay awake. He thought about plotlines for *Wenzel & Frankly*, developing hundreds of new ideas. Unfortunately, he didn't have his notebook to write those ideas down. He counted the books on the shelves in the study outside of his cell. He memorized the titles of the books nearest him. All of it did little to help.

And with only a non-verbal bird-beast for a companion, Peter rapidly ran out of entertainment.

Talking to the valravn seemed foolish. He didn't know how much of his conversation the beast understood, but it let out those menacing trills and ruffled its feathers in response to his voice, which were almost as disturbing as his dreams.

Though he fought sleep, Peter's exhaustion inevitably wore him down. No matter how hard he tried, he couldn't keep his mind occupied enough. He constantly lapsed in and out of fitful bouts of sleep, confusing his timekeeping even more. Plunged back into the nightmares again and again, he woke trembling and gasping in dream-induced pain, making his head swirl with delirium.

The dreams were getting worse. Peter didn't know if his exhaustion was causing it or if it was due to the presence of the valravn. He had noticed the bird-beast's eyes always gleamed brightest right after he startled awake.

Every dream started the same, with Peter running through the forest, numb from the cold and his pulse pounding. He would run from the beasts, the shadows swooping in at him from all sides. He wasn't even making it to Occasus anymore. He'd only made it inside the gates in the first few dreams. Since then, he wound up just outside the property line a handful of times and miles away in the rest.

Peter would have been grateful not to watch Gerard murder his brother again. However, this was almost worse. Alone in the forest, he started hearing the voices as he ran. Bone-chilling screams, and voice-breaking cries. The sounds of his family calling out to him—begging him to help them. To save them.

Spencer. Cassandra. His mom. His dad.

And no matter how hard Peter tried, no matter how furiously he struggled and ran, he couldn't get to them. He would sprint for endless miles, his body slowly breaking down with its weakness. The beasts would close in, and he would hear his family call for him. "Peter!"

He never made it. And in every dream, the beasts would be there—clawing, ripping, biting, breaking.

The first time that Peter woke with tears on his face, he felt somewhat embarrassed. He was a grown man. He could handle nightmares.

But after the sixth—or was it the sixtieth?—he'd grown numb to the sorrow and pain.

Now, Peter slouched against the corner, staring unseeingly into the fireplace, desperately hoping he wouldn't fall asleep again for a long, long time.

~

Eyes heavy and body hollow, Peter's mind began the slow descent into dreamy-awakeness. That strange place between reality and imagination that played tricks on your mind. Shaking his head and readjusting regularly, he fought against sleep like a Spartan defending Greece, knowing that, eventually, he'd fall.

The *click* of the study door startled Peter, saving him from another torturous turn in his nightmares. Alexander entered, ignoring him as usual to head straight for his desk. Dressed in dark slacks and a light green button down, he looked like a country-club poster man as he rifled through the desk drawers.

"Off to hit some tees?" Peter asked, then furrowed his brow, turning to the valravn. "What's the correct slang for going golfing?"

"I don't golf," Alexander said.

A loud *whomp* drew Peter's attention back to the doctor. There on the desk lay a massively hefty tome. Probably three thousand pages, at the very least. Or maybe the pages were just super thick.

But Alexander wasn't done digging treasure out of his desk. He retrieved a wooden box before shutting the drawer with a flick of his wrist. Stepping around the desk, he met Peter's gaze for the first time in . . . was it days?

"I have a meeting to get to," he said, crossing the study. "But I want to show you something first."

Peter scrambled to sit up straight, wary of the Druid's proximity. He hadn't come this close to the bars since Peter woke that first day, except for the times he brought in food or checked his vitals. "Whatcha got there?" he asked, eyes flickering from the oak box to the man's face.

A dangerous grin worked over Alexander's face as his fingers grazed the box's intricately carved lid. "Something very special."

The reverence in the doctor's tone made Peter's skin crawl. "Is this my lucky day?"

"More like *my* lucky day."

"That's disappointing."

Alexander's smug smile was almost as troubling as the fact that he was engaging in conversation. It didn't escape Peter that this man was a narcissist or that little he did was impulsive. Alexander Frossard led the Druids; he'd earned that role, even if he had inherited it. And for him to take time out of his day to show Peter something special creeped him out to no end.

"This," Alexander said, lifting a small golden object from the box, "is my prized possession. Unfortunately, I've had to hide it my entire life."

Peter's heart stalled, his eyes locked on the object. The firelight shone on the thick golden band, catching in the deep grooves of its broad face. Held aloft between his thumb and forefinger, Alexander proffered the ring for Peter's continued inspection.

"What is that?" Peter muttered, his mouth drying up.

Alexander's light eyebrow rose in mocking humor. "Seems as though you know what it is."

Of course, Peter knew what it was. How could he not recognize that crest? A dagger emblazoned on the beams of a star, nestled into the hollow of a V. The same sigil that was welded into the gates of Occasus.

The Varon family crest.

Peter glared at the ring, his eyes glued to its facets even as his anger burned hot in his throat.

"Your family has caused quite a lot of trouble for mine over the past century," Alexander said. "But *this*? This is a testament, Mr. Varon. Proof that my family won."

It didn't escape Peter's notice that this was the first time Alexander had called him *Varon*. This was the first time the man had legitimized his parentage. And it sat like a lead weight in Peter's chest.

Tearing his eyes from the ring, Peter glared at the man. "If you have to hide it, I'd say you haven't won anything," he taunted.

Alexander's dry grin didn't falter. "You have a point, I suppose. But you see," he tossed the ring into the air, catching it in his fist, "these are the final days, my friend."

Pulse stuttering and hands shaking, Peter wanted to leap through the bars of the cell and wrench that ring out of his grimy claws. The titter of the valravn tugged at the back of his brain, making him wonder if the beast could read his thoughts.

"After the full moon," Alexander continued, placing the ring back into the box with tender care, "I will finally accomplish what my father and his father before him never could. Then, I will wear this ring as a sign of our family's success and your family's destruction."

He shut the box with a firm *snap*. His cerulean eyes flashed up to hold Peter's. "And the name, Varon, will never be uttered as anything but a cautionary tale ever again."

Forcing his fingers to curl into a fist instead of reaching through to rip the box free, Peter ground his teeth together. He didn't know why this rage boiled up inside of him. Varon had only been his name for—well, he didn't even know how long he'd been down there. The lineage of being a Varon was still new. Should he feel so attached to the name already? Or was there something more to it?

Alexander wasn't just demeaning some unknown family—some spooky DeVerrean gossip, some psycho who murdered his dad and killed himself. He was demeaning Michael Varon, the man who'd sacrificed everything, including his life as a devoted husband and father, for what he believed in. He was also demeaning Seraphine Varon, the woman who'd stood up to her family, risking her life as a double agent, to do what she knew was right. He also demeaned Diane, the daughter who never forgot the mother she lost, giving her entire life to the family she'd barely known.

And in his dishonor of their family, Alexander also threatened Spencer. He mocked Peter and his brother. He discredited them as two pests to be crushed. Two pitiful, annoying boys with no more value than the family members his ancestors had already murdered.

Peter's eyes flashed to the dull red line on Alexander's forehead, the mark Spencer had left on the Druid leader. He smirked, thinking of his brother's defiance. "Spencer should have killed you when he had the chance," he said.

With a bored smile, Alexander rose, the oaken box still clasped in his hand. "You should get some rest, Mr. Collins," he said. "You're not looking so well. And I should hate for you to miss our appointment in three days."

Peter frowned. Three days? What was happening in three days?

As Alexander returned to the desk, Peter racked his brain. Had the Druid said something else that might give him a clue? Down here in the bowels of the beast, everything felt important. Every little detail might give him some inkling of hope or a source of salvation. Three days. What was happening in three days?

"After the full moon," Alexander had said.

Peter's heart sank.

"These are the final days."

Heart stuttering, Peter stared out of his cell at Alexander. The doctor set the box on the desk, lovingly adjusting it to face the cell. "There," he said. With a smug glance over his shoulder, he gestured to the box. "Now you can have something nice to think about while you wither away down here."

Peter did think about it. His eyes locked on the box and never moved away from its carvings. The Celtic knots and lush trees mimicked the desk it rested atop. He thought about it for hours, maybe for days. And with every second, his nails digging furiously into his palms, he thought about Alexander's taunts.

The full moon.

Three days.

"This is a testament, Mr. Varon."

Peter's jaw hurt from how hard he held it clenched. But he didn't care.

A testament.

Yes, the Varon signet would be a testament. But not to the Frossard's victory.

The lines of a letter to Michael Varon, crackled and yellowed with age, hummed through Peter's head. *"The finality of the Varon line within DeVerre will last for not a century but will resurrect to restore that which was stolen from you."*

A prophecy. A legacy. A promise.

"Your own blood will restore the cracks that have marred the surface of the glass."

Michael's blood.

Peter and Spencer.

And whatever it took, whatever hell they had to go through to get there, Peter would tear the whole of DeVerre to the ground to restore what was stolen from the Varons.

CHAPTER SIXTEEN

Cassandra

After a long day of working in the vault and getting to know Silas, they finally left for the meeting with Gabe and his friends at sunset. The winter light burned vibrant orange against the violet sky as the four of them piled into the Jeep. Ava and Aaron were supposed to meet them at the funeral home. As Anna had the evening shift at the tavern again, Haley chose to keep her company as part of their "no one's left alone" agreement.

Given the Lambert siblings' fervor to save DeVerre, Cassandra couldn't help wondering what might have been. If Diane had been less focused on her ancestry and more interested in the spirit world like the brothers, could they have made these discoveries sooner? Diane had always treated their study of the spirit world as a far more academic pursuit. Fine for concepts and abstract notions, but not for daily living. Her interest in ghosts surrounded her assurance that it was linked to her family. And she turned out to be correct, but it went far deeper than Diane had ever known.

When they parked at the funeral home, Cassandra frowned. There were only a few cars. Sam and Tom stood together by their shared ride, and Ava leaned against the door of her hatchback, Aaron and his motorcycle in the space next to her. Other than them, there were no other vehicles in the lot.

"I thought Gabe said he had friends," Cassandra said.

"I'd imagine they didn't want to draw attention to the meeting by filling up the front of the funeral home," Owen said from the backseat.

"Right," she murmured as Spencer parked.

They stepped out into the frosty evening, making a short introduction to Silas. Their large group crowded into the foyer to find Gabe sitting at a small desk. "Evening," he greeted, his sharp blue eyes scanning them. "Looks like we've got quite the party gathered."

Cassandra shifted nervously at Spencer's side. Meeting in a funeral home was a whole new level of creepy, even for her. She couldn't help fearing they'd made a mistake.

Gabe rose from his seat, beckoning with a lazy wave. "We're in the back."

The mortician held open the door, letting them file through. "Keep going," he instructed. "Double doors at the end of the hall."

Down the dingy, narrow hall, they pushed through the white-painted metal doors into a bright, sterile room. Shallow but wide, the center of the room lay clear. A silver embalming table was pushed against the left wall near cabinets and shelves bearing medical implements she didn't care to decipher or name. A hook next to the entrance bore a singular white lab coat. Along the back wall, ten silver doors filled the space.

The startling realization that they stood in the preparation and storage room made Cassandra cringe. Then she took in the group of people awaiting them. Ten men and women clustered comfortably amidst the morbid space. She recognized several of them—if not by name, then by looks. Most shared Tom's thick, dark hair, strong, pronounced jawline, and fierce, no-nonsense stare. Some were middle-aged like the marshal, but three looked closer to Anna and Spencer's age. Garniers, the lot of them.

On the far side of the room, Juliet Chapelle sat atop a cabinet, a teen boy heavily resembling Gabe with auburn hair and a strong brow lounging at her side. A man Cassandra didn't recognize hovered near one of the elder Garniers, a ragged work coat hanging open over an equally worn flannel.

But the member that caused Cassandra's heart to seize stood like a shadow at the back of the crowd. Mousy brown hair, burly-shouldered, and upturned brown eyes that haunted Cassandra's memories.

"Travis?" she said.

The son of Debbie Mercier raised his chin in a somber greeting. "Hey, Cass," he said.

"You're—I—" Cassandra's mind raced, trying to process the presence of the Druid's son in the meeting. She'd never been close with Travis. He was seven years older, preferring to hang out with her brother, Isaac. He'd always seemed so distant to Cassandra, and she'd never bothered to bridge that divide. Now, she wondered what she'd missed.

When the initial shock passed, panic seized Cassandra's chest. "What are you doing here?" she demanded.

Tension filled the room, the team from Occasus bristling nervously as Gabe's friends drew up warily.

Travis's bewildered expression seemed sincere. "I'm a member of the Militia," he said.

"The Militia?" Tom repeated, his tone accusatory as he looked at Gabe.

The mortician shrugged, standing by his son and niece. "We needed a name," he said. "It seemed fitting."

"What's the problem here?" an elder Garnier asked.

Spencer shifted closer to Cassandra, and she took strength from his presence. "I don't trust him," she said, unsure exactly how much to share. If Travis was amongst Gabe's friends, there was a chance several of them were Druids.

A chorus of "whys" rang out, but Travis quickly came to his own defense. "I don't exactly trust you, either," he said. "But I do know that you have experience with the spirit world. And I'm willing to listen because Dad and I want answers."

Cassandra flinched. "Mike's a part of this too?"

Travis nodded. "We've been working with Gabe for years. Just like Grandpa Clarence worked with Reverend John-Daniel."

"Dad was involved in this?" Sam asked his brother.

"Just because you chose not to care didn't mean the rest of us did too," Gabe said.

Travis kept on without any more prompting. "The Merciers have worked alongside the Chapelles, Garniers, and Ozannes since 1915. We weren't satisfied with the choice to simply *forget* the spirit world's existence. We want to destroy it. And after what happened to Mom—"

Cassandra tensed, the guilt welling up inside of her. Travis's eyes—replicas of Debbie's and Rene's—bored into her. He didn't know. He *couldn't* know. The accusation in his stare wasn't directed at her. He simply didn't know who to blame.

"Dad and I know Mom's condition isn't natural," he said. "We know that one of those monsters did that to her. And whatever took Rene to Occasus that night . . ."

A tremble worked through Cassandra's hand. *She* was the monster he sought, the one who'd killed both his mother and sister. Worse than killed, she'd shattered their souls, the scars of her actions lingering within her own.

Spencer's hand brushed the back of hers.

"That," Travis continued, "is why the spirit world needs to be destroyed. It's why all of us are here."

A round of support came from the Militia members.

Silas cleared his throat, drawing their attention. "That's a really stupid reason," he said steadily. "Seeing as how the spirit world is indestructible."

The Militia froze, glaring at Silas. One of the eldest Garnier men scanned him. "And who are you?" he asked.

Owen stepped forward. "This is my friend, Silas Varon."

The other side of the room went rigid at the name.

"Like me, he grew up in Harmony, Saskatchewan," he continued. "We've been friends for years."

"A Varon?" Gabe asked, scanning Silas.

Silas shrugged. "Through and through."

"What are you doing here?" one of the young Garnier women asked.

"As Owen said, we're friends," he said. "When he called to tell me that some of my family needed help, I couldn't say no."

The whole of the Militia was confused.

"Your family?" Gabe asked.

Silas gestured to Spencer. "We're distant cousins."

A low murmur filled the group, but the man in the work coat spoke the loudest. "You're saying these boys are Varons?" he asked.

Spencer stepped up then, moving to the front. "We are," he said.

"You got proof of that, son?" the eldest-looking Garnier asked.

"We do," he said. "We found Michael Varon's journal, which specifically states that he married Seraphine Frossard and that they had two children together: Diane, our great-aunt, and Phillip, our grandfather."

Ava added from the far side, "They also have a photograph that shows Lee Frossard delivering Diane and Phillip to the Collins family for adoption."

The murmuring grew louder as the group conferred.

"Well," Gabe said, bringing the mutterings to a halt, "it seems that we've got better odds than we thought." He eyed Spencer with a renewed interest. "Varons. Biological, ancestral, and here to inherit, huh?"

"Something like that," Spencer said.

"Good." Gabe motioned to his group to relax. "Now that we've got that all straightened out, how about you tell us *why* the spirit world can't be destroyed?"

Silas scoffed. "It's the *spirit* world," he said. "The spirit is far more real than anything physical. It can never be destroyed, no matter what form it takes. It lives on—forever."

"So, what do you all want with it?" the most talkative Garnier asked. "If you have no interest in destroying it, what are you trying to accomplish?"

"We're trying to protect it," Spencer explained.

"From what?"

"From the people who murdered Brendan," Sam said. "And Jessica. And Taylor."

"You mean the ones sending the hellhounds?" the Garnier man asked.

Tom's scoff echoed through the room. "Seriously, David?" he demanded. "I've been working to track down a supposedly rabid wolf, and you've all known this whole time? You didn't think to say anything?"

"You're the marshal, Tom," David said. "We couldn't risk you being on their side. Nor did we want to put you in a compromising position."

"We are highly selective of whom we talk to," Gabe said. "It's a pact that we have. We don't discuss the spirit world with anyone outside of the meetings. Our roles in this group have been inherited just like your job as the marshal."

The man in the work coat puffed his chest. "You may think you're protecting this town," he said, eyeing them. "But *we're* the ones who've worked to stop the spirit world for the last century."

"And you've done a bang-up job," Cassandra said caustically, earning narrowed glares from several of the Militia, including Travis.

Cassandra stepped up to Spencer's side. "While you've had your secret little club, the Druids have taken over your town. They've murdered your family while you've mastered your secret handshake."

"You think we don't know that?" Gabe demanded. "They're *our* family. Jess was David's daughter, Taylor was William's brother—" He gestured to the man in the work coat. "And Brendan was Juliet's boyfriend."

Cassandra took in the Militia and their sorrowful expressions.

"The Druids are working to pick us off," Gabe said. "That's why we're asking for your help."

Sam looked at his daughter. "Brendan was one of you?" he asked.

"No," Juliet said, playing with the end of her braid. "I didn't realize he knew anything about this until the hellhound."

"But the hound wasn't coming for Brendan," Gabe said. "It was meant for Juliet. Another of our members."

"But Brendan *was* a Wielder," Cassandra said. "Which means he was somehow involved in this. And he likely knew more than he said."

"His mother was a Guillaume," Ava said. "And we now know that they're aligned with the Druids."

"Brendan wasn't a Druid," Gabe insisted, his voice hard. The rest of the Chapelles shared his opinion.

"Perhaps *he* wasn't," Ava said. "But we know that children don't always follow in their parents' footsteps."

Cassandra knew that better than most. "There are likely dozens of families in DeVerre that have Druids hidden in their tree—past and present."

"What do you mean?" Gabe asked.

"The journal Spencer mentioned," she said, "lists the names of several Druidic families within DeVerre. The Frossards, MacDonalds, Guillaumes, Alaries, Dumonts, Laflammes, and—" She looked to Travis pointedly. "The Sauveterres."

Confusion lit her cousin's face for several seconds before anger surged across his features. "That's our family, Cass," he said like an accusation.

"Yes."

"That's—" Travis cut himself off, shaking his head.

"We have proof," Tom said. "Not only were the Sauveterres linked to the Druids back in the '40s, but we have firsthand evidence that they are members of the cult today. Namely Sarah Sauveterre . . ." He paused nervously before continuing, "as well as Debra Mercier and her daughter, Rene."

"No!" Travis spat, his voice breaking around the word.

Tom kept going with a clinical air like he was reading a report. "The Druids have infiltrated the town from its foundation. Our family and friends have duped us. The attack in 1915 was the work of the Druids. They conspired to cover up the town's connection to the spirit world to end any and all opposition to their attempt to take control over it. The fourteen men and women who died Saturday were Druids who came to Occasus to murder the Collins brothers and Miss Clement for standing in their way."

"We have to stop them," Sam said. "They've deceived us for too long. They've murdered our families. Now they're trying to take our home."

"But if the spirit world can't be destroyed, how do we stop them?" David Garnier demanded.

"Well, first off," Silas said, "it'd probably be a good thing to reveal them for who they are. The town is divided at the moment. Half the people are living in the dark. If you want to fix this—if you want to stop them— you need to reveal them."

Travis shuffled at the back of the group, tears in his eyes. "My mom . . . my sister—they weren't—"

"They were," Cassandra said apologetically. "They both tried to kill me. They tried to kill Spencer and Peter too."

While Travis dropped his head in his hands, the Garnier man next to him put an arm around his shoulders.

Gabe pressed on. "What else do we have to do to stop them?"

"Well, once we reveal them . . ." Silas hesitated, glancing at Owen. The men shared a knowing, disappointed look. Silas gave the blunt truth. "Then, we kill them."

The words scraped uncomfortably along Cassandra's heart. She hated that truth. She hated having killed and that she'd have to kill more.

The Militia gaped at them.

The young Garnier woman spoke up. "Kill them? But they're—they're our friends. And—killing is never the answer!"

"The only other option is letting them kill us," Silas said. "The Druids don't value life. Not even their own."

"Druidic tenet states that death brings about the most natural form," Owen said. "They hope to release the spirit world to release that form here in reality. If it means killing anyone—any of you, their friends, their family—they'll do whatever it takes to assure the grand design."

"The unleashing of the spirit world," Silas clarified. "Which seems to go against your group's mission statement."

The Militia shared worried looks, but none of them spoke. The truth was too weighty to argue. And it couldn't be ignored. If the Druids had their way, they'd destroy DeVerre and all its people. If they were to be stopped, it was *them* who must be destroyed.

"We're with you," Gabe said, speaking for his group. "Whatever you need to stop them, you have our support."

Cassandra felt hope burgeon within her like the bud of a flower cracking through a boulder. They had help now. With every new addition to their numbers, their odds grew with it.

"What do you need from us?" Gabe asked Spencer.

"Oh, uh—" Spencer gaped before turning to Owen.

"The vigil is tomorrow," Owen said, taking his cue. "It would be a good idea to make a showing and get people to understand that Peter, Spencer, and Cassandra *aren't* to blame for this tragedy."

"Is it a tragedy?" Gabe asked.

"People died," Owen said. "Of course, it's a tragedy."

"Murderers and cultists died," Gabe argued. "People whose lives were already forfeited, according to your friend here. If their deaths have prepared the way for the reconciliation of this town, shouldn't we be grateful?"

"We could use the vigil as an example," William Ozanne suggested, scratching at his scraggly beard. "Take the opportunity to point the finger at the Frossards and their cultists. Get the town to band together and hunt down these bastards."

"No," Sam exclaimed. "This is a vigil to honor the sanctity of life. We will not dishonor their memories—no matter what they did."

"It would make a point, though," Gabe said. "The whole town will be there. We could—"

"No!" the reverend repeated.

Tom tipped his chin up. "If any of you make a scene tomorrow night," he said, scanning the Militia, "I will interfere before you can get a single word out." The glint in his eyes threatened violence. He might be the "probationary" marshal, but he was still the marshal. And in his eyes, that made this his town.

"I thought we needed to reveal these people," Gabe said. "It seems we ought to take whatever opportunity we have."

"Do you think people will stand at your side while you dishonor the deaths of their family and friends?" Sam asked. "We want them to trust us, not hate us."

Watching this argument devolve, Cassandra couldn't blame the Militia for their response. They were angry. Why shouldn't they be? They'd been the Druids' number one target until Peter and Spencer arrived. Of course, they wanted revenge. But blind vengeance didn't bring justice.

Spencer suddenly gripped Cassandra's arm, drawing her gaze. His eyes were wide, fixed on the far corner. She followed his direction to the empty corner just beyond Travis's head.

Then she saw it.

The stark white wall and ceiling began to dim into soft gray. The gray bled, darkening like a stain into charcoal and then obsidian black.

"We have to get out," Spencer whispered.

Cassandra's brain tripped over itself. Should they alert everyone else, potentially causing a mass panic? Or would it be best to urge them cautiously to leave? There was only one exit—back the way they'd come. If the Druids managed to block the door, they could slaughter them all.

Spencer tugged on Cassandra's arm, beginning to back away as he spoke louder. "We have to get out!"

The whole room stared at him.

Silas followed their sight line. "Oh, yep, time to go," he said, pushing Owen and Ava toward the door.

"What's—"

"Druids," Silas interrupted Gabe's question with his sharp retort.

The lights flickered over their heads. Cassandra's breath hitched. In every corner, the shadows doubled in size and depth.

Silas swept his arm through the air, attempting to herd the group. "Come on," he ordered. "We've got about two seconds before beasts start—"

Aaron was inches from the door when the fluorescents scintillated above their heads like fireworks, and the shadows began peeling out from the walls, the shapes of beasts emerging. A scylla's long tentacles dangled from the ceiling directly in front of the door, cutting off Aaron's exit. One of the Garnier women cried out in horror, the other members of the Militia beginning to gasp and grumble in their fear. But Silas didn't waste time.

Stepping into the center of the room, Silas splayed his hands out to the side in a violent shove. All around them, a bright copper energy burst to life. It surrounded the group—those from Occasus and the Militia members—encasing them in a cylindrical wall of light.

Cassandra gaped at the display. She'd not seen anyone use their power as anything more than a quick burst of a shield. To hold onto the spirit world's essence, forming it into a wall of power and protection, would take fierce will and control.

Beasts slunk out of the darkness, morphing to life in the shadows. Lumbering wendigos paced the copper rift-wall. Scylla clung to the ceiling, their tentacles writhing patiently. A massive, bear-like beast shook out its muscled shoulders, smoke coiling off its fur. All forms of beasts filled the space as the group drew closer to Silas.

Aaron went for the handgun at his waist, but Tom halted him. "It doesn't work as well as you'd think," he said.

Silas let out an effort-filled grunt. "Owen," he called.

"Yeah," Owen said, an amber rift lighting up his hand. "We got this."

While Gabe and his Militia cowered, Cassandra turned to Spencer. His fear had gone, determination lighting up his eyes. Neither of them said a word. They knew what came next.

Summoning forth her will, Cassandra felt the tremor roll across her skin. In near unison, Owen, Spencer, and she all sent out arcs: amber, bronze, and pale gray. A scylla, the bear-beast, and a hydra all crumbled into smoke.

The Militia gasped in awe. The trio didn't stop. Beasts evaporated as the rifts hit them, though more came from the shadows creeping through the room. The overhead lights pulsed like strobe lights.

"We're gonna have to leave," Silas ground out, his voice strained. Cassandra imagined holding that wall required far more strength than the short bursts they were producing.

While the wall of light held the beasts at bay, a handful of new monsters rose in the time it took for them to take down three. And the tension in Silas's expression said that his wall couldn't hold forever. They might not be in immediate danger, but eventually, they'd all run out of energy and the beasts would attack.

Cassandra edged toward Spencer. "I have an idea," she said, sending out another arc.

"I'm all ears," he said, the light of his bronze arcs flickering over his face like flames.

"It's potentially stupid."

"More stupid than what we're currently doing?"

"Probably not."

"Let's hear it."

Cassandra sent a final arc at a hellhound, which poofed into disintegrating ash, then held her hand out to Spencer. "Teamwork," she said.

Whether he understood her idea or not, Spencer took her hand without hesitation.

Power rippled between their joined palms, Cassandra thrusting all of her will into a single thought. Together, she knew their power would be an uncontestable force. He was a Varon—the most powerful Wielders known to mankind. She was an anomaly—a Wielder so unusually gifted the Druids would rather her dead than oppose them.

The tremor of the spirit world's essence grew to a near-unbearable sting of prickles along her skin. The hair on her arms was raised underneath her sweater. The sense of lightning about to strike surged through her body.

Whatever Cassandra had intended, it hadn't been exactly this. But it worked.

A blast of light—bronze and pale gray twisting together—erupted from Spencer and Cassandra. The power burst from her body, ripping a gasp from her lungs. She saw Spencer grimace against it, but he didn't let go of her. The light seared through the room, disrupting Silas's copper wall. It tore apart nearly every beast, their shadow forms whisked away to dust. The fluorescents whined overhead, struck by the power.

Cassandra realized as soon as the surge died that it had been a mistake.

Her knees buckled, and though Spencer jerked forward to catch her, she could see the cost in his pained expression. His dark eyebrows drew close together in concentration, his mouth twisting into a grimace. And his grip on her wasn't as strong as she was used to.

They'd practically depleted themselves, wiping out all but a handful of remaining beasts.

But more were coming.

Silas fought to maintain his hold on the wall, resetting his feet.

"Owen," he yelled above the furious lights and the panicked DeVerreans. "Get them out!"

"There could be Druids in the building," Owen warned.

Spencer supported most of Cassandra's weight, his arm around her waist. "I can help," he said.

"Cassandra?" She heard the question in Owen's simple call.

Clinging to Spencer, she had the urge to lay her head on his shoulder and fall asleep. She knew they had to help, to get these people out of the building safely, but she was in a daze. She didn't have the energy to do more than lean into Spencer's side and breathe. "I'm tapped," she murmured, unsure if her voice carried.

But Spencer heard.

As Owen continued to manage the beasts, Spencer adjusted Cassandra's weight against him, beckoning for help. Aaron and Sam hurried forward, accepting Cassandra's weight. She rested her arms over each of their shoulders like a body carried off the battlefield.

The second she was secure, Spencer sprang back into action. She could see in his gait that he wasn't as sure-footed as usual. Whatever energy he still possessed, it was waning. And she'd been stupid enough to do that to him.

"I'll take the front," Spencer said, pushing through the doors before anyone could stop him.

Cassandra wanted to tell him that he was being an idiot. He couldn't take the front. He was weakened, like her. Well, not exactly like her. With each step and arc, his footing became surer and his gestures steadier, even if his power wasn't quite as impactful. Weakened but readily recovering.

"Go with him," Silas told Owen. "I'll take the back."

Owen took hold of Ava's arm as he rushed to follow Spencer. The rest of the group didn't hesitate to follow. Cassandra struggled to keep her feet underneath her, attempting to ease her weight on Aaron and Sam.

The hall leading to the front of the funeral home was dark aside from the bronze and amber rifts of Spencer and Owen. They took down a small handful of beasts, but it seemed that the focus of the Druids—wherever they were—was on the preparation room.

Cassandra looked over her shoulder as Silas barreled out behind them. She released a sigh of relief a second before Juliet Chapelle let out a scream. Sam cried out for his daughter, guttural and piercing in Cassandra's ear.

She watched in horror as a hydra unexpectedly burst through the wall on their right and snapped its tendrils around Juliet's arms and legs. Its serrated maw opened, ready to tear into the girl.

Then Gabe was there, diving for his niece. Dozens of tendrils slammed his face and body, knocking him back. It provided enough distraction for his son to wrench Juliet from the hydra's clutches. But the hydra's jaws still sliced shut over the space the girl had been a second before—where William Ozanne had stepped in to help.

The hydra's teeth severed through half of William's face, ripping the flesh away. Blood spurted, slashing across Juliet, her uncle, and her cousin. Cassandra's heart rammed against her chest. She'd never seen such a horrific death.

A copper arc streaked past them, tearing the hydra to smoke. "Come on," Silas demanded, shoving them back into motion. "We have to get out of here."

Sam shook as he helped carry Cassandra around the body. She couldn't tear her eyes from the mutilated man's head. Acid burned the back of her throat. She gagged, but she was too tired to be sick. Her muscles were in shambles, her head swimming with fear. Someone held the door to the front of the funeral home open, sputtering yellow lamplight beckoning them. She couldn't find Spencer.

Aaron and Sam carried her into the entryway, the amber bursts of Owen's arcs tearing down a hellhound that leaped at them as they stepped through the door. Freezing air flooded the space, the front door opening as someone called, "Out, out, out."

They burst out of the building, winter tearing into them as Cassandra caught sight of Spencer. Her heart eased a fraction as she saw him sprinting toward a man. Night crowded over them, the sole streetlamp gone out.

Cassandra frowned. Just one man? Had this been the work of one Druid?

In the blink of an eye, the air around the Druid shifted. A faint tinge of charcoal swept through the air, like a fold of shadow over light. And then he was gone.

Cassandra's jaw dropped as Spencer staggered to a stop. The man had disappeared into thin air.

And just like that, the streetlamp hummed back to life, its soft, burnt yellow glow pushing back the darkness.

The Militia members clustered around the front of the funeral home, muttering and crying. Gabe stepped to the front, his expression equal parts haunted and intent. "What happened?" he demanded.

The team from Occasus all exchanged looks as Spencer returned to the group. "Well," Silas said when the rest of them were silent. "Somehow, the Druids knew we'd be here and tried to ambush us."

"We lost a man in there," Gabe exclaimed, a fury in his tone that Cassandra didn't think was called for. Neither did she have the energy to say so.

"I'm sorry," Owen said, head dipped in sympathy.

At his side, Ava crossed her arms. "I'm not," she said.

Gabe opened his mouth, but she cut across him. "Don't pin this on us," she said. "You knew the risks involved. They've been murdering your people for months. Death is what we all face if we don't stop them."

Shifting at her side, Aaron spoke up next. "I need to go," he said, fear causing his voice to tremble. "Haley and Anna—"

Testing her weight, Cassandra found that she had enough strength to stand. "Go," she told him, lifting her arms from his and Sam's shoulders.

The young man clapped Spencer on the shoulder before barreling over to his motorcycle. The engine roared through the night air as he slipped on his helmet, then peeled off toward Harmony Plaza and the tavern.

Jaw tense with barely restrained anger, Gabe turned to Cassandra and Spencer. "You should go too," he said.

"Why?" Spencer asked, taking Aaron's vacated spot at her side. He didn't move to support her, but she knew he'd catch her if her strength gave out.

"We have a dead man inside," Gabe said. The group behind him bristled but remained silent. "I've got to call the station and report it. However, there's no reason for them to know that you two—" He glanced at Silas. "That you *three* were here. I have a feeling that would only make matters worse."

Tom nodded. "They named Tony MacDonald interim marshal," he said. "After the way you attacked Alexander, he's looking for any excuse to lock you up."

Cassandra noted Spencer's tightened expression, but he only nodded.

"I'll stay here," Owen offered, "and report back."

"We're your ride," Spencer said.

Ava sighed. "I can bring him back."

The arrangements made, Spencer turned to Cassandra. "You good?" he asked, gaze overly concerned.

Taking quick stock of herself, Cassandra surmised that she was— more or less—good. "Yeah," she promised. "Just tired."

"You should get going then," Gabe said.

Cassandra turned back to him and his Militia. "You understand what's at stake here?" she asked.

Gabe tipped his head in acknowledgment. "You call," he said. "We'll answer."

The clarification did little to help settle the internal debate at war within her. Even as they moved for the Jeep, Spencer following close at her side, Cassandra knew this wasn't a victory. They had more people on their side, but the cost had risen too. Another innocent life had been taken. How many more would die? How many would they fail to save?

Spencer held the passenger door open for her, shutting it as she buckled her seat belt. Cassandra stared at the frosted windshield. How many more would die because of her? She'd made a mistake tonight. That stupid idea of hers had nearly dropped her entirely. What would have happened if Spencer wasn't a Varon? What would happen the next time she got a bright idea? Would she wind up killing them?

Cassandra twisted her ring. She traced the imprint of the S with the pad of her finger. How many she wound up killing didn't matter anymore. Something was wrong with her. She shattered souls on instinct, inflicting the worst form of death. She impulsively reached for dangerous ideas: tethering phantoms, summoning beasts, and channeling vast amounts of power. This was why the Druids wanted her.

She spun the ring again. She wasn't a Wielder. She was a weapon.

And eventually, whether she intended to or not, she feared she'd implode, taking down everyone with her.

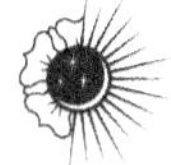

CHAPTER SEVENTEEN

Owen

Tony MacDonald threw his weight around with impunity. Most of the Militia members managed to pull themselves together, giving their reports of the event to the interim marshal and the still-employed deputy. Hunter took pictures of the crime scene while Tony interviewed the witnesses.

Owen watched from the sidelines, alert to everything. The fact they'd gotten out alive didn't surprise him. It was that they'd only sustained one death in the whole ordeal that baffled him. Whatever it was that Cassandra and Spencer had managed to do, it had saved their skins.

At his side, Ava observed Tony as he surveyed the damage from the attack. He'd finished his interviews rapidly, taking none of their allegations seriously. "A horde of monsters?" he said. "Seriously?"

No matter how much the Garniers, Chapelles, and Travis Mercier insisted, Tony shut them all down the moment they'd suggested there were cultists in their town intent on murdering the members of their families. "You'd best keep these slanderous accusations to yourself," he threatened. "I'm the law in this town now, and you'll find yourself facing more than imaginary monsters if you keep this up. Now, get out of here. I've got a crime scene to investigate."

While the rest of the Militia filtered out, Gabe remained to do his job. Typically, Alexander did autopsies, but in this case, the town mortician could help preserve the body until the morning when a proper search could be made. Owen and Ava stayed behind with Tom and Sam, loitering even as Tony grumbled about their presence. He never threw them out, and Owen assumed it was because he got a kick out of shoving Tom's probation in his face.

Leaning closer, Ava whispered to Owen. "So, Tony's a Druid?"

Owen kept a cautious eye on the man in question, inspecting the now brightly lit hallway. Still-wet blood splattered the cream walls. "We don't have official evidence," he said quietly. "But yes, all signs point to it."

"Mm." Ava eyed Tony, her expression unreadable. "Think we should just kill him now?"

He immediately frowned down at her.

"It's a joke, Owen," she said, a humorless smirk on her lips. "An admittedly dark one, but Peter's not here. And someone's got to bring some levity to this otherwise hellish situation."

Begrudgingly, Owen found himself smiling. His wife's sense of humor was notoriously dry, occasionally verging on morbid. On a normal basis, he found it charming. After a Druid attack, he found it conflictingly distasteful and endearing.

With the interviews taken and the crime scene investigated, Tony told Hunter to head out. The deputy moved for the door, sending his old boss an apologetic glance. Tom gave the young man a nod of approval. Hunter was doing his job. There was no reason for him to get fired too.

As Tony made his move for the doorway, Tom raised his chin. "What's going in your report, MacDonald?" he asked smugly. "How do you plan to explain away William's death with fourteen witnesses who say it was a shadow monster?"

Tony scowled, his bulldog face scrunching with the action. "I'm going to investigate, Garnier," he said. "Something you never did."

The door shut behind the interim marshal, as Sam muttered something about "good riddance." An eerie quiet fell over the funeral home's parlor. After the fight, tears, and anger, it left the room buzzing with raw emotion.

Gabe emerged from the back where he'd laid William's body to rest in a preservation cabinet. He wore his lab coat and scrubs. A speck of blood marred the coat's sleeve. Resting against the doorjamb, he surveyed them. "Seems we have a traitor in our midst," he said.

The accusation within his words did not go unheard.

"It has to be someone on your side," Ava said.

Gabe bristled. "What makes you think that?"

"You think Spencer or Cassandra are going to talk to the Druids? How about my siblings? Tom? Sam?" She shook her head. "None of our people would have any reason to betray us."

"What about that new guy?"

"Silas is a Varon," Owen said. "He's more dedicated to the Warden and its cause than any of us. Beyond that, he doesn't know anyone in this town."

"Fine," Gabe said. "But my people are Chapelles, Garniers, Merciers, and Ozannes. People who have suffered at the Druids' hands for generations. You think any of us would betray the cause?"

"What about Travis?" Ava said. "His mother and sister were Druids."

Anger flared in Gabe's eyes, but Owen held up a hand to stop him. "I think we ought to be very careful at whom we point the finger," he warned. "We need to be unified. Until we have proof, we can't blame anyone for this."

Tension strained the room, but Sam nodded. "Owen is right," he said. "For generations, we've hidden the truth from one another, and it's making us all paranoid. DeVerre is supposed to be a good, wholesome, safe town. It's up to us to *make* it what we once believed it to be."

"I never believed it to be that, Sam," his brother said. "Dad never believed it either. While you're over here buddying up to these . . . *Warden* folks, I'm still dedicated to what I was taught: The spirit world is evil. We need to cut it out of DeVerre."

"It can't be cut out," Owen said.

"How do you know?" Gabe demanded. "Who's to say there's not a way, and you just don't know it?"

"It's the *spirit* world, Gabe," Sam said. "Can you ever truly destroy a spirit?"

"I'm willing to find out."

Owen shook his head. "Whatever you think about the spirit world, you know the Druids will bring only death. We want to return DeVerre to safety. Now," he set a hand on Ava's shoulder for the briefest of seconds, nudging her toward the door before him, "I'm going home. If you need me, call me."

Tom and Sam moved to follow, Owen holding the door for Ava to exit first. The frosty night nipped at their faces. Owen tugged his coat closed, looping the buttons through their holes.

"Gabe will come around," Sam said as they stood on the stoop. "He's hardheaded, but he means well."

"He's brash," Ava said, her words coming out in a fog. "But perhaps that will be beneficial."

Sam nodded in acceptance.

They gave their farewells, the marshal and reverend climbing into the SUV they'd ridden in together. Ava moved for the hatchback on the far side of the lot, Owen following. A single streetlamp lit up the parking lot with its muted yellow glow. He always liked how few lights there were in DeVerre. Given the size of the town, there wasn't much need for them, even on the backroads. And it made for spectacular night skies. A black-blue curtain sprinkled with silver stars.

The cold burned through Owen's coat as he walked at Ava's side, maintaining a foot of distance. He didn't think they'd walked this far apart since their first date. From that night on, they either walked arm in arm, hand in hand, or close enough to brush arms at the very least. And this distance, this divide between them, Owen couldn't take it.

Owen reached for the driver's side door on instinct, holding it for her. Ava pulled her keys out of her mustard-yellow corduroy coat. He hated that coat, and she knew it. She'd found it at a yard sale in Spokane during college. When she showed it to him, he'd frowned at the garish color and frumpy fit. She purchased it because she liked how he scrunched his nose when he looked at it.

Moving for the open door, Ava drew closer. Close enough that Owen could smell the scent of their home and the library mingled in her presence: the must of books, her herbal teas, and the earthy dampness of plants.

Before Ava could climb into the car, Owen spoke. "I'd like to talk with you soon."

Ava paused, looking up at him. In the dark, her usually creamy brown complexion looked a vastly richer shade of cedar. She only stood to his shoulder, her black braids puffing around that horrendous coat's collar. Her almond-shaped eyes always gave her a fierce, calculating appearance. But Owen's favorite feature of Ava's was her small, pert nose. It counteracted the harsh effect of her sharper facial structure, reminding everyone that there was a soft, tenderhearted woman under all that fierceness.

"I'd ask about what," Ava said, her dry sarcasm reminding him too much of happier days. "But I think it's pretty obvious."

One hand resting against the frame of the car door, Owen held her steady gaze. He wanted to address the issue now. They'd had the opportunity to talk when Cassandra had first brought her to Occasus. However, Ava made it clear then that she wasn't comfortable returning to what they'd been. Not yet. She needed more time to process the past decade of lies, and she needed to figure out who her husband was before she allowed him back into her life. And he understood her reluctance.

But that was before he'd known she was carrying their child.

Another cold breeze cut through the open lot, the SUV carrying Tom and Sam out into the night. They were alone now. Just him and Ava in the parking lot. They could sit in the car, out of the cold, and have this talk for as long as it would take. They could share their sides, argue about whose lie was more wrong, and eventually come to some conclusion—be that a longer separation or a return to their marriage.

Owen took a deep breath of icy air that cut into his lungs. This wasn't the time for personal problems. And he wasn't selfish enough to beg for clemency when they had other, much more important things to focus on. So he chose to ask the only question he *needed* her to answer. "How are you?"

Those slanted, cunning eyes narrowed knowingly. "You mean, how am I doing with the baby?"

"Yes."

"I'm fine," she said, crossing her arms to keep her hands out of the cold. "There's barely been any nausea, nothing that tea hasn't been able to solve, anyway. And I've not been abnormally tired."

Owen couldn't help but frown as he surveyed her. "That's different," he noted.

Ava nodded, her eyes dropping to the corner of the open door. "It's why I didn't tell you," she said. "I was concerned it meant it wasn't real, that it wouldn't . . . last. But as of last week, I'm officially in the second trimester, so. . . ."

They'd been trying to have a child for the past seven years. Or rather, they'd not been *not* trying. Neither of them had fully committed to being "ready" for children, but as they both *wanted* multiple—at least three— they thought they ought to start sooner rather than later. Yet, it hadn't seemed in the cards for them.

Ava had been pregnant only twice before, both following all the regular patterns of extreme morning sickness, fatigue, and every other thing the pregnancy books warned of. And both had ended abruptly at the start of the third month.

This deviation from the past two pregnancies worried Owen. What if it meant something was wrong with the child? What if their baby was at risk? He didn't think he could handle that. "Have you seen a doctor?" he asked.

She shook her head. "I didn't want to go alone."

Owen's heart pricked with both affection and sympathy. But his head rankled with irritation, needing confirmation of their child's safety. "You should have seen a doctor."

She scoffed. "This isn't the time to start acting like a father."

"You're pregnant. I'd say this is the exact time to act like a father."

"Owen." Her sharp tone broke through his male pride, revealing their shared fear. "I'm fine."

Tightening his grip on the door frame, Owen's arms twitched to reach out and hold her. He wanted to feel her, to assure himself of her solidness and safety, to know that she and their child were whole and well. He wanted to engulf himself in her scent. He wanted to feel the velvety ridges of that awful corduroy coat under his hand.

Instead, he relaxed his expression and sighed. "I'm glad."

Ava shifted one step closer to the driver's seat. Her whole demeanor softened as she held his apologetic stare. "I was waiting to tell you," she whispered. "I didn't want to get your hopes up only to. . . ."

"I know," he promised, hoping she heard his sincerity. Hoping that she would know he wasn't angry. After all, he'd withheld far more from her. And however long it took her to forgive him—*if* she chose to forgive him—he wanted her to know that he would be there—for both her and their child.

Ava turned to the car, chewing on the inside of her lip. "I, uh—" She shuffled her feet, edging farther from him. Her head dipped, a trio of braids slipping from behind her ear. She reached up to tuck them back.

"I'm staying in Anna's room, but . . . Well, with Silas here now, and after everything that happened tonight . . ."

Hearing the forthcoming question before she spoke it, Owen drew his shoulders back, unsure how he'd answer.

She shifted another inch closer to the car, lips smashed together around words that he knew she was fighting to say. Words that she desperately wanted to say but felt foolish for. The last time she'd been this awkward with him was when she'd asked him to kiss her for the first time. A memory that often brought him a smile. But in this context, it made him anxious.

Ava cleared her throat, one of her more stoic expressions coming to her face as she met his eyes. "It would make both Anna and me feel safer if you would return to stay in the house."

Processing the statement, Owen stayed quiet. Ever intentional, Ava had given him all the information he needed to understand. She wasn't asking him to come back to her. This was a request for a bodyguard.

And yet . . .

Owen could read his wife's expression. Twelve years of marriage gave you a near-magical ability to read your spouse—if you paid enough attention, at least. And he could see it clear as if the sun had broken over the edge of the forest. He could see it in the nervous flicker of her eyes to his, in the tension that drew her shoulders to curl inward, in the set line of her jaw. She *wanted* to ask. She *wanted* him to come back to *her*. She was simply too scared to ask for it—to resume their relationship too early. As though accepting him back was negating the anger she felt.

But she wanted to ask. She wanted him back.

With a sharp nod, Owen looked beyond his wife to the snowy roof of the funeral home. It was up to him now. That's what she'd offered in her noncommittal intentionality. She'd laid the offer at his feet—make me choose, she'd said.

Ava wasn't one to buck responsibility. When it came time, she would answer the call. But she often needed a shove to make that decision. And perhaps it was selfish, but Owen knew what he wanted.

"If I'm coming home, Ava," he said, meeting her uncertain gaze with a steady one of his own, "then I'm coming home."

The whisper of winter, still and silent, hummed in the air between them. Ava's uncertainty was clear, her expression shifting to calculating and thoughtful as she stared up at him. This was the time for her to make the choice. Would she accept him back, or would she demand more time? Owen already had a contingency for if she said no; he'd planned for Silas to stay with her and Anna from the outset. He'd be a stronger defense.

But if Ava was offering, he wasn't about to miss his chance.

Like a strike of lightning, Ava's hand sprang forward to grab the collar of Owen's coat. With a fierce jerk, she tugged him down, standing on her toes to meet him halfway. Years together summoned instinct as their lips met, the kiss familiar, comfortable, and restoring. Owen's body reacted as it always had, arm slipping around her waist to pull her closer, even as his head reminded him that resolution was still unreached.

Ava didn't seem to hold the same hesitation. Her hands framed his face as she drew him deeper into the kiss. Their embrace held twelve years of love, promises, and hope. Twelve years of pain, fear, and lies. And an entire future together in spite of all that.

Breaking the kiss, Ava didn't let him go. The heat of their breath coiled in wisps of fog between them as she pulled back just enough to whisper, "Come home, then."

CHAPTER EIGHTEEN

Spencer

The anger grew to an almost stifling pounding in Spencer's head. He could feel it welling up in his chest, burning like a flare up his sternum and into his face. He wondered if Silas and Cassandra could see it reddening his cheeks. Was his body betraying his internal battle?

The attack on the funeral home brought the shaking back. Spencer had finally calmed the anxiety, thinking that after kissing Cassandra, he'd gotten ahold of himself. When Owen taught them to feel the spirit world's essence, connecting to it, he'd felt the vibration—he'd heard the sound beyond sound—and he was sure he'd mastered himself. He thought he'd gained control of this boiling rage, this monster prowling in his chest.

But now it was back, growling and pacing, growing and pressing against his ribcage.

Cassandra had almost passed out back there. Whatever they'd done together had zapped so much of his energy that he began to see spots. His arcs weren't nearly as powerful after that. Fear pressed in, the knowledge that even Varons weren't indestructible taunting him.

Pulling through the wrought iron gates of Occasus, the Jeep's tires rumbled against the gravel drive. Snow capped the dark, tiered rooftop, the white glowing like crystals in the moonlight. The ominous stillness of Occasus tugged at Spencer. The monster in his chest pushed harder to break free. His hand began to rise to press back, but he forced himself to reach for the keys instead.

"We should check out the house," Spencer said, eyes locked on the building. "They might be waiting to ambush us here too."

The *click* of Silas's seat belt rang from the back. "Let me take the lead," he said. "You two are still weak."

With a glance at Cassandra, her dark eyes rimmed with exhaustion, Spencer opened the car door. "I'm fine," he said.

He climbed out of the Jeep, a flash of movement by the pine trees in the yard making his pulse spike. But he quickly recognized the wiry coats of Anguis and Nex, enjoying the snow.

They made their way up the porch, its overhead light a steady beam. More golden light flooded through the windows from the interior. Gerard must have turned them on when they'd left. Even phantoms needed light to read.

Spencer unlocked the door, then let Silas step in first. With slow, deliberate steps, they entered Occasus's foyer. Eyes alert and searching, they scanned the building. The light was a good sign. If there were beasts, the lights would have gone out. That was a clearly defined trend. Darkness equated beasts. Light meant safety.

Still, Silas crept through the hall, silent and attentive to any sound.

Then, Cassandra jumped to Spencer's left, letting out a low curse.

Spencer jerked around to find Gerard on the staircase, frowning at Cassandra. "You're all jumpy," the phantom observed.

"Have you seen anything suspicious in the last couple of hours?" Spencer asked.

Gerard's dark gaze narrowed. "No. Why?"

With the relief of knowing the home was safe, Cassandra drifted toward the living room. "We were attacked," she said, voice hollow.

The men followed her. Silas leaned against the doorframe, watching as Gerard charged through the room. "What happened?" the phantom demanded.

Cassandra sank onto a couch as she pressed her fingers against her temples. Spencer wanted to sit beside her and wrap her in his arms. He didn't think now was the moment. Instead, he stood behind her and told Gerard about their evening. "We have more allies now," he concluded. "But it's pretty clear we need to be more careful."

"What you need to do," Gerard growled, turning to Cassandra, "is leave."

"We can't leave," she said, her voice weak but her gaze determined. "There's too much left to do."

Gerard's face contorted with rage. "What do you think, Cassandra? They're just going to let you go?" His arms flailed in agitation. "Pretty soon, they aren't going to wait anymore. They're going to send their beasts into this house, night or day, and you won't be able to stop them. Then we're all dead."

"Drop it," Spencer ordered. "I've lost count of how many times you've tried to get us to leave DeVerre, but it seems you're too dense to realize that we aren't going to listen. This is our home. We're not abandoning it."

Gerard snarled. "You're going to get her killed," he said.

"In case you haven't noticed," Spencer said sharply, "I care more about her than you do. If anyone is going to keep her safe, it's me."

They stood there, facing off. Spencer had always disliked the more possessive way Gerard regarded Cassandra. He understood why; she was his only means of retaining this semblance of "life" he had as a phantom. Without her, he'd dissolve back into a ghost, untethered and wholly alone. But his obsession with keeping her alive was riddled with selfishness that Spencer didn't trust.

"Get yourselves killed, then." Gerard's dark eyes shot back to Cassandra's face. "I did what I could for you. Remember that."

Then he was gone.

Silas let out a hum of thought, drawing their gazes. "That phantom's a real piece of work," he noted.

Cassandra sighed, slumping against the couch. "He's hurting."

"We're all hurting," Silas said, then stepped farther into the room. "What's next?"

"What do you mean?" Spencer asked.

"I mean—" Silas motioned to the house around them, "what's next? We just fought for our lives. I don't know about you two, but my adrenaline is still pumping. Sleep won't be easy to come by for some time."

Cassandra looked up at Spencer. "We could show him the essays," she said.

With a nod, Spencer moved to the office. Now that they had multiple digital copies, they'd been much less cautious with the essays. The stacks remained sprawled across the desk, the two chairs awaiting Spencer and Cassandra's return to their studies. Side by side, the legal pad of notes and the essay about the Great Wolf rested at the top, cast in an amber haze from the antique desk lamp.

Silas stood on the other side of the desk across from Spencer and Cassandra. "This is them?" he asked, gesturing to the stacks.

"All eleven of them," Spencer confirmed.

"Eleven?"

Spencer looked up to see Silas's brows arched. "Yeah."

"Hm."

Cassandra exchanged a look with Spencer before replying, "You find that strange?"

Silas shrugged. "I'd heard there were twelve."

"You'd 'heard'?"

"There's always talk," Silas said. "Particularly regarding the

Lawrence family and their work. Lots of times, it's hearsay or simply rumors. But then, rumors do start somewhere."

Cassandra pursed her lips as she met Spencer's gaze. "You think the reverend kept one back?"

Running a hand through his hair, Spencer considered his communications with the Irish reverend. The man had seemed plenty up front. But it was hard to get a gauge on a person through email. "Maybe," he said. "I don't know why he would."

"You said that your friend Diane had these essays before?" Silas asked.

Cassandra nodded. "She and her husband visited Elijah's church in Bushmills almost twenty years ago. The reverend at the time gave them copies."

"Of all of them?"

She shrugged. "I mean, from what I know. There's a chance that if this reverend is holding back, that reverend did too."

"How many essays did she have?"

"Eleven. Just like these."

Silas didn't show any sign that it surprised or bothered him. He regarded the stacks for a moment before replying, "There's a chance that neither reverend was holding back. As I said, the Lawrences are protective of their family's work. For the reverends to give you these essays surprises me."

"Neither reverend was a Lawrence," Spencer said.

"Doesn't matter. Bushmills is a Warden town. The reverends there are Warden members, and they wouldn't give you *any* information if not approved by the Lawrences who remain there."

"There are still Lawrences in Bushmills?"

"Our family is everywhere," Silas returned dryly.

"*Our* family?" Spencer asked.

Silas looked momentarily confused before raising his chin in understanding. "Oh, right. You wouldn't know." He swept a hand through the air to encompass Occasus as a whole. "The Varons are connected to the Lawrences. Back in the 1600s, Gabriel Varon married Rachel Lawrence, the great-great-granddaughter of John William."

Spencer gaped at him. "We're descendants of the Warden's founder?"

Silas shrugged. "Yeah."

Spencer scrubbed a hand over his face. He'd thought DeVerre's family tree was complicated. It seemed the Warden's was even more complex.

"Doesn't make us any more popular, though," Silas said. "We may be the most powerful and some of the most ancient members of the organization, but we're also some of the most disliked."

"Why?"

"People don't like legacies of power. They find it potentially untrustworthy." Silas paused, head cocking to the side in thought. "Or perhaps it's better said: They find it uncontrollable. And people fear what they can't control."

Spencer knew that fear. It was the foundation of all his anxiety. "What if" only came from unknowns. And unknowns only came from the chaos of the uncontrolled.

Leaning against the desk at his side, Cassandra's fingers tapped against the surface. "I take it that means your connection to the Lawrences doesn't afford the luxury of asking after a twelfth essay?" she asked.

The wry scoff Silas let out was answer enough.

Cassandra pursed her lips, disappointed. Spencer scanned her, noting how tired she looked. He thought about suggesting they drop the subject and get some sleep. The haunted glimmer in her eyes made him hold his tongue. Did she feel as anxious as him? Cassandra was so rarely scared. It was what drew him to her in many ways. She faced fear and danger unblinkingly. Yet the way she twisted her signet ring suggested that her seemingly magical ability to stare fear in the eye was dwindling.

Her words from two weeks ago rose in his mind: *"I've just learned the difference between what's actually dangerous and what's not."*

Spencer stared at Cassandra as understanding hit him. She *was* afraid. Because now, they were facing real danger.

Needing answers, Spencer turned back to Silas. "We told you that Diane had the essays before and that we reached out to the reverend in Bushmills because they were stolen, right?" At the man's nod, he continued, "Do you have any idea why the Druids would take the essays?"

Silas's blue eyes glinted with confusion. "What makes you think the Druids took them?"

"Because of Diane's murder," Cassandra said. "My mother confirmed that Diane's death was orchestrated by the Druids."

"Your mom is a Druid?"

"No," she said, then continued without giving the details of that particular convoluted facet of her life. "The essays were missing after Diane's death. Which suggests that they were taken at the same time."

"Druids would have no use for the essays," Silas said.

"Owen thought the same thing," Spencer said. "But we wondered if they didn't take them simply to keep them away from Cassandra. That maybe they took them to keep her from learning something."

That caused Silas to tip his head in consideration. Still, he hesitated to agree. "Who had access to the essays?" he asked. "Realistically."

"Whoever murdered Diane," Cassandra said.

"Yes, but what was the cause of Diane's death?"

"We don't know. Alexander's report said it was natural causes, which obviously wasn't accurate."

"Who found the body?"

"Hunter," she said. "I was with my family in Spokane, but Diane and I spoke regularly. I checked in daily to be sure she was all right and see if she'd learned anything more. When she didn't respond to me for an entire day, I got worried. I called the DeVerre Police, and they sent Hunter to check on her. When he got here, the dogs ran up to him on the lawn, basically herding him into the house. Diane didn't lock the door, so he walked right in. He found her lying on the couch."

"Did he mention the cause of death?"

"He's not exactly proficient in medicine, and he assumed it was natural causes."

"So, no signs of injury."

"No."

"Likely poison, then," Silas suggested.

Cassandra nodded. "That's what I always assumed too."

"In which case," Silas continued, "the murderer might never have entered the house that day. They could have been lacing something she ate or drank for weeks. Or even slipped it in something while she was out."

Spencer frowned at Cassandra. They'd never considered that. "Possibly," she said.

"But that doesn't explain the missing essays," Spencer said.

"They could have waited for her to die before entering the house," Silas said.

Cassandra shook her head. "No one knew we had them. Whoever took them had to be in the house."

"Then the murderer did enter the house," Spencer concluded. "And they could have taken the essays when they planted the poison."

"Diane would have noticed if they'd gone missing," she said. "And she would have reported it right away. Which meant Tom would be aware of the theft, which would lend suspicious circumstances to her death."

"Maybe the poison worked fast enough for her not to notice," Spencer said.

"Gerard was with her the final hour of her life. He said she'd complained that she'd had stomach pain and sickness most of the morning. It was a drawn-out death."

Silas tapped a knuckle repeatedly against the desktop. "Then whoever took them did so after her death." His sharp stare flicked over to Cassandra. "Who might have had access to them?"

Dropping into the seat behind her, Cassandra rested her head in her hand. "There was about a thirty-six-hour window between the time of Diane's death and when the lawyer, Nicole, took over the estate," she said, tiredness clinging to her tone. "Anyone could have snuck into the house in that time."

"But who *knew* about them?"

She pulled her bottom lip between her teeth, considering.

Spencer glanced at the essays. How many people had the opportunity to come through Occasus after Diane's death? Who *would* have come through? Not many, surely. Whoever had entered either already knew the essays were here or discovered them upon planting the poison.

For the second time that night, Gerard appeared out of thin air. He'd slicked back his dark hair, and his eyes no longer shone with agitation. Instead, he looked merely indifferent to the situation. He moved to stand by Cassandra at the fireplace.

"There were seven people who came through the house after the discovery of Diane's body," he said. "The marshal and his deputy who gathered the evidence, the doctor and mortician who took care of the body, the woman who came by to take care of the dogs, and the lawyer and her assistant who retrieved the draft and other items listed in the will."

Spencer ran through the people, visualizing the faces he could. "So, we know Tom, Hunter, Alexander, Gabe, and Nicole. Did you see any of them take the pages?"

"No," Gerard said. "Only the lawyer lady touched it from what I saw. Admittedly, I wasn't watching them closely. I felt it best to make myself somewhat scarce."

"What about the lawyer's assistant," Silas asked. "What did they look like?"

"Like the lawyer lady, but younger."

Cassandra frowned, but Spencer put two and two together. "Her niece, Jill."

"I wouldn't know," Gerard said.

Spencer added Jill to the suspect list, remembering she was the first

DeVerrean they'd met. He gave a chin up toward the phantom, prodding him for more information. "What about the woman who was taking care of the dogs?"

Gerard took a moment to think. "About your age. Dark hair, short, really pretty. The dogs seemed to like her."

"Danielle?" Spencer asked.

"She *is* a MacDonald," Cassandra added, a tinge bitterly.

He looked down at her in the chair beside him. "Would she have known about the essays?"

With a snide grin, Cassandra arched her brow. "You tell me. She's your girlfriend."

Spencer couldn't help bristling. He didn't know how much more obvious he had to make it that his interest didn't lie in Danielle. "She's not—whatever. How would she have known about the essays?"

"I don't know," Cassandra said. "We never talked about them in public. But if she is a Druid, then maybe she was the one who killed Diane, saw the essays, and then volunteered to watch the dogs so she could take them."

Pursing his lips, Spencer considered the idea. It wouldn't be beyond belief. But could Danielle—the nice girl who read *Wenzel & Frankly*—really be a Druid? He sighed. "I could try meeting with her," Spencer said. "She has been texting me."

Cassandra let out a derisive snort, but Silas nodded. "That might be a good idea," the man said. "Even if she isn't a Druid, she may have seen something while she was here."

The sharp vibration of Spencer's cell caused him to jump. "Sorry," he mumbled, slipping his phone from his back pocket. "It's from Owen. He's, uh—he's going to be moving back home. Starting tonight."

A soft smile tugged at the corner of Cassandra's mouth. "Good for him."

"Yeah," Spencer said. He turned to Silas. "Guess this means you'll be taking the guest room."

While Silas looked about to ask questions, he accepted the place to stay with thanks.

Cassandra rubbed her eyes drowsily. Spencer felt weariness flood his own body. The fatigue settled into his muscles. Nothing sounded better than the comfort of his mattress and heavy blankets upstairs. Though he doubted even this level of exhaustion would help him get rest. Especially not after the attack at the funeral home.

Shadows loomed in Spencer's peripheral. What if the Druids were waiting for them to go to bed, only to send in beasts and wipe them all out? His heartbeat stuttered, the monster in his chest rising. This was why he'd gotten so little sleep lately, thoughts like this. What if, in their most vulnerable moment, everything was finally taken from them? Why wouldn't the Druids kill them that way? What would it take? A single beast? A single slice of a wendigo's razor-sharp claw across their neck, silent and efficient. None of them would know. They'd die in their sleep, and DeVerre would be lost.

Curling his hands into fists, Spencer shoved down the thoughts. "We should get some sleep," he said, knowing it wouldn't come for him. He couldn't sleep. Not anymore. Not with Peter's room lying empty across the hall from his own.

Spencer offered to show Silas to the guest room. They stopped in the foyer to pick up the man's suitcase before trudging up the stairs. Cassandra stayed downstairs to call the dogs in from outside, Gerard promising to watch for any danger.

When they walked through the hall, Spencer gave him a quick rundown of the floor. "That's your room, and that's the bathroom. Pete and I—" He broke off, clearing his throat. "We share that bathroom. Cass is in the master at the other end."

"Great. I appreciate you letting me stay," Silas said.

"We appreciate you being here."

A gentle patter of claws harkened the dogs' and Cassandra's arrival on the staircase, and Silas said his final goodnight before entering his room. The door clicked shut as Spencer turned back to the dark hallway. He intended to say goodnight to Cassandra before heading straight for his room but froze when he saw her standing there. Her hand rested on her bedroom door, the lamplight from inside creating a halo around the frame. But she wasn't looking at him. She was staring at Peter's door, her expression blank.

The floorboard creaked under his feet as he moved for her, and she flinched. Her eyes blinked rapidly as though waking from a stupor.

"Hey," Spencer whispered, coming to her side. "You okay?"

With a low scoff, Cassandra passed him a faint smirk. But Spencer knew her flippant grins now. And he could tell when they weren't wholly felt. "I'm fine," she lied.

Raising his brow, Spencer made sure his expression said he didn't believe her even as he remained silent.

Cassandra took a step back, pushing the door farther open with her. Anguis slipped in past her. She gave a weak chuckle even as she tried to roll her eyes at his concern. She was doing a terrible job of brushing him off. "You know, that's pretty cute," she teased, motioning to his face. Her voice was too thin to pull it off. "That little worried wrinkle on your forehead."

"Cassie," he began, but she cut him off.

"Seriously, Spence," she rambled, "I'm perfectly fine. I'm just tired, which isn't really surprising after this day. And I—I think I should go to bed because—" Spencer caught the glimmer of tears a second too late when Cassandra's voice cracked. "Be—because—"

Spencer hurried forward, closing the gap between them. He set his hands on her arms, drawing her nearer and keeping his voice low. "Cass, what's wrong?" he asked.

Shaking her head, Cassandra tried to scoff through the brimming tears. "It's nothing. I—I just keep thinking . . . about Diane, and . . . about Debbie, and Rene, and—and now . . ."

Her dark eyes flickered over Spencer's shoulder toward the door that hung ajar to his brother's vacant bedroom, alerting him to what she'd left unsaid.

Cassandra's next words came out in a hollow whisper. "Do you hate me?"

Shock punched Spencer in the gut. "Why would I hate you?" he asked.

"It's my fault, Spencer." Her raspy voice was more ragged than normal. The tears now pooled so fully that he was sure they'd fall any moment. "Peter's gone because of me."

With a sharp intake of breath, Spencer prepared to contradict her, but then he remembered where they stood. He glanced over his shoulder, sure they shouldn't have this conversation in the hall, at risk of drawing Silas's attention.

Spencer reached around Cassandra to push open her door, guiding her inside with the other hand. Nex managed to make it in just before he shut the door behind them. He whipped back around to take hold of her shoulders. "That's not true, Cass," he said, desperate to stop her tears before they could fall. "You're not the reason for any of this. Peter's not gone because of you. He's gone because Alexander Frossard is a sadistic bastard."

A pained laugh erupted from her at his vehemence, and Spencer knew he was on the right track. "This isn't your fault," he said. "And I'd be an idiot to blame you—for any of it."

Though her lips turned up in a grateful smile, it was clear she didn't believe him. "People keep dying, Spencer," she said, dark eyes flickering back and forth between his. "Even tonight. That man—William—I didn't even know him, and he died."

"Cass—"

"You can say it isn't my fault as much as you want," Cassandra interrupted. "Maybe you're right, and maybe you're not. It doesn't really matter. The fact is: The people around me keep dying."

"It isn't because of you."

"No?" The first tear broke free.

Spencer's heart constricted, seeing that single tear slip from the corner of her eye, staining her skin as it wove down her cheek.

"My fault or not," she choked out, "people keep dying. And I'm so scared, Spencer, that if—if we lose Peter . . ."

The monster rumbled in Spencer's chest.

"If we lose him," she continued, "then you *will* blame me—you *will* hate me. And then, I'll lose you too."

It was too much for Spencer, seeing her like this. Cassandra Clement was fearless; she was strong and driven, and she'd unflinchingly faced death multiple times to save him and his brother. Yet here she stood, broken, all because she feared what he thought of her.

In one fluid motion, Spencer stepped forward, drawing her into his embrace. Her arms instantly wrapped around him, fingers gripping his jacket as if it could keep her from falling apart. Yet her body remained tense with emotion and tears. He could hear her sniffle as she tucked her head into his neck. He rested his temple against hers. "I could never hate you," he promised in a whisper. "No matter what happens."

Spencer didn't know how long he held her. Or how long she clung to him, her body shaking at random intervals. He just closed his eyes and held her, still and steady, the calm he knew she needed. It was the calm he needed too.

Quiet enveloped them; the *thunk* of the heater, their breathing, and her erratic sniffles were the only sounds. Spencer found himself dragging his fingers through the ends of her hair as they stood there. She smelled of pine, vanilla, and a heady floral. He realized for the first time that she wore perfume. A really lovely perfume.

Spencer supposed that happened when you developed a relationship. You began to notice all the little things about the other person that you never would have expected. The tiny things, like how she didn't use a bookmark when she read. Or how she always tucked the corner of her shirts into her jeans. Or how her thumbs massaged little circles on his back when she hugged him.

Spencer smiled to himself, quite pleased with that last revelation. If this was what having a girlfriend was like, he didn't know why he'd been so scared of it in the first place.

The subtle loosening of Cassandra's arms signaled to him that the embrace was at its end. Spencer relaxed his hold on her, both of them drawing back slowly. But he didn't let her go.

Cassandra's dark eyes flickered nervously over his face, inches away from hers. Spencer wanted to kiss her again. It wouldn't be difficult. Just a short lean in, and their lips would meet. But he could see in the tension of her tear-stained face that something still bothered her, and now wasn't the time to indulge in that side of their relationship.

Spencer loosened his grip, hand rising to brush back the strands of hair stuck to her cheek. "I should probably go," he whispered, one arm looped around her waist.

She nodded but didn't pull away. Either she wasn't ashamed of her tears, or she was just as distracted by his nearness as he was by hers. She let him tuck those damp bits of hair behind her ear, then he continued to run his fingers through her dark brown waves.

"Spencer," she whispered, eyes locked on his face. "I don't want to be alone."

Spencer's heart lurched, and his hand froze.

"I'm not—" Cassandra hurried to say, noticing his hesitation. "I'm not asking you to—to sleep in here or anything. I just don't think I can handle being alone right now. Not when I keep seeing beasts in every corner."

Spencer's eyes drifted to the room, realizing for the first time that they were alone in her bedroom. The curtains hung open, revealing the black night beyond the windowpanes. Only the lamp on her nightstand gave off any light, black-brown shadows clinging to the walls and furniture. Anguis and Nex lounged at the foot of the four-poster bed, their amber eyes blinking in sleepy intervals.

While quite appealing in many ways, spending the night with Cassandra was not an option. However, those fears plaguing her were the same ones that kept him from sleeping the past two nights. Twice now, the Druids had sent beasts into their midst without ever entering their walls. Those memories—of wendigos and hydras peeling from the walls and ceilings of Occasus—were the very thoughts that haunted him only moments ago. And holding Cassandra, seeing her this close, Spencer now saw the dark circles under her eyes that told him she likely hadn't gotten much more sleep than him.

"Hang on," he said, then strode over to the grand bed in the turret corner. He swept the throw blanket from the end, then grabbed the quilted comforter. Without a word, Spencer turned on his heel, took Cassandra's hand, and pulled her out of the room with him.

Taking the immediate left out of the bedroom, Spencer started up the stairs to the third floor, the dogs following.

"Spencer, what are you doing?" Cassandra asked, her confusion clear, though she didn't resist him.

Tossing a glance over his shoulder at her, Spencer started down the hall. "Where's the safest place in DeVerre?"

Cassandra hesitated for only a second. "The vault."

"Exactly," he replied, dropping her hand to open the door of the spare room. "Even if the Druids tried to send beasts into Occasus, they couldn't get into the vault."

An amused chuckle escaped her, and he could imagine that not-quite dimple forming on her cheek as she smirked. "So, what? We're gonna have a slumber party?" she teased.

"No." Spencer depressed the latch on the vault's door, letting it swing open. He grinned at her, pleased to see he was right about the smirk. "Slumber parties are for kids. We're simply camping indoors."

Cassandra dipped her chin, eyes narrowing at him. "You don't have to do this, Spencer."

Spencer hefted the blankets higher in his arms. "We both need sleep, Cassie," he said, then stepped into the vault. The dogs were already at his side, and he looked over his shoulder to be sure she followed as well. "I don't know about you, but I can't go off four hours of sleep anymore."

"You only slept for four hours last night?" she asked.

"Oh, no," Spencer said. "It's been roughly four hours since Sunday."

Ignoring her look of total shock, Spencer headed farther into the vault. He heard her shut the door, hurrying to catch up. Walking down the plush navy and golden runner that lined the center aisle of the vault, Spencer's gaze drifted up to the chandeliers over their heads. They were dim and comforting, casting a soft amber glow over the room rather than their usual sunshiny cream. It seemed the vault knew the reason for their late-night visit.

Spencer led Cassandra to the couches. The fireplace crackled with gentle, glittering embers. In the warm, coppery light, the sitting area held the perfect cozy comfort. Bright enough to chase away the beasts of their imaginations but dim enough to allow for sleep.

Coming to a stop, Spencer gestured to the two couches. "Pick one," he said.

Cassandra eyed him rather than the couches. "Spencer—"

"You really gonna make me carry these back downstairs?" he asked, brandishing the blankets at her.

Laughing, Cassandra turned to the sitting area. "That one," she said, pointing to the couch farthest from the door.

"Cool." Spencer tossed the comforter to her. "Try not to snore, okay? I'm a light sleeper."

She slugged his arm. "I don't snore."

"We're about to find out."

Though she glowered at him, he could see the sparkle of humor in her eyes. Spencer plopped down on his couch, tossing the throw blanket over himself. They took their time settling in. After much shuffling with pillows and adjusting blankets, they lay still, facing one another on opposite couches.

From across the coffee table, Spencer smiled at seeing Cassandra bundled up in the white-and-sage-green, vintage-patterned comforter. She beamed like a beacon in the firelight, arm propped under her pillow. He'd always thought of her as beautiful, but in the last two days, he'd come to know it differently. Yes, she was strong and confident and unshakable. But she was also soft, and kind, and protective. And that made her far more beautiful than he'd ever expected.

"I just realized something," Cassandra said, holding his gaze.

"What's that?"

"We didn't brush our teeth."

Spencer slapped a hand over his eyes. Some romantic gesture this turned out to be. In an effort to make her feel cared for, he'd forgotten basic hygiene. "Well, I feel stupid," he muttered. He lifted his hand to peek around his fingers at her. "I guess we should do that, huh?"

She shrugged, the quilt brushing her cheek. "Probably," she said. "I should wash off my makeup too."

"Mm."

The fireplace let out a hearty *crack* of heat.

"Well," he sighed, tossing back his blanket to sit up, "may as well get to it."

"Spencer."

He looked over at her, drawn by the softness in her voice.

"Thank you," Cassandra whispered.

Returning her smile, Spencer nodded. "Anytime," he promised, finding that he meant it. Anytime, anywhere, anything. He owed that much and more to this woman. And he was very glad he had the chance to prove it.

CHAPTER NINETEEN

Cassandra

The bright, cheery light of the chandeliers overhead woke Cassandra the next morning. After traipsing back into Occasus to take care of their nightly routines, she and Spencer had returned to their separate couches. Granted, it was more awkward the second time. The sweet atmosphere had diminished with the mundane activity and separation. Even so, last night had been the most romantic experience of her life. And he wasn't even her boyfriend.

Cassandra glanced over to the far couch to find it empty. Only the throw blanket remained to assure her the romantic gesture hadn't been a dream. She sighed at the thought. She needed to talk with him. She didn't think she could handle this new, affectionate Spencer much longer. Not without serious damage to her psyche.

Rising, Cassandra gathered the blankets and returned to her bedroom. The overcast morning shaded everything gray, leaving the untouched room feeling even emptier. She dressed, fixed her hair and makeup, and gathered her devotional supplies before heading to the kitchen.

She could hear activity from the top of the stairs. An unusual, deep laugh met her ears, reminding her of Silas's arrival yesterday. Thankful for the man's presence as a buffer between her and the too-sweet-for-her-sanity Spencer, Cassandra entered to find them talking.

"You're a park ranger?" Spencer asked.

Silas nodded. "Yep. Gold Mountain's got beautiful parks. You should visit if you like hiking or nature in general."

"I thought you worked for the Warden," Spencer said, then greeted Cassandra as she stepped over to pour a cup of coffee.

"Oh, I do," Silas said. "I'm part of the town's council, amongst other things. But my full-time job is as a ranger."

Though Cassandra was intrigued by the conversation, she moved to the dining room to complete her devotionals. Soon after, Owen arrived to do more research while Anna spent the day with Ava, and Haley spent it with Aaron at their respective jobs. Spencer and Cassandra set to work on the essays, this time in the vault with Silas to lend Warden knowledge to their studies.

Cassandra tapped her pen on the legal pad of notes. Her eyes kept drifting from the essays in Spencer's lap to the rest of him. His decidedly muscular arms rested on the arms of the chair. His long, deft fingers ruffled his grown-out hair. The waves fluffed with the action, sticking out before slowly dropping onto his forehead. He tapped his pen to his mouth, absentmindedly chewing on the end.

Cassandra's eye twitched.

"This is incredibly boring," Silas said suddenly.

She jumped, sending the legal pad flying to the floor.

Spencer glanced at her while Silas smirked. "Sorry," he said. "Didn't mean to scare you."

Waving him off, Cassandra bent to pick up the notepad and hide her flaming face.

"We're actually making pretty decent headway," Spencer said. "This essay is almost complete. Unfortunately, I'm a pretty subpar linguist, so it's taking way more time than necessary."

"Mm." Silas scanned the vault around them. "Seems like this place was built for work that takes a lot of time."

Cassandra agreed. A lot of time that they didn't have.

Silas stood. "I think there's a better use of our day."

"But the Druids—"

Silas brushed off Spencer's argument. "Look, for whatever reason the Druids took those essays, it can't be as beneficial as what I can teach you."

"Oh, yeah?" Cassandra asked, intrigued. "And what's that?"

"I'm an exceptional trainer," Silas said. "Taught Owen everything he knows about wielding. And about women, but that's beside the point."

Cassandra smiled cynically. "Really?"

He smirked. "I hate to brag, but I'm a Varon, so why not?"

Spencer scoffed. "You and Pete'll get along just fine."

"Glad to hear it."

They walked back through the vault and headed out to the snowy lawn of Occasus. When they stopped in the foyer to pull on their coats, Spencer began to ask more questions. "Are all Varons Sage Wielders?"

"No," Silas said, slipping the last button of his coat into place. "We're impressive, but we're not unstoppable. While our heritage allows us the potential to be a Sage, not everyone *wants* that sort of responsibility. Some people prefer to stay as Clerics and leave it at that."

Cassandra backtracked through the quick lesson Owen had given them on the ranks of Wielders. "Clerics can summon beasts but not wield arcs, right?" she asked.

"Exactly," Silas said. "Don't mistake the lack of arcs as a weakness, though. I've met some Clerics with even greater strength than some Sages."

"How does that work?" Spencer asked as they stepped onto the porch.

"Not sure," Silas said. "Maybe they have a stronger faith. Or maybe it's their willpower that's stronger. Your powers are your powers, but I have seen some who lose their strength during seasons of disbelief or fear."

"Your emotions can affect your power?" Cassandra asked.

"Of course. If you lack either the will or the faith to wield, then your spirit knows it. It can't connect to its rightful plane of existence."

Coming to a stop by the same trees as yesterday, Cassandra frowned. "That sounds unnervingly similar to what the Druids believe."

Silas's grin grew dry. "The best lies often hold an element of truth to them. Our spirits aren't tied to the physical world. When we die, they leave this realm and return to where they belong. That's a fact, not Druidic mumbo-jumbo. It's their choice to take that truth and turn it into a dogmatic tenet of their cult."

"They want to release the spirit world to unleash their spiritual forms on Earth," Spencer said.

Silas nodded. "And we—the Warden—want to keep the spirit world protected and in its rightful place. If God wanted us to live in spirit alone, he wouldn't have given us these physical forms now, would he?"

Spencer looked at Cassandra with a bewildered stare. She'd noted that neither he nor Peter had strong theology. She didn't doubt their faith, though their devotion could use some growth. But she thought their time in DeVerre might be changing that.

Silas slapped Spencer's shoulder. "Come on," he said. "Let's get going."

Even in the overcast noon light, the blanket of snow brought the world to an almost unbearable brightness. They settled into the banks of powder, ready to try Wielder training for a second time. Or at least Spencer seemed ready. Cassandra's nerves clung to the back of her mind, reminding her what a failure she'd been last time.

"Owen told me he got you started on feeling the spirit world around you," Silas said, rubbing his hands together. "That's good. Did you both feel it?"

Cassandra shook her head, but Spencer shrugged. "I think I started to," he said. "He told us to listen, and I thought I heard something, but I can't say for sure."

"All right, that's good. And don't worry, Cassandra, it can take some time to figure it out."

His encouragement didn't help her doubts.

"So, we're gonna stick with that approach," Silas said. "Whatever you did last time, Spencer, do it again. And, Cassandra," he met her stare, "try something new. See if you can tap into that state of rest, of stillness, and from there, we'll take the next step."

Cassandra chewed on the inside of her lip but nodded.

Out of the corner of her eye, Cassandra watched Spencer reset his feet and stare off into space. He'd picked one spot to focus on, and it had worked for him last time. Her short attempt at that had failed her, but perhaps she hadn't given it enough time.

Turning to the world around her, Cassandra scanned the property of Occasus. She looked at the gates, the fence, the dogs, the trees, the snow. Nothing caught her lasting attention until her eyes tracked back to Spencer's dark brown boots. The worn leather repelled the wet snow, leaving spots on the toes and sides. Both Peter and Spencer wore those military-style boots everywhere, rather similar to her own. She wondered if that was a new thing with their move to DeVerre or if they'd worn boots in Norfolk too.

She knew most things about their lives in Norfolk. The statistical, conversational sort of things. All the details that Diane's adopted family members could tell her. But she didn't know the small things, the daily things that made up their life. Like whether or not that denim jacket Spencer always wore had any emotional significance like the Jeep. Or why Peter always preferred to write in a notebook over the laptop.

Spencer's hand flexed in her periphery, drawing her attention upward. She wondered if he was struggling to focus as much as her. Or had he already tapped into the spirit world and could hear that unreachable "sound beyond sound"? She guessed it was the latter. His powers were already much stronger than hers; why shouldn't he be better at tapping into the spirit world?

Silas cleared his throat, breaking through Cassandra's reverie. They both looked up at him, expectant. He wore a droll expression like he was equal parts amused and annoyed.

"What is it?" Spencer asked.

The man's sharp blue gaze flittered from Spencer to Cassandra and back. He crossed his arms. "Did either of you even *try*?"

Cassandra wrinkled her nose, confused, as Spencer tossed his hands to the side. "I mean, I thought I was getting kind of close," he said. He pointed to his head. "There was a buzzing."

"Well, at least *you* were trying."

Mouth falling agape, Cassandra glared at him. "What makes you think I wasn't trying?"

Silas smirked. "Look, I get it," he said. He set a hand against his chest. "I adore my wife. And I remember those early days perfectly well. It can be distracting."

Mortified by his insinuation, Cassandra forced herself not to look at Spencer. "That's not—" Her rebuttal failed her, and she wound up shaking her head as she tried again. "I'm not distracted by Spencer. I just have a hard time focusing in general."

She sensed more than saw Spencer adjusting awkwardly at her side.

Silas kept staring at Cassandra as though trying to puzzle out the problem. "Why do you think that is?"

He sounded so much like a therapist that Cassandra wanted to laugh. She held the gut reaction in as she breathed the frosty air. "I don't know," she said. "I've just always been this way. I don't—I do better when there's noise. Like, you know, in coffee shops or down in the dining room."

"You do better with people around?" he asked.

"Yeah, I guess."

"Huh."

Annoyed that he was so blatantly studying her like a test subject, Cassandra set her jaw. She wanted to tell him to forget it; she could figure this out on her own. But after last night, she knew that wasn't true. She was powerful—everyone knew it—but she was unpredictable. She was dangerous. And without training, without control, she might wind up getting them all killed with her impulsivity.

"What does 'huh' mean?" she asked.

Silas's dry grin tipped up in the corner. "Spencer, would you mind if I work with Cassandra alone for a bit?"

"Uh . . ." Spencer looked between the two of them. His quirked eyebrow and gaping mouth said he was as befuddled as Cassandra. "Sure. I'll just—" He gestured to the house.

On his way past, Spencer gave Cassandra's arm a supportive tap. She tried to smile at him but struggled to feel anything beyond irritation and embarrassment. It was bad enough being the dangerous one. Now, she needed special tutoring too.

Once the front door shut behind Spencer, Cassandra turned back to face Silas. "You know," she said, "you should probably be more focused on him. Varons are more powerful, right?"

Silas pursed his lips, an amused twinkle in his eyes. "Yes, but . . . I have a feeling something's different about you."

"Right." That was what she was afraid of. She didn't want to be different. She wanted to be powerful, controlled, and acceptable. She didn't want to be dangerous or intimidating; she wanted to be safe and lovable.

Realizing that Silas was still staring at her, Cassandra leveled him with all her frustration. "By the way, we're not dating."

"No?" Silas looked genuinely surprised by that. "You should."

That shocked her so much that she didn't have a quick enough response.

"What's stopping you, Cassandra?" Silas asked.

She fumbled for an answer. "Stopping me from . . . dating Spencer?"

"From connecting," Silas said. "You know how to do it. From what Owen's told me, you've done it under stress multiple times. And what I witnessed last night confirms that you have quite a strong, natural inclination for it. So, why is it that you can't do it now? What's stopping you?"

Cassandra swallowed past the dryness in her throat. She felt her irritation dulling, softening to a tangle of emotions she couldn't name. "I don't know," she mumbled.

"Then why did you hesitate?"

The irritation spiked again. "Listen, I get it," she said sharply. "There's something wrong with me. I've always known that."

"Who said something was wrong with you?"

"Everyone," she said. "My parents. All of my family, actually. Everyone in DeVerre. Even Owen."

Silas tipped his head to the side. "Owen tends to be overly cautious."

"Said the Varon."

He laughed. "We are rather incautious sometimes. And no, we don't care what other people say. But when you have power—when you have responsibility—you can't be concerned with opinions. You have to do what's right, regardless of the pushback you experience."

"Right, but I'm not a Varon," she reminded him. "I shouldn't have that kind of power."

"You have the exact kind of power that God intended."

She shook her head. "Look, I—I know that this is who I'm supposed to be, and I've never cared before . . . But I do now."

Silas watched her thoughtfully. "What changed?"

She angled toward Occasus. "Diane died," she whispered. "And my mother was in a coma. Which I recently learned was a ploy of the Druids' to get me out of DeVerre so they *could* kill Diane . . . who was more of a mom to me than my own mom."

Silas's sarcastic countenance shifted as his expression took on a sympathetic understanding.

Cassandra didn't want his sympathy. These things—these deaths and tragedies—they were on her. She'd chosen to return to DeVerre no matter how many times her parents begged her to stay in Spokane. Whether or not they were wrong in keeping the truth from her, they *were* trying to keep her alive.

"I know I can't blame myself for what the Druids chose to do," she heard herself whispering. "What's done is done, and whatever role I played in it . . . I can't take it back."

"Guilt?" Silas said. "Guilt is getting in your way?"

Cassandra felt her lips twist into a self-mocking smile. "No."

"Then what is?"

She shrugged. "Myself."

His eyes narrowed, prompting her to explain.

"I'm getting in my own way," she admitted. "Faith and will. That's what Owen told us. It takes faith and will to wield. I have the faith, but my will is faltering. I know I can do it; I just don't want to."

His eyebrows drew together in consideration. "Why not?"

The truth stuck in Cassandra's chest. The words didn't even make it up her throat and to the tip of her tongue. Her mouth remained closed, and her mind resolute. She didn't want to tell him. She didn't want to admit it to anyone. She didn't want to face their judgment.

But then, what was the harm? Everyone already judged her. They'd condemned her as the dangerous ghost-whisperer almost twenty-five years ago. She'd been branded a monster long before she ever became one.

Cassandra stared at her feet. "I don't want to kill anymore," she whispered. "I don't want to be a murderer."

Silas remained silent.

Crossing her arms tightly over her chest, Cassandra hung her head. "I don't want to be irredeemable," the words slipped out of her brokenly, "and I'm terrified that if I give in to this . . . version of myself, this person that I was born to be—the Druid that I was born to be . . . then I'll lose everything I care about."

In the frigid atmosphere of Occasus's grounds, Cassandra's confession gave her no relief. It didn't soothe or alleviate her fears. It didn't make her feel any better about herself. Because she knew it wasn't the whole truth. Yes, she was afraid of giving in to the monstrous killer she'd become. But even more than her fear was her desire.

The will that Owen lacked—Cassandra had it. She'd always had it. The power that coursed through her, the essence that had covered her body in gooseflesh last night—she liked it. The urge to try new things, to grow her skills, and to wield the spirit world with greater control than even Silas when he summoned that forcefield of light—she craved it.

And that scared her.

Because if she gave into that side of herself—if she truly became the Wielder she'd been born to be, what would that mean for the people she loved?

Silas watched her in the silence, his eyes flickering over to Occasus only once. "I don't think you're gonna lose him," he said.

Though still slightly embarrassed that Silas could so blatantly see the attachment she felt for Spencer, Cassandra smirked. "It isn't just him," she said. "It's both of them. They're my family now, and with Peter gone . . . it's like I've lost my brother. Somehow, in the past month of my life, Peter became my best friend. I miss him. And I feel like it's my fault that he's gone."

"How could it be your fault?"

"All of this is my fault," she replied on instinct. It was such a part of her DNA that Spencer's logical arguments *against* her case hadn't yet found their home in her heart. She knew he was right, theoretically. But she didn't feel he was right, emotionally.

"It's kind of a long story," Cassandra said, holding Silas's steady blue gaze. It reminded her quite a lot of Spencer's. It was quite like Diane's too. A Varon family trait, she was now certain.

Silas shrugged. "I'll listen if you'd like to tell it."

Did she want to tell it? Cassandra didn't think so. But she needed to.

If she was going to save Spencer and Peter—and all of DeVerre along with them—she needed to get past this faltering will of hers, this fight between the woman who wished to be loved and the woman who wished for power.

So, she told him. She told him about her childhood in DeVerre, about her tea parties with ghosts, and her first memory of helping the woman, Katherine, find peace. She told him about how her abilities were discovered and how the then-reverend, John-Daniel Chapelle, had ordered her parents to remove her from the town—which, in the end, had been an agreement with the Druids: Take Cassandra from DeVerre, keep her away from the spirit world, and we'll let her live free from the demands of becoming a Druid. She told him about the twenty years she'd lived in Spokane, about the loneliness and the constant sense that something was wrong with her, about the lies her parents told her and their insistence that she never return. She told him about Debbie, her mother's cousin and best friend; the woman who had made bargain after bargain with the Druids to keep Cassandra out of their grasp; the woman who'd murdered multiple people and attempted to kill Peter, Spencer, and Cassandra.

"I shattered her soul," she said. "I didn't know what I was doing. But she was going to kill us, and Spencer told me . . . he told me to do what I knew I had to. I didn't realize that there was a difference between killing and destroying a soul."

Cassandra met Silas's understanding stare. "I didn't know what I was doing," she repeated. "I just touched her chest and willed that—that she would die. I didn't know that it was such a horrible death."

Silas took a deep breath, studying her carefully. "You shattered her soul without knowing that was a possibility?" he asked.

"I do that sort of thing a lot," Cassandra said. "I tethered Gerard without really understanding what I was doing. I controlled and sent the hellhound that attacked Spencer and Peter away without ever having tried to control a beast before. I wielded an arc after only having seen Owen do it once. According to Peter, I created an entire portal and summoned a whole host of light beasts without even knowing that was possible either.”

He took it all in stride, nodding as he listened. “I’m assuming you didn’t know what you were doing last night either? Joining powers with Spencer.”

“No. I just had the idea, and I thought—” Cassandra shrugged. “Well, it was stupid and impulsive. But that’s what I do. The more power I discover, the more it seems I try it out.”

Silas’s severe gaze swept over her face, and somehow, she knew he was divining the truth from her unsaid words. “So, it isn’t that you don’t want your power,” he concluded. “It’s simply that you’re afraid that by reaching your potential, you’ll be dangerous to the people you love?”

“Yes.”

“Well, how about this?” Silas said with a sardonic grin. “If you *don’t* reach your potential, you *will* lose the people you love.”

Cassandra blinked, the threat sinking into her heart.

“They don’t care about how dangerous you are,” Silas told her. “They aren’t scared of you. Neither am I.”

“But my powers are dangerous,” she said, Owen’s warnings lingering at the back of her mind.

Silas smirked. “Good for you. Don’t brag about it.”

Cassandra gaped at him, surprised at his flippancy.

“Power isn’t something to fear, Cassandra,” he said, his stare weighty as he leaned toward her, impressing his sentiment. “It’s a burden, yes. It’s a responsibility too. But it is also the greatest ability you can have to care for those you love. You have the potential to keep them safe—to keep this whole town safe. So, don’t let your fear stop you.”

Finding that her fingers had begun to twist her ring without any conscious awareness on her part, Cassandra forced them away. Could he be right? He knew great power. He *was* a Varon.

But he was a *Varon*. She was some anomaly that they didn’t yet understand.

An anomaly that could save them all.

Cassandra drew in a long, unsteady breath. She closed her eyes and clung to that truth: She could save them. Because of the power that made her different, dangerous, and unknown, she could save everyone. Whatever the reason, whyever God had granted this power to her, it was hers. She could use it to become a monster, or she could wield it to protect her family.

Instinct made Cassandra screw up her face in concentration, but she heard Silas speaking softly, "Relax. Be still and listen."

Purposefully, Cassandra loosened her facial muscles. Her shoulders drew back, and her hands hung limply at her sides. Tension remained in her lungs, so she took another long breath in, letting the rest of her body ease while she exhaled.

Silence greeted her. It pressed in on all sides, hollow and empty. She wanted to strive after the sound of the spirit world, to press with all her might and hear it. But she forced herself to stay relaxed, at peace.

The world of winter sang its quiet tune to her. A whistle of wind. The rustle of pine branches. A crunch of snow as Silas shifted his weight. The creak of the swing on Occasus's porch behind her—Owen and Aaron had taken the time to fix it the other day.

Cold bit her nose as the breeze whipped hair across her face. She didn't reach up to move it. She didn't do anything at all. She just listened.

Her breath rattled in her head. Silas swallowed as he waited patiently.

Cassandra's hands began to fist. She wanted it too badly.

Resetting her feet, Cassandra took another breath. She held it. One . . . two . . . three . . . four. She let it out. The gasp of her breath erupted into the air.

Silence.

And then . . . a sound. A gentle, almost hum that she couldn't quite describe. Soft and calming. A sound beyond sound.

Cassandra's skin tingled. Her pulse steadied. Her mind stilled.

"That's it." Silas's voice broke through, sounding distant though she could feel he stood only a few feet from her. "I can sense it too. You're channeling it here, giving me access to it. You can hear it. Now, *feel* it."

Cassandra did feel it. The sound beyond sound reached into her core, touching the atoms of her body. It wove through her like a second skin. She recognized the sensation immediately. The tremor of the spirit world's essence flowed through her, connecting to her, waiting on her. An intangible but very present tingle that hovered over her like a shell.

"Draw on it, Cassandra."

At his order, Cassandra listened. Her will met her faith in an effortless command. The tremor traveled from her head to her feet, a burst of energy flying out of her.

"Whoa!" Silas cried out.

Cassandra's eyes flew open, the fear that she'd hurt him immediately dampening the sensation that had taken over her. "Are you okay?" The words tumbled out before she processed the man before her, totally unharmed and staring at her with his mouth hanging open.

Then, Silas started laughing.

"What?" Cassandra asked, her heartbeat slowly resuming its natural rhythm. "What happened?"

"Well, you're right," he said with a smug grin. "You're far more powerful than the average Sage."

Not quite sure if she wanted the answer, Cassandra asked, "What did I do?"

"There are these things called holoforms," he explained. "That's the new name for them, at least. The early Wielders called them spirit-forms. It's kind of like having a spirit animal or a Patronus if you're a fantasy nerd like my wife."

"A Patronus?" Cassandra pressed her lips around the urge to laugh. "Like, a spirit guardian?"

"Pretty much. They require extreme power to raise and maintain. Few Sages ever manage it."

"And I summoned one?"

"Yep."

Cassandra crossed her arms, intrigued. "What'd it look like?"

"It replicates your arc, surrounding you in beast form," Silas said. "So, yours was really light gray with ivory around the edges, and it took the shape of a nyct."

"What—" Cassandra did laugh then. "I don't know what a nyct is."

"They're batlike creatures."

Cassandra bit her bottom lip in thought. "Peter and Spencer said that I summoned batlike creatures when I opened that portal Saturday night."

Silas shrugged. "We all have our favorites. Seems like you prefer the nyct."

"But I didn't think summoning beasts was a good idea."

"Who told you that? Owen?"

"I haven't really talked to Owen about it," she said, then frowned. "I haven't really talked to anyone about it. I guess I just assumed that beasts were bad."

"They can be," Silas said. "Just like Wielders can be bad. But they aren't inherently evil. There are shadow beasts and light beasts. Did you think the ones you summoned were evil?"

"I didn't know."

"Look, as long as your heart is in the right place, you're not gonna summon shadow beasts," he said. "Stop worrying so much about doing the wrong thing. Just start doing what you *know* is right."

"Even if it's dangerous?"

"Most things worth doing are dangerous."

Cassandra smiled, knowing that he was right. Every time she'd made some leap in her abilities, it had always been with the right intentions. And she'd managed to keep her friends alive because of it.

"Thank you," Cassandra said, looking up to Silas.

His mouth curled up in that apparently genetic Varon smirk. "Happy to help."

They turned to walk toward the house when Cassandra had another revelation hit her. "Did you say my arc was light gray?" she asked.

"Yes. Why?"

She furrowed her brow. "Well . . . I don't know. Maybe we should ask Spencer to confirm, but I could have sworn it was darker. Kind of an ash gray, you know?"

Silas nodded. "They can change."

"They can?"

"There's a spectrum. Like I said, as long as your heart is in the right place, you'll summon the right sort of power. The purer the heart, the brighter the arc."

"So, the ideal color would be white?"

"I suppose technically," he said. "Though that's not likely."

"Why not?"

"We're fallen. Total purity is only accomplished in Christ. The potential for our heart to be 100% pure is there, but it's practically impossible. Inevitably, there will be some level of fear staining our intentions, keeping us from being wholly selfless in our pursuits."

"And that's not a problem?"

Silas let out an indifferent hum. "Not really. So long as you keep pursuing trust over fear, you'll be just fine."

Cassandra decided to leave the subject alone. She liked that, pursuing trust over fear. Hope over pain. She didn't mind pain; she didn't mind difficulty. She minded isolation and rejection. But this hope, this trust that she might not be the dangerous creature her parents always claimed—it gave her a new focus.

Pain was pain. She knew that.

Danger was danger.

But if she could embrace her power, this unexpected, anomalous power that made her some grand threat to the Druids, she might be able to save her family yet. And she had an idea of just where she might start.

CHAPTER TWENTY

Anna

Standing in the entryway of DeVerre Chapel, Anna held a basket looped around her arm, passing out hugs and candles to each vigil attendee. The somber mood ate at her. Nearly everyone had tears in their eyes as they stepped into the building. She had to fight to maintain her own emotions, both sorrow and anger threatening to breach her tear ducts.

After spending the day at the library researching all she could with Ava, she felt like her ability for compassion was at an all-time low. This was the last place she wanted to be. Especially now that Owen had informed them of Cassandra's plan. While everyone else was at the vigil, she and Spencer would break into the DeVerre Clinic.

With the town distracted, the two of them could search the clinic without fear of discovery. As it was Alexander's place of work, they hoped to find the files for Diane, Michael, and Seraphine, looking for evidence to support their biological connection and possibly, their murders.

"The clinic would also be a perfect cover to conduct Druidic business," Owen had explained to Anna and Ava. "Meetings could be covered as appointments so that he could give orders and receive updates. They're hoping to discover information about the Druids' plans *and* where they're keeping Peter."

A part of Anna still struggled, feeling as though she was betraying her lifelong friends. The stronger part reminded her that the Frossards didn't deserve her loyalty. Their lies and deceit had wormed their way into her mind over the years. So much that she naturally wanted to defend them despite all the evidence of their nefarious intentions.

Ready to prove her renewed allegiance, Anna spoke up. "What about their house?" she asked. "Shouldn't they search there too?"

Owen shook his head. "They can't search both in one night. It's too dangerous. The clinic is a safer bet, being the less obvious choice. Once we rule that out, we can pursue other options."

So, while Anna and her family attended the vigil, Spencer and Cassandra would search the clinic, and Silas would remain at Occasus, working in the vault. If the clinic proved fruitless, they would find a way into the Frossard home another night.

Now, Anna couldn't help her heart's erratic pounding as she greeted the solemn arrivals at the chapel foyer. Though every Frossard in DeVerre stood in the building, she worried that Spencer and Cassandra would get caught. It didn't matter how carefully they'd planned or that they'd chosen to wait until after the vigil began to leave Occasus, avoiding any chance of being seen. They were putting themselves at risk, and all she could do was stand there and wait.

Anna kept her eye on the clock, anxiously awaiting the agreed-upon time for Spencer and Cassandra to enact their plan. As Giana Frossard's right hand, Anna had been the one to help them formulate their timetable, the very reason Owen came to confer with them at the library in the first place. If anything went wrong, it'd be her fault.

Gia had the vigil planned out to the second. The mourners would arrive from 6-6:25 p.m. Sam would step up at 6:30 to lead them in a welcoming prayer, followed by a short eulogy. Then the mayor's seventeen-year-old niece, Madelyn Guillaume, would sing some hymns, accompanied by Melanie Chapelle on the piano. Anna had suggested that Spencer and Cassandra leave at 6:45 to be safe.

Anna kept her expression soft with compassion as she handed out candle after candle. Some of the attendees spoke with her, muttering about the tragic loss in hushed tones. They gripped the vigil programs tightly in their hands. The tri-folded papers bore the pictures of each lost DeVerrean, along with individual obituaries and Bible verses. Ivory candles littered the church, lighting it up like an ancient cathedral. An adequately depressing and moody amount of floral arrangements lined the platform.

With an eye and ear always alert for Gia's presence, Anna responded to each mourner with noncommittal apologies and well wishes. The whole evening, Gia relied on her as though nothing had changed. It was as though Anna and Connor were still best friends, and Gia and Alex weren't leaders of the Druidic cult in their town.

Anna's skin crawled every time the woman came near. Gia acted as she always had, treating her like a beloved daughter, doting on her, whispering praise, and checking in regularly.

Anna wanted to throw the entire basket of candles at the woman's beautiful head.

Instead, she smiled sadly and sighed mournfully. She played the part, acting as the devoted DeVerrean they expected her to be. If the Frossards could lie to her for twenty years, she could lie to them for a few days.

She wondered if it even mattered. The Frossards knew that Anna sided with Peter, Spencer, and Cassandra. Which meant they were aware that Anna knew of their lies, right? But if so, why was Gia still treating her like such a dear friend? Why pretend at all?

Looking to the front of the chapel, Anna watched as Alex spoke with Tony MacDonald. Even Alex had pulled her into a tender, fatherly hug when she'd joined to help prepare for the vigil. It seemed the couple was performing some malicious drama. The problem was that she couldn't figure out the point of it all. Why would they pretend to love her when she'd already taken a stance against them?

Anna shivered as the door opened for the hundredth time, letting in the cold November air. She handed a candle to the man standing before her, then turned to the new arrivals. The door *whooshed* shut, and her whole being froze.

He was back.

Taking up the majority of the entry hall with his broad shoulders and towering height, Connor Frossard had returned. Perfect, handsome, and like a dream. His golden blond hair glowed even in the candlelight, the black button down and slacks he wore only amplifying his suntanned skin. Ava always teased Anna that Connor had a jawline that could cut diamonds and a smile that could melt graphite.

Anna felt her knees go weak.

Then her cheeks blazed with a furious inferno that rivaled Mount St. Helens.

At Connor's side stood his adorable fiancée. Of all women, Lily Montgomery was Connor Frossard's perfect match. Her soft brown hair framed her face with waves that only a model could achieve. Petite and dainty, she looked like a fairy. Even in her sleek black dress, she looked elegant and refined. Her sweet round eyes were moss green, and her full lips a natural rosy pink. If Anna hadn't been so jealous of her, she might have called her the most beautiful woman in the world.

The instant Anna saw the happy couple, Connor's sky-blue gaze locked with hers. Her stomach flipped. She hated that it did that. When had that started? She couldn't remember. Was it since they'd first met? Or had it come on gradually?

Connor took a step forward, and Anna panicked. She shoved the basket into the arms of Evelyn Durand, who was handing out programs beside her. She muttered an excuse and stormed away.

Immediately, a rush of Frossards pressed forward, headed for their golden child and his fiancée. Anna stumbled through them, slipping deeper into the chapel to seek refuge from his presence. She wished she was stronger, that she could be indifferent and nonchalant. If only she carried a fraction of the elegance Lily exuded and could manage to greet them serenely. Maybe that's what she'd been missing. Maybe that was why Connor had never loved her back. She wasn't the sophisticated, gorgeous goddess of a woman he wanted. She supposed she couldn't blame him. He was worth that sort of woman.

Pain lanced up Anna's arms. She stopped dead in her tracks, realizing that her nails were cutting into her palms, hands curled into tense fists at her sides. She panted shallow breaths, her eyes stinging with unshed tears. She hated that he could make her feel this way, that he could make her cry by stepping into the room. She hated that she didn't hate him despite his lies. She hated that even though their entire friendship had been a sham, a cover while he and his family were working to destroy everything she loved, her heart still ached for him.

A hand landed on Anna's shoulder. She whirled around to find Danielle there, tears in her eyes as well. "Are you okay?" she asked.

Smoothing down her black blouse—she didn't own anything nearly as sophisticated as Lily's dress—Anna forced herself to smile. She took her friend's hand and squeezed. "I'm fine, Dani," she promised. "I just got overwhelmed for a moment."

Danielle nodded, her dark gaze flitting around the sanctuary. "It's really strange," she whispered, inching closer. "Being here and knowing—knowing everything you and Aaron told me."

After they'd opened up to Danielle, the young woman asked to help. She didn't understand everything fully, but she wanted to stop the Frossards and their plans for DeVerre. While Anna hadn't invited her to help at Occasus—she didn't want to make it awkward for Spencer or Cassandra—she'd given her friend an equally important task.

Danielle worked at her Uncle Tony's diner, putting her in a unique position to hear what the MacDonalds were up to. She'd agreed to listen and report back. Anna had warned her not to prod; she didn't want her friend putting herself in unnecessary danger. But already, Danielle's help had proved useful. She'd texted Anna earlier that day with an update about Tony's attempts to write William Ozanne's death off as an accident with some ridiculous story about a party gone wrong involving lots of booze and hallucinations.

Anna didn't know who would buy that Gabe Chapelle had hosted a rager in his mortuary, but that was the story Tony MacDonald intended to sell.

At Anna's side, Danielle went rigid.

Gia appeared, giving them a soft, apologetic smile. "It's 6:25, dear," she said, setting her hand lovingly on Anna's shoulder. "Would you help me guide people to take their seats?"

Tensely, Anna nodded. "Of course."

Gia brushed down one of Anna's wispy curls. "Thank you, sweetheart," she said, a glimmer of tears in her eyes. "What would I do without you?"

Anna's stomach roiled, her throat burning with bile as she watched the woman walk away. The charade made her want to grab the nearest vase, smash it against the carpet, and scream in rage. They were liars. Hypocrites. Murderers. And she'd unwittingly helped them, unknowingly loved them for twenty years.

Danielle's hand brushed Anna's arm. "Do you want help?" she whispered.

"That'd be great, thanks," she said, the words tight in her throat.

Once all the attendees were ushered to their seats, Anna lingered at the back of the chapel. Connor entered the second aisle seat, compassionately greeting the openly weeping Alan Sauveterre.

DeVerre liked its traditions, and since the chapel's grand opening in 1889, the Frossards sat in the second row on the left-hand side of the chapel. Anna's family sat three rows back.

Years ago, Anna and Connor took turns sitting with each other's families. One week, she sat in the second row with him. The next, he sat in the fifth row with her. Everyone knew they were the exception to the chapel's seating rule. Everyone always made room, because the pair were inseparable.

Now, Anna couldn't bear the thought of having only three rows of distance. She needed a whole chapel, a whole town, a whole state between them.

Danielle invited Anna to sit with her, seeing her discomfort. As a teen, Danielle had lost her parents. Since then, she sat with friends near the back of the church, almost as far from Connor as Anna could get.

Whether or not Danielle had guessed her embarrassing predicament, Anna didn't care. She sat with her friend gratefully.

Sam stepped onto the platform to open with a prayer. His ginger hair shone in the candlelight. Though he gave a genuine, sorrowful eulogy, she could see the fire in his eyes as he scanned the audience. His voice held a fierce edge, his words a charge of goodness over evil, love over hate, and justice over personal gain.

All around the chapel, people wept. It was painful to witness. Be they cultists or not, these people were mourning, and Anna couldn't stop her own tears from falling. To varying degrees, she'd known every person who'd died at Occasus, most of them for her entire life. And still, they'd been Druids, cultists intent on murdering her friends.

Anna's gaze caught on the glint of Connor's blond hair, his head bowed. Lily sat close at his side, dark waves obscuring her expression. Treacherously, Anna's imagination gave her a vision of their fingers woven together in sympathy and support.

A spear of jealousy cut through her. She shouldn't be sad that it wasn't her at his side. She shouldn't wish that it was her fingers entwined with his. Not when he was just as bad as the rest of them. Why was he back anyway? Had he come to rub his happiness in her face?

Guilt slapped Anna across the face. Selfish. Bitter. Remorseless.

Of course, he'd come back. This vigil honored three of his family members. He'd be callous not to return.

Tears of sorrow and anger burned down her cheeks. Her heart ached through every second of the service. When it finally ended, she excused herself from Danielle's side to clean up. She couldn't handle sitting and crying, hugging and sympathizing. She needed to move, to work, to distract herself.

As the non-family members filed out, Anna gathered their candles upon their exit. She collected the left-behind programs. Then she started organizing the floral arrangements to send home with each family. She moved for the final arrangement at the front of the emptying chapel, ready to complete her tasks and head home. She wanted a hot shower where she could cry out all her sorrow unseen.

Anna moved to pick up the blue vase. She gave a passing glance over the chapel, finding the very person she *didn't* want to see heading her way.

Steadily, Connor worked across the church with caution and purpose. He glanced over his shoulder at his family suspiciously. She could always tell when Connor was defying his parents. She could read his every emotion, whether happy, annoyed, angry, or frightened. And right now, she read desperation in those shockingly blue eyes of his.

Panicked, Anna abandoned the flower arrangement, nearly sending it toppling to the floor. With one final shove back in place, she rushed away from Connor's path. He whispered her name pleadingly. His voice slammed into her back, sending warmth racing across her neck, chest, and face. She loved his voice. Deep but refined. Strong but friendly. Masculine but affectionate.

Anna squeezed her eyes shut, banging into the pew at her side as she attempted to slip around it. He called again, but she refused to acknowledge him, doubling her speed to slip away. A group of weeping Dumonts blocked his path, helping her escape. She skirted around them, heading straight for Ava on the opposite side of the room.

Sure that her face was coated in mascara lines, Anna didn't bother to rub them away. Haley's cheeks were stained with signs of tears, and Aaron held her close. Unmoved by the emotional evening, Ava's expression remained stoic. Her sharp stare darted to the chapel behind Anna, reaching out a hand to her.

"Do I need to kill him?" Ava muttered under her breath.

Anna took a deep breath, knowing Ava's defending presence would be enough to halt Connor's pursuit. "I'll do it myself," she whispered back.

Ava passed her a proud grin, then turned back to Owen, who spoke with a stranger. The man was about Owen's height, though with a much narrower frame, and in his early thirties with a professional look. He wore a dark brown, elbow-patched blazer over a black shirt and slacks. In the dim light of the chapel, his pale skin took on an orange cast. Through the conversation, Anna quickly understood that he was the new teacher. The one hired to take Debbie Mercier's place.

"I didn't plan to come tonight," he said, voice hushed as his light eyes flickered over the mourners. "I feel like an interloper. But the other teachers insisted that I should. I was very sorry to hear about the whole situation."

Owen nodded with his usual steady demeanor. Anna was happy to have him back home, even if it meant she had to sleep alone again. For the last week, Ava's presence had helped her sleep after the horror she'd faced. But having Owen home made them both feel vastly safer and happier.

"It's good you came," Owen told the man. "DeVerre likes to see its newcomers getting involved. It shows they mean to be part of the community."

The teacher gave him an appreciative smile. He met Anna's gaze, giving her a polite wave.

Owen noticed and gave the introduction. "My sister-in-law," he said. "Anna, this is Jacob, the new English teacher at DeVerre School."

Anna accepted Jacob's offered handshake. "Nice to meet you," she said.

"Sorry that it has to be under these circumstances," he replied. She liked his smile, she decided. It was friendly without being pushy.

"DeVerre's having a particularly bad stint," Aaron said, his arm tightening around Haley. "But it's about to get better."

"Well, I've heard great things about DeVerre, so I'm sure you're right."

Ava's brow rose. "You've heard about DeVerre?"

He nodded in confirmation.

"That's a first," she muttered.

"How'd you hear about us?" Anna asked.

"Oh, uh—" He hesitated. "My best friend's sister lives here. I heard about the job through him and thought, why not apply?"

"Really?" Haley asked, her bubbly demeanor slightly less enthusiastic but no less genuine. "We probably know her. What's her name?"

"Oh, I doubt it," Jacob said. "She's not lived here long."

A nagging suspicion drew Anna and Haley to exchange a look.

Haley's blue eyes crinkled as she smiled. "Anna and I know pretty much everyone in DeVerre. I'd be surprised if we *didn't* know her."

"Uh, well, her name is Cassandra," he said. "Cassandra Clement."

Anna's jaw dropped. "You know Cass?"

His expression showed equal surprise. "*You* know Cass?"

"Yeah, we're—well, she's kind of one our closest friends."

"Really?" Jacob asked, elated. "That's great! Like I said, I'm best friends with her brother and . . . well, Cass and I—we, uh—we were close for a time. I know she can be a bit of a loner, so it's good to hear that she's made friends. Ike's been worried about her."

With a newfound skepticism, Anna found his explanation less forthcoming than she'd like. "Ike is her brother?" she said.

"Yeah."

"Why's he been worried?"

Ava squeezed her arm in gentle warning, but Jacob simply shrugged and said, "As I'm sure she told you, things have been difficult for their family recently. I wouldn't normally discuss this, but since you all know Cassie, I assume you're already privy to the details. After her mother's accident and her cousin's condition, well . . . things have been difficult. And then, she had that falling out with her parents, and . . . I'll admit, I'm worried about her too. It's hard, watching all these things happen and not being able to help."

Owen shifted beside Ava. "That's understandable," he said. "But I can assure you that in spite of it all, Cassandra is okay."

Jacob sighed, and then his gaze drifted beyond them to the clearing chapel. Only a handful of people remained to finish cleaning. Sam's wife, Melanie, flipped on the overhead lights to make the work easier. The LEDs shone white, revealing the departing figures of Connor and Lily as they exited the chapel. Anna's heart squeezed with relief and anguish simultaneously.

Jacob cleared his throat. "May I be honest?" he asked.

Tucked into the corner of the chapel, no one paid attention to their group. The conversation was wholly private. And Anna knew that's what Jacob had ensured moments ago.

"Of course," Owen said.

"The teachers," Jacob began, "the ones who invited me tonight. They—they told me that some new residents . . . that they don't care to be . . . friendly. They said that the men and women we remembered tonight went to try and talk with them and that these people . . . they killed them."

Anna tensed.

"And the way they were talking . . ." Jacob shook his head. "They said that Cassandra was part of it. But I *know* Cassie. And while she's always been different," he said it almost fondly, like her being different was charming and not off-putting, "she's not malicious. And she's certainly not a murderer."

Anna did another scan of the chapel. Only Sam's family, Tom and Hunter's wives, and Gia remained.

Anna looked to Ava, questioning. Was it safe? Could they trust this man? This stranger? They'd trusted Peter and Spencer. They trusted Cassandra. And Jacob said he was here because he knew the Clement family—because he cared about Cassandra too.

The reserved glint in Ava's eyes made her uncertainty clear. She didn't know what to think either. But they couldn't play it safe anymore. Not when they needed to convince all of DeVerre of the truth.

Anna turned back to Jacob. "Cassandra didn't murder anyone," she said, keeping her voice low. "Neither did Peter and Spencer."

Jacob's shoulders relaxed.

"But if you want to know more," she continued, "then you'll have to talk to them."

His gaze shot up to meet hers. "Of course. I want to help Cass in whatever way I can."

Anna nodded, hopeful. "I'll see if I can set something up."

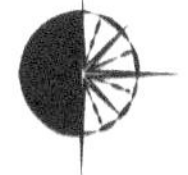

CHAPTER TWENTY-ONE

Spencer

"**I** can't believe you talked me into this," Spencer muttered, following Cassandra as they snuck around the back of DeVerre Clinic. They'd parked the Jeep on the square, creeping around the buildings while the rest of the town attended the vigil.

"What, would you rather mourn the lives of the people who tried to kill us?" Cassandra whispered over her shoulder. They scanned the doctor's office for a backdoor, finding nothing but brick walls and locked windows. "Guess we'll try something else."

"We could go in the front," Spencer said.

She raised an eyebrow. "Do you know how to pick a lock?"

"No," he said. "But apparently, small towns don't believe in basic safety."

She chuckled. "They leave their *homes* unlocked. This place has medical records. I doubt Alexander would keep it open to the public. Another reason the clinic is a better hiding place than his home."

"So, how do you suggest we get in?" Spencer asked. "Break a window?"

Cassandra rolled her eyes, then grabbed his hand. Spencer fought to damper his immediate delight. "Come on," she said, leading him to the far window. The blinds were open—another trusting small-town trait—revealing a storage room lined with file cabinets.

Fingers still wrapped around his, Cassandra raised her other hand to hover over the panes of the window.

"What are you doing?" Spencer whispered.

"I want to try something," was her only reply before she pressed her palm to the window.

Suddenly, a muted light shimmered around them. Spencer's stomach lurched, and the world dropped out from under him.

The urge to cry out leaped into Spencer's throat, but he held it in as he scanned the space around them. His head spun as his equilibrium worked to rebalance. In the blink of an eye, they'd left the frigid exterior of the clinic, and now, they stood inside the storage room, surrounded by beige cabinets.

"How the—?"

"I can't believe it actually worked!" Cassandra exclaimed, quietly laughing in joy at her success.

Spencer gaped at her. "When did you figure out how to do that?"

She shrugged. "I saw the Druid do it last night. And then, I was thinking, Gerard walks in and out of the spirit world all the time. Why couldn't I?"

He blinked at her incredulously. "So, you just thought, why not try something that could kill us?"

"Calm down, dear." Cassandra patted his arm placatingly. "I wouldn't have tried it if I thought it would kill us."

His stomach still rolled uncomfortably. "I'm never doing that again."

She smirked. "You intend on spending the night here, then?"

"No," he said. "I'll be going out the front door."

Cassandra chuckled under her breath, moving for the file cabinets. She scanned their labels, then opened a drawer. "These are marked alphabetically by last name," she noted. "Do we start with Michael and Seraphine or Diane?"

Forcing himself to get a grip, Spencer heaved a final sigh, then joined her. "Probably best to start with Diane," he suggested. "We *know* there'll be a file on her."

"The L's then," Cassandra said, shifting along the rows. When she found the correct cabinet and tugged on the drawer's handle, Spencer held his breath, inordinately worried it would be a trap or trigger an alarm.

The drawer slid open without any resistance. No alarm sounded. Nothing moved. And Spencer grimaced at his paranoia.

Cassandra crouched down to shuffle through the numerous hanging file folders. "LAF, LAM—ah-ha, LAR." She pulled out the two folders labeled LARKIN. "This is Liam's, and this is Diane's."

"Do we have any reason to look through his?" Spencer asked.

"Not really," she said, then opened Diane's.

Laying the file on the top of the cabinet, they arched their necks to read it. The file held years of records, though none were particularly detailed. Diane had few health concerns. All the records were from routine checkups, dental appointments, and other minimal visits from the thirty years of her life in DeVerre.

The one piece of paper that held their lasting interest rested at the bottom of the stack: the record of Diane Larkin's death.

"*'Natural causes,'*" Cassandra read aloud.

Spencer frowned. "I guess we shouldn't have expected anything else."

"He didn't even request a toxicology report," she said, glaring at the paper. "He marked it as unsuspicious, and that was that."

"It doesn't matter," Spencer said. "If he had reported anything, Tom would have investigated her death. And that would have led back to him."

Cassandra nodded begrudgingly, closing the file with a flick of her wrist. "Why don't you look for Michael's file," she said, refiling the paperwork. "I'll try to find Seraphine's."

Spencer moved straight for the far side of the room. On the very last drawer of the very last cabinet, he found the files marked V. Though he'd been skeptical of the clinic keeping records more than a decade old, Cassandra had reminded him that this was a small town that cherished its records. Sixty-year-old medical records of their founding families would be highly prized.

Spencer only found six files labeled *Varon*. Matthias, Cecile, Marcus, Lena, Matthew, and Nathalie. Three couples from three generations. But no Michael.

"His file isn't here," Spencer said, turning to Cassandra.

She crouched next to the cabinet on the far side of the room. "Really?" she asked, her eyebrows pulling together in surprise. Her hand stilled over the files. "Are the rest of the Varons' files there?"

"Yeah," Spencer double-checked even as he replied in confirmation, "all the Varons are here, except for Michael."

Cassandra tweaked her mouth to the side, the hollow appearing on her right cheek. "That's odd. Maybe they kept it secret. If they falsified his information, they may not want it to be easy to find."

"We found Diane's easily enough."

"Yeah, but who can prove that he falsified anything? Maybe Michael's file holds discrepancies."

Spencer supposed that was possible.

"Come on." Cassandra waved him over. "Help me search for Seraphine. There's a horrifying amount of Frossards in here."

Spencer gave her a dry grin. "I am just as much Frossard as I am Varon, you know?"

"Maybe," she replied as he knelt beside her. "But having met Silas, it's pretty clear which bloodline runs truest in your veins."

"Wonder where he got his height, though," Spencer said absentmindedly as he perused the files. "Both my dad and grandfather were short."

"Short like you? Or short like Peter?"

Spencer paused to think about it. "Like Pete. I got Mom's genes in that department."

"Your mom's particularly short?"

"Five-three," he recited from memory, "and a half."

Cassandra chuckled. "That has to be the only thing you inherited from her. You look too much like Silas otherwise."

"Pretty much," he said. "Mom and Pete are far more alike—in every way."

"And you're more like your dad?"

"From what I remember."

She hesitated, and Spencer could tell she was worried she'd asked too much.

He looked up from the files. "It's okay to talk about him," he promised. "I *like* talking about Dad. Just not his death."

Cassandra nodded, though she didn't seem convinced.

Rather than take the time to prove it to her, Spencer slipped the last Frossard file back into the cabinet. "Seraphine's file isn't here," he said. "I don't think it's a coincidence—both of their files missing. They have to have them somewhere else."

"But why?" she asked.

Spencer sighed. "I have no idea."

Turning her ring, Cassandra frowned at the files. "Maybe they destroyed them," she said.

The thought tasted sour.

"I hope not."

Cassandra raised her chin. "They could be in Alexander's office," she said.

"Even if they aren't, there's nothing left to find in this room," he said. He didn't add that he was less concerned about finding the files because he mainly cared about seeking information on Peter.

They rose together, moving across the linoleum-tiled floor to slowly open the door. Spencer glanced down the hall to be sure they truly were alone. Though they spoke in hushed tones and moved with quiet caution, he didn't think they could be too careful.

The hallway was dark and laid out in an L-shape. Silence whispered through the building. A door hung open to their left—a vacant restroom. Other rooms lined either side of the hall leading to the front of the clinic. And across from them at the back, two more doors waited.

"May as well check back here first," Spencer whispered.

They drifted across the hall to the first door on their right, finding a shallow supply closet, shelves full to the brim with gauze, medical tools, and medications. Cassandra moved past him for the second door. She set her hand on the knob when Spencer heard a distant *click* echo through the space.

Panic rolled through his chest. He reached over to grab her hand, stopping her from opening the door.

Cassandra froze, her eyes wide as he held his other hand up to tell her to be quiet. They listened for a painstaking second before the *swoosh* of a door sweep reverberated back to them.

Spencer didn't wait to hear more. He pulled Cassandra with him as he backed into the supply closet. Ever so carefully, he shut the door until he felt more than heard the near-silent *snap* of the latch. Heart thudding furiously in his chest, Spencer's ears rang in the silence. He could hear the softest sound of voices and movement, but it wasn't urgent or worried.

A relief washed through Spencer. They weren't coming for them. It was just a coincidence.

Relaxing, another more immediate revelation hit him. He blinked in the darkness of the closet, his eyes adjusting to see the barest outline of Cassandra's face. The details didn't come through in the black-on-black that permeated the closet, but he was suddenly aware of how closely they stood. Face to face, he had one arm around her waist as her hands pressed against his chest.

Spencer's pulse spiked. He was pretty sure his face was burning, and he was suddenly grateful she couldn't see him. The gentlemanly thing to do would be to give her room. But with the shelves digging into his back, that wasn't an option. If he attempted to adjust, he feared that he'd knock into the supplies, revealing their presence.

Breathing became difficult, his skin grew clammy, and his senses began to buzz. Spencer's hand flexed instinctively against her lower back as the dumbest idea he'd ever had shouted through his mind: He *really* wanted to kiss her.

Not quite sure what possessed him, Spencer leaned in, his nose brushing hers.

Cassandra gasped, drawing back as far as the door behind her would allow—which wasn't very far. "Spencer," she hissed his name. But he could hear the dry edge of humor woven into the shock.

"What?" he said, heart still hammering.

"We're hiding."

"I know."

Darkness enveloped them so fully that Spencer couldn't be sure, but he thought her mouth dropped open in shock. He could feel the breath leave her lungs as she let out a silent scoff. "I'm aware that this is an anxiety-inducing situation," she whispered hurriedly, "but seriously?"

"Sure, it's not ideal, but you can't exactly blame me." Spencer tried— he really did try to pull back, but there wasn't anywhere to go.

"It's *your* coping mechanism."

It didn't sound like a joke when they stood this close.

"I've never had a more enjoyable coping mechanism," he returned, mouth only inches from hers.

"Yeah, me either."

Cassandra's fingers latched onto Spencer's coat as he closed the distance. His head roared victoriously, the hand on her back pressing her closer still. He ignored the potential disaster looming on the other side of the door, reveling in the moment. Kissing Cassandra for the first time had frightened him. This time, it confirmed everything he'd ever thought about her.

Impulsive or not, Spencer wanted this relationship with Cassandra. He didn't care that they'd known each other for a month or that they were fighting for their lives. She was worth every reckless choice in the world.

A voice broke through the moment, feminine and ringing through the hall as muffled footsteps grew nearer. Spencer and Cassandra jerked apart, holding their breaths. Which was intolerably difficult as they'd just been kissing.

Spencer's heart felt like a hammer against a brick wall inside his chest. He feared that they'd made noise, drawing attention to themselves. Did he knock something off the shelves? Somehow, his hand had drifted from Cassandra's arm to her neck, his thumb brushing her jawline. He didn't even remember doing that. What else had happened when he'd lost control of his senses?

"Look," a man was saying. "I just had to put up with you for five straight hours, so I'd really appreciate a single minute of relief from your bitching."

"Oh, is someone grumpy after his girlfriend refused to talk to him?" the woman said mockingly.

They both sounded around Spencer's age, but the animosity between them charged the air, seeping under the door and through the walls.

The man didn't respond, his heavy footfalls banging terrifyingly close to the supply closet. Spencer instinctively tightened his grip on Cassandra.

"Hate to break it to you, sweetie," the woman continued, her tone filled with derision, "but you and I have a lifetime ahead of us. And I didn't sign up to be the consolation prize."

A door opened with a soft creak, their voices now startlingly loud. The couple stood right in front of the closet. "Let's just get the codex and get out of here," the man returned.

Spencer blinked into the darkness. Cassandra must have been right. The Druids *were* keeping things in Alexander's office. But who were these people that he trusted enough to retrieve this special book?

Their footsteps marked their path into the office. Spencer could hear the sound of a drawer opening as the woman began to speak again. "You know, you've been getting rather feisty lately. It makes me wonder . . ."

"Wonder, what?"

There was a pause, and Spencer imagined this young woman goading the man, daring him with some knowing look. "It makes me wonder if you're planning to do something brash," she said.

The silence stretched, Cassandra's leg brushing against Spencer's as she slowly shifted her weight.

A drawer slammed shut, making both of them cringe with tension.

"Let's go," was the man's only rebuttal.

There was a shuffle of footsteps before they came to an abrupt halt. "You agreed to this," the woman said sharply. Then her voice shifted, softening, almost pleading. "We could be happy. We're *meant* to be happy."

Spencer flinched in the awkward silence that followed.

After a short pause, the man's gruff voice came back. "*I* never agreed to anything."

As he began to leave, she called after him. "You're going to have to forget her eventually," she said. "It's that or force your father's hand. Is that what you want?"

"What I *want*, Lily," the man growled, the agitation biting in his tone, "is for you to get the hell out of my life."

She huffed. "Maybe it isn't your father's hand you'll force. Maybe I'll take care of her myself."

Without warning, the chaotic rustle of aggressive action erupted from the office. It sounded like the man had shoved the woman against the wall. Cassandra curled into Spencer, and he found himself wrapping both arms around her as though she were the one in need of protection.

The man's voice came out in a rumble of fury, low and threatening. "If you so much as touch Anna, I will *kill* you."

Anna.

Spencer's jaw dropped. This was . . . Connor Frossard? And his fiancée?

They certainly didn't sound like the happy couple Peter had witnessed. But then, maybe the secrets in DeVerre were more convoluted than even they realized.

A vicious, scornful laugh broke through the air. Slow and insulting, Lily was responding to Connor's violence as though it was amusingly quaint, like he'd shown his hand, and now, she was about to play the trump card.

"Calm down, darling," Lily said, her voice achingly patronizing. "Hasn't your daddy's new pet taken her from you already? That's what the phantom said, right? That Collins boy has got her wrapped around his finger. Probably every other part of his body too. I bet he told your little angel all about your devilish ways. No wonder she couldn't run fast enough from you tonight."

There was no immediate response. Only painful, cruel silence. Spencer lost all pity for the woman. If he were faced with her malicious remarks, he might've shoved her into a wall too.

Cassandra's breath was hot on Spencer's cheek, reminding him of the other words that Lily had said: *That's what the phantom said, right?*

The Druids had a phantom? One that knew about Peter and Anna?

The blood drained from Spencer's face. A phantom that said snarky things when there was no real evidence behind them. One who would perceive the relationship between his brother and their friend to be more than it actually was. One who had first-hand knowledge of her connection to the Collins brothers.

Lily's voice brought Spencer back to the terrifying present. "It's your fault, really," she taunted. "I might've let you keep her if you showed me even a hint of the devotion you give to her."

A horrifying moment of absolute stillness passed when Spencer was sure that Connor would resort to far greater violence. Angered, unsteady breathing was all he could hear coming from the office. The tension snapped.

Heavy stomping marched out of the office, past the supply closet, and down the hall. Connor was leaving. He'd chosen to ignore Lily's dare, and he was leaving.

But she hadn't left yet.

Spencer held his breath, Cassandra's forehead dropping onto his shoulder. He wondered if she'd picked up on the same words as him. If she'd put two and two together and was left wondering. . . .

The slower, more calculating footsteps of Lily crossed out of the office and to the front of the clinic, mumbling under her breath.

Spencer's head roared with fury, her previous words sinking in deeper now.

The phantom.

The damn, traitorous phantom.

Spencer held Cassandra for several minutes after he heard the front door open and close. He didn't want to take any chances that the couple would return. He didn't want to wake the monster he'd worked so hard to calm in his chest. He didn't want to see the guilt that he knew Cassandra would feel, accepting this revelation as her fault.

The closet grew stifling and hot, and he finally eased the door open, letting cool air wash over them.

Cassandra pulled away to step into the hall. She wore an expression of something between resignation and horror. He shut the closet behind him, then stepped up to her side.

"Spencer," Cassandra whispered his name, it alone telling him that she'd come to the same conclusion.

He took her hand. "I know," was all he could think to say. The monster of anxiety rose, pressing furiously against Spencer's ribcage. He couldn't panic now. Fear wouldn't help Cassandra. He had to remain strong and steady to support her.

Her fingers clamped down on his like a vice. "Gerard betrayed us."

Spencer flexed his jaw, grasping for his anger. Rage was better than fear. And right now, it burned through his body like a surge of lightning.

Holding her panicked stare, his voice came out in a dangerous rasp. "I know."

CHAPTER TWENTY-TWO

Peter

Peter was dreaming. He knew it was a dream because he was running again. The pines surrounded him, the fog tingling against his sweat-dampened skin. Shadow-beasts chased him, racing through the trees, hissing, growling, chittering. They were moving to box him in on all sides. It's what they did every time.

He tried to avoid their tricks. He'd run from them enough times to know them all by now. If he went left at that tree, they'd back him into the rock outcropping covered so thickly in moss and lichen that his fingers would slip no matter how desperately he tried to climb. If he dropped off the nearby overhang to his right, they'd be waiting, swallowing him up before he even reached the bottom. And if he went straight . . .

Peter's foot caught on the overgrown root even though he knew it'd be there. He crashed into the forest floor. Rocks and twigs dug into his palms, the snow stinging the cuts.

And the voices began.

"PETER!"

His heart twisted, his throat raw from screaming his brother's name back to him. "I'm coming, Spencer!"

Even as Peter pushed himself off the ground, he knew he wouldn't make it.

He'd done this too many times. His muscles ached, his head pounded, and his limbs wouldn't move quite like they should. He was so tired, so worn down. What had Alexander said when he'd first woken in the Frossard vault?

"I will relish the opportunity to break you."

Gritting his teeth, Peter refused to break.

He doubled his speed, head down and lungs spasming. His side felt like it would split open any second. But he ran as he listened to his brother call for help. If he could just get there, if he could make it through those gates. . . .

Peter's skin crawled as the needle-like claws of a wendigo slashed through the night, inches from his left side. He leaped back on instinct, crashing into a pine tree. His face stung as the needles scratched his skin.

Spencer's scream ripped through the air, a summons to Peter's deepest psyche. He couldn't have ignored it if he'd wanted to.

Pushing off the tree, Peter bolted forward. "Hold on!" he cried out. "Hold on, I'm coming!"

He ran and ran and ran.

Spencer kept screaming.

And then, the forest fell frighteningly silent, the scream cut short.

Peter gaped into the darkness. This was new. "Spencer?"

He started forward again, picking up speed. Only the sound of his boots crunching over snow and fallen branches echoed in the space. Not even the beasts were there anymore.

Hope beyond hope filled Peter's chest. "Spencer?" he yelled again, beginning to jog.

A flash of black nearly struck him in the face.

Peter drew up short, his feet slipping on the ice beneath him. He fell onto his back with a hard *thump*. "Ow," he grumbled, a dense cluster of roots digging into his back.

Without the beasts harrying him any longer, Peter pushed himself up to a seat slowly. He surveyed the silent forest suspiciously. Mist drifted lazily through the pines, the moonlight reflected in its dew. No cries pierced the darkness. No growls, no snarls, no snaps.

Only the flutter of wings as a raven landed on a branch to his right.

Peter eyed the bird. Its glittering black orbs blinked, then its ebony beak opened in a single, "Caw!"

Swallowing past his unbearably raw throat, Peter shifted to his knees, eyes locked on the bird. It cocked its feathered head, blinked again, then, with a flurry of its wings, flew off into the mist.

Peter watched as the thick fog parted around its beating wings, its feathers magically clearing the path. Coiling wisps of mist lifted, drawn back like a veil to reveal a figure. But not the hulking, horrifying figure of a beast he'd expected.

His breath caught, and his body relaxed, fear melting away into awe as he stood.

Moonlight drove back the shadows, falling like an ethereal spotlight on a woman who faced away from him. Her head was tipped back, staring up at the full moon overhead. Gilded in the silver light, her hair shone like molten copper. The cold winter wind sent the hem of her long navy coat fluttering around her calves. It rushed through the forest, nipping at Peter's face with its icy chill.

The raven folded its wings, landing on the woman's shoulder. It crooned in her ear, drawing her attention. The silhouette of her profile glowed in the misty haze.

Peter's body thrummed with something like recognition. He knew her, somehow. That had to be it. Why else would he feel this intense relief at the sight of her?

He took a step forward, the whisper of snow shifting beneath him.

At the sound, the woman turned, the raven taking flight at her sudden movement.

Then it all went black.

~

Peter jerked awake from the dream as he always did, sweat on his brow and his mind reeling. The valravn fluttered its wings unhappily in the corner. He slouched against the wall, blinking away the stupor of sleep.

Peter didn't know what to make of this version of his dreams; how many times had he had it now? He wasn't sure how to tell time anymore, waking and sleeping in strange intervals thanks in part to the drudgery of his existence. In greater part, he thought, thanks to the valravn's influence on his mind. These dreams weren't natural. His regular return to sleep had to be due to the bird-beast's presence.

He raked his fingers through his hair. How long had it been since the raven overtook his dreams? How long since the woman haunted him? Days ago? Weeks? At first, he thought it had to be a bad omen if it disturbed the valravn. Then he realized that was likely a good thing.

What did this change in the dreams mean? The first time the dream shifted, it had only been the raven that made its appearance. That freaky bird flew right in front of his face, knocking him down, and that was the end of it.

It wasn't until the third dream that the woman appeared, outlined in moonlight. Over the course of time, the details started filling in. The red hair. The raven on her shoulder. The navy coat. The profile of her face. She had a cute nose; he could tell that much. But he'd never actually seen what she looked like. He wondered if he ever would.

Yet, in every version of the dream, he'd felt that tingle of familiarity. The sense that he should know her.

In his isolation, Peter had started cataloging every redhead he'd ever met with little success. Most of the gingers he knew were guys. And what few girls he did know personally, none of them had the same tone of rosy copper to their hair.

That was the thing—she wasn't just a redhead. Her hair was a very particular shade of not quite red, not quite orange, highly saturated silky copper. And it was baffling.

After untold hours of consideration, Peter concluded that he had never met this woman. Whatever that strange sensation was, it wasn't true recognition. And he still found her perplexingly disconcerting.

But attempting to place Forest Lady—as he'd taken to calling her—gave him something to think about in his solitude. Thus, think he did. He knew a couple of redheaded girls in college. Both were almost certainly bottle-red. His second cousin, Stacy, had carrot-red hair—which led him to realize that she wasn't even biologically related to him at all. There were a handful of girls throughout his school days. Probably half a dozen others that he'd met through work, church, or wherever. None of them came even close.

It wasn't until today—however many dreams later—that his thoughts dredged up the memory he'd repressed in the farthest recesses of his mind.

Peter pursed his lips, not wanting to relive that particular time in his life. It wasn't so much that specific memory as the ones that followed that he wanted to forget. Now, with the echo of his fourteenth summer pried from the depths, he found himself examining it with fascination.

He didn't even remember her name. That was the cruelest part. Every other detail—every dainty freckle, every toothy smile, every girlish giggle—he remembered that. After all, she had been the first girl he'd loved . . . or whatever it was you called the thing between two fourteen-year-olds at summer camp.

Peter scoffed but allowed himself to linger in the memory of Summer Camp Girl. He didn't want to move past that summer. In many ways, he felt stuck, as though he never *had* moved on. He still felt as he had at fourteen—eager to prove his value. Desperate to earn the respect of both his peers and his elders.

Summer Camp Girl was the one person he hadn't felt the need to impress. Because she was the one person who made him feel seen. She was clever and funny and far smarter than the other girls their age. They were from separate towns, separate churches, seemingly separate worlds. But they'd been put on the same team, and over the course of a week, she became the best friend he'd ever had.

She talked to him—actually carried on conversations with him like he was intelligent and serious rather than a goofy teenager. And she had snark that could rival his. How was he *not* supposed to fall in love with her?

Peter was ashamed he couldn't remember her name. Of all details, he should remember that. Had it started with an A? Abigail, maybe? Or was it an H? Hannah? Harlow? Haley?

The valravn chittered in the corner.

"Yeah, I know," Peter said, resting his head against the concrete wall. "I'm an idiot. I'm imprisoned in a pocket dimension, and my biggest concern is the name of my first crush?"

The valravn fluttered.

"Nah, getting her number wasn't an option," he said. "I wasn't allowed to have a girlfriend then."

In the silence, Peter found himself admitting, "I need to remember her name."

Because Summer Camp Girl wasn't just a girl from summer camp; she was Peter's last memory of being a young, carefree kid. That week with her was the last time he lived without fear of making a mistake. They were the final days before getting in trouble for goofing off or talking too much in class made him feel like a failure.

After her—after those simple memories and rosy feelings—came the worst days of his life. And in the wake of losing their dad, in his effort to take care of his mother and brother, Peter let go of the boy he'd once been. Including the memory of that particularly important name.

The vault door opened, interrupting Peter's sorrowful reverie. He remained slouched against the wall as he glanced over his shoulder. But Alexander wasn't alone.

Both men wore all black, dressed as though for a special event. Their matching golden hair shone in the light. Their tall, muscular builds filled the space with refined egotism. Father and son—near duplicates of one another.

Surprised, Peter sat up. Connor was back?

"I thought that went rather well," Alexander said, dropping a large book onto his desk. Peter recognized it as the book from the other day. Apparently, its use outside of the vault had been fulfilled.

The thought made Peter nervous.

"You made a good showing," Alexander said to his son.

Connor gave Peter a dismissive glance. "You sure we should be discussing things in front of . . . ?" he said, tipping his head toward the cell.

Alexander didn't deign to look Peter's way. "He's not going anywhere," he said, taking a seat.

Though Peter would have disagreed, he wanted to hear the father and son's discussion. So, he did his best to appear non-threatening, slumped in his cage with the valravn.

Connor continued to hesitate. His gaze swept over the cell, focusing on the beast in the corner. His eyebrows pulled together for a fraction of a second. Then his expression relaxed, and he turned back to his father, taking a seat.

"I did what you asked," Connor said. "As I promised."

Alexander huffed. "How gratifying," he said, "to know that I need my son's promise to trust his word."

"When have I proven untrustworthy?"

"Don't pretend that I wasn't there tonight."

Connor turned away.

"I need to see continual evidence of your dedication if you want my trust," Alexander said. "I need proof that your loyalties won't falter."

"They won't."

"Says the boy who nearly caused a scene at a vigil in remembrance of his own family."

Though Connor lounged in his chair, it was clear that he wasn't as relaxed as he pretended. "I beg your patience," he said, jaw tense. "I'm working to erase old habits."

"Yes, they are awfully hard to kill."

Connor's gaze shot to his father's face.

Alexander held up a hand. "A figure of speech only, I assure you."

The tension didn't leave Connor's body.

A sudden memory sprang to Peter's mind. One that had completely eluded him until now. Standing in front of the Frossard house at the town-wide Halloween party, while talking with Anna, Haley, and Cassandra, he'd seen two men talking—arguing—in the shadows. Alexander and Connor. Aggressive pointing, shoving, and collar-grabbing. Father and son in a heated fight about . . . what? Peter never had figured that out.

Seeing the men together again today, it was clear the argument was not resolved.

The charged atmosphere made Peter squirm. What must it be like to feel such anger toward your father? Of course, he'd gotten mad at his dad as a kid. But never like this. Never seriously. Never with such animosity that Peter could only call it seething hatred.

Peter suddenly, irritatingly, felt sorry for the Frossards in their twisted reality of life.

"Everything is in place," Alexander said, ignoring his son's discomfort. "Tony is keeping the town off our backs as the interim marshal. Lloyd is keeping the mayor in line. And Alan is stirring up as much discontent and outrage as he can amongst the townspeople."

"What about the Chapelles?" Connor asked.

Alexander sighed. "We've lost them. But that was a matter of time. We only have to make it another forty-eight hours—" He checked his watch. "Less than that now, and honestly, how much trouble can they cause."

Connor thrust a hand in Peter's direction. "It's been a month since he and his brother showed up, and look how much trouble they've caused."

Alexander's laugh grated on Peter. It was like the man thought he'd already won. Which maybe he had. Peter didn't know much beyond these spirit-induced walls. Maybe the Druids had finally been successful, and his brother and friends weren't alive anymore.

The thought sat painfully in his stomach.

"While the Collins brothers have proven a more challenging obstacle than anticipated," Alexander said, "their end will be no different. I have my plans and contingencies, and the phantom assured me they're blind to them. They're too busy wasting time with those essays to discover what we're up to."

"Essays?" Connor asked.

"The old Lawrence reverend's essays," Alexander said with a wave of his hand. "They're meaningless."

Peter turned away from the father and son to frown.

"Why are they so focused on those?" Connor asked.

"They think they have something to do with us."

"Did the phantom feed them that?"

"Unintentionally, I believe."

"Hm."

In the resulting seconds of silence, Peter turned back to study the pair. They sat in an almost identical fashion, leaning heavily against the back of their chair, elbow on its arm, fingers brushing their jawlines in thought. It seemed that Connor noticed this shared quirk as well, his hand going still before dropping into his lap.

He straightened in his seat. "Do you need anything else from me?"

Alexander's sharp gaze rose from his desktop to his son's face. "No, you can go."

Connor began to rise.

"But first," Alexander interrupted, "I need your word that you won't go after her."

Connor drew in a sharp breath. He towered over the desk, expression blank. "When would I have time for that?" he asked sourly. "You've got me babysitting Lily around the clock."

"We have to be sure she's safe."

Connor scoffed. "You think she can't handle herself?"

Alexander wasn't impressed. "Your mother is taking Lily along to visit the Guillaumes tomorrow."

Connor's brow furrowed. "Why?"

"We want to reinforce their faith in us. After Friday night, we'll need additional support within the town," he said. "We've always known that. We can't have people running to the feds."

"I thought that was Tony's job," Connor said.

"It is. Now, shut up and listen." Alexander leaned forward, propping his elbows on the desk. "I need your word that you won't go looking for Anna Lambert."

That caused Peter to perk up.

Connor rolled his shoulders as if trying to shrug off his father's charge.

Alexander pressed on. "I want you to swear to me that you will not seek her out. Should you find yourself in the same room with her for whatever reason, I need to know you won't so much as look at her, let alone talk to her. I want you to vow on her blood that you will turn around and walk out."

Though Peter was sure it only took a couple of seconds, he could have sworn the following silence lasted ages as Connor glared at his father. The men held each other's furious gaze. Connor's jaw went rigid as Alexander waited.

Connor let out an almost inaudible huff. "Go to hell," he told his father, then walked out of the vault.

Peter watched as the door closed behind the young Frossard's retreating form. Then he turned back to the father at his desk. Alexander glared into space, his mouth covered by clasped hands.

The words of the conversation rolled over and over through Peter's head. Something more was going on than any of them knew. The plans were set. The essays were a distraction. But the Frossards were at odds.

All that nonsense about demanding that Connor not see Anna . . .

Peter wondered why Connor cared so much. He was engaged to Lily. It wasn't like he'd ever loved Anna the way that she loved him. Maybe he just felt guilty. Perhaps apologizing was his last-ditch effort before taking over the whole of DeVerre with his family.

But why?

"Whatever puzzle you think you're solving, Mr. Collins," Alexander said, rising from his seat, "I'd advise you to stop trying so hard."

Peter leaned heavily against the cell bars. "Why's that?" he asked.

"Because valravn feast on the mind," the Druid said. "The more you think, the more you give the beast to work with."

A clack of a beak came from the corner, and Peter flinched.

Alexander's eyes shone with cruelty. "And the darker your dreams will get."

But as the man walked out of the vault, Peter thought of the woman with the raven and wondered if there were some things even the Druid leader couldn't control.

CHAPTER TWENTY-THREE

Cassandra

Rage blinded Cassandra. They jumped back through the wall to leave the clinic, crossed the icy field to the town plaza, and wound through the black night in the Jeep. But like highway hypnosis, she didn't remember any of it. Her mind had fixed itself on one thing: Gerard was a traitor.

The moment she'd heard the words "the phantom," Cassandra felt a missing link lock into place. The familiar sensation she'd felt at DeVerre Chapel when they'd discovered Peter was gone. The missing traitor who'd told the Druids of their secret meeting with the Militia. The Druids' early arrival to Occasus when they'd finally solved the puzzle.

She'd tried to deny it at first, telling herself that the Druids had another phantom. Gerard couldn't betray them. She'd set up rules with him. Hard and fast rules that Elijah Lawrence's essays said could not be broken without also breaking the tether. So, there was no way for Gerard to be a traitor. He couldn't lie to her; he couldn't have hidden the truth for so long.

But Cassandra knew it. Standing in that supply closet, held in Spencer's arms, she knew it like she knew Diane had never become a ghost. Gerard *was* a traitor.

The second Spencer parked the Jeep in front of Occasus, Cassandra leaped out of the vehicle. They'd been silent the entire drive back. He must have known that anger boiled under her skin. It seared across every nerve of her body with such heat she thought she might spontaneously combust.

Stoically, Cassandra moved up the porch steps, waiting patiently for Spencer to unlock the front door, then pushed inside. Nex and Anguis bounded up to them. Spencer was gracious enough to give both dogs a pat on the head before hanging up his coat. Cassandra didn't bother with trivial housekeeping.

She yanked off her scarf as she reached into her mind, scanning for the sensation of Gerard's tether. The cool thread linked them at the back of her consciousness. One tug and he would appear before her. But Cassandra didn't care to force him into the foyer. She sought his precise location and moved for the stairs.

"He's in the vault," she said, the fact damning.

He was in the vault.

They'd trusted him. Completely. And he'd repaid them with . . . with what exactly? What all *had* he done? What villainy had he participated in?

Cassandra replayed the words he'd said to her so many times, reminding herself of how foolish it had been to trust him in the first place: *"I will do whatever it takes to have my justice."*

Had he been telling her? All this time, had he been warning her? *"I'm betraying you for the sake of my vengeance."* Was that what he'd meant?

Determination reverberated through Cassandra's every step up the wooden staircase of Occasus, to the third floor, through the hall, and into the spare room. The door to the vault hung ajar. Silas was still there, then.

Good. She'd need his help with this.

Cassandra and Spencer entered the vault. He walked at her side, silent and steady. She'd had a moment of fear in the clinic. She worried that he'd blame her for Gerard's betrayal. She should have seen it, and she knew that. His blame would be justified. She knew that too.

But he hadn't blamed her.

He was at her side, ready to be the support she needed.

Under the bright light of the chandeliers, they stepped past the final row of bookshelves. Silas sat by the desk, a book in his lap as he chewed on the tip of his reading glasses. *"Thirty-six shouldn't be old enough for reading glasses,"* he'd lamented to them just that morning.

Silas looked up from the page. "Welcome back. Find what—" He broke off when he caught their expressions. "I'm gonna guess that's either a 'no' or a 'yes, and it wasn't good.'"

Cassandra wasn't particularly in the mood for the Varon snark. "Where's Gerard?" she asked. She could feel him somewhere on the second floor, but she didn't want to summon him. She wanted *him* to do the work, to come sulking to her, knowing his betrayal was at an end.

Silas frowned. "He said he was tired of studying useless information. I haven't seen him for hours."

She turned to scan the second story. "Gerard," her voice echoed around the bookshelves, "make yourself visible."

The reaction was immediate. He stood a few paces from the rail with a book in his hands. His expression was somewhere between annoyed, surprised, and disinterested. He lowered the book, stepping the rest of the way to the rail. "Did you need something?" he asked.

"Come down here," she said. "And bring that book with you."

In a flash of gray light, Gerard shifted from the second floor to the space before her. He proffered the book to her. Cassandra scanned the spine. "What is this?" she demanded.

"A book of poetry," Gerard said.

"Why were you reading it?"

"It looked interesting."

Narrowing her eyes, Cassandra questioned everything she'd ever known about phantoms. Was it possible that every rule she'd set had never been effective? Was he lying to her now?

Cassandra glared at him. "Is it true?" she asked.

Gerard blinked, his warm brown eyes ever cunning. "Is what true?"

Fury made her voice shaky. "Are you working with the Druids?"

Gerard froze, Silas grimaced, and Spencer stepped closer to Cassandra's side.

Cassandra slammed the poetry book on the desk next to her. "Answer me!"

"Yes," Gerard said flatly.

The shock of the truth hit her full force. Involuntarily, Cassandra stepped back, her mouth hanging open.

Yes.

Gerard was working with the Druids.

The heat of anger began to cool like molten lava, turning to hardened rock as the betrayal sank in. Her body felt numb, her head swimming with hurt. "How?" she eked out. "How have you—you can't lie to me."

Gerard showed no sign her emotion moved him. "Not to you, no."

Cassandra frowned, confused.

"Oh, God," Spencer said. "You can't lie to her, so you've been lying to Peter and me. Did you lie to Diane too?"

Gerard gave him a disinterested side-eye.

"Answer him, honestly," Cassandra ordered weakly.

The command took control. "Yes."

Tears sprang to Cassandra's eyes. "Why?"

Gerard pressed his lips together as though debating his answer. He couldn't lie to her—they'd confirmed that—but he was good at manipulating the truth. If he never answered her directly, he could lie because she hadn't been smart enough to enact such an all-encompassing standard.

After several seconds of hesitation, Gerard stretched his neck like he was fighting himself. "You have to be more specific, Cassandra."

"What?" she asked, too desolate for smart retorts.

"If you want me to answer questions truthfully, you need to ask them with specificity," he said. "Otherwise, I *will* find ways to lie to you."

His blunt reply curdled in her veins. "Why would you tell me that?"

"Because, believe it or not, I care about you."

Cassandra had to believe him. But that didn't make it any better. "You are just like those DeVerreans you claimed to hate. You know that, don't you?" she said. "All those people you called selfish and cruel, the ones you called self-serving and manipulative? You're just like them."

Gerard didn't respond. He didn't even react. He only stared at her.

"Why did you betray us?" Cassandra demanded.

"I didn't," he said.

Cassandra's anger flared, but he kept talking. "In case you think that's some attempt at a lie, it isn't. You include yourself when you say 'us,' and it isn't accurate. I never had an agreement with these people you call friends. And *you* were never part of the deal."

Gerard's intensity filled his heavy voice. "I never betrayed *you*," he said. "I only betrayed *them*."

The first tear fell, streaking down Cassandra's cheek. She felt Spencer's fingers brush the back of her hand, but she didn't accept the comfort. She couldn't. Not when the truth pointed back to her. She'd made a mistake with Gerard. A horrible, terrible mistake that got her closest friend killed.

"You betrayed Diane?" she whispered, framing it as a question so he would have to respond.

For the first time, Gerard showed regret. He dropped his eyes to the rug. "Yes," he admitted, his voice dull and . . . was that apologetic?

So many questions rang through Cassandra's mind. All the details she'd needed to know for so long, all the secrets and missing answers they'd never managed to find, Gerard held them all.

Cassandra's body shook weakly, and she took the seat next to Silas. "Tell me everything you know," she ordered, making sure to be specific as he'd advised. "Every last detail. Don't lie about anything. Don't hold back anything. Start with when you chose to work with them until this very moment."

Gerard pressed his lips together as though attempting to fight the command.

Spencer sat on the edge of the desk by Cassandra's side, near enough that he could touch her, though he didn't. Silas set a hand to his mouth as he listened. They were all settled in, ready for the truth.

"Four months ago," Gerard said, voice clipped, "while Diane went to church one Sunday, the Frossard boy came for a visit."

Cassandra and Spencer shared a look.

"He didn't seem to want to be here," he said. "The kid's a prick, I can tell you that much. I got the sense that he was here on orders. Like he didn't want anything to do with the job. But he stood on the porch and knocked. I didn't make myself visible, but I listened. It was interesting, and life's boring when you're dead. He introduced himself as Connor Frossard, the son of the man who could solve my problems in exchange for my help."

Cassandra frowned. "How did he know about your past?"

"He didn't," Gerard said. "They only knew that you'd tethered a phantom. The kid said the ghosts at the lake had heard us make the deal. Then he made his offer, saying that whatever you'd promised me, his father could deliver ten times more."

Gerard leaned against the bookshelf. "I didn't buy it, but it was amusing, so I kept listening. The prat began running through various services his father might provide. Useless things, mostly. Information, reconnection with someone living, a new tether to a better location. But eventually, he stumbled upon it."

He stared into the distance as though reliving a memory. "'Is it someone dead?' he asked. Then he said, 'My dad can give you that. If there's someone dead that you want back, he can give them to you.'"

Air swelled tightly in Cassandra's lungs.

"I thought he was talking about Kristina," he whispered. "That he would bring back my wife and child."

Spencer tensed, and Silas shifted. They didn't know. They couldn't have known. Gerard had never told anyone but Cassandra and Diane about his murdered family. His pregnant wife had been slaughtered at the hands of his brother in retribution for not joining the Druids. And everything he did was in pursuit of vengeance for them.

Gerard ran a hand over his mouth as though wiping away the emotion from it. "You have to understand," he said. "I wouldn't have done anything if I hadn't thought . . ." He struggled then, his facial muscles twitching. "Well, maybe that's a lie. But I genuinely thought he was talking about my wife. So, I appeared to him.

"I didn't hold anything back. There wasn't any point if his words got me to reveal myself. So, I told him: If they could bring back my wife, I'd do whatever they asked."

Cassandra didn't know whether to be heartbroken or irate.

"He told me that it wasn't that simple. He had to ensure the spirit was viable before he could promise anything, that some spirits can't be brought back."

"Brought back?" Cassandra repeated in shock.

Gerard nodded. "Evidently, there are certain spirits that can be returned to life. Resurrected, like your Christ."

Silas held up a forestalling hand. "That's hearsay," he said. "Raising the dead—it's theoretical. It happens, but to suggest that anyone could do it at will—"

"Whatever your own cult has told you," Gerard interrupted, "I don't give a damn. The Frossard brat promised me his father could raise the dead—given the right circumstances. So he made me a deal: He would find out if my wife could be brought back."

Gerard paused. "He came back the following Sunday," he said, more subdued now. "He told me that my wife's spirit wasn't in DeVerre anymore. She'd moved on. But he had an alternative."

Cassandra knew the answer before Gerard said, "He would give my brother, Franklin, to me. The man who murdered my wife and then murdered me two years later."

"How could any brother ever . . . ?" Spencer whispered, his voice hollow.

Cassandra knew his confusion came from someone who didn't understand the complications of a toxic family. His brother and his parents—they were all part of some fairytale, only marred by the premature death of their father. Spencer could never fathom a brother being so cruel because he and Peter were wholly devoted to one another.

Hatred gleamed with greed in Gerard's dark eyes. His lips twitched into a cruel smile. "They promised to resurrect Franklin and let me have him," he said. "After sixty-three years, I'd finally have my revenge."

"How? You can't hurt anyone," Cassandra said.

Unflinchingly, Gerard held her glare. "Not this way," he said. "Alexander agreed to bring me back too. Then I'd take Franklin's life as he'd taken my wife's, my child's, and my own. But only after I'd made him suffer the same way he tortured me."

The growl of his voice vibrated across Cassandra's skin. Whatever his explicit plans included, she didn't want to know. His words were violent enough.

"You sold Diane's life for your brother's?" Cassandra said.

"I did."

"So, that was your deal with them? They would give you Franklin if you helped them murder Diane?"

"Not—not quite."

"Then what was it?"

Gerard tensed, fighting the compulsion to answer. "The original deal," he ground out, "was Franklin's life in exchange for my help unlocking the Veil."

At Cassandra's side, Silas pinched the bridge of his nose.

"There was information they needed from Occasus," Gerard said, "information from the vault. They knew they'd never get Diane to let them in. But they also doubted her ability to find it. They'd watched and saw that she showed little signs of power. I didn't understand at the time, but I didn't care to. So, the deal was that I would share information with them to aid their plans until we both got what we wanted."

Gerard shrugged. "It wasn't until I overheard Diane arranging to include you in her will that we saw a way forward. I informed them, and they kept me ignorant of their plans, so I wouldn't have answers if you asked for them. A month later, Diane was dead."

"She trusted you," Cassandra whispered accusingly.

That made Gerard's head dip. "I know."

Cassandra closed her eyes, imagining Diane's face. Her snow-white hair, those bright blue eyes, that pale, joy-wrinkled skin, her typical no-nonsense expression that often twisted up into that signature Varon smirk. The old woman had born a heart of gold, a keen mind, and an unwavering loyalty. She'd cared about Gerard's redemption just as much as Cassandra. She'd been the one to insist they go through with the tether. *We should help a suffering man find his peace,* she'd said. *Besides, I'm a lonely old woman. I could use some company when you're not here.*

And he'd killed her.

The whole scheme hit Cassandra then. He hadn't just been part of Diane's death; he'd also been a part of her mother's accident—the means of getting Cassandra out of town. Everything she'd labeled as her fault was all because of Gerard's betrayal.

Which, in the end, was also her fault because she'd trusted him. *She'd* been the one to tether him.

"The unfortunate part," Gerard said sullenly, "was that I misunderstood."

Cassandra straightened.

A cynical scoff slipped from the phantom. "The whole plan hinged on you inheriting everything," he said. "You inherit and it was only a matter of time before the Druids found their way into the vault. They promised they could win you over and said they had some ace up their sleeve. They never told me what it was, but I think they're still banking on that if everything else fails."

Gerard glanced at Spencer with contempt. "But then, the will revealed that you *weren't* the sole beneficiary. No, you weren't even listed as a true heir. Merely a personal representative and a recipient of a special bequest. Granted," he added, "there was the caveat."

Everything came together, and Cassandra turned to Spencer. "The hellhound," he said. "They were trying to kill us so that the house would fall to you."

"An inconvenience," Gerard said. "Easily handled, they claimed. Turned out that wasn't quite the case."

Cassandra twisted her ring, the weight of all the answers overwhelming her. "What about the essays?" she asked. "Do you know who took them?"

Gerard flinched. "Yes."

His withholding made Cassandra suspicious. She narrowed her eyes, scanning him. His chin dipped lower under her inspection, his dark hair framing his face like a curtain. He wore guilt as visibly as the red tie around his neck.

"It was you," Cassandra realized. "You took the pages?"

Gerard nodded.

"Why?"

He snarled. "I didn't want you figuring it out."

"Figuring what out?"

"That you're a Vessel."

His response was harsh, like a slap to the face. And yet Cassandra didn't know what it meant.

"A *what*?" she asked, completely baffled.

Silas sat straighter in his seat, eyeing her with interest. Then he turned to Gerard. "You're sure about that?" he asked.

"Alexander Frossard told me himself," Gerard said.

Silas sat back. "Huh."

Cassandra gaped at the man. "'Huh'?" she repeated. "What's that supposed to mean? What is a Vessel?"

Silas's expression pinched in consideration. "It's a subject for another time," he said, then cut off her rebuttal. "Trust me. You've just learned a lot. Dealing with what it means to be a Vessel—or a potential one, at least—isn't something else you want to add to tonight's agenda."

Cassandra didn't like that response. But she could see in his intent gaze that he meant it. Whatever this news meant for her, the truth would be too much in the midst of everything else she was processing.

Spencer stood rigidly behind her, his hand resting on the back of her chair. His knuckles brushed her shoulder as she sat back, reminding her of other important answers they needed from the phantom.

"What did the Druids want from the vault?" she asked.

Gerard gritted his teeth. "A location," he said.

"What location?"

He swallowed as though trying to keep the answer in. It ground out of him anyway. "Mapleton, Virginia."

Spencer's brow furrowed. "What's in Virginia?"

"I don't know," Gerard said, his eyes locked with Cassandra's to prove he wasn't lying.

"I do," Silas muttered defeatedly. "Or at least, I know what they're looking for. This is . . . *bad*."

"What's bad?" Spencer asked.

Silas tapped his reading glasses against the book in his lap. "They're after something—someone," he corrected. "And if they get to her, things are gonna go sideways, real fast."

Spencer and Cassandra shared a worried look.

"I gotta make a call," Silas whispered.

"Could that wait a moment?" Cassandra asked. "I—I need your help with this next part."

With understanding, Silas nodded.

Gerard understood as well. "Don't do it, Cass," he said desperately. "You need me, still."

"I don't," Cassandra said.

"Cassandra, don't." Gerard held his hands out as though she were about to attack. "Think about it. Put yourself in my shoes. If you were me—if you had your one shot at vengeance, at getting justice for your wife and child, wouldn't you have done the same as I?"

The question burned in her brain. What would she do for her family? She'd killed for Spencer and Peter. Wasn't that all that Gerard was attempting to do as well?

"They were going to give me Franklin," he reminded her, his words hissing with reckless need. "What was I supposed to do?"

Finding her heart and mind conflicted, Cassandra shook her head. She still wanted to help him—she wanted so desperately to see this man she'd once called ally and friend find peace. But he'd sold Diane's life for selfish gain. Could there be any redemption left?

"What if they've lied to you?" Cassandra asked. "What if they never intended to give you Franklin from the start? Like Silas said, raising the dead is theoretical. What if you chose to work with them, to betray Diane, all for a lie?"

"Would you have given him to me?" Gerard demanded, his voice strained. "If I asked you to, would you have raised my brother from the dead? If I'd asked, would you have shattered his soul for me?"

Cassandra didn't need even a second to consider it. "No."

Hurt crossed Gerard's face before it resolved to his typical cynicism. "*That's* why I did it," he said. "That's why I lied and helped them murder Diane. Because I knew you'd never fulfill your promise. Even if it was a lie, I had to take my chance. I had to know that I'd done everything in my power to avenge my wife and child."

Finding her cheeks wet with tears, Cassandra turned to Silas. "How do I remove his tether?" she asked.

"Cass, don't," Gerard pleaded.

She refused to look at him.

Silas held her stare with a compassionate one of his own. "Will it," he said. "Feel the link connecting the two of you, follow it to where it's tied to the house, and will it to dissolve."

"Cassandra!" the phantom begged, the panic in his voice tugging at her resolve. "Please! I just wanted to—" His words broke off into a growl of anger. "Don't do this! Don't pretend that you're any less guilty than me."

The accusation twisted like a knife in her heart, and she felt her lips tremble. He was right. She was as guilty as Gerard. She'd killed for the same reason he wanted to see his brother suffer—because she loved her family. She'd do it again. And she couldn't forget that every choice he'd made, he'd only made because she'd given him the opportunity.

Diane's blood wasn't just on Gerard's hands—it was on hers too.

Sensing her struggle, Spencer touched Cassandra's shoulder supportively.

Gerard caught the touch, and his furious expression turned calculating. His dark eyes flared with wild hope. "I know where your brother is," he spat. "I can lead you to him."

Spencer's fingers flinched. "You're lying," he said. "You're just trying to save yourself."

Gerard grinned bitterly. He turned to lock eyes with Cassandra. "I know where Peter Collins is, and I can lead you to him."

Cassandra gaped at the phantom. Gerard deserved to be untethered; he deserved to return to the purgatory of his own making. But he could take them to Peter.

"Where is he?" she demanded.

Gerard shook his head. "I won't tell you."

"You have to," she said. "If I order you to do something, you have to, or your tether will dissolve on its own."

"Compel me all you like," he said. "I will lose my tether either way.

But I'll make a new deal with you." His eyes glimmered with one last effort at staying in the land of the living. "I'll lead you to Peter Collins tonight if you, Cassandra Clement, promise to keep me tethered to Occasus, find a way to resurrect my brother, and shatter his soul upon his return to this world."

Cassandra stared at him, horrified yet considering.

"What's to say she won't break the deal once we have Peter back?" Silas asked bluntly.

Gerard held Cassandra's gaze, a frightful knowing within his own. "Because she's just as guilty as I," he said. "She's desperate to save me, to prove that she's not irredeemable too. And she can't do that if I'm gone."

Cassandra couldn't breathe. He was right. And, if she were honest, she wanted to accept the deal. Her sacrifice would lead them to Peter. The death of Diane, her mother's accident, the murders of DeVerre, bringing Peter and Spencer danger from the Druids—she could have absolution from those crimes. And more, she could keep her first promise to Gerard and help him find peace.

That, Cassandra knew, meant the most to her. She had the urge to take the deal, to show Gerard this mercy and work with him one last time—to redeem them both.

Spencer crouched next to Cassandra's seat. He set a hand on her cheek, drawing her gaze to his. "Don't take it," he whispered, low enough that only she could hear.

She blinked back her tears as he brushed his thumb along her skin, a gentle caress of encouragement. "It isn't worth it, Cassandra," he said. "End this now. Be free of him."

"I don't want to," she admitted.

He frowned, his bright blue eyes searching hers.

"What if this is my only chance?" she said.

Spencer shook his head. "You can't save him," he said.

Cassandra sucked in a sharp breath. "Am I beyond redemption too, then?"

She could see Gerard looming in the background, working out his plan if she said no.

"That's not what this is," Spencer said. "Everything that's happened—whatever role you played, you're not at fault. And you don't need to redeem yourself."

Gently, Cassandra removed Spencer's hand from her cheek. "What about Peter?" she asked.

His jaw flexed, a sure sign that he was fighting off the temptation. "We will find him," he said. "But not like this."

She studied him to be sure. It hardly felt right, leaving his brother to the Druids when they had their chance to save him. But Spencer was right: She couldn't sacrifice her integrity in an attempt to prove her goodness.

"Okay," Cassandra whispered.

Spencer stepped back, letting her rise from the chair.

Cassandra squared her shoulders, facing Gerard. The phantom had forsaken all signs of remorse or bargaining. Now, he was angry, seething in his selfish drive for vengeance.

"End me then," Gerard said caustically. "But never forget, Cass: That blood on your hands won't wash off. You will always be the reason Diane's dead."

Cassandra opened her mouth to reply but the words stuck in her throat. So, she closed her eyes and felt for the tether, the cool, wraithlike sensation that gave him a tangible form. In her mind, Cassandra gripped the thread, following it to its source—to the front door of Occasus. She'd chosen the front door when she'd tethered Gerard three years ago to symbolize her and Diane welcoming the phantom into their home.

Into their lives.

Into their family.

Mentally, Cassandra reached for the door, fingers wrapping around the cold thread. She felt a sudden jerk on the cord, a pulse similar to a heartbeat. A quiet, violent plea. Gerard's last request: *"Don't take this from me. Don't send me back into darkness and isolation."*

Cassandra felt a tear slip free, dropping off her lashes and onto her cheek. "I'm sorry," she whispered. And then, she pulled the tether free.

For the first time in three years, there was no extra pressure at the base of her skull. There was no cold thread tying her to another spirit. And she knew that when she opened her eyes, there would be no more Gerard Alarie within the House of Occasus.

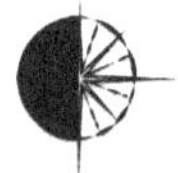

CHAPTER TWENTY-FOUR

Spencer

Nex's snuffling nose tickled Spencer's cheek, waking him the next morning. Sleepily, he opened his eyes, instinctively patting the dog's head. His fingers wove through the wiry fur as consciousness came to him.

He lay on the plush leather couch staring at the vaulted ceiling and ornate chandeliers overhead. After the events of last night, Spencer decided that Cassandra shouldn't be alone. So, he'd suggested they sleep in the vault a second night. She readily accepted, and now, she slept peacefully on the couch across from him.

Spencer rolled onto his side, the woven throw pillow rough against his skin. Silent and still, Cassandra lay bundled up to her neck in the quilted comforter. He could hardly see her ivory face beneath the blanket and her dark waves of hair.

Smiling to himself, Spencer would have lain there longer, enjoying the moment. The dogs had other ideas, however. Anguis joined Nex, prodding Spencer to attend to their morning needs.

"All right," he whispered to the dogs, tossing his blanket away.

Under the still dim lights of the vault, Spencer led the dogs down the hall and into Occasus. Once he'd shut the door quietly behind him, he no longer worried about moving stealthily. He'd learned the previous morning that Silas was a man of routine—up at 5:30 a.m. each day. Checking his phone, Spencer knew the man had been up for at least two hours.

He'd also found a notification from Anna.

She'd texted him only thirteen minutes ago. *"Hey! I'm working the morning shift today. Would you and Cass be able to swing by? I have someone you should talk to."*

Spencer didn't think she was being intentionally cryptic, but he didn't like how ambiguous "someone" sounded.

Spencer followed the dogs into the kitchen. Rich, full-bodied coffee filled the air, the sizzle and pop of bacon a morning melody. Silas stood at the stove, tossing a greeting over his shoulder. Anguis and Nex pushed through the pet door.

When Spencer poured his cup of coffee, he caught Silas eyeing him.

Slipping the pot back into its tray, Spencer turned to the man.

Silas dropped his gaze to the pan of bacon.

Spencer frowned at the quizzical look on his face. "Everything okay?" he asked.

"Hm?" Silas shuffled the bacon with a spatula. "Oh. It's . . . well, it's undecided."

The coffee tasted abnormally bland on Spencer's tongue. "What happened?"

Silas cleared his throat, his eyes flickering to the side. Spencer tried to follow their path. What was he directing him toward? The cabinets? The tiling?

"I think you should look out the window," Silas said.

A shiver raced down Spencer's spine at the intonation of his words. He set his coffee mug on the counter, drifting around Silas to the sink.

The antique frame of the window gave a clear view of the back lawn of Occasus.

Overcast as ever, new snowfall misted down to add another foot to its blanket. Every tree on the property looked tired, limbs drooping under heavy snow. Nex and Anguis crept warily through the yard, their tails tucked as they skirted around figures of gray.

Spencer's jaw dropped. Dozens of men and women stood around the yard, their faces unknown yet familiar to him. They shared the likeness and image of so many other DeVerreans he'd seen. And they were all slightly transparent.

"Ghosts?" Spencer gasped.

Silas tended to the bacon, only mildly disturbed. "You've not seen one before?"

"No," he murmured, unable to find his full voice.

The pet door gave a *slap*, announcing the dogs' retreat. They pressed into Spencer's legs as though seeking shelter. But he didn't look away from the lawn.

Each ghost stared at the house, determined and diligent. Their ages and appearances ranged from youthful to wizened, from modern to centuries vintage. Every bit of them—skin, hair, clothes, everything— was some shade of gray, like a black-and-white TV show come to life. Most of them bore no visible signs of death, but he saw one man with a bloodstain across his shoulder and a woman with a streak of gore splattered down her front. Their numbers were so vast they wrapped around the house, out of Spencer's field of vision. He had no doubt they surrounded the entire property.

"What are they doing here?" he asked.

Silas scooped the bacon out of the pan. "Not sure yet. I assume they were sent to watch us, but I thought I'd wait for you and Cassandra before going to ask."

That got Spencer to turn away from the window. "You plan to talk to them?"

Spencer couldn't tell whether Silas was feigning nonchalance or if several dozen loitering ghosts really didn't bother him. "It'd be nice to know why they're here," he said. "Typically, ghosts don't just hang around one place unless they have a reason. We can speculate why, or we can ask them."

Spencer didn't have a response to that.

"When do you think Cassandra will be up?" Silas asked.

Suddenly, a male ghost made eye contact with Spencer through the window, and he jumped back, no longer interested in studying the host anymore. "I don't know," he said, returning to his coffee mug. Its warmth burned his palms rather than soothed his anxiety. "She's typically not a late sleeper, though."

"Huh." Silas didn't sound overly interested. He tore off a piece of bacon, glancing out the window as he popped it into his mouth. As he chewed, he lifted a hand and waved. Then he smirked. "Well, we won't be talking to that one."

"Why not?"

Silas raised his brow, amused. "He flipped me off," he said. "Typically, that's not a sign of cordiality."

"You think any of them are gonna be cordial?"

"They might be." He took another bite of bacon. "Ghosts are completely alone. They can't even see one another, let alone talk to one another. Sort of like being in perpetual solitary confinement. Only Wielders can give them a break from their isolation."

Spencer shuddered at the thought. "So, you think they'll be grateful to talk to anyone?" he asked.

"Not all of them," Silas said. "But some of them, sure. I've met many ghosts who will talk about pretty much anything just to feel like they're alive again. I'm sure it's why Gerard was so terrified of being untethered."

The memory plagued Spencer. He wasn't sure why. The phantom's betrayal ran deep. If he'd stayed loyal, Diane would still be alive,

Cassandra would be safe, and he and Peter would still be in Norfolk with their mom, stepdad, and extended family.

Perhaps that was why it bothered Spencer. If Gerard hadn't done what he'd done, they wouldn't be here. They wouldn't have met Cassandra—at least, not yet—they wouldn't have learned of their true ancestry, and they wouldn't have gained their inheritance. There was even a chance, that without Gerard's interference, Diane and Cassandra still wouldn't know about the Druids either, which meant that Owen would still be without answers too. And that meant that the Frossards and their disciples would still be living under the radar, uncontested in their attempt to tear the Veil.

Spencer owed a lot to Gerard in a screwed-up way. He had him to thank for their life in DeVerre, the reclamation of their family name, and the pleasure of knowing that incredible, powerful, beautiful woman upstairs.

And now, the phantom was gone, thrust from Occasus the instant Cassandra had dissolved the tether.

As though his thoughts had summoned her, the back stairs creaked. Dressed in her uniform of black sweater and jeans with her makeup done and hair swept back into a ponytail, Spencer was suddenly aware that he'd forgotten to change out of his pajamas in his haste to take care of the dogs. He smoothed down his baggy Norfolk State University tee.

"Morning," Cassandra called, her voice abnormally gentle.

Spencer and Silas returned the greeting as she poured herself a coffee.

Watching her carefully, Spencer wondered if he should try to reassure her. She'd cried for several hours after breaking the tether, silent, contained tears rather than sobs. He'd sat next to her on the couch, arm around her shoulders for most of it.

Now, Spencer felt inept. How should he treat her? Would she like to move on from the events of last night? Or would it be better to be open and direct, regardless of emotional fragility?

"We have a potential problem," Silas said, taking the initiative.

Cassandra looked up from her seat on the other side of the island.

Silas indirectly motioned to the window. "There are ghosts outside."

"Oh." Cassandra gave a bored shrug. "I know. I saw them from the bathroom window."

Spencer felt his eyebrows shoot onto his forehead. "And that didn't worry you?"

She passed him a smirk. "I've seen ghosts since I was a kid, remember?"

"Yeah, but have you seen this many all in one place?"

She thought about that for a second, then shook her head. "No."

"You're really strange," he found himself muttering.

"So are you, dear," she said. Then she looked to Silas. "Did you want to talk to them?"

The man nodded. "I thought we should try, at the least," he said. "But I see no reason to delay our breakfast because of it."

In less than half an hour—after they'd eaten, Spencer took the time to dress himself properly, and they'd put on their coats—they stepped onto the front porch. The ghosts stood everywhere across the snowy lawn. Spencer guessed their numbers reached into the hundreds. Owen had told them that Druids always became ghosts, clinging to the physical world as a tenant of their faith. He wondered if every dead Druid in DeVerre now stood on the property of Occasus.

Silas led them down the steps, out onto the driveway, and straight up to a ghostly, middle-aged woman at the front of the lines. Her cunning eyes surveyed them as they approached, her light hair cropped to frame her sharp jawline. Her floral print dress, straight out of *I Love Lucy*, flared from the waist to settle around mid-calf. A pearl necklace rested atop its high neckline.

"Morning, ma'am," Silas greeted, a broad smile on his face. "Mind telling us who you are and why you and your friends are here?"

The woman scanned him with a bored sweep of her eyes. Then she looked past him straight at Cassandra. "You removed the phantom," she said, her words edged with disdain. "We're his eyes and ears now."

"You mean Alexander's?" Spencer asked.

The woman turned her fierce stare to him and curled her lip in disgust.

"You didn't tell us who you were," Silas said.

"I didn't care to," she replied.

"Why not?" he asked, undeterred and mockingly sweet. "After all, you've come to pay us a visit. It'd be nice to know who we're—well, who he's," he pointed back to Spencer, "hosting."

"We already know you're a Druid," Cassandra added. "So, really, there's no point not to tell us."

"Unless you're afraid," Spencer said. "I could understand that—us being Varons and all. It's no wonder Alexander sent you to watch us. He's scared too."

The woman laughed bitterly. "Oh, no, dear one. Our Elder has nothing to fear from you."

Spencer tucked that title away, hoping his expression didn't show his surprise.

"We made our mistake eighty years ago—letting the blood of traitors and heretics go," the woman said. "But it will have no lasting effect. The plan is in place, boy. The Veil will be torn, and the Varon line will be ended once and for all."

"Well," Silas interrupted, a sly grin on his face. "That's a tad farfetched. There are an awful lot of us these days. You'll have a tough time ending *all* of us."

She sent him a scathing look.

He smirked. "About that name?"

"You're a Varon?" She spat the name like it was poisonous.

"Oh, yeah."

"Of Matthias's line?"

"No," Silas said. "I'm of Edgar's line, his great-uncle. Still from Harmony, though."

"Well, then, Varon, you are still my enemy. Therefore, I have nothing further to say to you."

Before he knew what he was doing, Spencer stepped forward, eyes locked on the woman's face. "Do you know who I am?" he asked.

Her lips curled. "The progeny of a psychopath and a bastard."

Though Spencer knew half of that equation was technically true, he rejected the woman's defamation. "I'm Spencer Varon, great-grandson of Michael, a man selfless enough to put aside his life and future for what he believed in," he said. "And of Seraphine, a woman brave enough to stand up to her sadistic family no matter what it cost her."

"Don't speak of that bitch to me, boy!" the woman spat. "She wasn't brave. She was a whore, prostituting herself to that weak-willed bloodline of yours. Lloyd should have drowned her in the lake the first chance he got."

Despite the contempt filling him, Spencer's mind caught on the name. He scanned the ghost's clothing once more, placing her from the 1950s like Gerard. "You knew Lloyd Frossard," he said.

A glint passed through her eyes that Spencer recognized. It was the same look that went through his mom's eyes every time someone mentioned their dad. Sorrow. Loss. Longing.

"You were his wife," Spencer said.

Cassandra gasped. "That's why you hate Seraphine," she said. "She was a reminder of your husband's infidelity."

The ghost raised her chin in a proud tilt. "That wretched child was a mistake made by a boy," she said. "When we met, Lloyd had long before realized his weakness for what it was. He was faithful to me to his last breath."

Silas cleared his throat. "Well, this has been an interesting history lesson. Do you have any more tidbits to share, Mrs. Frossard?"

She glared at him.

"Fantastic." He took a step back. "You and your ghosty friends have a lovely time being creepy out here. I'm going inside." With that, he turned and walked back to the house.

Spencer eyed the ghost of Lloyd Frossard's wife. She was his great-grandmother through marriage. Not biological but a relation, nonetheless. Did that mean Lloyd and the rest of the Frossards were out there on the lawn of Occasus too?

Spencer looked over his shoulder at the ghosts filling the snowy landscape. Did Seraphine's family stand on the lawn? Were the people she'd stood against, the ones she'd died trying to stop, watching him now?

A strange sense of connection filled Spencer, a link to the Frossard woman who found the strength and courage to defy family. He wished he could thank Seraphine for her sacrifice, giving birth to two children with only the glimmer of hope that she might one day join her husband in this home that now belonged to him.

Spencer and Cassandra followed Silas back into the house. Locking the door, he asked, "Should we be worried about them?"

Silas lifted one shoulder in a dismissive shrug. "Not really. They can't get in the house," he said. "That's the thing about ghosts. Unless they're invited in, they can't enter. Which, I'm guessing, you don't plan on doing."

He glanced over his shoulder at the gray specters. "Nah, I'm good."

"But," Cassandra interjected, "I saw ghosts inside all the time when I was a girl. In my house, in the school."

Silas took it in stride. "You or someone else must have invited them in."

"I—" Cassandra furrowed her brow in thought. "Maybe I did. I don't remember."

Silas shrugged. "Regardless, these ghosts don't pose a threat. They may watch us, but they can't *do* anything else."

The three of them exchanged looks, considering the new development. It wasn't much of a problem, Spencer supposed. A nuisance, sure. But easily forgettable. After all, they'd be spending most of their day in the vault with no means for the ghosts to watch them. Though he supposed that might be a problem all its own. If they knew they were up in the vault, the ghosts might inform the Druids that there was no one in the main building, thus giving them the perfect opportunity to set an ambush for them when they reentered.

He shuddered at the scenario his imagination conjured.

"Did we have any specific plans for today?" Silas asked, breaking Spencer's trance.

"Oh, right." He turned to Cassandra. "Anna texted me this morning. She wanted us to come down to the tavern to meet with someone."

Cassandra frowned. "Who?"

"She didn't say."

She sighed. "It's Anna. There's no reason to be paranoid. Whoever she wants us to meet is probably important."

"When does the rest of the crew get here?" Silas asked.

"Uh—" Spencer thought through their group. "Like I said, Anna's at the tavern this morning. It's Thursday, so Ava's got work, but she said something about taking off early. Though I think Aaron said he's got to work late. So, I'm guessing that Owen and Haley are keeping them company with the whole 'no one's alone' deal. I believe—" he cleared his throat with a glance at Cassandra, "Anna said something about Danielle helping out with that too, so I'd guess she's at the tavern."

"And the marshal and reverend?" Silas asked. "They don't care to help out?"

"I think they're a bit preoccupied with figuring out what's going on with their family and friends right now," Cassandra said.

"So, what do you think?" Spencer asked. "Should we head down to visit Anna now?"

"Did she say when her 'special guest' would be available?" she asked.

"Oh, no, she didn't. I guess I should call her."

While Spencer checked in with Anna, they all parted to continue their morning routines. The "special guest" wasn't available until lunch, and since Anna's shift ended at lunchtime, she could join them for the conversation. Danielle was spending the morning with her at the tavern but would have to leave early to get to work herself—Spencer couldn't help feeling relieved that he wouldn't have to see her. After the meeting, Anna would return to Occasus with Spencer and Cassandra.

"Did she give you a name?" Cassandra asked when he got off the phone.

Spencer sighed at his forgetfulness. "I didn't even think to ask. But she did say that Ava decided to close the library early, so she and Owen would join us in the afternoon too."

Deciding to trust in their friend, they went about their morning. Since Gerard had revealed the Druids' disinterest in Elijah Lawrence's essays, he worried that studying them was a waste of time. Then he remembered that Gerard had taken them to keep Cassandra from learning about being a Vessel. If the phantom found that information important, he thought he should too.

So, while Cassandra finished her morning routine, he sat at his desk in the downstairs office in search of the word *Vessel*.

CHAPTER TWENTY-FIVE

Cassandra

The streets of Harmony Plaza were plowed free of snow and ice. Being in the Pacific Northwest, they'd prepared for the weather. All the sidewalks were salted and clear. The windows of each building fogged from the heaters blaring inside.

Cassandra and Spencer stepped into The Glass Tavern, the late morning light filling the usually dim room. The lunchtime rush brought a reasonable number of customers to the tavern. They worked their way to the bar where Anna stood, filling a tray with freshly plated meals.

"Hey," she said, smiling brightly. Lifting the tray with one hand, she motioned for them to take a seat with the other. "Hang on just a second, okay? This is my last delivery before I clock out."

While Anna delivered the food, they sat backward on the barstools, surveying the room. Despite all her years in DeVerre, Cassandra only recognized the customers by looks and not names. A coil of guilt made her wonder if that was another mistake. If she'd been more willing to connect with the townspeople, could she have avoided the need for Gerard's help at all?

Spencer leaned over, his arm brushing hers. "Who do you think we're meeting?" he asked.

Cassandra shrugged as she scanned the room. All the customers were in groups, with no sign of anyone waiting to meet with them. She opened her mouth to respond when the bell above the tavern door chimed. Her eyes flashed to the man who walked in, and her stomach dropped.

"You've gotta be kidding me," she muttered.

Spencer turned to follow her gaze, but she set a hand on his arm affectionately, drawing his attention back. "Just, uh—look," she said, forcing herself to smile. "Just pretend like we're talking, okay?"

Utterly baffled, Spencer blinked. "We are talking," he said.

She squeezed his arm playfully. "Yeah, but I mean like *really* talking. To the point where I wouldn't have noticed anyone else in the room," she said, casting a surreptitious look over his shoulder.

Spencer began to angle to see what she was looking at, so she let her hand drop to his knee. She felt bad, but he'd used her to get over a panic attack, so she decided this was a fair enough equivalent. He gaped down at her hand as she whispered hurriedly, "Just play along, okay?"

"Play along with what?" Spencer barely got the words out before the man stepped up to their side.

"Hey, Cassie," Jacob said in a mild, cautious tone.

Cassandra looked up, throat tight. Trim and refined, Jacob Howser looked the same as ever. His dark hair was nicely styled, and his silver-blue eyes shone along with his smile. He wore a chunky sweater under his coat, the blue and green Seattle Sounders FC logo on the front. Typical.

"Hi, Jake," she said tightly. "What are you doing here?"

Spencer kept glancing from Jacob to Cassandra, to her hand still on his knee and back.

Jacob's gaze also flickered down. He cleared his throat. "Here in the restaurant or here in DeVerre?" he asked.

"Take your pick."

"Right," Jacob said, resigned. "I'm in DeVerre because I'm the new English teacher."

Cassandra's hand flinched, and Spencer shifted uncomfortably. She removed it to cross her arms.

"And I'm here in the restaurant," Jacob said, "because I came to talk to you."

Anna returned then, beaming at them. "Sorry about that," she said, slipping behind the counter. She tapped the computer to clock out. "I met Jacob last night at the vigil. He told me that you two have been friends forever and that he'd really like to learn about what all is . . . *up.*"

She'd said the last word so pointedly that Cassandra didn't think anyone could have missed her meaning. Though she doubted that Anna understood exactly *why* Jake wanted to talk.

Sending him a hard stare, Cassandra raised her brow. "Really?" she asked.

Disrupting the tense moment, Spencer held out his hand to introduce himself.

"Spencer," Jacob repeated with dejected understanding. "Right."

Cassandra flinched as Spencer's forehead furrowed. He didn't know that she'd told her parents they were dating, and she didn't particularly want him to find out.

Jacob gave Spencer a polite nod. "Nice to meet you," he said. "Call me Jake or Jacob. Whichever you prefer."

Another young waitress that Cassandra vaguely recognized switched places with Anna. "Why don't we grab a table?" she suggested. "It'll be easier to talk that way."

Though Cassandra was sure this could only end in disaster, Jacob and Spencer readily followed Anna. They sat in the booth farthest from the rest of the patrons, the same one she'd shared with Peter and Spencer after they first met. Now, she had to share it with her ex and the guy she'd made out with in a storage closet.

Cassandra grimaced internally. She'd never liked Jacob the same way she liked Spencer. She'd only dated him to make her family happy. They'd parted on good terms—or as good as you could part with a guy who claimed to have loved you since you were teens. They'd even met up for coffee during her time in Spokane after her mother's accident. Still, she wasn't looking to welcome him back into her life.

Anna got to the booth first, scooting in. In a move of desperation, Cassandra bolted forward to sit beside her. There was no chance she was getting stuck sitting next to Jacob. While Spencer eyed her curiously, Jacob wore a knowing frown and cleverly offered for Spencer to take a seat first.

Cassandra glared at him across the table. She didn't trust Jacob, whatever he'd done to convince Anna that he wanted to help. While she'd had other reasons, his insistence that she forget the spirit world led to their breakup. She couldn't believe that he'd changed after all this time.

She twisted her ring, hands resting on the table. "Care to tell me why you took a job in DeVerre?" she asked.

Anna frowned at her acerbic tone, and Spencer's eyes narrowed, but Jacob wasn't fazed. He relaxed back against the brown leather booth. "Ike mentioned that the position was open," he said.

"And why'd you take it?" Cassandra asked.

Her brother, Isaac, and Jacob had been best friends since elementary school. The Clement and Howser families had grown closer ever since. It wasn't surprising that Isaac had confided in Jacob. What was surprising was Jacob's move to DeVerre.

Jacob raised his brow. "If you don't know, then I wasn't as clear the last time we talked as I thought."

The waitress, Reagan, chose that moment to bring water and take their lunch order. Cassandra didn't order anything. She didn't have the stomach for it.

The instant the waitress was out of earshot, Cassandra turned back to Jacob. "You were perfectly clear," she said. "It seems I'm the one who wasn't direct enough."

Jacob blanched. Yes, he'd been clear when they'd gotten coffee. He'd told her that he missed her, he wasn't over her, and he wanted to give their relationship another shot.

Now, Cassandra regretted letting him down easily.

"I told you in August, Cass," Jacob said. "I'm sorry for what happened between us. I was young and stupid. And I didn't understand."

Spencer drew up in his seat.

Cassandra tried to ignore the understanding light in his eyes.

"Oh," Anna muttered, then grimaced. "Oops."

"Cassie—" Jacob's hand landed on Cassandra's in a placating gesture, and Spencer's eyes went wide.

Cassandra yanked back. "You told me that I was meddling in witchcraft, Jake. And yet, you suddenly show up in DeVerre, eager to help?"

He hung his head.

"Why are you here?" she demanded.

"Because I'm worried about you, Cass," Jacob said. "All of us are—Ike, your parents, and me. I know things have been . . . *rough* these last few months. But that doesn't mean we don't care."

"You folks sure have a funny way of showing it," Spencer said, red creeping up beneath the collar of his denim jacket.

Jacob eyed him for a moment, then slowly began to nod. He turned back to Cassandra. "Ike mentioned that too."

Cassandra tried to ignore Spencer's confused expression. "Answer the question, Jake," she said.

He sighed. "Listen, I'm not here to win you back, okay?"

She wanted to scoff.

"I just . . . after what happened with Debbie, things started to become clear," he said. "Everything you'd said all those years ago—everything you talked about, it made sense."

"Because of Debbie?" Cassandra asked.

"Ike and I talk regularly, and . . . well, he was telling me that some weird stuff has been going on with your family. He said that after your last visit, your mom started *acting* weird. And he was concerned about you and your safety. So . . . I dunno, when he mentioned the job up here, I just thought . . ."

"You thought you'd come to protect me?" she said incredulously.

He shrugged. "I thought I'd come to help you."

"How could you possibly help me?"

"In whatever way you want me to, Cassie."

Spencer let out what Cassandra assumed to be an unintentional snort. "So much for not trying to win her back," he muttered.

Jake leveled an annoyed glare at him while Cassandra repressed a smirk.

The waitress appeared with their meals then, summoning an awkward silence.

Anna cleared her throat and offered to pray. They all bowed their heads as she muttered a fast grace. Once it was concluded, she picked at her fries. "So," she began shakily, her eyes flickering to Jacob, "you didn't say that you and Cassandra were, uh . . ."

"Exes?" Cassandra finished. Her eyes flashed to Spencer for the briefest of seconds. He looked adequately uncomfortable.

Jacob sighed. "I didn't think it was relevant."

Ignoring the sandwich on his plate, Spencer turned to Jacob. "What sort of help are you offering?" he asked.

Jacob stabbed a few potatoes on his plate, gaze cautiously averted. "To be honest, I don't know," he said. "I just wanted . . ."

"You wanted," Cassandra picked up where he left off, "to bring me back to Spokane."

A long pause hung between them as Jacob and Cassandra held each other's stare. It felt nothing like holding Spencer's gaze. There was no anticipatory charge, no hopeful patter in her chest, no feeling of comfort.

Jacob let his fork clatter to the plate. "Fine, you know what? Yes," he admitted. "Yes, you're right. Everything I felt ten years ago? It's all still true, Cassandra. I've been in love with you since I was seventeen. But believe it or not, I'm not here to break up you and your *boyfriend*."

He said that word—boyfriend—with such disdain that it was clear he'd love nothing more than to come between Cassandra and Spencer.

"I'm here because you're my friend," Jacob said. "And Ike is my friend. More than that, you guys are my family. And whatever you want to think, if I can be there for you—if I can help you in *any* possible way— I want to. I know I don't bring much to the table. But whether you believe it or not, I still care about you. We all do."

"My family lied to me," Cassandra said, a tremor of hurt in those words.

"Ike told me that too," he said compassionately.

Cassandra blinked. "He knows?"

"Your mom came clean," Jacob said. "To your dad and Ike. I don't think Sandy and the boys know, but . . . Ike told me. Then he mentioned the job here, and I knew—you shouldn't be alone in this, Cassandra. Whatever is happening here, you need people beside you."

Her eyes met Spencer's, and she found herself smiling. "I'm not alone," she said, knowing it was true for the first time in her life.

Jacob caught the look and sighed. "You can never have too many friends, Cass."

Cassandra turned to study him. Whatever his personal feelings, she believed his sincerity. And while she didn't think he could do much to help them stop the Druids, his presence might give them another ally in DeVerre.

Pushing away all her discomfort, Cassandra met Jacob's gaze. "I appreciate the offer," she said honestly. "But right now, Jake, there are things that we need to take care of. Dangerous things that you'll only get in the way of. So, I do—I appreciate you coming here. And when I think of a way you can help, I'll let you know."

Jacob nodded hopefully. "Anything you need."

Spencer pursed his lips, and Cassandra bit the inside of her cheek to keep from laughing at the ridiculousness of the moment. "Thank you," she said, then added, "However, until that time comes, I need you to give me space. Can you do that?"

He took a deep breath, then said, "I can."

"Great." Cassandra turned to Anna. "Thank you for setting this up, but I need to go."

Without waiting for a response, Cassandra got up and headed for the door. She heard Spencer say "excuse me" as more of a demand than a request. But she didn't stop.

The bell rattled above the door as she pushed into the frigid air. Cassandra sucked in a sharp breath, staring up at the gray sky. Her fingers were on her ring, twisting recklessly. Her mother had confessed everything to her dad and brother. What did that mean? Would they support her now? If she went back to Spokane and talked to them, would they finally accept her for who she was? Or would things remain as they always had been, a stilted, pressure-filled exchange?

The door opened behind her, and Spencer was there, Anna right behind him.

Cassandra eyed them both. "You left him in there alone?" she asked.

Anna halted to give them space, and Spencer stepped to her side. "Didn't see any reason to stay," he said.

Cassandra sighed. "I'm sorry."

"For what?"

The matter-of-fact way in which he said it made Cassandra laugh derisively at herself. "Well, I guess I'm not sorry for *you*," she said, then looked back at their friend. "I'm sorry to you, Anna. You were trying to help, and it's Jake's fault he didn't tell you we aren't on the best terms."

Anna finished shrugging on her coat, a playful smile on her lips. "You really dated him?" she asked.

Cassandra grimaced. "He's my brother's best friend," she said. "It was an attempt to placate my family."

"Obviously, it didn't work out," Anna noted, her eyes darting to Spencer.

"Obviously," she said, smirking. She turned to Spencer. "Can we get out of here?"

Pulling the keys from his pocket, Spencer nodded. "With pleasure," he said.

They all climbed into the Jeep, idling to let the heater clear away the ice crystals that coated the windshield. While the classic rock hummed through the speakers, Spencer began to chuckle under his breath as they fastened their seat belts.

"What?" Cassandra demanded.

"Nothing," he said.

Cassandra bit the inside of her lip, fighting a smile. No matter the awkwardness, she thought the meeting was good. If nothing else, it gave her a semblance of hope. Regardless of what her parents and brother thought of her, she felt resolved in the truth she'd told Jacob. She wasn't alone.

Her heart tried to cling to Gerard's accusation that she was Diane's true killer. All night, she'd had nightmares, worrying that he was right. When she stared at her hands, she saw the blood on them.

But every time she looked at Spencer, she remembered she wasn't alone. Whatever her mistakes, whatever her flaws, he wasn't afraid of her. Her power might be dangerous, but she had to trust what Silas taught her. She had the potential to save the people she loved, and whatever the Druids intended, she could stop them.

Cassandra looked at Spencer, his eyes on the road as they drove back to Occasus. Then her gaze moved to Anna in the backseat. She wasn't alone anymore, and together, they *would* stop the Druids.

But first, she decided, it was time to find Peter.

CHAPTER TWENTY-SIX

Peter

Sprawled on his back, foot propped onto the crossbar, Peter kicked out a rhythm on the bars, bored out of his mind. Somehow, the sporadic rhythm morphed into a nearly unidentifiable version of "I've Got a Lovely Bunch of Coconuts" from *The Lion King*. As Peter didn't know much of the melody beyond what they'd played in the movie, banging out such an erratic melody line didn't sound quite clear when the drummer's skills as a rhythmist were notoriously lacking.

"Ever heard of Zazu?" Peter tipped his head to the side to look at the valravn. The cold concrete floor pressed against his temple. "He was a bird too. And he was also put in a prison-cage thing."

The valravn's neon eyes slowly blinked.

Peter stared back up at the ceiling. "Though that one was made out of bones, I think. And he didn't want to be there. Though I guess you didn't ask to be put in here either."

A flutter of wings.

The beast had yet to emerge from its shadowed corner. Peter couldn't say it disappointed him, not knowing exactly what the valravn looked like. Albeit not as strong as Spencer's, his imagination wasn't lacking. The glowing eyes, clacking beak, and fluttering feathers conjured a horrifying enough vision. To discover the valravn's true form would probably wind up causing his nightmares to return to their full force.

Sure, he was still tearing through the woods, hearing the screams of his family begging him for help. That sucked. But ever since that raven flew in his face, ever since that woman showed up, the dreams weren't quite so terrifying.

Plus, Peter had to admit, there was something alluring about that redhead. Even if it was just the fact that she kept him from going completely insane.

The soft *whoosh* of air pressure around the vault door opening met Peter's ears. He raised his head, letting his foot drop from the crossbeam. Time didn't mean much to him anymore, but he was rather certain it wasn't time for lunch.

If he were being honest, Alexander wasn't a cruel captor, beyond the whole bird-beast torturing his nightmares thing. But it wasn't the doctor visiting this time.

Shutting the door softly behind him, Connor Frossard stepped into the vault. In the dim light of the room, his pristine, angular face caught the shadows just right, making him appear rugged and moody. A picture of the morally gray Greek gods that liked to seduce unsuspecting mortal women.

Connor stepped across the room and sat on the desk's edge, eyes locked on Peter.

Peter dropped his head back to the concrete floor. "Sup, man?" he said, tone more cheerful than he felt. "You here to gloat?"

Absolute silence met his quip.

Peter turned back to see Connor sitting there, hands shoved into the pockets of his dark denim jeans. His sharp eyes were focused, scanning his captive warily, like he was looking for something.

Peter raised his brow at the inspection but let it happen. Whatever the guy was looking for, there wasn't much to hide.

Finally, Connor raised his dimpled chin and muttered, "Is she happy?"

"What?" Peter said lamely.

"Anna," he said, his deep voice taut. "Is she happy?"

Peter couldn't help scoffing. "Last I checked? No. She's actually very *un*happy."

Connor's eyebrows pulled together as though disappointed. "Why?"

Baffled, Peter glared at the guy. Then he sat up, resting his arms on his knees. "Well, let's run the playback, shall we?" He lifted a hand to tick off a list on his fingers. "First, you string her along for the past twenty years. Then, when she finally tells you how she feels, you play the biggest douchebag card in the world and kiss her before telling her, 'We're just not right for each other.' Which, seriously, is super cliché, dude. You couldn't think of anything better?"

Slowly, Connor drew his shoulders back with an abashed air. "She told you about that?" he asked.

For a fleeting second, Peter wondered if Connor might be ashamed of that particular mistake. He couldn't help feeling a sense of justification on Anna's behalf. "She did," he said.

Connor's gaze dropped to the rug under his boots, head hanging.

"Next on the not-so-instant replay," Peter continued, "we've got the fact that the last time you were in town, you got engaged to Thumbelina without so much as a word of warning for your supposed 'best friend' who very clearly still has feelings for you. And most recently, she's learned that your daddy's the leader of a cult, and everything you've ever told her is a lie. So, yeah, I'd say she's doing pretty well to be simply unhappy."

"I didn't mean to—" Connor's eyes flashed up to Peter's, words rushing out of him before he cut himself off with a shake of his head. "It doesn't matter," he muttered almost to himself.

Peter frowned. Something wasn't right here. This wasn't the behavior of a douchebag trust-fund boy who got all the girls and didn't care when he broke their hearts. It looked an awful lot like a man who'd royally screwed up and was trying to set it right.

"Do you love her?"

The question hit Peter like he was standing on the road and a car came careening down the bend. "Excuse me?" he squeaked.

Connor worked his jaw before repeating himself. "Do you love her?"

"Uhhhhh." Peter squirmed in his seat on the floor. "I mean, she's Anna. She's hard not to love."

Connor nodded as though he expected as much.

"But I've only known her for a month and a half, dude." Peter found himself laughing. "If you're asking if I'm *in* love with her . . . then the answer is no."

A flare of anger passed across Connor's face. "You're not?" he practically demanded.

"No?" Peter said it like a question, unsure why that was the wrong response.

Connor stood up. "Why not?"

That was *definitely* a demand.

And Peter was more confused than ever. "Do you *want* me to be in love with her?" he asked.

Connor looked somewhere between irate and mystified. "I *want* her to be happy," he said, a thread of desperation lining his voice.

And in that single admission, it all connected for Peter.

"Wait—" He held up a hand as he ran through the details, starting with Connor's return to town weeks ago and the chemistry between him and Anna that practically sizzled the air in the tavern. The frequent glances Connor sent her the entire night of the party. The fight between Connor and Alexander. The way Connor had pointed not at *Peter* as he'd assumed but at Anna. The flurry of apologetic texts and calls just after his engagement.

Connor's behavior wasn't that of a man stringing along a girl, neither blindly nor intentionally.

"You're in love with her," Peter said. "You always have been, haven't you?"

Connor shifted, his furtive gaze keeping well away from the cell now. It was a plain enough admission.

"Why date Lily then?" Peter asked, trying to make sense of the madness. "Why get engaged?"

Shaking his head, Connor's expression twisted. "I didn't have a choice," he said.

Peter felt his eyebrows rise, incredulous. "You do have a mind of your own, don't you?"

"You don't understand," Connor said. "My marriage to Lily has been planned for more than a decade. I never had a choice."

"Hold up—" Peter couldn't help his bemused laughter. "Are you saying it's an arranged marriage?"

The pieces were starting to fall into place, but the concept was so bizarre that Peter struggled to process it.

Connor shrugged. "I guess that's the technical term."

"Wow. Didn't know those still happened," Peter muttered. He ran a hand over his face, the truth sinking in. "You could have said no."

Connor frowned sardonically. "Gee, why didn't I think of that?"

Another piece of the puzzle snapped together, and Peter sighed. "It's why you kissed her," he said. "When she told you how she felt. It wasn't some consolation for her. You did it because you thought it was the only chance you'd ever get."

Connor dropped his head, his expression ashamed. "Everyone in my life is so . . . so loud," he said, the admission coming out strained. "They all demand everything I am and even what I'm not. But Anna . . . From the first moment I remember seeing her, I loved her. And I was only five," he laughed the words with a bittersweet tone.

He rubbed his hands together as though desperate for some warmth, some comfort to ease the pain. "I've wanted to marry her since I can remember," he murmured. "On her sixteenth birthday, I was going to ask her to be my girlfriend. I was gonna tell her that I loved her and that the minute we were old enough, I wanted to marry her. But I wanted to do it right. So, I talked to my dad. I told him my plans and asked for his advice. And do you know what he said to me?"

Peter shook his head even though he knew it wasn't needed.

"He said no." Connor's eyes blazed with fury. "He said, 'We don't mix bloodlines with the ignorant and the weak. Don't degrade yourself by loving a Rayne.'"

After his time as Alexander's prisoner, Peter could hear the words clearly, as though the man himself spoke them now.

"Then," Connor continued, "he told me about my engagement to Lily. He said if I didn't follow orders, then he'd be forced to take Anna from me."

Peter's heart lurched.

Connor gulped as though reliving the moment. "I didn't know what he meant by that—whether he would send her away from DeVerre, or if he would actually . . . But I was too afraid to test him. I was too afraid to find out."

Peter didn't know what to say to that. It was awful—horrible—to be so afraid of your father that you felt you had to abandon the woman you loved to keep her safe. "I'm sorry," he said.

"Don't be," Connor said apathetically. "Just take care of her, okay? Love her because I can't."

Connor's charge made his misunderstanding blatantly clear.

Peter sighed. "We're not together, man," he said.

Connor frowned. "Why not?"

"Because of you," Peter said. "She's still in love with you."

A rapid succession of blinks preceded Connor's broken voice, "She shouldn't be."

"Maybe not."

He nodded like it was confirmation.

Peter scoffed. "But that doesn't mean she should be with me either."

Connor furrowed his brow. His eyes shot back to the valravn in the corner. "You've been having nightmares?" he said rather than asked.

"Yeah," Peter said with a humorless chuckle.

"Is she in them?"

Peter's immediate thought was of Forest Lady. Then he realized by the intensity of Connor's gaze that he meant Anna. And on the heels of that revelation came the other that, surprisingly, she wasn't. In his dreams, he heard his mom's voice and even Cassandra's. But not Anna's.

"No," he admitted.

Connor's lips parted in near irritation like he expected her to mean more to Peter than that.

Without warning, Connor lifted his hand, sending a streak of charcoal energy straight for the cage.

Peter scrambled back, expecting the seizure of the arc to take hold of him. Instead, it sailed right past him into the depths of the cell. A piercing cry rent the air, rising like a siren, high and ringing. The beast exploded into ash and smoke.

Immediately, a pressure released in Peter's head that he hadn't realized was there.

"You won't have them anymore," Connor said as Peter raised a hand to his forehead. He stepped up to the bars, hand on the door. It swung outward, opening.

"Come on," Connor said. "My dad will sense the valravn's expulsion."

Peter couldn't seem to move. He was too shocked to do anything but stare at the man.

"Peter, we *have* to go."

Slowly, uncertainly, Peter settled his feet underneath him, pushing himself off the concrete floor. He scanned Connor, unsure if this was some cruel joke. Maybe it was another of those twisted dreams. The hope of escape, only to be thrust back into the prison once he awoke.

"Why are you . . . ?" Peter didn't finish the question, realizing why Connor was helping him. This was a man ready to overcome his abusers, a victim desperate to become the victor.

Taking his first step out of the cell, Peter looked up at the towering Frossard. "Thanks," he said.

Connor shrugged as though this meant nothing. "Follow me," he said, moving to the door with purpose.

Peter scanned the Druid's vault one more time. His eyes caught on the desk, and his heart leaped. "Hang on," he said. He rushed to the desk, grabbing the small wooden box on its surface. His fingers brushed the smooth grooves of Celtic knots as he opened the lid. There, on the emerald-green velvet lining, lay a smattering of trinkets. He bypassed them all for the gold signet ring resting in its center.

Peter took up the Varon ring and, on instinct, slipped it onto his right ring finger. It fit—snug and secure.

"Okay," Peter said, leaving the box open as he joined Connor at the door.

The young man glanced at Peter's hand, then at the desk with a sly grin. Connor opened the door and led them out into the modern white halls of a house. He headed down the hall, the hardwood thumping under his boots.

Peter snuck after him, trying to keep his footsteps quiet. "Don't we need to, I dunno, be more careful?" he said just above a whisper. "This is a rescue mission, right?"

"I don't know that I'd call it a mission," Connor said, his volume normal. "Besides, Dad's at work, and Mom took Lily to visit family."

Realizing this was the time in which Alexander had charged Connor *not* to go visit Anna, Peter mouthed an "ah" of understanding. They passed through the Frossard's house, a slightly larger and fancier replica of the Merciers'. They walked down the stairs and through the living room. White furniture, glass nicknacks, family portraits, and famous paintings decorated the space. There wasn't a single book in sight, which confirmed for Peter that this could *never* be called a home.

Taking a right off the staircase, Connor led Peter into another hall. He reached for the first door, guiding them into the garage. He flicked on the light and hit the garage door opener in succession. A solitary vehicle sat in the bland interior.

Peter's jaw dropped. "Dude, *that's* your car?"

Connor paused at the side of the shiny black, vintage Land Rover. "Aaron helped me fix it up," he said as though that was what everyone did.

Though Peter hadn't quite picked up the same love of cars, their dad regularly schooled the boys on the most beautiful and often temperamental vehicles, instilling a respect for such antiques. This SUV was undoubtedly from the 1980s and in impossibly good condition. Whoever had paid for it—be it Connor or his wealthy parents—they'd shelled out a ton of cash not only at the date of purchase but to refurbish it.

Going for the passenger seat, Peter eyed the car thoughtfully. "You're friends with Aaron?"

"Well, yeah," Connor said. "After Anna, he's probably my closest friend. Anna and I did everything together, but Aaron was there a lot of the time too. We'd play video games while Anna sketched or painted on the couch next to us. Then I asked him to help me with this guy, and we spent almost every Saturday together for the next year trying to fix it up and get it running."

Shaking his head, Peter wondered what life might have been like if Connor had stood up to his dad years ago. Would Anna be Mrs. Frossard by now, living with Connor in Spokane while he finished medical school? Would Connor have even gone to medical school? He didn't know much about the guy. Everything he'd assumed about the man came from his limited knowledge of his and Anna's relationship, and he'd filled in the rest.

As Connor backed out of the garage, Peter studied the Druid-turned-savior, running through the details he knew. Anna and Connor were the same age—twenty-five. He was in his final year of school and planned to return to DeVerre upon graduation. His dad was the leader of the Druids, and his mom was the leader of the DeVerre party planning committee. He'd broken Anna's heart but not for the reasons she'd thought. That was it.

Now, it seemed frightfully inadequate.

Free from the Frossard house, Peter squinted in the bright light of the afternoon. He marveled at the world around him as they drove down Haven Boulevard. He'd not seen the sun for . . . how many days? DeVerre looked just as he'd left it. Snow-covered and quiet. That meant he couldn't have been gone long, right? He hoped Spencer hadn't gone mad without him.

Pulling onto Whitehill Way, Connor glanced at Peter. "Um, I know this is kind of weird, but . . . I'm not really gonna be able to go home after this, so. . . ."

Peter took a deep breath, trying to steady his rising emotions in the wide-open world around him. "Say no more," he said. "You can stay with us."

"You sure?"

"Well, my gut reaction is to doubt you," he admitted. "But to be honest, I can't believe this is some elaborate trick."

"No?"

"No."

Connor adjusted his grip on the steering wheel. "Why not?"

Eyes locked on the pines surrounding the road, Peter's heart swelled. He was going home. He was going to Spencer.

He cleared his throat, forcing down the tears that welled at the revelation. "Anna," he finally answered.

Connor didn't ask for more.

After watching Connor refuse his dad's order the previous night and seeing his adamance today, Peter couldn't doubt his intentions. This wasn't some trick of the Druids. And for the first time since hearing the name Connor Frossard, he found that, disappointingly, he liked the guy.

"So . . ." Peter said, turning to Connor. "Your dad's a dick."

Connor scoffed. "Yeah."

"We could use your help stopping him."

"It'd be my pleasure."

"Good."

The road rose, giving them the first glimpse of Occasus. Its haunting, Victorian exterior summoned Peter, tugging at his very core. Home. He was going home. Back to the refurbished halls, vintage furniture, large windows, and overstuffed bookshelves. Back to his comfortable bed, a shower, and a toothbrush. Back to Spencer, Cassandra, and the dogs.

"You ever been to Occasus?" he found himself asking.

Connor hesitated. "Yes."

"Oh, yeah?" Peter turned to him. "When?"

"Uh—about four months ago . . . to talk to the phantom."

Peter blinked. "The—you mean Gerard?"

"Yeah."

The understanding came readily. "*You* were talking to Gerard?"

"I was his contact," he confessed. "Dad was too high profile. No one would ask if he was talking to *me*, so it was my job to contact him with our offer. I gave him a burner phone, and we kept in touch."

"He had a burner?"

"He couldn't figure out texting."

A snort slipped out of Peter before anger took back over. "You talk to him recently?"

Connor shook his head. "Dad took over the past week. Said something about things getting too complicated for a middleman."

"Well," he said, "that's gonna be the first thing we take care of."

They passed through the wrought iron gates, the Varon sigil welcoming them. Peter touched the ring to be sure it was still there. Then he saw them, the smatter of ghostly gray figures lining the entire property.

Connor nodded to them. "It's already been taken care of, apparently," he said.

"What—"

"Gerard's tether was broken last night."

Peter gaped over his shoulder at the horde of ghosts as they pulled up next to the line of vehicles: the dark green Jeep, the red vintage truck, the white sedan of Owen's, and an unfamiliar silver SUV.

Peter tore his gaze away from the ghosts. "How do you know?" he asked.

"He showed up at our house last night," Connor said. "With his tether to Occasus, he could only go within a specific radius from the house. That's why he was meeting with Dad at the church when you discovered them. Now that he's a ghost again, he can technically go wherever he likes within DeVerre. Though it takes a lot of effort. He'll probably be stuck at the lake again for a while after the energy he expended to alert us."

"Huh." Peter hardly found it in himself to be interested anymore. Not when he was sitting before Occasus, his brother only a handful of seconds away.

Connor seemed to notice his anticipation. "Real quick," he said, a layer of panic in his voice. "Just—if they . . . they might not accept my being here, you know?"

Peter waved him off. "Ah, don't worry, man. I'll take care of it."

Though Connor didn't show much confidence, Peter wasn't willing to wait any longer. He leaped from the Land Rover, racing for the stairs. A tremulous bark ripped through the air, the patter of paws through snow bringing him to a halt. Anguis and Nex bounded across the lawn, through the eerie lines of ghosts, and straight for the porch. They passed Connor blindly, barreling straight up to Peter. Their paws struck his chest, whining excitedly at his arrival.

Shocked at their enthusiasm, Peter didn't hesitate to crouch and wrap his arms around the dogs' necks. Their wiry fur scratched his cheeks and tickled his nose. Unexpectedly, inexplicably, he had the sudden urge to cry.

Frantic, sloppy dog-kisses assaulted his face then, and he pressed them both back. "All right, all right," he muttered, standing up. "Don't push it."

Peter made his way across the porch, smoothing down his flannel. He realized suddenly that he didn't have his coat or his phone. He couldn't find it in himself to care. They were unimportant, replaceable things. And he was home.

Hand trembling, Peter grabbed the doorknob. Then he froze.

"What is it?" Connor asked, his tone wary.

"Nothing, I just—" He cut himself off to laugh. "I don't have keys."

"So?"

"We always lock the door."

Connor tipped up his chin. His time in the "big city" as a medical student would have taught him the importance of home safety that small towns didn't understand. "Do you think we should call someone?" he asked.

"I guess," Peter said disappointedly. It would be a lackluster return. "I don't have my phone, though."

"Oh, right." Connor snapped his fingers, then pointed to the Land Rover. "I loaded up before coming to get you. Thought it'd be prudent to pack some stuff if I wasn't going to be headed back home, ya know? I grabbed the stuff Dad took from you while I was at it."

"Cool."

Peter was about to suggest that Connor grab his phone when he realized it would probably be dead. He played with the doorknob absentmindedly, considering having Connor make the call himself. But then he frowned, trying to remember Spencer's phone number. He got stuck two digits after the area code.

With a sigh, Peter leaned his shoulder against the door. It gave, and his heart stuttered. The door was unlocked. Something must have happened to Spencer. He'd never leave the door unlocked.

Peter pushed the door, letting it hover open.

Voices hummed through the halls.

Peter's eyes welled up again. That was Spencer's voice.

Summoned by his brother's presence, Peter stepped into the foyer of Occasus, Connor following hesitantly. Anguis and Nex trotted past them both, headed toward the voices. They spoke casually, soothing any worry of danger. Peter didn't care to process their words. He was too focused on the fact that those were the voices of his brother and Cassandra.

An excited bark cut through the conversation, and Spencer chided Nex, who simply barked again.

Following the commotion, Peter rounded the corner into the living room. His pulse soared at the sight of the office. Cassandra sat on the desk's edge, Spencer on her other side, the seeming leader of the meeting. Across the desk, Owen, Ava, and another man—who was that?—stood looking down at something on the desk. And there was Anna, leaning against the frame of the French doors, watching the discussion.

Nex let out another resounding bark, and Anguis nudged Cassandra's hand. She turned to the dog, her gaze drifting toward the living room. Then she did a double take.

Peter grinned, lifting his hand in a wave.

A gasp ripped out of Cassandra's lungs, and her hand shot out to grab Spencer's arm. "Spencer!" she exclaimed, drawing the whole party's attention.

Spencer's gaze flew to her face, then followed her sight line. Straight to Peter.

A flurry of movement burst from the office. Half in the room already, Anna took a step forward, but Spencer was faster.

His brother raced across the floorboards of Occasus and barreled into him, their arms going around each other in a desperate hug. Joy and relief washed over Peter, the tears stinging once more. Laughter shook his lungs as he and his brother clung to one another. The knowledge that Spencer was safe—that he was alive—rippled through him. He didn't realize how afraid he was, how unsure he'd been of his safety, until now. The nightmares had convinced him, however subtly, that his brother might be dead.

And now, a smile indelibly plastered onto his face, Peter took his first easy breath in a long, long time.

Loosening his grip, Peter pulled a step back from the hug. He took in Spencer's face, which was exactly as he remembered it. Wavy, shaggy hair. Scruffy, slightly-more-full beard. Deep-set, sharp blue eyes. Round, youthful cheeks. Strong, annoyingly masculine jawline. Safe and sound.

"Hey, Frankly," he said.

"Connor?" Anna's gasp broke through the moment.

Peter and Spencer both shifted. The others had filtered into the living room, the dogs wagging their tails at Cassandra's side. She stood, one hand on the far couch, a bright smile on her face. Owen, Ava, and the stranger stood behind her, watching with approving, tempered grins. And then there was Anna, mouth hanging open in shock and—was that horror?

Connor shuffled his weight from one foot to the other, a nervous lift to his lips as he held her stare. "Hi, Banana," he said.

Spencer's nose scrunched. "Banana?" he whispered to Peter.

Peter waved him off, intent on seeing this reunion.

"What are you doing here?" Anna's voice trembled.

Glancing at Peter as if for direction, Connor looked like a lost child. "Uh, well . . ." He turned back to Anna, swallowing under the weight of her accusatory glare. "I guess I'm finally doing the right thing."

Anna's usually cheery brown gaze was cold. "The right thing?" she repeated hollowly. She turned on her heel, muttering a flat "excuse me" before rushing past Ava through the office and out of sight.

They all listened as Anna marched through the kitchen, and the back door slammed. Connor hung his head, standing dejectedly to the side.

Ava sighed. "I'm going to check on her," she said. Her gaze swept over Connor before landing on Peter. With a dry grin, she gave him a nod. "Peter."

"Ava," he returned.

After retrieving Anna's coat, Ava hurried to attend to her sister.

Cassandra stepped forward then, welcoming Peter home with a hug. He smiled, looking between her and Spencer. "It's good to be home," he said.

Spencer's eyes glimmered wetly as Peter's vision went fuzzy. Not in a particular mood to cry, he took a deep breath. "Now," he said and slapped Spencer's cheek. "First things first, I'm in dreadful need of a shower. Then you're gonna tell me what the heck has happened in the last . . . How long have I been gone?"

"Four days, two hours, and—" Spencer glanced at the clock, "twenty-six minutes."

Peter smirked so that he didn't collapse. Such a short time. Four days. Only four days. It had felt like an eternity.

"I missed you," Spencer whispered.

Forcing his body not to shake, Peter pointed a finger at his brother's face. "And don't you forget it, J.B."

CHAPTER TWENTY-SEVEN

Anna

Anna's whole body trembled with a fury she didn't know she could ever feel.

How dare he? How dare he!

She'd barreled out of the kitchen onto the small back porch of Occasus only to stop dead in her tracks. She scanned the frozen and snow-covered lawn, the sparkling white pine trees, and the cloudy gray sky. They'd told her about the ghosts that surrounded the property. Dozens, they'd said, maybe a hundred or more. But all she could see was the stillness of winter.

Breath caught in her lungs as Anna stared at the nothingness before her. She couldn't believe he'd shown up, that *he'd* been the one to save Peter's life. And he had the audacity to enter Occasus like nothing had ever happened, to call her "Banana" like they were still best friends.

How dare he?

Tears burned at the back of her eyes. She wanted to leave, to run all the way home and slam the door behind her. She wanted as much distance between Connor Frossard and herself as possible. But she couldn't get her feet to move.

The soft creak of the door behind her caused Anna to whirl. Her rapid heartbeat eased as Ava joined her.

"You forgot your coat," she said, holding the blue puffer out to her.

A momentary flicker of embarrassment heated her cheeks. What must she have looked like in there? She hadn't even said hello to Peter. One look at Connor, and she'd forgotten all about him.

"Thanks," Anna muttered. She jerked her arms through the sleeves. "Did I, uh—I kind of ruined that homecoming, didn't I?"

Ava's wry smile was comforting to Anna in a way few people could understand. Her whole life, her sister had been her role model. She was strong-willed, intelligent, and determined. She wasn't moved by wild feelings or overwhelming sympathy. She stood up for what she believed in and took care of her loved ones with unflinching loyalty.

Since their parents moved to help with their dad's parents in Canada seven years ago, giving their ancestral home to Ava and Owen, Anna had lived with them ever since. And in a strange way, they'd become her surrogate parents, the people she most looked up to for advice and direction.

The very thing she needed at this moment.

"You didn't ruin anything," Ava said in her signature deadpan tone.

Anna dipped her head, uncertain if she believed her.

"Do you want me to take you home?" she asked.

Anna stared at her feet. Did she want to go home? The well of tears that kept rising and rising within her chest to clog her throat told her that maybe she should. She'd never been good at separating from her emotions. Sometimes, she thought that was a problem. Other times, she found it to be a strength. She was, for good or ill, a tenderhearted person. Oftentimes, it served her. She found that people liked someone with such a warm, affectionate nature. They welcomed compassion and gentleness like a blanket on a cold, rainy afternoon.

These moments, however, were the times she hated her soft, emotional heart. She wished she could be strong and unblinking like Ava and Cassandra. Both of them were so sure and levelheaded. They didn't let emotions run their lives. They didn't crumble when the man they loved didn't love them back.

Even the way Cassandra had faced Jacob at the tavern shocked Anna. She couldn't fathom having the guts to say the sort of things that Cassandra had said to him. And she'd even *dated* Jacob.

Anna had only ever been friends with Connor.

Could she do that? Could she go back and face Connor? She doubted it.

Deep down, Anna wanted to walk back inside, go back into that living room, and march right up to Connor to tell him exactly what she thought of him. She wanted to yell at him and tell him they didn't need his help. She wanted him to know that he wasn't welcome in Occasus, he wasn't welcome in DeVerre, and he wasn't welcome in their lives. She wanted to hurt him with cutting ferocity because he'd hurt her.

The thought sent chills across her skin.

She could never do it. She could never have that kind of brutal strength.

Ava's steady presence reminded Anna that she was waiting for her answer. "Should I go home?" she asked.

"It's up to you."

Truly unable to read her sister's thoughts, Anna sighed. "I shouldn't be okay with this, should I?" she asked in a desperate plea for validation. "I *should* be mad at him."

"Maybe," Ava said. "I only know what you've told me and what I've seen through the years. But I'd imagine that if he's here, the situation is more complex than we ever realized."

She couldn't help glowering at her and her diplomatic reply. "He's a Druid."

"Seems that way. But maybe there are things that we don't understand."

"He lied to me."

The moment Anna said it, she realized who she was talking to.

A knowing grin came to Ava's lips. "Speaking from personal experience," she said, "sometimes, people lie to the ones they love to protect them. Doesn't make it right, but . . . sometimes, we don't know what else to do."

Anna played with the pendant on her necklace, considering. When they'd learned of Owen's lies a week ago, she'd chosen to forgive him, to trust him, and accept that what he'd done, he'd done out of love. She'd argued with Ava constantly, telling her sister that she should listen and take Owen back.

But this was different, wasn't it?

Owen and Ava were married. Connor and Anna were . . . nothing. They'd always been nothing. Just a childish dream built on lies and imagination and impossibility. She couldn't take him back because he'd never been hers in the first place.

Anna wrapped her arms around her waist. "I don't trust him."

"You don't have to trust him," Ava said. "You don't even have to have a relationship with him. But it does appear that he saved Peter's life, so . . . I think we need to hear him out."

"What could he possibly have to say that will fix everything he's done?"

"Nothing."

She turned to look down at Ava.

"Nothing he could say will *fix* anything," Ava said. "But that doesn't mean it might not *solve* some things. Such as answering questions we've had for a long time."

Anna couldn't quite manage to rid herself of the threatening tears. "I don't want to hear him out," she whispered. "I don't know if I can handle it."

There was nothing else to say. Ava wrapped her arms around Anna, knowing words wouldn't help. Words were useless in the wake of a broken heart. Platitudes or encouragement wouldn't soothe her. The presence of another was all that could mend such an ache.

Anna fought against her tears for another minute before she let them fall. She didn't sob or sniffle. She simply let the lost and twisted memories slip out of her in silent sorrow. Whatever Connor said—whether or not he offered an apology—the past was irrevocably shattered in her mind.

Twenty years of growing up together, of sunshine and rain, of laughter and quiet, of happiness and sorrow—every memory she had of Connor was bound to the dreams she'd carried in her heart. The hope of their life together, what they might have meant to one another, had been tainted by the knowledge that he'd kept such a dark, crucial secret from her.

In all that time, she saw him as perfect. The most handsome, kind, generous, and loving man in the whole world. She put him on a pedestal from that first day coloring together in kindergarten. He was all that was good and right with the world.

And through it all, he had duped her. He'd let her see him as the perfect hero when he was the villain.

Somehow, the tears dried up, and Anna pulled back. "Thank you," she murmured, working to regain her composure. "Am I a mess?"

Ava gave her a scan, a sure sign that she was *actually* checking. "No, you're good," she promised. "You might want a tissue when we get inside, though."

Anna let herself chuckle, then followed her sister inside. The kitchen remained empty, cast in the gray light of the afternoon. She stopped for a glass of water to soothe her tense throat and settle her fragile nerves.

Reasonably recovered, Ava led her back into the living room, where the rest awaited. Or most of the rest, Anna corrected. Habitually, her eyes fell on Connor first, sitting on the far couch. His arms rested on his legs, hands clasped together, and his head hung like a student awaiting the principal. The wingback chairs from the turret corner now rested across from the fireplace, Silas ensconced on one, Owen on the other. Cassandra sat alone on the couch across from Connor, the dogs at her feet.

The group looked up at their arrival. "Peter went to shower and change," Cassandra said, a dry smirk lifting the corner of her mouth. "And Spencer's probably pacing the hall as we speak."

Anna didn't blame Spencer for his anxiety. If she were in his position with Ava or Aaron newly returned to her, she'd probably hound their steps for eternity too.

Ava brushed Owen's hand as she passed to sit on the far side of the couch, and Anna took the seat between her and Cassandra.

Connor returned to staring at his hands.

A painfully long silence stretched before Silas spoke. "So," he said to Connor. "You're a Frossard?"

Clearing his throat, Connor shifted to face the men. "Yes."

"I'm new to town, but from what I understand, that means your family are Druids."

He hesitated. "They are."

"But you're not?"

"Not anymore."

Anna didn't know whether to laugh or cry. Was that the truth or another lie? Either way, she didn't know how to take that. He wasn't a Druid *anymore*. Meaning he had been, and he'd, what? Renounced his past life?

"I think we should wait for Peter and Spencer," Cassandra said. "Before learning more, I mean."

"I'll repeat myself if I need to," Connor said. "I don't mind. Ask me anything. I'll tell you whatever you want to know as many times as you need to hear it."

The sincerity and desperation in his voice made Anna's stomach twist. A month ago, she thought she knew him better than anyone. She would have sworn that she could tell when he was lying. Now, she wondered if she was watching the world's most proficient liar.

"Just one quick question," Owen said. "Did your family know that I was with the Warden?"

"Not until the phantom told us," Connor said. "You weren't on our radar until about three weeks ago."

A look of relief came to Owen's face.

But Anna wasn't relieved. She was irritated.

"The phantom," she said, drawing Connor's attention. He stared at her with something like fear as she continued, "You mean Gerard. Who gave you information on Peter, Spencer, and Cassandra?"

Connor's chin dipped even lower. "Yes."

Emotion pulsed through Anna. She couldn't for the life of her name what emotion it was—perhaps because so many emotions blended together. Sorrow, hurt, anger, shame, fury, panic. She crossed her arms as though they could hold in the building chaos within her.

Connor's lips parted, but he never got to speak as pounding footsteps came down the staircase. Peter's low, playful laugh sailed through Occasus, lightening everything. Cassandra smiled, sitting up as the brothers burst into the room.

Watching Spencer following on Peter's heels made Anna forget her conflicting emotions. Seeing them together again was strangely restoring. Spencer, without Peter, was like a man without a home.

Peter's ever-wild hair hung more limply than usual, weighted down and damp from the shower. He'd donned a fresh thermal and jeans, his face looking more alive despite the clear signs of exhaustion hollowing out his features.

Rounding the couch, Peter whacked Connor's arm. "They giving you the third degree?" he asked.

"Uh, no, actually," Connor said, shifting awkwardly as the brothers sat next to him. He'd never had siblings, and aside from Anna and Aaron, he'd been a loner through most of his life in DeVerre. Being around the easily accepting Collins brothers would be a shock to his standoffish system. "They wanted to wait for you two."

"Cool." Peter turned to the group. "So, I guess you'd like to hear what I've been up to the last few days. Let me just tell you, Frossard Inn and

Suites is a two-star establishment, at best. The food's not bad, though."

Anna repressed a laugh as he gave a true recounting of his days in the Frossard vault. He told them about his cell, the valravn, the nightmares of the bird-beast's design, the full moon Alexander had mentioned, and the Varon ring he wore now.

It was strange seeing Peter and Connor sitting next to one another. They looked and acted so little alike. Connor had hair like the sun, while Peter's was darker than usual with its lingering dampness. Connor's eyes shone sky blue; Peter's were the richest coffee. The planes of Connor's face were rugged and chiseled; Peter's were rounded and gentle. Their pale skin held such different undertones too: Connor's golden, Peter's rosy. Even their personalities differed so vastly: Connor was quiet and steady; Peter was outgoing and direct.

Anna was so caught up in her mental exchange that she realized she'd completely missed the entire explanation of Connor's rescue.

"So," Peter said, "I know that bringing an ex-Druid into the group isn't something we're probably all gung ho about, but I really think he deserves our trust."

Though no one jumped to contradict Peter, there was a notable unease in the room. Spencer clamped his jaw tight, Cassandra shifted nervously, Ava eyed Connor suspiciously, and Owen held a hand to his mouth. However, Silas leaned forward with interest. "I'm open to hearing more," he said.

As Peter gave him an appreciative nod, Anna assumed the introductions had been made while she was outside.

Owen sighed, turning to Connor. "After the past dozen years of knowing you," he said, "I'll admit I'm equally hopeful as I am skeptical. So, I'd appreciate hearing your story, Connor. I'd like to know why you've suddenly changed your allegiance."

With a nervous nod, Connor scooted to the edge of his seat. "I'll just . . . start at the beginning, I guess," he said, deep voice unsteady. "So, obviously, my dad is the Elder of DeVerre."

"Obviously," Peter repeated sarcastically.

Connor's eyebrows pulled together. "What?" he asked.

"None of us know what that means," Spencer explained. "The assumption is that he's the leader of the Druids, but . . . does Elder have some other meaning beyond 'leader'?"

"Oh, right. Uh—" Connor scrubbed a hand over his face. "No, more or less, Elder is just the name for our leader. Every faction has one."

"Faction?" Owen prompted.

"The divisions of our people that live in specific areas. For example, my dad's faction is the DeVerre Faction. As Elder, he makes all the decisions within the town and represents the Brothers and Sisters of Gaia to the Priests."

A tense laugh escaped Silas. "I'm sorry, did you say Priests?" he asked.

"Yeah." Connor shrugged. "They're the Council of Gaia. They give Dad and all the other Elders their assignments, and the Elders make sure the Council's will is done."

Spencer swore under his breath as Silas and Owen shared a dubious look. Anna didn't like how unnerved they all appeared while Connor regarded them as though they should know this already.

Connor held out his hands as he went on. "Listen, we can get into the hierarchy of the Druids another time. First, I want to assure you guys I'm not one of them anymore. I—" his words began to rush out of him so fast that he stuttered as he grappled with the words, "I'm—I'm not even positive that I ever *was* one now. It was never a conscious choice, you know? Sort of like being born a DeVerrean. It isn't something you choose. You're just born here, and then, that's it. This is your life."

Anna could understand that. DeVerre was a strange black hole of a town. It didn't matter who you were; you never left forever. Even her parents intended to return as soon as they were no longer needed in Canada. DeVerreans didn't leave; they just went away for a short while.

"That's how it was," Connor said. "I was born a Frossard—which meant I was a Druid, whether I wanted it or not. Worse, I was the only child of the Elder, which meant I was destined to take his place. I was never asked. It was assumed. And as a kid . . ." He paused as though thinking through the past twenty-five years of his life.

Connor licked his lips and swallowed. "As a kid, I didn't understand what that meant," he said. "I listened to my parents with the blind allegiance every kid has for their mom and dad. I thought they were next to God, you know? Of course, I'd do what they said. It wasn't until I was twelve that I started realizing just how—" He cut off, his eyes darting to Anna.

She pursed her lips, knowing he'd stopped himself from swearing. He never used to curse before college. It was a trait he'd picked up from his time away from her. But he always caught himself when he was back.

"How screwed up they were," he corrected, then added, "I think—I think it was probably because of my time with your family."

He didn't look at Anna. He didn't look at anyone, for that matter. His eyes were glued to the rug like he was afraid to keep talking.

"My parents were always so . . ." He grimaced. "They were so cruel and—and proud about it. Like they didn't care that they were ruining people's lives. They almost took pleasure in it. And then, I would spend the day with you and Aaron and all the rest of your family, and I'd see that families weren't like that. They weren't full of greed and this insatiable need to control everything."

Compassion threatened Anna. She could easily imagine twelve-year-old Connor—quiet, gentle, accommodating Connor—learning that his parents weren't the paragons he'd imagined them to be.

"Anyway," Connor sighed. "I didn't realize how bad it was until it was too late."

"Too late, how?" Owen asked.

Connor blanched. "Um . . ." He squirmed in his seat, glancing at

Peter. "Dad, uh—Dad sort of made it clear that if I didn't do as he said, I'd regret it."

That, Anna realized, wasn't the whole truth. Not that she had to be any great reader of Connor to pick up on that. What she couldn't figure out was why Peter was staring at her.

Brow furrowing, Anna stared back at him.

Peter tipped his head toward Connor.

Anna frowned, confused.

Peter rolled his eyes.

"So, I followed his orders," Connor said, oblivious to their silent exchange. "Until today. Now, I want to do what I should have done the minute I turned eighteen. I want to stop him."

"How do you plan to do that?" Silas asked.

Connor held the man's direct stare. "A couple of ways. Mostly, I plan to help you as much as you'll allow. I'll tell you everything I know, give you whatever information I can, and if it comes to it, I'll fight beside you."

A drawn out silence met his offer.

Owen and Silas studied Connor suspiciously. Ava crossed her arms. Cassandra twisted her ring while Spencer wrung his hands.

"Wow," Peter said with a scoff. "You guys are really paranoid these days, aren't you?"

"You *were* captured right under our noses," Cassandra said. "And we've got a whole host of ghosts on our lawn. Yet when the son of the *Elder* shows up, we don't have Druids knocking down our door to get him back?"

"They don't have the time or energy to waste on getting me back," Connor said.

They all looked at him in surprise.

"It's why they've been so lenient with you," he said. "We—*they* only have a limited number. If they waste all their energy chasing you down, they won't have what it takes to accomplish the Unleashing."

Anna felt her mouth drop open at the ominous statement.

"The unleashing of what?" Ava asked.

Connor sat up, brows drawn together in worry. "You don't know?" he asked, the question directed mostly at Owen and Silas.

In the prolonged silence, Connor scanned the group, his gaze meeting Anna's for a second. She felt the tug in her gut, the pull she always felt when he was near. Then he looked away.

"Tomorrow night," Connor said, "the night of the full moon, the Druids will tear the Veil."

CHAPTER TWENTY-EIGHT

Spencer

The announcement should have flooded Spencer with horror. It should have sent a tremble through his hands, a shiver down his spine, and a constriction in his chest.

It *should* have.

But with his brother back at his side, Spencer couldn't find it in him to be afraid of anything. He had Peter back. What was there to fear?

The rest of their friends didn't share the sentiment.

Cassandra stared at Spencer as though worried he'd have another panic attack. At her side, Anna played with her necklace, and Ava looked about ready to charge the Frossard home herself. Owen seemed to be taking intentional deep breaths. Silas's forehead was furrowed so intensely that his tenish years on Spencer seemed doubled.

However, sitting next to Spencer, with his shoulders back, head held high, and dark eyes narrowed with calculating confidence, Peter held his gaze, undaunted. Together, the brothers would take on these Druids, no matter what their plans. They would stop them, save DeVerre, and finally have the future they'd always longed for.

"How do they plan to do this?" Silas asked.

Connor, who was far nicer than Spencer had expected due to Peter's past descriptions, kept his head lowered as he replied, "I—I don't know exactly. Dad's not super . . . forthcoming with his plans. I know some things, but most of the information he kept to himself."

"Why?" Spencer found himself asking.

"Because he's the Elder," he said. "It's the Elder's job to keep the sacred precepts and prophecies safe. They give their orders, and the Brothers and Sisters of his faction follow them blindly. The only reason I know what I know is because I'm his son, and—well, he was *beginning* to train me."

Spencer massaged the palm of his hand habitually. His first instinct upon recognizing Connor was to toss him out. They'd just rid themselves of the phantom who'd worked with this very Druid. Could it be a coincidence that he showed up the next day?

Yet, for some reason, Peter trusted him.

"Can I ask?" Spencer said. "If you realized you didn't want anything to do with the Druids, why'd you come back? You moved away. Why not stay away?"

Connor squinted at him in confusion. "This is my home."

The answer resonated deep within Spencer. For weeks, he'd been asking himself such a similar question. Why stay in DeVerre? With Druids to fight, a spirit world occupied by his nightmares, and his and his brother's lives on the line, why stay? Why not go back to Norfolk, their mother, and the rote comfortability of unreached dreams?

Spencer's gaze flickered to the golden ring now on Peter's hand. In the hallway upstairs, Peter had shown it to him. *"I don't know why I put it on,"* he'd said. *"I could have just put it in my pocket, but . . . I don't know. It just felt like the right thing to do."*

Staring at the Varon family sigil now displayed on his brother's hand,

Spencer couldn't help agreeing. It felt right, seeing it there on his ring finger like that's where it'd always belonged.

They were Varons, and DeVerre was their home.

Spencer turned back to Connor. "Yeah," he said with an understanding smile.

Gratitude flashed through Connor's eyes, then he returned the smile.

"So," Silas said, "what *do* you know about their plans?"

Connor's eyes flashed to the couch where Anna sat between Ava and Cassandra. "Like I said, they intend to tear the Veil," he repeated. "The how is a little fuzzy, but to my best understanding, they need the power of every Druid left to accomplish it."

"Which is why they only sent twenty of their members after us this last week?" Cassandra asked.

"Exactly," Connor said. "We—*they* were planning to wait until the spring solstice, but then you two got here—" He gestured to Peter and Spencer. "And that kind of screwed things up."

"How did we change anything?" Spencer asked.

Connor's shoulders nearly brushed his ears as he shrugged. "You're Varons," he said. "You weren't supposed to be here in the first place. The house was supposed to fall to Cassandra, at which point we'd—*they'd* get her to let them in."

Cassandra scrunched her nose, indignant. "And just how were they planning to do that?"

Bright gaze flashing to Cassandra's hand as it twisted her ring, Connor tipped a blond eyebrow up. "You're a Sauveterre," he said, and she dropped the ring. "Most of your family are already Druids. It was Debbie's job to get you on our side. With Diane around, that was difficult. Which—" he interrupted himself, eyes growing to twice their size. "I'd like to make it clear that I was *never* cool with what they did to Diane or your mom. Not that I was asked. But . . . I didn't approve."

"You were still Gerard's middleman," she said.

He dropped her gaze, abashed. "I was."

"So, you played your part."

"I—I did."

Cassandra nodded as though validated by his recognized guilt in the scarring of her life.

After a deep breath, Connor continued in an apologetic tone. "With Diane out of the way, Dad said you'd be vulnerable. Debbie was supposed to capitalize on your grief, winning you to our side in whatever way possible. He suggested that she embitter you, make you want revenge, and then lie to say that it was at the hands of those opposing the Druids.

"She was supposed to trick you into letting her into the vault, finding the address, and . . . well, the next step was dependent on how committed you seemed."

"Best case scenario?" she asked.

"They'd accept you as a Druid and use you to their ends."

"And the worst case?"

Connor shrugged. "She'd kill you."

Cassandra held Spencer's stare across the room. He wondered if they were thinking the same thing: Debbie was following orders that fateful night nearly three weeks ago. The Collins brothers had been a fly in the ointment, but Cassandra had become a problem, securing her death.

"What about us?" Peter asked. "Sure, we made it harder for them to get the house. Why did that push up the timeline?"

Connor gave him a "this should be obvious" look as he said, "You started asking questions. You were literally digging up their skeletons."

"Metaphorically," Spencer heard himself correct. He moved on too fast to allow the young man to recognize the amendment. "You mean because we started looking into the spirit world, we forced them to move faster?"

"What were we supposed to do?" Connor said. "If you three kept uncovering stuff, soon the whole town would know what we—*they* were up to. And then, they'd be up a creek, you know? Dad's got most of the council and higher-ups in the town in his back pocket, but the majority of the populace aren't Druids. If they found out that Dad was a murderer, do you really think they'd just let him do whatever he wanted?

"They were running out of time," Connor said. "It was either kill you three, which they tried and failed, or tear the Veil before the town figured out what they were up to. They just had to hold out until tomorrow night."

"Because of the full moon?" Owen asked.

"Yeah."

"Celestial events," Spencer said. "Do they really make the spirit world stronger?"

"According to Dad," Connor said. "Can't say I've noticed for myself. But then, I never practiced."

"'Practiced'?" Peter asked dubiously.

A twitch of discomfort came to the young man's face. "The, uh—the most devout of our people like to go out on the nights of the celestial events to commune with the Veil."

Spencer frowned as Peter pulled an apprehensive look.

"I'd be interested in learning more about that later," Silas said, then moved on. "Let me see if we're all on the same page now: Your dad, the Elder of DeVerre, orchestrated an accident that put Cassandra's mother in a coma for almost three months. Then he ordered the murder of Diane Larkin, under the impression that the house would fall to Cassandra. When it was discovered that it actually fell to the Collins brothers, and they arrived to make their claim on the inheritance, the Elder then attempted to have them murdered too. Why? Wouldn't it just fall to their next of kin?"

"No," Spencer answered. "In the eventuality that Peter and I didn't want Occasus, or that we didn't take good enough care of it, or failed to bring in an income, Diane left a provision for Cassandra to inherit."

"Which," Connor said, "they didn't know until the news had fully circulated. Dad didn't think you two would be much trouble, so they figured they had time to make plans. And they had Gerard here to watch you completely unknown. But then, you started digging around on your own, and while you weren't really hitting on anything important, Dad knew you weren't going to be easily handled. You were Varons, after all. It was dangerous to let you learn anything. So, he told Debbie to kill you."

"The hellhound," Spencer concluded.

"Why Debbie?" Peter asked.

Connor wore a wry grin. "Well, after Dad, Debbie was our strongest Sage," he said. "Though Tony has always been his public right hand, Debbie was his true second. If he needed something done, he went to her. Every death at the hands of the Druids in my lifetime was dealt by Debbie."

Cassandra dropped her head into her hands. Spencer's heart tugged on his compassion.

"Okay, then," Silas said. "So, the attempted murder failed. This prompted the sped-up timeline because . . . ?"

"Because of the prophecy," Connor said.

Silas's eyes narrowed knowingly.

"Years ago, we lost the actual date," Connor said. "But this year marks the Final Unleashing. Or, at least, the prophecy states that the Final Spirit will find its home then. Like I said, the dates got murky, so we're not totally sure when it's supposed to happen, but we *do* know that next year, something major is supposed to occur that requires the Final Unleashing to take place."

Spencer felt like these ambiguous terms and explanations were swimming around in his brain. The Final Unleashing of what? With Silas's reaction to the term "prophecy," Spencer thought it must be serious. But where did prophecies come into play with the spirit world? And why was this the first time they were hearing of it? Was it a distinctly Druidic thing?

Peter jumped in, asking his own baffled question. "How do you lose the date the whole plan hinges on?" he asked.

Connor shrugged. "Druidic tradition passes everything on through our Orators," he said. "They are our record-keepers, essentially like walking history books and encyclopedias. But the problem is, they've been playing a game of telephone for over a millennium. What one person thinks is a key bit of information, another finds to be irrelevant minutiae. Eventually, things get lost in retellings."

His voice took on an annoyed quality. "And *that's* how you lose the date to one of the most important events in the last century."

Spencer gaped at Connor. "Why didn't they write it down?" he asked, incredulous.

"It's against the Druidic code," Connor said. "Though, some are pushing for progress, and . . ." After a glance at Peter, he went on. "There is an unsanctioned codex."

Understanding dawned on Peter's face while Spencer looked at Cassandra. Last night, while they were hiding in the supply closet, Connor and Lily had come to retrieve the codex from his father's office.

Spencer began to fidget, his knee bouncing as Peter pointed at Connor. "That's the book Alexander took out of his vault," he said. "The one you two returned with last night."

Connor nodded in confirmation. "A copy of it, yeah. It's not widely accepted amongst purists, but Dad always thought they were being shortsighted. Passing everything down orally from generation to generation wasn't working. So, about five hundred years ago, some of the Druids began to write down the most important information."

"After they lost the Raven?" Silas said more than asked.

As the rest of the group stared at the man in confusion, Connor blinked in surprise. "Uh, yeah," he said. "When the Warden took Corva from us—from *them*, the Druids sort of freaked out. They had no means of sustaining her prophecies beyond memory. And lots of the details were lost, including the date of the Final Unleashing. So, an Elder took matters into his own hands and created the codex. Dad relies on it more than most, believing that knowledge is power. He lets it guide most of his decisions. Anyway, the codex explains the rough directions to tear a Veil and release the Spectral."

"Wait, what?" Spencer asked, mind reeling.

"What's a Spectral?" Cassandra added.

Silas sighed. "Oh, boy."

"You guys don't know?" Connor asked, scanning the group wide-eyed.

"No," Peter said.

"Wow, uh—" Connor turned to Silas. "You know, right?"

Silas looked like he was preparing to navigate a minefield. "I do," he said cautiously.

"You do?" Owen asked in shock.

"I'm a Varon," Silas said. "And presently, my job is to help protect the Vessel in Gold Mountain."

"I thought you were a park ranger," Spencer said, the term "Vessel" keying his memory. He looked to Cassandra, who had been named a Vessel last night. Silas had promised to explain what that meant, but in the chaos of the morning and Peter's return, the conversation had been forgotten.

"Amongst other things," Silas said.

Connor's brow furrowed as he took in Silas anew. "Gold Mountain?" he asked. "The Leviathan?"

"Not as far as you know," Silas said dully.

He shrugged lazily. "It wasn't that hard to figure out. Obviously, we've known about him and the Wolf for years. That all—" He huffed. "That was kind of a shit show."

"That it was," Silas said.

"When the Leviathan disappeared, they watched for him. I mean, the Druids have people in most Warden towns by now, so when we heard about Varons suddenly moving to Gold Mountain eight years ago, we assumed that was where you'd chosen to take him."

"What do you know about the others?" Silas asked worriedly.

"Well . . ." Connor considered it. "We've got no idea where you're keeping the Bear. He's well hidden. And while the Wolf remains in Porthaven, they won't be trying that again any time soon."

"Smart." Silas smirked dryly. "And the phantom gave you the location for the Raven?"

"He did."

Silas pursed his lips. "Which is the worst one."

"For the Warden, yeah," Connor said.

"They're going to make a play for her?"

"Eventually."

Silas's lips twitched. "I really need to make a call."

"You may want to focus on what's happening here first," Connor said.

Spencer's head felt ready to explode with the back-and-forth. The names. The creatures. The surreptitious language completely escaped his understanding.

"This is it," Connor said, voice taut as if to impress the seriousness of the situation. "If they open this Veil, they'll release the last Spectral."

Throwing his hands up in the air, Peter heaved a sigh. "What *are* Spectrals?" he demanded. "You two need to stop talking over our heads here. If this is such a big deal, then *tell us what it means*!"

Without waiting for Silas's approval, Connor answered. "They're the kindred, the sovereign spirits of the Ether. The mothers and fathers of all beasts."

Six blank, horrified stares fell on Connor. He said it so simply it took a second for it to click in Spencer's brain.

Spencer's knee stopped bouncing, Peter's eyebrows shot almost clean off his forehead, Cassandra froze with her mouth partially ajar, Anna blinked slowly and uncomprehendingly, Ava pressed her fingers to her lips in thought, and Owen's usually controlled expression contorted with shock.

"They're the source of the Veils," Silas said, his voice sharp. "Spectrals are effectively the beings that create the beasts. When a Wielder summons a beast, they're really connecting with the Spectral and drawing forth after its kind."

"And the Druids want to *release* one of these things?" Spencer exclaimed.

"They want to release the *last* one," Connor corrected.

"Oh, God." The words gasped out of Spencer like a prayer.

"That's—that can't happen," Owen said.

"We're going to ensure it doesn't," Silas said, then turned to Connor. "Who do they have prepared?"

"Lily," Connor said tensely.

Peter grimaced while Anna flinched.

"Prepared for what?" Cassandra asked.

Connor met her gaze apologetically. "Spectrals can't live outside the Veil without a tether," he said. "At least, not in their full form. They'll survive, but they won't be corporeal."

"Like a phantom?" she asked.

"Sort of," Silas said, meeting her stare as though trying to impart a warning. "But instead of tethering to a location, they tether to a being."

"A Vessel," Connor said.

Cold fingers of dread traced from the crown of Spencer's head into his neck, shoulders, and chest, draining the blood from his body. He looked at Cassandra on instinct, their eyes meeting. He could feel the worry radiating off her. He wondered if her heart was beating with the same erratic rhythm as his.

"A Vessel?" she said.

"It's why they wanted you," Connor confirmed. "Vessels are extremely rare. So, the Druids sort of collect them as a precaution. They watch for the signs to ensure they have one when they need them. When Debbie begged for you to be spared, they only agreed because they already had a few Vessels prepared since none had been born in DeVerre yet. The only issue was if they didn't control you, they couldn't let you stay."

"Why not?" she almost demanded.

"Spectrals are selective beings," Connor said. "If there are options, they'll choose whichever Vessel pleases them most. To have you in DeVerre—within the radius of the Veil—would be to risk the Spectral choosing you over the Vessel aligned with the Druids."

Spencer's breath escaped his lungs as Connor concluded, "They can't risk your presence in DeVerre because they can't risk the Spectral choosing you over Lily."

"Those freakin' bastards," Peter muttered, drawing their attention. "They were forcing you to marry her because she's the Vessel?"

Anna's sharp inhale cut through the room.

Connor shrugged, plainly avoiding her gaze. "It was supposed to be a mutually beneficial deal," he said gruffly. "She'd get a future Elder for a husband, and I'd get a Vessel for a wife."

"They didn't bank on you being a better man than that," Peter said.

Connor didn't respond.

"Do you have a name for the final Spectral?" Silas asked abruptly.

"No," Connor said. "We simply know that she's female, and they call her the Ancient One."

Spencer spared a glance for Peter at the ominous name.

"Oh," Connor added, "and she takes the form of a bat."

Cassandra's gaze flew to Silas's face. The man was already looking at her, a knowing glint in his eyes. Spencer wanted to leap up and demand answers. Silas was supposed to be helping them, preparing them to stop the Druids. And the whole time, he'd kept this sort of knowledge secret? They were his family. He should have been honest with them.

Peter scrubbed a hand over his face before dragging his fingers through his damp hair, sending a few drops flying to spatter on Spencer's cheek. "That's not horrifying in the slightest," he muttered. "What do we do, then? How do we stop them?"

"You don't," Connor said. "Unless you manage to kill every last Druid before they can open the Veil, there's no way to stop them."

"But you said they won't try that Unleashing thing until tomorrow night. Doesn't that give us the chance to stop them now?"

"You don't get it," Connor said with a humorless grin. "They will do whatever it takes to ensure the Veil is torn, the Spectral is released, and Lily is chosen as her Vessel. If that means killing all of you in the process, they will."

"Right, so why not take the fight to them?" Peter demanded. "We can end all of this tonight *before* they ever get to the Veil."

Spencer nodded, the possibilities falling into place. They could stop this. All of it. They could end it, and the Veil would be safe. Cassandra would be safe.

"We can call Tom," Spencer suggested. "He may be on probation, but he's still got a large number of townspeople on his side. Then we get Gabe and his men to help us too. That's an additional fourteen people right there. Plus, Aaron. And with you on our side now, Connor, we can easily convince the rest of the town of the truth."

Connor let out a heavy sigh. "It won't work," he insisted. "Sure, you've got three Varons, a potential Vessel, Owen, and me. That's it. The rest of the people on our side aren't Wielders. Meanwhile, Dad kept back all his most powerful members from the attack on you all last week.

"Twenty-four Druids against our six," he continued. "All of them more powerful than any that you faced last week."

Spencer looked at Peter. "Forty-four Druids?" he asked. "That's the total in DeVerre?"

Connor sighed. "Specifically, there were fifty-four, including the kids."

"Kids?"

"Teens, mostly. Technically, you have to be thirteen to become an official Druid."

Spencer ran a hand over his face. Teens were involved? Who was he kidding; of course, there were minors involved. The Druids weren't stupid. They raised their children to follow the grand plan just as the Varons had raised their children to protect the Veil.

"Going after them all tonight won't do you any good," Connor continued, "because they'll be expecting it. And they will do everything in their power to stop you, even if it means whittling you down as you go from one house to the next. You include the normal townspeople of DeVerre, and you'll lead them to their deaths."

"Then what's the point?" Peter asked. "If you're so convinced we can't do anything about this, why join us?"

"We *can* do something," Connor said. "I told you, there's no stopping the Veil from being torn. The prophecy ensures it."

"What prophecy?" Owen asked.

Connor blinked, looking at the man as though he'd forgotten he was there. "You guys don't know much, do you?"

"Nope," Peter admitted bitterly.

"The prophecy of Corva, the Raven," he said. "Her prophecy of the Final Unleashing. She specifically stated that the final Spectral would be released and affect an important event next year. And the Raven's prophecies are irrefutable."

Peter grimaced, holding up a hand. "When you say *'Raven'* . . . Do you mean an actual raven or, like, a metaphorical one?"

Connor looked baffled that *that* was what Peter had gotten out of his explanation. "I guess metaphorical," he said. "Though she's known to take the form of an actual raven, yeah."

With a frown, Peter nodded. "Cool, cool."

"And when you say irrefutable . . . ?" Cassandra prompted.

"I mean, they have never been wrong," Connor said. "Not in a thousand years."

Spencer looked to Silas, hoping beyond reason that the man would deny the claim. But he looked as disturbed as the rest of them.

"The Veil *will* be torn tomorrow night," Connor said. "And the Ancient One *will* be released. The only thing we can do to stop the Druids is to ensure *we're* the ones who gain control of her."

Spencer's gaze snapped to Cassandra's.

"Our only chance," Connor continued, "is to go to the Veil tomorrow night and kill Lily."

"She's your fiancée," Anna whispered.

Connor tensed but remained silent.

Peter sighed. "Not by his choice, Annie," he said.

Of that, Spencer had no doubt.

Owen cleared his throat. "I'm not in favor of murdering a young woman simply because she's in our way," he said.

"She's not innocent," Connor said. "There's a reason the Council chose her. She's calculating, cruel, and she'd kill any of you without a hint of remorse."

"And what if we do kill her?" Ava asked. "If the prophecy is true, the Spectral will still be released."

Connor raised his eyebrows. "Why do you think they wanted Cassandra out of DeVerre?"

Every nerve in Spencer's body flared to life. His chest constricted. "No," he said before he even realized it.

Everyone looked from Cassandra to him and back.

But Cassandra held his stare, her fingers aggressively twisting her ring.

"No," Spencer said, louder this time. "We're not using Cass as bait."

"She's not bait," Connor said. "She's a Vessel. This is what she's meant for."

"Eh—" Silas winced. "That's debated. There are more Vessels than Spectrals."

"All right, yeah," Connor sighed. "Just because you're born with the ability to be a Vessel doesn't mean you'll be tethered to a Spectral. They're called the kindred for a reason. The Spectral might not find her compatible."

Silas brushed that off. "Oh, if there's a Vessel around, it'll take the tether regardless of their compatibility. They hate being without a host."

Spencer didn't care about their facts. He didn't care about the details. He focused on Cassandra, studying her stunned expression. She was afraid, he knew. And all he wanted to do was take that fear away, to promise it wouldn't happen. He wouldn't let it happen.

A small, tender smile tugged at Cassandra's mouth, seeing the promise in his gaze. She gave a single shake of her head as though refusing it. Then she turned to Connor.

"If it's between letting the Druids win and becoming this Vessel," she said, voice strong and sure, "I'll do whatever it takes to stop them."

"It isn't easy," Silas warned. "Vessels live marked lives."

She turned to him. "I didn't expect it would be."

"Cassie," Spencer called, almost begging her to reconsider. He knew he didn't have a right—they'd had less than a week together. It wasn't fair of him to stake some claim on her; to demand that she was his and couldn't give her life away without his permission. It was her life to give, not his. It was her sacrifice to make. And he couldn't stand in the way of it.

But, God, did he want to.

"This is the only choice we have," Cassandra said. "If we can stop them from tearing the Veil, then great. But if we can't, then at least we'll know they won't hold this creature in their power."

Connor looked ashamed as he addressed Cassandra. "They'll hunt you if you take her. The Druids will always search for you. They'll always try to gain control over you."

With that signature confident grin of hers, Cassandra's eyes flickered to Spencer and Peter. "Then it's a good thing I've got such impressive friends."

Peter raised his chin in an acceptance of the charge. But Spencer couldn't help his frown. This wasn't right, letting her take on this life. Cassandra shouldn't be hunted. She shouldn't be tied to some dark, horrifying creature.

She should be happy. She should be free of the Druids and their twisted plans for her. This had been what they wanted from the start, wasn't it? For Cassandra to take on this Spectral, then work for them. If she accepted this fate, they would come for her. Again and again.

Angered at the thought, Spencer struggled to draw a full breath. Let the Druids come. He'd protect Cassandra no matter the cost.

CHAPTER TWENTY-NINE

Peter

Everything moved too fast after that.

Cassandra accepted her impending fate, while Peter and Spencer accepted the role of her lifelong guardians. Though they weren't entirely certain what all that title meant—they would definitely need to have a conversation with Connor and Silas to get more details once they figured out the whole Unleashing situation—part of Peter thought it was just how it ought to be. From the day they'd arrived in DeVerre, they'd known this was their job, right? Diane had even said it in her will: *"I ask that my great-nephews should take care of my dear friend—treat her as their own blood."*

Yet another part of Peter said this *wasn't* how things were meant to end. He couldn't put his finger on it, but he knew something was off. Cassandra wasn't meant to host some freaky bat creature. Not really. How could she? How could anyone that Peter loved?

He wasn't given time to dwell on it.

Connor laid it all out for them. Every last detail of the Druids' plans.

Or, at least, all the details that he knew. "I'm still a novice, technically, so Dad didn't tell me everything. I know enough to ensure the success or, in this case, the demise of the mission."

From there, Silas took over, giving his advice. "I've dealt with stuff like this before," he said. "It's sort of a Varon specialty."

Peter didn't know exactly how he felt about Silas yet. He thought he liked him, and the Varon resemblance was weirdly obvious, so it took any edge off suspicion. His direct, dry manner was even refreshing in some ways. But Peter couldn't help feeling perturbed that the man so clearly knew so much and wasn't telling them all of it.

A Warden trait, Peter supposed.

Hours and hours of planning began. Though he still wanted to take matters into their own hands that night, he understood Connor's points. It was too great a risk. If they failed, there was no one to stop the Druids tomorrow. "But if our big plan tomorrow is just to kill Lily," Peter said at one point, "why not do that tonight?"

"With my betrayal, they'll know I've told you everything," Connor said. "And there is no chance my father will leave Lily unprotected. It wouldn't surprise me if he's got nearly all of the Druids camped at his place tonight. He's probably even making her stay in the vault at this point."

That, Peter knew, would be a problem. The only way to get into someone else's vault was to be invited in. And even if he and Connor had access to the Frossard vault, that didn't bode well for their attempts.

"Speaking of vaults," Connor added. "I have a suggestion."

"What's that?"

"Anyone and everyone you love in DeVerre," Connor said, his tone ominous, "I'd bring them here. Let them in your vault, just in case. I don't trust my dad not to do something malicious. If only to get back at me."

Spencer immediately balked at the idea. "I don't think that's a good idea. There's a lot of sensitive information in there."

With a wave of his hand, Connor dismissed the concern. "You can revoke their access afterward," he told them. "And in the meantime, you can create a separate space for them—like a room inside the door that lets them stay there without having access to the space beyond."

Thinking back to his cell in the Frossard vault, Peter realized it wasn't a typical fixture. "We can alter the space whenever and however we want?" he asked, amazed.

Connor nodded. "I can teach you how."

"Which means giving *you* access to the vault?" Spencer asked.

With a knowing grin, Connor shook his head. "Not at all. I'd actually advise you *not* to give me access. Should everything fall to shit, I don't want Dad to have the chance to use me against you guys."

Within an hour, they had a new antechamber within the vault meant to house the innocents of DeVerre.

As the night progressed, Spencer and Cassandra filled Peter in on everything he'd missed. Ava compared notes with Silas, getting her fill of information to add to the Rayne family records. Owen called Tom, Sam, and Gabe to inform them of the updates. Aaron and Haley arrived at Occasus, shocked to find Connor there. Anna explained it in clipped tones, deftly avoiding direct interaction with Connor throughout the evening.

With everyone brought up to speed and safe in the House of Occasus, Peter felt a hollow sense of overwhelm. There was so much to do, and yet nothing left they *could* do. They'd made their plans. Tom, Gabe, and the rest of the Militia—sans Juliet, though Gabe's son, Malachi, was determined to join—would join their team to defend the Veil.

Though Connor warned against including anyone who couldn't wield the spirit world, Peter could tell he was more concerned that Anna would volunteer to fight than anything.

But she didn't.

Instead, she and Ava were to be their representatives, caring for the people who would hide in the vault while they were away. People like the Chapelles, the Garniers, the Ozannes, and others that Sam and Tom had vetted over the past week—including Elizabeth Chapelle, who had taken the news of the spirit world as a shock before adopting her sons' mission as her own. The vault would be full of people who wanted to stand up to the Frossards and their lackeys. People who'd never stopped supporting the Varons.

The one surprise addition to the Veil party was Haley.

Peter's jaw had nearly dropped as Aaron announced this detail, the bubbly blonde standing at his side. "You sure?" he asked.

Aaron nodded but let Haley speak for herself. "My dad and brothers are lumberjacks," she explained. "I grew up hunting with them, so I'm pretty good with a rifle."

"She's a crack shot," Aaron corrected. "If I need someone watching my back, I wouldn't trust anyone but her."

"I'll stay in the shadows," Haley added. "If things get too dangerous, I know to run."

Impressed by her tenacity and unexpected skill, Peter scanned her. "Would your brothers care to join?"

Haley gave him one of her bright smiles. "I can ask."

With the final plans in place, they broke off.

Though there was no need to search the vault for answers regarding the Druids and their plans anymore, Ava and Owen were eager to continue their work. "We need to learn as much as we can," he said. "Whether or not it helps us defend the Veil, there will be tomorrows after that. Days that we'll need to be as prepared for as possible."

"And," Silas said, "it won't hurt for the Druids to think we're still scrambling to create a plan. So, if we're all up in the vault, the ghosts can have something false to report."

While the rest of the group agreed, Connor shifted nervously at the side, reminding Peter of their earlier discussion. He didn't want to go in the vault. And though Peter trusted him, he wasn't sure he trusted him *that* much. He'd let him sleep in their house, but he wasn't ready to give him access to their most valuable assets.

The group shuffled around the living room where they congregated. They moved for the stairs, small clusters forming as they worked their way through. Silas began to speak with Cassandra—hopefully, Peter thought, explaining more of what he knew about Vessels—while Aaron, Haley, and Owen began to talk about how to approach her brothers about the spirit world. Ava and Anna rose, slowly making their way behind the group.

Watching them all walk past, Peter realized that no one had even considered leaving Connor alone in the house. Giving Spencer's arm a slap, Peter gestured to the ex-Druid on his other side. "I'll stay down here with Connor," he said. "Can't say I'm in the mood for research anyway."

"Oh, uh—" Spencer hesitated, clearly not wanting to leave him. "Yeah, good point. I'll join you."

After the past several days, Peter couldn't say he was altogether pleased with the idea of parting from his brother either. "Maybe we could work on those essays or something?" he suggested. He turned to look up at Connor with a lopsided grin. "What d'ya think? You up for some translation?"

Connor didn't appear to be listening. As Anna passed him, he leaned forward and whispered her name with near frantic desperation. Her head whipped in his direction, eyes wide with panic. Most everyone had already made their way up the stairs, only Ava and her remaining.

Anna came to an abrupt stop, Ava pausing at her side.

Connor swallowed but impressively didn't drop eye contact. "Could I talk with you a minute?" he asked.

"No." The word flew out of Anna with a knee-jerk reaction.

Dipping his head, Connor conceded. "Okay."

Anna moved to leave, but Ava grabbed her hand, pulling her to a stop. "The sooner you deal with it, the sooner it's fixed," she said.

"I don't want it fixed," Anna shot back.

"Anna," Peter began, hoping to defuse the situation, but she turned her icy glare on him.

"You're supposed to be on *my* side," she said accusingly.

"I am on your side," Peter promised as Spencer shifted awkwardly next to him.

"Then you wouldn't ask me to do this," she said, looking between Peter and her sister. "The only reason I have accepted him here is because he saved your life, Pete. I have no interest in 'fixing' anything."

Peter couldn't help frowning as Connor stepped back. For some reason, Anna's rejection stung like it was meant for him. Why? Peter and Connor weren't exactly friends. Sure, the guy had saved his life, but that didn't change the fact that he was a stranger.

But Peter realized it had nothing to do with feeling sorry for Connor. He sympathized with the guy, but it wasn't *his* pain that Peter was feeling. This was Peter's own insecurities, his own past rejections that stuck like a burr in his heart. It was infuriating. For years now, Anna had secretly pined after a love she thought unrequited. All the while, she'd never understood that the man she loved also loved her back—he was just a tad stupid. She hadn't been rejected; she'd been cared for. Connor made the wrong choice, but it was out of fear, not indifference. He loved her and didn't want to see her harmed. He'd made the wrong choice for the right reason.

And now, Anna was being too stubborn to listen. She was going to let go of everything she'd ever wanted—everything Peter wished he could have too—because she was angry.

Well, Peter was angry too.

Quite frankly, he was pissed off. He'd spent the last week alone with nothing but his thoughts and a valravn who fed off his terror. He'd had four and a half days to dwell on his worst memories and his greatest fears. And he wasn't about to put up with obstinance for the sake of anyone's pride.

Maybe Anna didn't want to fix it.

But he would.

Jaw set and mind made up, Peter met Ava's gaze. Either she read his mind or trusted him enough to let him take care of it. She dropped her hold on Anna and turned to head up the stairs.

"Right," Spencer muttered, clearing his throat. "I'm gonna. . . ." He motioned toward the upstairs, gave Peter an awkward shrug, and followed Ava.

As he passed Anna, she also began to turn toward the stairs, but Peter didn't let her make it a single step. "Sit down, Anna," he called.

She spun around, her mouth agape. "Excuse me?"

"Sit down," he instructed again.

Without giving her the chance to say no, Peter turned to Connor. He pointed to the couch and ordered, "Sit."

Then he moved around the coffee table to take a seat on the couch across from them.

Anna and Connor stood frozen, the sunset casting a burnt halo of light around them.

Waiting patiently, Peter gave them a pleasant grin. Connor kept blinking dumbly but sat. Anna gritted her teeth, and Peter thought for a moment she might storm out of the room. She huffed, perching on the couch as far from Connor as possible, arms crossed.

Peter couldn't help his amused grin. She was going to make this ten times harder than it needed to be. Which might actually make it more fun.

Looking between the pair, Peter suddenly realized what he'd signed up for. His grin slipped. Wow, he was stupid sometimes. He'd just set himself up to mediate a reconciliation between the girl he liked and her ex.

Well, not her real ex, but still.

Why had he even suggested this? He might not be interested in dating Anna anymore, but that didn't mean he wanted her and Connor together either. Though he supposed it seemed right. He couldn't put his finger on why. But from the moment he first saw Connor and Anna together in the tavern, Peter knew that they belonged to one another. Just like Spencer and Cassandra.

Even now, with Anna stubbornly ignoring him and Connor respectfully bowing his head, Peter could feel the charge in the air, the magnetic pull causing Anna to shift an infinitesimal inch closer to the man she swore she wanted nothing to do with.

With a self-deprecating smirk, Peter shook his head. Whatever insanity drove him to this, he'd chosen it. May as well make the most of it.

"So, this is nice and awkward," he said as he surveyed the pair. "Might be the worst idea I've ever had."

Anna kept staring at the corner while Connor shook his head. "You don't have to do this," he said.

"Well, no, I don't," Peter agreed. "And I'm probably not really qualified for it, but, hey—I'm the only one offering, right?"

Neither responded.

He sucked in an uncomfortable breath. "Mkay, well . . . Annie, I believe that Connor has something he'd like to say to you. I know you're not really in the mood to listen, but I think you should, so . . . maybe give it a shot, huh?"

Anna glared at him.

He returned it with a wink, then nodded to Connor.

Thumbing his nose, Connor shifted nervously. "I don't wanna—"

"Do it anyway," Peter interrupted.

Connor's brow furrowed. "You're really obnoxious sometimes."

"Yeah."

Connor pressed his lips together, obviously seeing that Peter was on a warpath—albeit a weird one. But this mattered. It mattered that Anna forgave Connor, even if she didn't accept him back. It mattered that they didn't go into tomorrow night with a strain between them. It mattered because Peter needed to fix it, to do *something* right for once.

With a heavy sigh, Connor turned to look at Anna even while she refused to look at him. "I just wanted to say that I'm sorry, Anna. I know it doesn't make up for anything that's happened. I know it can't make it right, but I need you to know, okay?"

Nodding along with Connor's words, Peter thought it was a good start. Apologetic, sincere, and not shying away from the blame. But then he realized that Connor had stopped talking.

"Go on," Peter prodded.

Connor shrugged. "That's all."

"Great," Anna muttered, pushing herself off the couch.

"Hey," Peter called, bringing her to a halt. "No. No, that's not 'all.' What the heck, man? You're just gonna keep all that stuff you told me back at your family's place to yourself?"

"It's not really relevant," Connor said tightly.

"Not relevant?" Peter scoffed. "Dude, you're freakin' in love with her! I'd say that's pretty relevant."

Connor glowered at him, irritation lighting up his face as Anna's expression shifted from agitated to baffled to enraged. "Peter!" she exclaimed.

"What?" he shot back. "He wasn't going to tell you."

"It doesn't matter!"

Peter rolled his eyes. "You've been in love with him since you were five—that's what you told me. And now, all of a sudden, it doesn't matter that he's loved you this whole time too?"

Anna's mouth worked open and closed around unsaid words. Her eyes brimmed with tears, and Peter immediately flinched. Had he gone too far? Had he pushed too hard? He didn't think so. The two of them needed to start being honest with one another. And if it took him forcing them to tell the truth, then so be it.

Leaning forward in his seat, Peter held Anna's watery stare. "He *loves* you, Anna."

"He's engaged to someone else," she said.

"It was never my choice," Connor mumbled.

Anna whirled to face him. "Don't you dare," she growled. "You had a choice. I told you before you ever met her that I—" She broke off, a gasp catching in her throat. She slapped a hand to her mouth as though refusing to say anything else.

Connor shook his head, desperation in his eyes. Slumped on the couch as he was, he looked pitiful and broken as he stared up at her. "It was too late by then," he said, deep voice thin with regret. "I wanted to tell you, Anna. I wanted to tell you everything, but Dad . . ." He paused as though realizing that he was making excuses. "That doesn't matter. I'm sorry. That's all I wanted to say. Whatever I feel for you—whatever you once felt for me, I know it isn't enough to overcome the mistakes I made."

Peter frowned. The guy really didn't get the picture, did he? "She's just hurt, you idiot," he said. "She still loves you."

"I don't," Anna insisted. Her shoulders straightened and her chin lifted, but she didn't meet Connor's eyes as she added, "I don't love you anymore."

Connor nodded, accepting her lie.

"Seriously?" Peter exclaimed, baffled by their ridiculousness. "This is how you're gonna handle this? You're just gonna pretend that you don't—wow, okay. You try to help someone."

"Peter," Anna said his name with the same level of exasperation as his mother when he'd tried to hotwire his broken remote-controlled car and burned a hole in the carpet. "Stay out of this."

"It's a bit late for that," Peter said.

Irritated, Anna huffed. "I don't love him! I don't."

Peter smirked to tell her he didn't believe her.

Her gaze hardened. It flashed to Connor, who watched her with resigned acceptance. Then it sailed back to Peter with what he could tell was renewed determination. Anna took a sharp inhale and then said, "Because I love you."

Yes, this was definitely the worst idea Peter had ever had in his life.

Silence hit the room like a tree falling to the forest floor. It slammed into them, kicking up the detritus of the charged atmosphere with its forceful blow. Anna's regret instantly clouded her expression, causing her jaw to quaver. Every emotion imaginable passed through Peter's mind as he held her stare—shock, disbelief, irritation, a twinge of unwelcome happiness. But one emotion smothered them all.

Connor's head hung as he stared at his hands and rose. "Excuse me," he muttered.

Somehow, Peter managed to keep himself from stopping the man. He let Connor escape up the stairs—presumably to Peter's bedroom, which he'd offered since Silas was in the spare—before speaking.

Peter clasped his hands between his knees. The cold metal of the Varon ring sat uncomfortably on his finger. He scanned Anna. Her wispy curls coiled daintily around her beautiful face, and her rose-colored sweater brought out a subtle pink in her brown skin. He'd always found her attractive; there was no use in denying that. And he wasn't afraid to admit it caused his early crush on her.

Peter was five months shy of being twenty-nine. Most guys likely wouldn't see that as the end of the world, but for him, it was a nuisance. He'd wanted a family for as long as he could remember. Probably because he grew up with David and Mallory Collins as parents. For the first fourteen years of his life, he'd watched the most perfect example of what marriage could be. His dad and mom were movie-level. Their romance was sweet and charming, friends-to-lovers with a dash of slow burn.

Not once in his lifetime had Peter ever seen his parents fight. Sure, they'd banter back and forth, but they were so compatible it was almost annoying. And it'd surely wrecked his expectations for his own love story.

One day, when Peter was nine, his dad told him, *"The greatest thing a man can do is have a family, Petey. Remember that. No amount of success in a job or a career matters if you don't have a happy family. That's the real measure of a man."*

And ever since Peter had known that was all he cared about—rising to the true measure of a man, caring for and protecting his family.

At the time, his family had been his dad, mom, and brother. Then, five fateful years later, it was just his mom and brother. Now, with his mom remarried, it was just his brother that he cared for. And in the midst of it all, Peter waited and waited, coming up empty as he searched and searched for his chance to start a family of his own.

Time was getting away from Peter. Twenty-eight and he'd not had one serious girlfriend in the past. Not for lack of trying. For lack of being chosen.

And as he stared back at Anna now, her false declaration hanging between them, he felt his whole body flush with anger.

"No," he said flatly.

Anna took a step back, running into the arm of the couch. "What—"

"I've been waiting my whole life for someone to pick me, Anna," he interrupted. He didn't care that his words were clipped and hard. She didn't have the right to lie to him to prove to herself that she'd moved on. "For someone to look at me, to think about me, the way you look at and think about Connor."

She sucked in a sharp breath as though to retort, but he didn't let her get a word out.

"I'm not new to this," he said. "My track record is roughly zero for thirty-five with girlfriends. Trust me, that's enough dates to know when it's not real. To know when it's not right. And you and me, Annie? We're not right."

Crossing her arms, Anna dropped his gaze. "I don't understand. I thought you—"

"Don't lie to me," he said. "Yes, I had an interest in you. You're cool, beautiful, and kind. Of course, I had an interest. But I told you weeks ago that I'm your friend. I wasn't looking to be anything else to you. So, don't tell me that you thought I loved you or that somehow, in the last five days, you suddenly realized that you loved me."

"How do you know that I didn't?" she asked. "You were gone, Peter. And I was terrified that it was forever. I didn't want to lose you."

"Great, thanks. I'm glad to know I was missed. But here's the deal: I'm not your boyfriend. And you don't get to treat me like I am when you need to prove to yourself that you don't love your ex anymore."

"He's not—" She cut herself off this time, scoffing as she dropped onto the couch across from him. "He *lied* to me," she said. "My whole life, he lied to me. Why would I ever want to be with him? How could I ever trust him again?"

"Trust him or not—be with him or not." Peter brushed the issue away. "It's not any of my business what you choose, Anna. But I'm not gonna be your rebound. I don't want to live the rest of my life knowing I was the second choice."

Anna stared at him in shock. But he could see as her dark eyes gleamed with tears that he was right. She didn't love him. She loved the idea of him. She loved the chance to get over Connor.

Guilt pressed into Peter's conscience as he watched the first tear slip out of the corner of Anna's eye. She quickly swiped it away, but his heart twisted, unable to take back his harsh words.

With a heavy sigh, Peter dropped his head into his hand. This had been a really awful, stupid mistake. All because he was jealous of her chance at the sort of love he wanted.

When would he learn to stop trying to fix things? When would he let things take their natural course? If he had let it go, maybe Anna and Connor could have figured this out themselves. Now, he'd not only caused a deeper rift between them, but he'd also caused a rift between him and Anna.

Why did she say that? Why'd she have to say the one thing Peter wanted to hear more than anything? That's what made him so angry, Peter realized. It wasn't that she was using him to rebound. It was that she hadn't meant it. Not the way he wanted her to.

"I'm not him, Anna," Peter said finally. He looked up at her, silent tears making tracks down her cheeks. Another pang of guilt hit him, but he pressed on. "And normally, I'd say that's a good thing when it comes to exes, but . . . in this case, I don't think it is."

Sitting with her ankles crossed and her arms wrapped around her stomach, Anna looked like a scolded child. "Shouldn't it be, though?" she whispered. "Shouldn't I want someone completely different than him?"

"Honestly?" Peter shrugged. "I don't know."

Anna looked let down by that reply.

Peter tried again. "I don't think you're ready to love someone else," he said. "Whether or not you want to, moving on isn't that easy. You love him. You've loved him for twenty years. You're not gonna move on in a week or a month, maybe not even a year. And that doesn't make you weak or stuck or . . . anything. It just means you've got more work to do."

Chewing on her bottom lip, Anna let his words sink in for several moments before sniffling. She met his gaze. "Can I ask you something?"

"Of course."

"And you'll be totally honest?"

Though nervous, Peter nodded.

"Do you love me?" Anna asked.

Somehow, that was the easiest question for Peter to answer. He gave her a soft smile and shook his head. "Not like that."

Anna looked conflicted, as though she didn't know what answer she'd hoped for.

"Not like *him*," Peter said. "Yeah, he's done some messed up stuff and made stupid mistakes. But it was because he was trying to do the right thing, and he had cult leaders as parents, so the right thing wasn't that clear to him."

She hung her head, listening dejectedly.

"He abandoned his family for you, Anna. He saved me because of *you*. Whether he'll say it or not, all of this—everything he's ever done, it's been for you. He loves you more than anything."

"Then why didn't he tell me?" Anna asked.

Though he knew it wasn't his story to tell, Peter explained anyway. "Because his dad threatened you."

She gasped. "Alex?"

Peter nodded.

Dropping her face into her hands, Anna began to cry again in muted snuffles. It stirred Peter's compassion, and he quickly went to her side. He put his arm around her shoulders, squeezing her close.

"I'm sorry, Annie," he whispered. "I shouldn't have brought this up. I shouldn't have made you two talk."

She leaned into him, her head pressing into his shoulder. "I trusted them, Pete," she said. "How did I miss it? How did I miss their lies?"

"Not everything was a lie," he promised. "Whatever Connor lied about, he loved you and was protecting you. And as Owen taught us, it's not always the worst thing."

"I don't want to be protected," Anna muttered through her tears.

He couldn't help his chuckle. "Why not?"

"I want to be strong," she said. "Like Cassandra."

"You think Cass doesn't need protecting?"

"I know she doesn't."

"Hm. She seems pretty happy to let Spencer protect her from time to time."

A soft giggle slipped out of Anna, and she pulled out from under his arm. "That's because she likes him."

Peter grinned, raising his eyebrows. "I thought you liked Connor."

A sly, shy smile tipped up the corner of her mouth as she brushed her cheeks dry. "I thought *you* liked me."

Something between disappointment and calm pulled at Peter's gut. "I do like you," he admitted. "And at another time, things might've been different."

"If I had moved on from him."

Peter nodded.

"I'm sorry that I didn't."

"I'm not," he said, and he meant it.

Reaching up to brush some of those wild, curly wisps off her damp cheek, Peter knew this wasn't the woman he'd been waiting for. He loved Anna, but it was in a purer, less amorous way than Connor. He didn't dream about her. He dreamed about the shadow of a redheaded woman he'd yet to meet. Someone with the same kindness as Anna but maybe a little less sweetness. Someone who looked at him the same way Anna looked at Connor—like he was the center of her world. Someone who looked at him the way Cassandra looked at Spencer—like he was her home, her safety, her hope.

No, Anna wasn't the romantic love of his dreams. But she was the first friend aside from his brother who never judged him, the first to accept him just as he was, overdramatic and interfering warts and all.

Peter gave Anna's arm a gentle squeeze. "I think you should talk with Connor," he said, then hurried to add, "Not tonight. Unless you want to, of course. But . . . I think you should hear him out, okay? He's actually a pretty decent guy."

"I'm not sure I'm ready for that," she said.

"That's okay," he promised. "Just remember that we're fighting Druids and sometimes . . . sometimes tomorrow never comes. So, don't wait until you're ready. Only wait until you can't bear the thought that you never got the chance."

Anna tipped her head to the side, scanning him with an awed look.

"What?" Peter asked, reaching up to rub his cheek. "Do I have something on my face?"

She chuckled, taking his hand and tugging it down. "No," she assured him. "You're just surprisingly wise sometimes."

Peter pursed his lips sarcastically. "Tell that to Spencer," he returned. "That kid never listens to a word I say."

CHAPTER THIRTY

Cassandra

Getting up that morning, Cassandra decided she hated sleeping in Diane's room. She couldn't stand how dark the heavy curtains kept the space. She charged around the room, tucking back each of their navy folds, banishing the shadows with the gray light of dawn. It didn't help the nagging loneliness that had settled into her chest.

After the past two nights, Cassandra had somehow grown used to having someone near when she went to sleep. Knowing Spencer was across from her in the vault had soothed her worried mind. And with everything they'd learned yesterday, she'd needed that peace.

Cassandra's hands trembled as she moved through her morning routine. She needed to talk with Spencer. Not to set up those boundaries she'd conveniently ignored for far too long. No, those things wouldn't matter soon. She needed to be upfront with him, to let him know what was coming.

Silas had drawn Cassandra to the side last night. He'd managed to sneak her away without Spencer noticing. And he'd immediately told her everything he knew about being a Vessel.

"You won't have a normal life," Silas explained. "If this Spectral tethers to you, you will never be free of it."

"What do you mean?" she asked.

"They latch onto you like a leech," he said. "You are their life source. They live in your head and feed off your power."

"Feed? Like, it'll kill me?"

"No. It needs you to survive," he said. "If anything, it will fight tooth and nail to keep you alive for as long as possible. But that's the thing, Cassandra. Spectrals are sentient spirit-beings with minds and wills of their own. They need you to have a tangible presence here within the world. And after you do die—because they can't keep you alive forever—they live on."

"If I die, wouldn't it just go back into the Veil?"

His expression turned haunted. "They attach to your bloodline. If you have children, it will pass to one of them. If you don't, it will search out anyone and everyone in your biological family to find a match."

"Why can't you just send them back?" Cassandra asked, desperate for some other solution. "If you don't want to be tethered, what's stopping you from getting rid of them?"

"The Veil is their domain," he said. "One Veil for each Spectral. Wherever the Spectral goes, the Veil goes with it. But once the Veil is torn, it's permanently opened. The Veil still follows the Spectral's presence, but they cannot be returned to its hold."

The terrifying understanding that if this Spectral was released, the Veil would be forever opened along with it hit Cassandra with visions of beasts pouring out of the glassy lake, haunting the woods, stalking through the town.

An open Veil. What would that look like? What would that mean for the people of DeVerre? What would that mean for Cassandra?

"How do, uh—" She paused, twisting her ring. "What happens once the Veil is torn?"

"It comes under your control," Silas said. "Yours and the Spectrals."

"What does that mean?"

Silas hesitated. "Honestly? I'm not sure."

"I thought you worked with a Vessel?"

"I do. I help protect the Vessel in Gold Mountain, but . . . well, I don't work that closely with him. I sit on the town council, and I'm a member of his protection detail, so I help make decisions, but that's a part-time thing. My cousin, Christian, works much closer with Sterling."

Cassandra knew she should be interested in hearing more about these two men. This other Varon and Vessel. But she only had one other question.

"How dangerous will it be?" she asked. "Being a Vessel."

Silas drew in a long, telling breath. "Let's put it this way," he said. "There are, at present, twenty-seven Varons in Gold Mountain. With the exception of my two daughters and the other six children, all of us are on his fifty-person detail. And we're on call, twenty-four seven, to protect him."

That was the answer Cassandra had needed. She'd nodded then, accepting her fate.

But in the new morning, she wanted to rail against it. To tell them to find another Vessel or insist that Lily couldn't possibly be that bad, even though she'd heard just how cruel she'd been to Connor that night in the clinic. But this future—being a Vessel—was far worse than she anticipated.

After her conversation with Silas, she knew that whatever came in the next twenty-four hours, her future was either to die at the hands of the Druids or to take on a frighteningly powerful creature. The first made her sad. The second terrified her. Because Cassandra knew that if she became the Vessel—if that became her future—she couldn't stay here. If she became the bearer of such a dangerous being, there was no way she could stay in DeVerre.

And that was why she needed to talk to Spencer.

Things had grown complicated between them over the last week. Now, she needed to put an end to it. And she knew that if she tried to convince both Peter and Spencer together, Peter would put up a fight. If she could get Spencer alone and appeal to his rational side, he would back her up.

Rushing through her morning routine, Cassandra hurried to get downstairs. As an earlier riser, she knew she'd find Spencer up, giving her the one chance to talk to him alone.

So, Cassandra went down the back staircase, pleased to find Spencer there, pouring his mug of morning coffee. The soft gray light kept the room dim, the windowpanes frosted over from the freezing night.

"Hey," Cassandra greeted, joining him at the coffee pot.

Spencer smiled, his bright blue eyes lighting up as he leaned against the counter. "Hey. You sleep okay?"

Grabbing a mug, Cassandra tried to keep her voice unaffected so he wouldn't hear her nervousness. "Not really," she admitted.

"Yeah, me either."

She couldn't help chuckling as she poured the coffee, knowing he'd had to share a bed with his brother. "I imagine Peter's a bed hog," she said.

He scoffed. "It's been at least ten years since we've had to share a bed. I'd forgotten that he steals all the blankets."

"Does he snore?"

"Surprisingly, no." Spencer smirked. "Unlike someone I know."

Cassandra poked his ribs. "I do not snore."

Spencer didn't respond as he took a sip of his coffee. His eyes twinkled playfully, flirtatiously.

Heart plummeting, Cassandra stepped away to lean against the island. She stared at the hardwood floor. Spencer hadn't put on his boots yet, his woolen-socked feet oddly intimate.

Shifting her gaze, Cassandra shoved down those feelings. "Hey, so I wanted to talk to you," she said.

Spencer hesitated at her tense tone.

"Last night, Silas explained life as a Vessel to me."

"Oh." Spencer sounded relieved. "I'm glad to hear that. I'll admit I was kind of annoyed that he hadn't been more forthcoming about all that."

Unsure if she should feel cared for or not, Cassandra shrugged. "Yeah, he, uh—he told me everything he knows."

"Good."

"Mm-hm." Cassandra forced herself to meet his gaze. "And I just wanted to let you know that he and I discussed the best course of action for after . . . after tonight."

Spencer set his mug on the counter behind him. "If you become the Vessel?"

Sure that there was no hope otherwise, Cassandra thought it best they squash all doubt. "*When* I become the Spectral's host," she corrected. "I'm already a Vessel, apparently. Just an empty one."

"It isn't like it's gonna possess you, Cass," he said, an irritated edge to his voice. "No more than Gerard possessed Occasus. It'll just . . . be connected to you, or whatever."

"You're right," she said. Silas had assured her of that very thing the night before. Whatever else the tie between Spectral and Vessel was, it *wasn't* possession. "But regardless, he said that being a Vessel is particularly dangerous. The one in Gold Mountain has a rotation of fifty or so Warden members watching out for him at all times."

A flash of concern crossed Spencer's face. "Really?"

Cassandra swallowed down her last nerve. "Which is why, after tomorrow—after we've dealt with the Druids . . ." The words caught, but she forced them through the strangle of her throat. "I'll be leaving DeVerre."

A long string of silence drew out between them.

Spencer reached up to scratch the back of his head, his mouth dropping open as if to speak, and then it closed. He crossed his arms, then uncrossed them almost immediately. "Why, uh—" He cleared his throat and started again. "Where would you go?"

This was something Cassandra had yet to discuss with Silas. But she'd come up with a few ideas on her own. "Maybe Harmony?" she suggested. "Or maybe Gold Mountain. Silas said that his cousin knows the Vessel there pretty well, so I thought maybe he could take me to him. For training and stuff, you know?"

Spencer pressed his lips together. He was fidgeting almost constantly. Hand to his jawline. Adjusting against the counter. Eyes darting around the room. "I don't understand," he said. "I thought—last night you said that you weren't concerned. You said that you trusted Pete and I to protect you."

"That was before I talked to Silas," she said. She didn't like how nervous he was growing. How agitated the idea of her leaving made him. He wasn't supposed to care. He was supposed to understand and accept it. That's why she'd come to him first. It was Peter who would make a big deal. Spencer was supposed to support her choice, knowing it was the right thing to do.

"Listen," she continued as he started to shake his head. "I know that it—well, it sucks. We were just starting to fix things here. And DeVerre is my home. I hate to leave it, but . . . I can't stay."

"Why not?" Spencer all but demanded. His eyes flew to hers with such intensity that she would have taken a step back if not for the island behind her.

"It's dangerous," she reminded him.

"So what?"

Cassandra frowned. "I literally just told you that the Vessel in Gold Mountain requires a guard of fifty people. You think that DeVerre can handle something like that?"

"They don't have Peter and me."

She laughed reflexively. "No, but they have nineteen other Varons."

He shrugged as though that meant nothing.

"I have to go, Spencer," she insisted. "If I'm going to be a Vessel, then I need to understand what that means. I need to be in a place where people can protect me and where they can protect others from me."

"From you?"

She nodded. "Silas said that every Spectral grants particularly strong, unique powers to their Vessel," she explained. "He doesn't know what this one will be, but he said that's why the Druids are so desperate to collect them all."

Spencer pinched the bridge of his nose.

"That's why I have to leave, Spencer," she pressed. "I'm becoming a collectible. One that the Druids will do whatever it takes to possess."

He tossed a hand through the air. "We won't let them," he said in exasperation.

Cassandra narrowed her gaze at him. "Spencer, what do you think is going to happen? Everything the Druids have done in the last three months is nothing compared to what's coming."

"Is this what Silas told you?" he demanded. "Did he tell you that you need to leave?"

Sighing, Cassandra wasn't ready to fight with Spencer. She'd wanted him to accept it. She'd *needed* him to accept it. "No," she admitted.

"Then why are you so convinced this is the right thing to do?"

"Because," she said desperately, "if I stay, I'm not only putting DeVerre in danger, I'm putting you and Peter in greater danger than ever before. I can't let you two give up your lives for me."

"What do you think we've been doing the last month?" Spencer said through an unamused laugh. "Cass, we don't care about the danger. We care about you."

Cassandra's heart warmed traitorously as Spencer smiled and added, "*I* care about you."

That, Cassandra couldn't handle. She'd been so stupid these past days, letting him kiss her and hold her. Letting herself pretend that this was ever anything but a distraction. She had to put an end to it. She had to get her head clear and free of the confusion that was Spencer Collins.

Cassandra set her mug on the island, then straightened up to face him. "Look, I get it," she said, ready to be an adult about the situation. "These last few days were stressful. And it was a good distraction, pretending that we were . . . something."

Spencer frowned.

"But you've got Peter back now," she said. "You don't need me to calm you down, or . . . whatever. And there's no reason for us to pretend—"

"Cassandra," Spencer interrupted, his expression a blend of irritation and utter confusion. "What the hell are you talking about?"

She blinked. Could he be that oblivious? She knew it had all been a whim, some strange way to cope with his panic, but she'd thought, at the least, it might have meant something to him too.

Glaring back at him, Cassandra crossed her arms. If he didn't care to acknowledge what had happened between them, then she wouldn't either. "I need to leave."

"Why?" he demanded.

"Because I don't want to be around you anymore." The words tumbled out in a desperate rush.

He drew back, hurt. "What?"

That single, frightfully quiet word broke Cassandra's resolve. She wanted to take it back. She wanted him to know it wasn't true. That in all reality, she wanted to be around him forever. That he was to her, the only place she wanted to be.

Breathing grew difficult as Cassandra held Spencer's pained stare. "I can't be around you," she whispered. "Not when I don't know what you want from me."

Spencer drew in a sharp breath, understanding. "Cassie," he sighed.

He pushed off from the counter to reach for her, but she pulled back, drifting to the far edge of the island, unable to bear his touch. "I'm not asking anything of you," she promised. "I just—I can't—"

Jaw clamped tight, Spencer lunged forward. Despite her attempt to evade him, he caught the barest hold on her sleeve. It was enough. He gave a gentle tug as he stepped to her.

Slipping his arm around her waist, Spencer pulled her close. He wore that horribly attractive Varon smirk. "If you're trying to break up with me," he said, brow raised, "you're not doing a very good job of it."

Cassandra fought to calm her pulse as she scanned his too-near face. "We'd have to be in a relationship for me to break up with you," she said.

"I thought we were in a relationship," he replied.

"A romantic relationship," she clarified. "Not a friendship."

His smile softened as he wrapped the other arm around her waist. "I thought we *were*," he said sweetly.

Cassandra tipped her head to the side, mouth agape as she realized he was telling the truth. He'd genuinely thought they were . . . what, dating?

"You assumed we were dating because we kissed?" she asked.

He shrugged. "We kissed multiple times."

"Spencer," she laughed, "you didn't say anything. How was I supposed to know that you took it seriously?"

He looked genuinely bewildered. "Cassie, why would I kiss you if I wasn't serious?"

A little dazed at their closeness and his hands resting on her back, Cassandra couldn't find a clever retort. "I don't know."

"Well, I wouldn't," he said.

Finding her hands on his arms, Cassandra swallowed. "So . . . you— we're . . . in a relationship?"

"As far as I'm concerned."

An embarrassed scoff slipped out of her. "Does that make you my boyfriend?" she asked, amused.

He grinned sheepishly. "I think so."

"Hm." The realization sent a funny jolt of peace through Cassandra's chest. "In that case—"

Cassandra leaned in, taking Spencer's face in both hands. She kissed him, knowing for the first time that it wasn't some fluke or heightened, stress-induced reaction. When he kissed her back, he was kissing her because he wanted her. Because he cared about her in a way he didn't care about any other woman.

The thought sent a chill tingling across her skin. What a strange thing to make her so bizarrely happy.

Lost in her thoughts and Spencer's kiss, Cassandra failed to hear the particularly important sound of someone coming down the stairs. "Good morn—whoa!"

Jerking away from one another, Cassandra and Spencer whirled to find Peter staring open-mouthed at them. His shock was already wearing off as a spark of humor lit his eyes.

"Huh," Peter remarked, a knowing smirk on his face as he scanned the two of them.

Spencer stood off to the side, rubbing the back of his neck as he studiously avoided looking at either of them. Cassandra thought she should probably feel embarrassed too. Instead, she grinned, feeling smug.

Peter waved a finger in their direction. "Is this new, or am I to take it you didn't miss me all that much?"

Moving for her mug still waiting on the island, Cassandra shrugged. "Someone had to keep Spencer sane."

Peter raised his brow. "Well, I can tell you I'll never try that method," he said, giving Spencer a shove as he walked past. "Don't worry. You can get back to whatever it is you two were 'discussing' right after I get my coffee."

"We weren't—it's not—" Spencer's fumbling came to a stop as he watched Peter grab a mug from the cabinet. His cheeks, flushed from embarrassment, now settled back to their usual rosy-pale complexion as his expression calmed. "Actually," he said, a hint of revelation in his tone, "you've got great timing. I could use your help."

Peter screwed up his face in disgust. "I have no interest in helping you with *that*." He said the last bit while tossing a thumb in Cassandra's direction.

Understanding where this conversation was headed, Cassandra frowned. "Spencer, I'd prefer to discuss this another time," she said, putting the island between her and the Collins brothers.

At her hesitant tone, Peter turned to study her. He narrowed his eyes, suspicious. "Discuss what?"

"Nothing," Cassandra blurted out just as Spencer said, "Cass plans to leave DeVerre."

Dark gaze shifting from his brother to Cassandra, Peter pursed his lips. "You tired of us already, Cass?" he asked, then smirked at Spencer. "We must be pretty bad roommates. First Owen, now Cassandra? Though this case might be more because of . . . well, you know." He said the last bit with a wink.

Cassandra rolled her eyes. "It's not because of either of you," she said, then realized that wasn't wholly true. "Well, it is. But it's because I want to protect you."

"I thought the whole deal was that we were going to protect you?" Peter said.

"That's what I said," Spencer grumbled.

"And then you kissed her."

Spencer glared at him. "The point is," he said, "Cassandra thinks that becoming a Vessel—"

"I'm already a Vessel," she reminded.

"Becoming a *connected* Vessel," he corrected, "will make her too dangerous to stay in DeVerre. She wants to leave because she's convinced that we can't take care of her with all the Druids that are going to flood the area trying to take her."

Peter quirked an eyebrow. "Is that all?"

"Pretty much."

"I fail to see the problem," he said with a shrug, then proceeded to take a nonchalant sip of his coffee.

With a heavy sigh, Cassandra pressed a hand to her forehead. "This is why I didn't want to talk to both of you," she said. "I knew—if I couldn't get you to see reason, Spencer, there would be no rationalizing with Peter."

"You saying I'm not rational?"

Cassandra gave Peter a bland glare. "I'm saying that I need you two to look at this without feelings getting in the way."

"Not sure what the point of that would be." Peter tapped his thumb on the rim of his mug as he looked at Spencer. "Didn't we say, like, two weeks ago that we were the only ones who could protect her?"

"As if our lives depended on it," Spencer said with a nod.

"Right," Peter said, then turned back to Cassandra. "Because our lives do depend on it."

"Not anymore," Cassandra said. "You do realize that, right? You don't need me anymore."

"That's—" Spencer began, but she interrupted before he could say something that made her want to stay even more.

"If I leave, the Veil leaves with me," she said

They stared at her in shock, their deep-set eyes wide—bright blue and rich brown. Both were so different and so similar. The past weeks of stress had resulted in neglect of their appearance, letting their facial hair grow in much more fully. Spencer's usually floppy waves now dipped into his eyes while Peter's, which typically stood on end, had begun to droop despite the number of times he'd dragged his fingers through it.

Cassandra smiled at the brothers, an unexpected affection filling her chest. "If I leave," she continued, "and the Veil leaves, then DeVerre becomes safe. And you two get everything you ever wanted."

Spencer and Peter exchanged a look.

Seeing her opportunity, Cassandra pressed on. "You moved here to pursue your careers. If I leave, then you get that chance. There will be no Druids to fight and no spirit world to defend. You'll have Occasus and all the time in the world to write every story you ever wanted to write. You can turn *Wenzel & Frankly* into a whole series if you want. You could spend the rest of your lives doing exactly what you always dreamed of."

"But you wouldn't be here," Spencer said emptily.

Cassandra felt disappointment twinge in her chest, but she forced herself to maintain her smile. "But you would have everything you ever wanted, and I think that's worth it."

Spencer frowned at the floor, arms crossed over his chest. An unexpected surge of memory reminded Cassandra that she knew what it was like to be held by those arms now. She knew how strong and warm they were, how safe and caring. The memory made her feel abnormally cold and lonely, sitting on the opposite side of the island from him.

An irreverent grunt drew her attention to Peter. His jaw was rigid as he glared at her. That famed Collins stubbornness—no, it was Varon stubbornness—rising to the surface. He set his coffee on the counter with a *thunk*, and a small splash of the liquid sloshed over the side. "How long will it take for you to get it, Cass?" he asked. "You're our family now. We don't care about the danger. We care about you."

At his side, Spencer drew his shoulders back, that same determined glint in his gaze. It echoed his brother's declaration but with a hint of something else in it. A feeling that Peter hadn't infused. One that made Cassandra's heart skip. "You're not allowed to leave us, Cassie," he said, low and sure.

"Not even if it gives you everything you ever wanted?" she asked.

"If you're not here," he said, "I don't want it."

Cassandra supposed it was stupid of her to be surprised by the sentiment. After all, they'd just declared their feelings, hadn't they? She'd been thrilled to call him her boyfriend only minutes ago. What else had she expected?

But Cassandra realized that she had never actually expected anything. Being with Spencer was a fun, unrealistic daydream to her. Something she'd never actually have. Something she didn't mean because she'd intended to leave.

Spencer meant it, though. He'd truly believed they were a couple from the moment he kissed her. He took every moment they had together seriously. And he would face a lifetime of danger to be with her.

The thought sent a tingle through her hands and arms. He would give up his dream of living a quiet life as a successful author with his brother to be with her.

Cassandra looked at Peter. "You're okay with the fact that he's putting himself in danger for me?" she asked.

With a flippant wave of his hand, Peter smirked. "Hey, I'm just glad he's finally worked up the courage to do something. Now, I can have a little time to myself."

Spencer gave his brother a side-eye. "Like you'll ever leave me alone."

"You're not as charming as you appear, J.B." Peter turned to Cassandra. "So, here's the deal: You aren't leaving. Especially not now that you've made out with my brother."

Spencer sighed as Cassandra bit her lip.

Peter ignored them. "Tonight, we're going to stop the Druids. Then whether they tear the Veil and release this Spectral-thing or not, you're sticking around to help us clean up this mess. We'll figure out the whole Spectral/Vessel thing if it comes to it. But the idea of you leaving and taking the Veil with you does us no good. After all," he tapped the new gold ring on his right hand, "we're Varons. Taking care of the Veil is our inheritance just as much as Occasus is."

Spencer nodded. "He's right. Michael and Seraphine gave their lives to defend the Veil. We'd be selfish to ignore that."

"Plus," Peter added, "Diane point-blank told us to take care of you. We're not about to snub our benefactor's last wish."

Cassandra twisted the ring on her finger, trying one last pointless argument. "She also asked me to take care of you two," she reminded them. "She wrote me a letter, specifically asking to be sure you made a home here. If I left—"

"If you left," Spencer interrupted, "you'd be abandoning us."

"I'd be protecting you," she argued.

"You can't care for us if you're gone, Cassie," he said. "And we couldn't take care of you either."

"So, you'd not only be ignoring Diane's wishes," Peter said smugly, "you'd be making us ignore them too."

Cassandra spun her ring. She felt like she should continue to fight. She needed to convince them that the danger of her staying outweighed any danger of her leaving. She could better care for them if she left them.

But she didn't want to fight them. She wanted to stay, to accept this new family of hers, to date Spencer, and see what came of it. She wanted to enjoy the friendships she'd developed with Peter, Anna, Owen, and all the rest of the people in DeVerre. She wanted to belong for once in her life.

Looking down at her hands, Cassandra's fingers froze on her ring. The Sauveterre family crest stared back at her, the gothic S imposed upon the budding tree. It was a symbol of the woman she was supposed to become.

Cassandra paused then.

Who was she supposed to be? A Sauveterre? A Druid? A Vessel? Did it even matter?

Slowly, Cassandra found herself twisting the ring again. Not with the normal, frantic rotations with which she worried it. Now, it was with a gentle wiggle, slipping it over her knuckles and free of her finger. She stared at the silver band and etched face, the ring off her hand for the first time in almost twelve years.

Then, she dropped it.

The metal tinkled against the granite countertop, wobbling until it came to a rest.

Cassandra blinked at it, somehow detached from the sight. Whatever her last name, whatever her ancestry, she wasn't a Sauveterre or a Clement anymore. She no longer considered herself a part of those families.

Looking up, Cassandra smiled at Spencer and Peter. They watched her with their steady Varon stares. "Well," she said with a lightness in her chest that she hadn't felt for years, "I guess I'd better stay then."

404

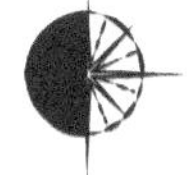

CHAPTER THIRTY-ONE

Spencer

All of two seconds after Cassandra left to gather her devotional supplies, Peter turned to Spencer with a huge grin on his face.

Spencer hefted a sigh, grabbed his mug, and promptly walked out of the kitchen. When he plunked down into his desk chair, Peter dragged a dining chair into the room. He sat across from him, resting his elbows on the desktop.

"Soooo . . ." Peter propped his chin on his hands. "You and Cass, huh?"

Spencer opened his laptop, working to keep his cool. "What about it?"

"You official or what?" he asked.

Spencer ran a hand over his face, heaving another annoyed sigh. "Yes, Pete, Cassandra and I are dating."

"I knew it!" he exclaimed.

"You caught us kissing," Spencer said, keeping his voice low in case Silas or Connor were nearby. "Of course, you knew."

Peter screwed up his face as though Spencer were being obtuse. "Kissing does not make it official."

Exasperated, Spencer tossed his hands in the air. "Why do people think that? Who goes around kissing other people at random?"

Peter's eyes narrowed. "Wait, how long has this been going on?"

Heat spread up Spencer's neck. "Since Monday," he mumbled.

"Wow, I really wasn't missed."

Spencer glared at him. "If you ever disappear again, I'll kill you."

"That's sweet of you," Peter said with an attempt at his signature grin. Yet something about it remained haunted and uncertain.

Expression softening, Spencer watched his brother carefully. "You have another dream last night?" he asked.

After everyone else went to bed, they'd sat up in Spencer's room, talking more about Peter's time as Alexander's captive. While he'd told everyone else about the valravn's nightmares, he'd left out many of the details. It hadn't been until the brothers were alone that he told him just how terrible they really had been. How he'd watched Gerard kill Spencer. How he'd been running through the woods, dying over and over at the hands of beasts. How he'd had to listen to his loved ones screaming for his help.

While Spencer was used to nightmares of his own, what Peter went through sounded far more vivid than what even he experienced. Yet, in the low lamplight of last night, Peter had managed to smile when he said, *"The dreams weren't all bad, though."*

"What do you mean?" Spencer had asked.

Peter hesitated, absentmindedly adjusting the Varon ring on his finger. *"Oh, just . . . I guess the valravn couldn't quite control them all, so I had a few that were pretty chill."*

Spencer could tell that his brother was holding something back from him. But after almost five days without him, he didn't want to push. So, he let it go and moved the conversation to things of less consequence.

Now, as Peter sat opposite Spencer in the office, he could see his brother's hesitation once more.

Peter shook his head, sounding almost disappointed as he said, "No, actually. I didn't have a single one."

Before Spencer could reply, Silas stepped through the kitchen doorway, greeting them with a chin-up gesture. "Could I interrupt for a minute?" he asked.

Face heating at the thought that the man had overheard them, Spencer cleared his throat. "Sure. Pull up a chair."

After taking a seat, Silas surveyed them both. "I thought it important to give you two some information," he explained. "Being on the Varon family tree is particularly unique and, quite frankly, pretty cool."

Spencer and Peter shared an amused look.

"That being said," his tone dropped into a more serious lilt, "it's also demanding. The sort of power we're granted isn't easy to carry. It requires responsibility and, oftentimes, sacrifice."

The once-amused glance turned nervous.

Spencer adjusted in his chair, closing his laptop. "We've sort of picked up on that," he said. "Not to say we aren't interested in what you have to say, just . . . it's become pretty clear that our lives are likely to look different than we once thought."

Peter nodded in agreement. "We're not afraid of responsibility."

"That's good," Silas said. "Because you two are going to get a lot of it."

Spencer raised his brow. "Us two? As in, we'll personally get an abnormal amount of responsibility?"

Silas opened his mouth as though to reply but paused before he spoke. His sharp gaze darted in Peter's direction. He angled toward him. "Could I see that ring you found?" he asked.

Peter instinctively reached for the ring. "Yeah, sure."

He began to work the ring off, but Silas's hand flew up to stop him. "Don't—don't take it off," he insisted, his words almost panicked. "Ever."

Peter frowned.

"I just want to take a quick look," Silas said.

Awkwardly, Peter held up his hand.

Eyes narrowed, Silas leaned close to inspect the ring. He gingerly touched the gold face, brushing the etching. "Mm," he murmured. Then he sighed. "Well, seems legit."

As Peter furrowed his brow, Silas looked him over with a renewed interest. "It's nice to meet the heir," he said. "At least of this line."

Spencer's mouth hung ajar as Peter screwed up his face. "The heir?" he asked.

Silas motioned for Peter to set his hand down. "This is why I wanted to talk to you two. It's a bit of a story," he said. "But you need to know the gist of it at the very least."

Settling into his seat, Spencer massaged his palm. "Because Pete's the heir to something?"

Silas nodded.

"What kind of heir?" Peter asked suspiciously.

With a knowing grin, Silas replied, "A good kind."

Spencer and Peter shared one of their questioning looks, asking one another if they were ready for another big revelation. Spencer didn't think they had much of a choice.

Peter turned back to Silas and nodded for him to go on.

"Again, it's long, so bear with me," Silas said. "But we need to start at the beginning for you to understand."

Spencer pressed his thumb deeper into his palm as Peter hunched in his seat.

"Back in the 1600s," Silas began, "the First Varon was born into the Warden. His mother, Brigid, was from Bushmills, Ireland, and while her father was a Druid, her mother was a devout Catholic. The opposing views of her parents stirred up an urge within Brigid for the truth. So, when she was old enough and the Warden came to Bushmills to reclaim the Veil there, she defected to help them."

"There's a Veil in Bushmills?" Spencer asked.

"Not anymore."

Understanding clicked into place. "Because the Vessel left?"

Silas looked momentarily surprised, and then his expression eased. "Cassandra told you that the Veils follow the Spectral?"

Spencer confirmed it.

"Well, yes," Silas admitted. "But don't go sharing that information. It's important we keep the details about everything connected to Spectrals and Vessels quiet."

Though Spencer was uncomfortable with the Warden's secretive nature, he wanted to get the rest of the story. "So, the Varons started with an ex-Druid?"

"More or less," Silas said. "It was because of Brigid's help in Bushmills that the Warden was able to get control there. They drove out the Druids, got control of that Vessel, and secured the next century of the Warden's growth. Brigid and her fellow defectors taught the Warden everything they knew about the Druids' plans and purpose with the Spectrals. They taught them how to be stronger Wielders. It was the first time we had anything more than Advocates amongst our people."

"Advocates?" Peter prompted.

"Wielders who can interact with ghosts and tether them into phantoms."

Peter nodded.

"Thanks to Brigid," Silas went on, "the Warden became an actual force against the Druids. They had a dedicated purpose and power rather than a vague hope. She became a close, trusted ally to the Lawrences. Or at least, to some of them."

"Why just some of them?" Spencer asked.

"People get uncomfortable when someone challenges their status," he said. "Brigid was a Sage and a powerful one. She became influential quite quickly. There were certain members of the Warden and the Lawrence family who didn't appreciate her rise through the ranks."

Silas took a breath before he continued, "But she left her mark in the

Warden anyway, training up Wielders and seeking out Druids to add to the Warden numbers. Because of her, the Warden was able to expand from the U.K. and into Mortemer, France, where the Druids had a particularly large encampment.

"Brigid moved with the Warden to Mortemer, with the intention of infiltrating the Druids," he explained. "That's where she met Jean Varon, a young, zealous Mortemer man who adopted the Warden's calling with open arms."

Spencer couldn't help thinking of Seraphine and how she'd been a double agent amongst her family. Then he thought of Cassandra and her rejection of her own family's lineage. Was it a coincidence that the Varon men were drawn to brave women?

Silas gave Peter and Spencer each a look as though to impress on them the importance of his next words. "Brigid and Jean married, and in 1630, she gave birth to Gabriel Varon, who became known as the First Varon."

Something in Spencer latched onto the name and title. It sounded familiar, and it took a moment for the conversation they'd had with Silas about Elijah's essays to resurface in his memory. "Gabriel went on to marry Rachel Lawrence," he said to himself as much as to inform Peter. "The two-times great-granddaughter of John William, the Warden founder."

"Right," Silas confirmed. "While Brigid was hugely impactful in the Warden's history and growth, Gabriel continued to expand her impact. The Varons became nearly as important to the Warden as the Lawrences. Another reason several of the Lawrences came to dislike them."

"But they became family," Peter said. "And they were on the same side. Why would they care?"

"Have you met us?" Silas asked with a chuckle. "We're sort of intense, and if we're being honest, a tad arrogant too. We know that we're strong, and we don't really care if people like us or not. We do what's right. We stand for the truth. That often alienates people.

"But we're powerful," he added. "And we're helpful. So, the Warden accepted us and all the great things we did for them. In fact, Gabriel went on to accomplish potentially the most impactful event in the Warden's history. He liberated the Vessel of Corva from the Druids in Paris."

"That name's gotten thrown around a lot," Peter said, strangely interested. "Corva, the Raven."

"She's a Spectral," Silas said. "A particularly important Spectral. And when Gabriel recovered her from the Druids, it ended the cult's upper hand. You heard Connor last night. Without Corva and her prophecies, the Druids are lost."

"Corva's the one prophesying?" Spencer asked.

"She sees the future," he confirmed.

Peter's jaw dropped. He snapped his fingers and pointed to Spencer. "She's Elizabeth!" he exclaimed. "The one who sent letters to Matthias and Michael and all the other Varons in DeVerre."

Silas frowned. "How do you know about that?"

"We found her letters in the vault," Peter said.

Silas considered this. "I *really* need to make a call," he murmured.

"To whom?" Spencer asked, realizing this was the third time he'd mentioned it.

Silas waved him off. "After liberating Corva's Vessel from Paris, Gabriel and Rachel Varon became close friends with her," he said, returning to the story. "Her name was Ariane Valente, and she was the one who told them to leave France to spread across North America. Apparently, Ariane's lineage stayed in contact with the Varons all through that time. Our family is of particular importance to Corva."

"How so?" Peter asked.

"I'm not sure, to be honest," Silas said. "I'm a Varon, but . . ." his eyes dropped to where Peter's right hand rested on his jaw, "I'm not of an heir's line."

Peter glanced at Spencer. "Back to the heir thing, huh?"

"What does that mean?" Spencer asked.

Silas shifted in his chair. "Gabriel and Rachel had three sons," he said. "Benedict, Edmond, and Henry. Three sons to carry on the family's motto: *Virtus, devotio, et cor, omnes pro Christo.*"

After days of working on Elijah's essays, the words came easily. "Courage, devotion, and heart, all for Christ," Spencer translated for his brother.

Silas nodded. "Courage, devotion, and heart," he repeated. "One trait for each son. Courage for Benedict's line, devotion for Edmond's, and heart for Henry's. As they spread across Canada, the Varon bloodline grew, but the strength of the Varon power always followed the true heirs of their fathers.

"You see, Gabriel had three rings made for his sons. And that," he pointed to Peter's ring, "is the ring of Benedict Varon. The symbol of courage and the inheritance of the Varon power."

"What does that mean?" Peter asked, his voice unsteady as he adjusted the ring self-consciously.

"It's like a Biblical blessing," Silas explained. "Each ring carries with it the inheritance of all the Varons before. When it passes from one Varon to the next, it passes the blessing with it, marking the next generation of Varon authority."

Peter and Spencer gaped as Silas continued. "The fact that it's come to you, Peter, means that *you* have now inherited the leadership of Benedict's line. You are one of the three Varon leaders," he said, then paused. An amused grin tugged at his lips. "Technically, it sets you as my leader."

"But—but," Peter stuttered, "we work for the Warden, right? Whoever's in charge of the Warden is your leader."

"That's not how being a Varon works," Silas said. "We prioritize family. We're kind of like those old mobster families in that way. We look to the head of our line for direction. What they say goes. It's one of the reasons the Warden doesn't like us much. We don't care about their instructions; we care about what the head of our family instructs."

Spencer frowned. "That sounds . . . weird."

Silas shrugged. "It rarely comes up. After Matthew Varon died along with his son, Michael, our line of the family lost its leader. Now that the ring found you," he said, gesturing to Peter, "we've got him back."

A look of horror crossed Peter's face as he turned to Spencer, eyes wide. As surely as Spencer knew his own thoughts and feelings, he knew what was going through his brother's head. This was simultaneously Peter's greatest desire and worst fear. Being marked as a leader granted him the respect and attention he longed for while also placing the weight of responsibility and success on his shoulders.

And Peter would crumble under that weight.

"It's just a ring," Spencer said, hoping to ease his brother's burden. "It doesn't mean anything."

Silas smirked. "Tell yourself that all you want, but every other Varon in the world will disagree with you." He scooted forward in his chair. "The three Varon rings mark the three heads of the family. They pass from generation to generation, father to son—or sometimes daughter if there is no son. And every time, the family listens to that leader without fail."

With a pause, Silas looked down as if considering his next words. "And, honestly, we need our leader back," he said. "We've sort of lost the other two."

"How do you lose people?" Peter asked.

"The same way we lost Benedict's line," Silas said. "People die without heirs, or they go into hiding, or . . . well, we don't actually know what happened to Henry's line."

He waved his hand then. "That's beside the point." He turned to face Peter. "We *need* a Varon leader back in the Warden. After that disaster in Porthaven, we lost our voice. The Warden views us as irritants at best. Powerful and necessary, but a nuisance they'd rather forget. Without the mark of the true Varon," he gestured to the ring, "we have no one to step up and make the Warden listen."

"Dude," Peter interrupted. "I know we just met, but trust me, you don't want *me* to be that person. Ask anyone. I'm known for screwing things up."

Spencer frowned. That wasn't true, and that was part of the problem. Peter didn't understand that he wasn't a screwup. He didn't realize that people saw him only as he presented himself—ever confident, sometimes overbearing, and habitually sarcastic. They didn't see the failures and flaws that Peter saw in himself. Sure, he was awkward, but Spencer knew better than anyone that his brother was intelligent, caring, and dedicated. He was a natural leader. And Spencer would follow him to the ends of the Earth.

Peter couldn't see that he inspired people's trust and devotion. And he'd never believe it, even if Spencer told him.

Peter ran his fingers through his hair, mussing the waves before they slowly drooped. "Can't I just . . . give the ring away?"

Silas laughed. "Not until you have a son who comes of age," he said, then shrugged. "Or unless you die. Then the ring will fall to the appropriate Varon."

"Great," Peter murmured, glaring at the ring.

Spencer wondered if his brother regretted taking it from Alexander Frossard. "So, Peter's our leader now," he said, keeping his voice light. "Works for me."

"It's bigger than that," Silas said. "Things are going to need work here. Not only do you need to clear the town of Druids, but with a torn Veil and a Vessel in your midst, you're going to have your hands full. Plus, I'm planning to contact the Warden and request they send us help."

"Us?" Spencer repeated. "Are you sticking around?"

Silas hesitated. "Maybe. As I told you, I'm assigned to the Vessel in Gold Mountain, and I have a family there. But if my wife is all right with it, I thought I'd ask to be reassigned to DeVerre."

A tug of relief lifted some of the pressure on Spencer's chest. He hadn't even realized just how tense he'd grown. Having others who knew more than them come to DeVerre to help save the town changed everything. It gave them a whole new hope for the future of their home.

"You think they could get here in time to help us out tonight?" Peter joked, though his voice was laced with bitterness.

Spencer looked at his brother with growing worry.

"Unfortunately, no one lives close enough for that," Silas said. "I'd have had to make that call of mine a couple of days ago to get the Warden to make a choice. They can be a bit slow. Another reason the Varons don't always wait on their word."

"So, if your wife is cool with it and if Peter asked, you wouldn't wait on the Warden's approval? You'd just move here?" Spencer asked.

"I *would*," he said. "But I'd advise against that course. I'm still on the detail for the Gold Mountain Vessel, and I'd not feel comfortable leaving until I'm sure the Warden can replace me."

Peter slumped in his seat, fingers tapping on the side of the chair. "What about our Vessel? Won't we need help protecting Cass?"

"Of course," Silas said. "As soon as I call it in, they will send somewhere around fifty new Warden members to DeVerre."

"Fifty?" Spencer gasped. "That's a lot of people."

"That's the standard detail for a Vessel."

"And who's gonna be in charge of this detail?" Peter asked.

"Whoever the Warden deems the most qualified," Silas said.

"Shouldn't Cassandra be a part of this conversation?" Spencer asked.

"I already explained most of this to her last night," Silas assured him. "I will warn you that the detail probably won't be the only members who show up. It's likely that they'll send a few others in to try and get the town back under firm Warden control. They've gone kind of corporate these days, and they're going to try to lock down the government and town leadership, extricating any Druidic sympathizers."

"They won't fire Tom or Sam, will they?" Peter asked, concerned.

"Maybe," Silas admitted. "But that's why *you* need to understand your role as the Varon heir. With that ring on your finger, any Varon sent to DeVerre will automatically support you. And I'd imagine the town will support you too. Which means any Warden member would be stupid to oppose you directly. Though there probably will be one or two."

Spencer scrubbed a hand over his face. "This is getting complicated," he murmured.

"It'll only get worse," Silas warned. "With a Vessel in DeVerre, you're about to see changes. Asserting yourself as the leaders—the *true* leaders is of the utmost importance. Above all else, you have to make sure the town is on your side. That way, when the Warden gets here, they'll have no choice but to listen to you."

"What if we don't want to lead?" Peter asked. "What if we'd happily give them control?"

Silas raised his brow. "Who would you rather make decisions about Cassandra's safety? You or someone else?"

That needed no response. Peter and Spencer both knew beyond a doubt that they'd do whatever it took to keep Cassandra safe. And they weren't about to let strangers make those decisions.

Seeing that they understood, Silas moved on. "One final piece of advice," he said, giving each of them a serious glare. "Start going by Varon."

Spencer opened his mouth to object out of loyalty to their dad, but Silas spoke over him. "Here in DeVerre and anywhere else amongst the Warden, people automatically respect our name. If you want to ensure Cassandra's safety, if you want to keep control over this town, you need to accept who you really are."

Spencer turned to Peter, who held his chin tucked.

"I, uh—" Peter cleared his throat. "I've sort of already done that."

A sharp stab of betrayal hit Spencer before he could shove it down. Was this why their Grandpa Phillip had gotten angry with Diane for seeking out their biological family? Spencer knew he was a Varon genetically, but he couldn't forget that their dad's name was David *Collins*. Losing that part of him, that shared name, felt wrong.

But it wasn't worth a fight.

Spencer gave a sharp nod, still uncomfortable and undecided. "Any advice for tonight?"

With a wry grin, Silas shrugged. "Don't lose your nerve."

Somehow, Spencer worried that might not be enough.

417

CHAPTER THIRTY-TWO

Anna

From the moment Anna, Ava, and Owen arrived at Occasus in the late morning, the day moved at an unnatural speed. She couldn't say why. There were just so many people and so much conversation that it seemed a never-ending cycle of one arrival after another.

Aaron and Haley arrived with her brothers, Devon and Logan. Her youngest brother, Nathaniel, was at university in Spokane, but her other two brothers were the epitome of burly lumberjacks. Their curly blond hair mimicked their sister's, and that's where the resemblance stopped. With a rifle strapped over their shoulders, the six-foot-plus, broad-chested, early-twenties lumbermen struggled to take anything about the spirit world seriously.

That was until Silas summoned a copper-coated hellhound. It looked like any normal wolf at first glance. But when you looked longer, you could see a subtle but present creamy glow emanating from its fur. Its unnaturally shiny, golden eyes were frightfully intelligent, and it had a monstrous build.

"There are . . . *good* hellhounds?" Cassandra asked, gaping at the creature.

Silas shrugged. "Beasts are amoral," he said. "You determine their intent. Same with arcs."

Though Silas dismissed the hellhound, no one questioned the spirit world the rest of the day.

Occasus turned into a boarding house from that point on. The Garniers, Chapelles, and other DeVerrean families began to show up to stay in the vault. Danielle had chosen not to join, determined to be their eyes and ears in the town while working at the MacDonald diner. While most of the arrivals couldn't see the ghosts on the lawn, some showed marked discomfort at their presence. They still remained invisible to Anna.

She walked up and down the stairs so many times that her thighs burned. She was tired of talking, answering the endless questions of the men, women, and children. She couldn't answer most of their questions anyway. She wasn't a Wielder, and it disappointed her that some of these people she'd known her entire life could see the ghosts even when she couldn't.

Throughout the day, Anna kept a wary eye out for Connor. He did a good job of avoiding her. And she couldn't decide if that made her grateful or immeasurably sad.

She felt like an idiot after her outburst the other night. Peter had been right; she hadn't meant it. She'd only wanted to prove to herself that she didn't love a man who'd broken her heart more times than she could count.

She was ashamed of the many ways she'd used Peter to get back at Connor. She'd known her feelings toward Peter were platonic, though she had little doubt they could grow if she gave herself the time and opportunity.

But Peter was right about that too. He didn't deserve to be second choice. He didn't deserve to have someone slowly grow to love him when they could have loved him from the start.

Now, Anna felt the need to apologize to Connor as well. After all, he'd apologized without expecting anything from her. It was clear he hadn't intended to confess his feelings for her. He'd been so upset when Peter had said it for him.

Anna could still feel her body shaking at the memory. Connor loved her. It didn't fix anything. It didn't change the fact that he'd hurt her. But somehow, it made her heart swell with compassion for him.

And now, he found a way to leave the room whenever she entered.

Peter's voice echoed in her head every time she saw Connor. *"Don't wait until you're ready. Only wait until you can't bear the thought that you never got the chance."*

Anna wasn't ready to forgive or forget Connor's mistakes. She wasn't even sure she wanted to. But she knew if he was going to risk his life to save her and the rest of DeVerre—if he didn't come back from the confrontation at the lake—she would regret that she never got the chance to forgive him or to tell him that she was sorry for everything he'd gone through with his parents.

That truth, Anna couldn't shake.

She'd always seen the Frossards as a perfect and loving family. Alex and Gia had welcomed her into their home as Connor's friend. They'd treated her like a daughter. They'd loved her. She'd never once seen the sort of cruelty that Connor spoke of. But his fear of them, his absolute loathing for them, radiated so strongly that she couldn't doubt it. And now she wondered how she ever missed it.

Yet Anna never had the chance to pull Connor aside and tell him. While he avoided her, she was helping people settle into the vault's new antechamber, a large room filled with couches, bunk beds, and a projector set up to play the original *Star Wars* trilogy.

Ava and Sam were in charge of running the place. The librarian and reverend kept the DeVerreans organized and the children calm throughout the day. It wasn't until the sun began its steady descent and the team prepared to leave Occasus that an air of fear began to rise. Men and women said goodbye to their families. Some children didn't understand this might be a dangerous excursion for their loved ones. Others displayed their fear through anger, tears, or anxiety.

Though some additional DeVerreans offered to join the fight, Tom, Sam, and Gabe had all determined they wouldn't allow it. As much as they needed numbers, they also needed the assurance of support for the town if they all died at the lake. And the Militia members who *were* joining the team at the lake were, at best, a plan B.

Stepping onto the lawn, Anna and Ava watched the team as they prepared to leave Occasus. She knew them all. Tom Garnier and his cousins, David and Mitchell, along with their sons, Joseph and Tyler. Travis Mercier, Cassandra's second cousin. Gabe Chapelle and his son, Malachi—only sixteen and determined to fight. Haley and her brothers. Aaron and Owen. Silas, Peter, Spencer, and Cassandra. And Connor.

The plan, Anna had overheard Peter saying earlier, was for the non-Wielders to hang behind the trees with rifles, covering the six Wielders who would work to stop the Druids. While bullets were nearly useless against beasts, the Druids were flesh and blood. The riflemen's job was to watch the Wielders' backs. Their focus wasn't necessarily to kill but to bring down the Druids by whatever means necessary.

All but Lily, Connor had reminded them.

"If you don't kill her," he'd said, voice dark and heavy, "I'll do it myself."

Anna didn't know what to make of this version of Connor. He'd always been quiet and tenderhearted. She'd never even seen him kill a spider. He always trapped the arachnid under a cup and escorted it back outside on a piece of paper.

Now, Connor stood by the gates, arms crossed and sullen, while Ava and Anna said their final goodbyes. Sam had taken control of the vault, Ava insisting she wouldn't leave Owen's side until he walked through those gates. The only reason she'd agreed to stay behind was because of the baby. And as Anna had no skill with a gun, she'd known she'd be more of a liability to their safety rather than a help.

"Be careful, please," Anna told Aaron as she hugged him. While she hated being so helpless, she hated letting her family walk into danger even more.

Her brother's arms tightened around her. "I will," he promised.

"Don't do anything stupid," she charged. "Mom already blames me for letting you get a motorcycle. What am I supposed to tell her if something happens to you?"

Aaron pulled back with a raised brow. "You're gonna tell her it wasn't the motorcycle's fault."

Anna couldn't help laughing with Haley, who scooped her into another hug. Her friend's fluffy blonde curls tickled her cheek. The scent of lilies and vanilla surrounded their embrace. Over the years of working together, Haley had become more of a sister than a friend. When Aaron and she started dating, the bond between Anna and Haley had grown almost as strong as the one she shared with Ava.

"Don't worry," Haley said with a final squeeze. She pulled back and grinned at Aaron. "I won't *let* him do anything stupid."

A funny look crossed Aaron's face then. His serious expression softened, and his eyes scanned Haley's face. Anna knew that her brother loved the woman. He'd had a crush on her for a whole year, always finding random excuses to show up at the tavern during her shifts before working up the courage to ask her out. Aaron was a slow mover, more out of worry that he'd make a mistake than because he didn't know what he wanted.

Suddenly, Aaron started digging in his coat pocket. "Screw it," he said. "I've been planning this for like a year now, but we may die, so . . ."

Aaron dropped to one knee. "I love you, Haley Roux, and I want to marry you."

Anna and Haley gasped at the same time, drawing the group's

attention. Everyone turned to watch as Aaron opened the box in his hand, an elegantly simple diamond ring twinkling in the dim evening light.

"I—I had a lot of plans for this," Aaron said. "Which is why it took so long, but—that doesn't really matter now. I love you, and I want to spend the rest of our lives together. So, if we make it through tonight," he stared up at Haley hopefully, "would you marry me?"

Tears were already on Haley's cheeks as she leaned down to hold Aaron's face. "I'd marry you even if we didn't," she promised through her joyous laughter. Then she dropped into his arms and kissed him.

The lawn of Occasus erupted with cheers. Ava and Owen smiled at Anna from the other side of the group. On the cusp of a night filled with death, this was the reminder they'd needed. This was what they were fighting for—love, joy, and family.

Beyond them, Anna caught sight of Connor hovering near the gates. A small grin was on his lips. He'd been nearly as close to Aaron as he was to Anna. If he hadn't gone off to Spokane for medical school, she didn't doubt that Aaron would have asked Connor to help him plan the proposal. He belonged in their family nearly as much as Haley and Owen.

And yet he stood on the outside of the group.

Suddenly, Anna didn't care anymore. She didn't care about Connor's mistakes or his lies. She didn't care that he'd not been brave enough to stand up to his father. She didn't care that he'd gotten himself engaged to a Druid. And she needed him to know—if he was going to risk his life, he needed to know that she would be waiting for him to return.

As Peter slapped Aaron on the shoulder in congratulations, and the group wished them well, Anna snuck around the edge. Her brother held Haley close, tucked under his arm, his glasses askew from their kiss. Their loving smiles filled her with desperate hope.

Anna doubled her speed. The celebration would end soon. She was running out of time.

As she broke free of the group, Connor did a double take at her approach. He stepped back, looking around in search of somewhere to hide. Anna couldn't help smiling, wondering if this was how she'd looked at the chapel two nights ago.

Seeing nowhere to go, Connor turned back, jaw tense. Anna stopped, leaving a distance between them. Her heart did its usual erratic patter even when she was this far from him. It gave an extra jolt as his sky-blue eyes met her waiting gaze.

The chatter behind her was dying down, and Anna reminded herself that she didn't have time to spare. "Hi," she said lamely.

Connor rubbed his hands on the front of his coat. "You, uh—you don't have to do this," he said.

"Do what? We're sending everyone off. I wasn't going to forget you."

He attempted a wry grin that fell flat. "Right. Well . . . bye, I guess."

Anna scrunched her nose. "That's it? That's your goodbye to me?"

Connor stared back at her as though afraid to speak.

Hearing their friends nearing, Anna hurried to say her piece. "I'm sorry," she said, and he blinked in surprise. "I—I should have listened to you. When you texted—when you called, I should have answered. If I had, you might've—"

"I wouldn't have," he interrupted.

It was Anna's turn to blink. "Why not?"

Connor's voice was almost lost on the frosted wind. "He threatened you. And I couldn't risk it."

"Your dad?" she asked.

He nodded.

Her heart twisted in pain. Alex had threatened her. The man she'd considered a second father.

Anna looked up at Connor, her vision blurry. "You have to come back," she said.

Ducking his head down, Connor didn't respond. And Anna knew— in the same way she knew when Connor was happy or scared or ashamed—she *knew* he wasn't planning to come back. He would do whatever it took to stop his family and end the Druids' attack on DeVerre.

Even if that meant giving his life.

Barreling forward, Anna threw her arms around Connor with a force that pushed him back a step. Whether it was instinct or habit, Connor's arms wrapped around her in response. His chin pressed into her forehead, his breath heating her skin.

With a vice grip, Anna held onto her own wrist around his back, unwilling to let him go until she extracted his promise. "You *have* to come back," she hissed into his collar.

"Anna, I—"

"No!" She leaned back to look up at him. "Promise me," she demanded. "Promise that you'll come back to me."

Anna could feel his hands shaking as they slipped to her shoulders as though to push her away. She tightened her grip, refusing to let go.

The shock and hope in Connor's expression broke her heart in the best way. "Why?" he breathed.

Tipping her chin up, Anna kissed Connor's cheek. "Because I've waited twenty years for you," she whispered. "And I won't let you go now."

Instantly, Connor tugged Anna closer, tucking his head into her neck. She felt his muscles ease as he pulled her even closer. She breathed him in, tears openly streaming down her face. But it wasn't from the same pain she'd felt the last month of her life, imagining that she'd lost him.

It was in joy—pure joy knowing that he was hers. Whatever mistakes either of them had made, that was in the past. Whatever happened that night, that would become the past too. All they had was the future. And ever since she was a five-year-old coloring in her kindergarten class, she'd known that Connor Frossard belonged in her future.

The voices had long fallen silent, and Anna squeezed once more. "Promise me, Connor," she whispered.

She'd barely gotten his name out before he said, "Always. I will *always* come back to you."

Connor pulled back then, hands on her shoulders once more. He held her gaze, serious and sure. "I've loved you since I saw you color that wagon blue," he said, and she laughed. "I'm sorry I didn't tell you sooner."

Reaching up, Anna brushed his smooth jawline. "You told me now."

Connor's eyes scanned her face tenderly. Anna's breath hitched as he wet his lips, thinking he would kiss her. He'd done it once, seven years ago, when she'd told him that she loved him. After everything, her heart stilled in both fear and hope that he'd kiss her now.

Grip loosening, Connor stepped back even as his hands trailed down her arms, fingers grazing hers before pulling away entirely. "Always," he repeated his promise.

Anna nodded, letting him walk away from her and out of the gates of Occasus. His eyes flickered over her shoulder, and Anna looked back to see Owen, Peter, Spencer, and Cassandra waiting there. In quick succession, they each hugged her. Peter took an extra second to whisper, "Proud of you, Anne," then gave her shoulder a playful slap. Owen gave Ava one last lingering kiss. Then they followed the group off the grounds of Occasus and into the forest.

Ava stepped up to her side, slipping her arm through Anna's. "We've picked some reckless men, haven't we?" her sister said, a hand brushing over her still-flat stomach.

Anna drew her closer. "Yeah," she said.

A light sprinkle of snow dotted the hazy sky, painted blush, violet, and terracotta in the sunset. DeVerre was most beautiful in the winter, Anna always thought. Still, silent, and steady. Like Connor.

Giggling at herself, Anna tugged on Ava's arm. "Let's go inside," she said.

The warmth of the house comforted Anna, creating a pleasant flush on her skin as she and Ava took off their coats. "Here," she said, reaching for Ava's corduroy monstrosity. She turned her back, slipping it onto the hanger, and into the closet just as she heard a rapid shuffle of feet and a loud *thud*.

Anna whipped around just in time to see Ava drop to the ground. She was about to scream when something struck her in the chest, sending her sailing into the closet doorframe, her body numb. Floaters spotted her vision. She tried to blink them away as a distorted figure stepped over Ava's prone body, but she couldn't get her eyes to work. And she couldn't breathe either.

Agony ripped through Anna's chest. She could tell her muscles were spasming, though she had no control over them. She couldn't fight any of it. She couldn't even grimace from the pain.

Her vision began to come together, still fuzzy but slightly clearer. Someone crouched in front of her, a feminine hand reaching out. "I'm sorry, Anna," the woman said, taking hold of her arm.

Anna knew that voice. She knew it well. She tried to speak, but she couldn't get the name out.

The face came into focus then—thick, black-brown hair, rich and tawny complexion, and lovely, gentle features. "I really am," Danielle said, sincerity lacing her tone. "But you picked the wrong side."

Then the floor dropped out from under Anna, and her vision went completely black.

CHAPTER THIRTY-THREE

Peter

The permeating chill of Washington's approaching winter drove Peter to tuck his hands into his coat pockets as they trekked through the Blackwood Forest. His breath fogged as they scrambled up the frozen rocks of a rise. The last of the sun's light cast an ember-like glow on the clouds.

Looking around at the jutting roots, snow-heavy pines, and craggy outcroppings, Peter felt a creeping sense of familiarity with the forest. He'd run through it so many times in his dreams that now, he knew it as well as Occasus. He could predict every turn, every step, every low-hanging branch. He tried to tell himself that that was impossible. They'd been dreams, after all. Yet he couldn't shake the strange sensation.

Their large troop moved through the forest at a slow, cautious pace. Peter drifted back from Spencer's side to walk next to Connor. "Question," he murmured, not wanting others to overhear. He'd been honest with Spencer about his time in the Frossard vault but hadn't fully opened up about every facet of the dreams quite yet.

Connor gave him a sideways glance before turning back to watch his step.

"The valravn," Peter said. "What do they do, exactly?"

"They control your mind," Connor said. "In the simplest terms, at least. They can't actually control *you*, just your thoughts."

"Mm." Peter suspected as much. "Does that include your dreams?"

"That's where they do their best work."

"Great."

Connor looked down at him, eyebrows raised. "You have any dreams that might be relevant to this particular situation?"

"Huh? Oh, no," Peter assured him. "At least, I don't think so."

"Then why did you ask?"

"It's just—I was running through this forest," he explained. "In every single one of them. And now, in reality, I realize it's exactly the same. Like, there's literally nothing different."

Connor wasn't surprised. "The valravn can't create," he said. "Everything they put into your mind is something you already know."

Peter scrunched his nose, thoughts immediately going to the raven and Forest Lady. "Nah, that—that can't be right."

"It is," Connor insisted. "Whatever you saw, you'd seen before."

"But I saw—" Peter stopped himself, not wanting to talk about her.

Connor eyed him. "What did you see?"

Something in Peter urged him not to say. A near compulsion kept him silent, the memory drifting through his mind. He stepped over the dense growth of roots that he knew all too well. He'd fallen onto them every time that raven flew in front of his face.

Peter looked to his left. He scanned the hollow in the trees where moonlight and mist shrouded the woman. He could almost see her now, standing in the skeletal pines, the flash of her rosy copper hair catching the last rays of the sunset.

But the hollow was empty.

Peter swallowed down the rising tightness in his throat. "Nothing," he said. "I must have misremembered."

Unconvinced, Connor let it go. He glanced back over his shoulder. "You know," he muttered, "this would go a lot faster if we could just plane-walk to the lake."

"Plane-walk?" Peter asked, incredulous. "Did you just say 'plane-walk' as though it were perfectly normal behavior?"

Connor gaped at him. "It is perfectly normal. We do it all the time."

"You walk through different planes of existence all the time?"

"We walk through the Ether," Connor corrected. "It's really easy."

"Easy enough to do with eighteen people?" Peter asked.

Connor's lips twitched down. "No."

"Then that's not very useful, is it?" Peter said. He paused. "Though, it *is* very interesting. You'll have to show me that trick tomorrow."

Sticking out his hand, Connor smiled. "Deal."

Peter shook his hand. "It's a deal."

Over the next twenty minutes, the group fell into tense silence. The woods were difficult to traverse on a good day. With the snow and ice, it was twice as taxing. They slipped and shivered, reaching out to steady one another regularly. Surprisingly, Haley and her brothers moved easily. They often drifted through the snow without a sound, their eyes sharp and ears alert.

Though Connor assured them that the Druids wouldn't ambush them in the forest, they couldn't shake the worry. Every crack of a branch or rustle of wind caused the team to tense. Peter stretched his back at the top of the next hill, sure that he'd never be able to relax again.

Looking over the team as they walked through the forest, Peter's throat began to close up. He reached to rub at his neck, the memory of the bruises from the scylla's tentacles rising.

Had it really been only three weeks since the attack at the Mercier house? It felt like a lifetime to Peter. But then, he'd been locked in a vault for four and a half days with no way to track time. He'd nearly lost his sanity to the torture of a bird-beast.

Peter flexed his hand, forcing himself not to touch the signet ring that weighed down his finger. He didn't want to wind up like Cassandra, constantly twisting and turning the thing whenever he felt self-conscious—not that she wore her ring anymore. But the urge was strong, as though the ring was calling out to him, asking him to touch it.

Looking up from the snowbanks at his feet, Peter curled his fingers into a fist to quell the compulsion. He watched as Spencer and Cassandra walked side by side, arms brushing and regularly sharing sweet looks. He smiled to himself at their adorable behavior. He envied it, but he was happy for them.

At the front of the line, his eyes caught Silas walking with Owen, both men carrying a manner of strength and calm that Peter couldn't understand. They weren't that much older than him. Yet he felt like a child walking behind them.

The way they carried themselves, their surety and resolve—their baffling lack of concern for what others thought of them. *That* was what Peter couldn't understand. *That* was what made him feel like a kid.

While Owen and Silas were men, he was still stuck as that fourteen-year-old whose dad had just died.

Peter hadn't been ready to take care of a family then. To his great shame, that was his first thought when he heard of his dad's death. *"I'm not ready."*

He'd still had too much to learn. He hadn't been ready to care for a grieving mom and brother. He hadn't been ready to take on the emotional responsibility of protecting them. He hadn't been ready to make decisions or lead. And while their mom never asked it of him, Peter had been too young to understand.

Maybe he'd seen too many movies or read too many books. Maybe he'd idealized the role of a man in the household. Maybe he'd just been too narcissistic.

But when David Collins died, Peter accepted the new truth: It was *his* job to care for Mom and Spencer, no matter what.

How could he have been so selfish all those years ago? His dad died, and his first thought had been about himself. *"I'm not ready."* Ready for what? His dad's death wasn't a demand for him to grow up. No one forced him to take on the role of his dad. No one told him that he was the man of the house. He'd selfishly adopted it himself like the world would stop turning if he didn't step up.

"I'm not ready."

No one had asked him to be ready.

Peter's thumb brushed against the band of the signet ring. No one had asked until now.

The moment Silas explained the ring's meaning, the minute he'd looked at Peter and told him that he'd inherited the leadership of Benedict Varon's line, he'd thought it again. *"I'm not ready."*

Silas's words rang through Peter's head over and over again. *"We prioritize family . . . We look to the head of our line for direction . . . The family listens to the leader without fail . . . We have no one to step up and make the Warden listen."*

Peter *wasn't* ready for that. He couldn't be a voice for the Varons. He'd only just learned that he was a Varon a week ago. He didn't know half of the things that Silas knew. If anyone should lead, it should be Silas.

Who would listen to Peter anyway? He bumbled through life, making one mess after the next while he tried and failed to care for his family. And Silas wanted *him* to be a leader?

"I'm not ready."

The refrain echoed in Peter's chest, clogging up his throat as they climbed the final ridge of the forest. When they crested the climb, the lake would lay before them. Tom, Gabe, Aaron, Haley, and the rest of the team split off to find their positions, hidden in the trees. Owen, Silas, Spencer, Cassandra, Connor, and Peter slowly worked their way to the top of the hill.

"I'm not ready."

But Peter took the last step anyway.

The pines cleared around the massive expanse of the glass lake. Mist danced through the night air, the sky inky black and glittering with stars. High above them, the full moon glowed silvery-white. Cold swept off the water, freezing the air around them.

A shiver ran down Peter's spine as he stood next to Spencer. Everything remained silent as they scanned the lake. There was no sign of Druidic activity.

"You think they decided against it?" Peter whispered to Spencer.

Spencer took a step forward, his eyes on the lake's surface as though drawn by its presence. "Why would they?" he asked.

Connor stepped up to their side, his gaze flashing all around the edges of the forest. "They're here," he said. "They're just waiting for the moon to reach its peak."

"When will that be?" Peter asked.

"Around midnight," he said, then shrugged. "It's preferred, but if we make our move, they'll make theirs."

"So, they'll wait to tear the Veil unless we make them do it now?" Peter asked.

"Yes."

"Cool," he grumbled.

Cassandra turned to Silas and Owen. "What do we do?"

"You know their plans," Owen said to Connor. "Do we press them?"

Without hesitation, Connor nodded. "It's our best bet," he said. "Dad won't want to start the ritual until the moon's zenith. But he can't risk letting the Druids weaken their strength fighting us. He needs them to focus on tearing the Veil."

"How does that work, by the way?" Peter asked. "Do they just, I dunno—reach into the water or something?"

Connor frowned. "The Veil and the lake aren't physically linked."

"Right, so, how do they tear it then?"

"We don't have time for a detailed explanation," Silas interrupted. He turned to Connor. "Where would we find them? If they won't show themselves, we have to take the fight to them, right?"

Looking at the lake, Connor scanned the trees again. "I have a feeling," he took a step farther out of the tree line, "we just need to show ourselves."

The other five all exchanged worried looks but followed Connor's direction. Moving free of the shadows, they walked into the moonlight-drenched mist. The lake stretched for a mile, its kidney bean-like shape heavily obscured in the dense fog. Peter wondered if the Druids could even see them. What if they were on the far side? Even from their height on the hill, Peter couldn't see that distance.

A flicker of movement came from their right. A single figure stepped out of the forest, dressed for the cold winter night. Head held high, the moonlight lit up the man's golden blond hair. The smooth, raised voice of Alexander Frossard echoed across the large span of water between them. "Have you come for a fight, son?" he said.

Connor took a step in his father's direction. "Only if you refuse to stand down," he said.

A caustic scoff cut through the night. Alexander raised his right hand, summoning a rustle in the trees behind him. Twenty-some men and women emerged from the tree line. The DeVerrean Druids all came to enact the Unleashing. And along with them, an entire horde of beasts.

Hydras, hellhounds, wendigos, scylla, valravn, and every other kind that Peter still didn't know the names of yet. Their black forms haunted the water's edge like a storm cloud. Their neon yellow eyes pierced the night. They numbered somewhere near a hundred, he guessed.

One hundred beasts and twenty Druids.

Peter looked to Spencer, pulse elevated. He had the sudden, suicidal urge to charge the cult members. This was the whole of them. Every last Druid in DeVerre, there to tear the Veil. If they killed them all, the town would be saved. In one fell swoop, they'd rid DeVerre of its enemy and complete the mission their great-grandparents had set out to accomplish.

"We could do it," Peter whispered, knowing his brother had the same thought.

Eyes bright even in the darkness, Spencer clenched his jaw. "Probably," he said.

Cassandra stepped between them. "Definitely," she added.

A hand clamped onto Peter's shoulder, and he jerked around to look up at Owen, Silas standing just behind him. "That's not how we handle things," Owen said.

Peter was ready to argue his case—these twenty-odd lives in exchange for the whole of DeVerre's safety. Over twenty murderers and liars in exchange for hundreds of innocents. Why *wouldn't* that be the right way to handle it?

But he never got the chance as Alexander began to speak again, calling to his son. "You've made promises to me," he reminded Connor. "We don't break our word."

"You've manipulated this whole town my entire life," Connor spat, edging farther away from the group in his agitation.

Peter made to follow. Spencer and Cassandra kept at his side as Connor continued to talk. "Don't tell me you keep your word," he yelled.

"When have I lied to you?" Alexander demanded. "When have I not kept up my end of the bargain?"

Connor didn't reply, his shoulders trembling in rage.

But Peter knew his lack of response wasn't out of the same anger. It was because Alexander spoke the truth. He never had lied to his son. Perhaps to others, but not Connor.

"This is your last chance, Connor," the Druid leader called. The lake twinkled in the night, reflecting off Alexander's pale face. "Abandon these fools and come back to us. Every deal we made will hold if you come back."

"I wouldn't trust you," Connor snarled, "if my life depended on it."

Even from the distance, Alexander's sigh whispered through the mist.

He raised a hand with an almost regretful air. "What if her life depended on it?" he said.

Peter furrowed his brow as the tree line rustled again. He knew even before he saw her. Peter knew, and his heart dropped into his stomach. "No," he whispered. "No, no, no, no."

A petite, lithe woman led the way out of the woods, a hulking, monstrous figure half-carrying, half-dragging another behind it. Connor shuffled forward, Peter and the rest of the group on his heels as they watched Anna struggle to keep up with the wendigo's long strides.

"Hi, love," the woman called with a wave, the wendigo at her side.

Peter recognized that fairylike face.

"I swear to God, Lily," Connor ground out, "if you touch her—"

"Oh, please," Lily interrupted. "I've already 'touched' her. She's got a nice new memento courtesy of my charming wendigo here."

With a panicked gait, Owen scrambled to Peter's side. "What did you do to her?" he demanded.

"I'm fine," Anna promised, her voice trembling.

Though they'd shuffled forward, they still stood a good distance away from the Druids, the lake and its ice and snow-laden rocky beach between them. In the mist and the darkness, the details were obscured, but Peter's throat dried up as he saw something dark and damp glimmer on Anna's coat.

"Anna," he heard himself calling before he realized it. "Anna, what did they do?"

"I'm fine," she promised again, tears lacing her words. "I'm—I'm fine."

Connor's whole body shook. "Let her go," he ordered. "Let her go now, or I swear, I will kill you."

"You've sworn that in the past," Alexander said. "So, you'll forgive me if I don't take you seriously this time."

Drifting toward Lily, Anna, and the wendigo, Alexander kept talking. "It is not in my preference to hurt someone I consider a friend," he said, stopping at Anna's side. "But sometimes, the people you care about the most turn their back on you."

Alexander reached out to brush back some of Anna's hair that had fallen free of her ponytail. She jerked back, but the moonlight glinted off her skin, revealing the Druid's handiwork.

Peter's jaw dropped as the light shone on the slowly bleeding quartet of slits that sliced across her temple, cheek, and jawline. Connor swore under his breath, staggering forward.

"It's superficial," Alexander promised. "But she'll carry the scars as a reminder to you and everyone else. We keep our word."

"You promised not to hurt her!" Connor yelled.

"So long as *you* did as *I* ordered!" Alexander roared back. "*You* broke the deal. Don't complain to me when your actions have consequences."

Peter felt his hands curl in and out of fists at his side. Fury and fear fought an unending battle in him. They needed to get Anna away from that wendigo. But the beast held her in front of itself like a shield. The riflemen in the forest would do no good. Bullets meant nothing to beasts. And if any of the Wielders sent an arc at the thing, it might hurt her too.

Maybe they could override Lily's control of the beast. Was that even a possibility? Cassandra had taken control of the hellhound Debbie sent after them. Surely, they could do the same with Lily's wendigo. But if she was a Vessel, that meant she had the same power as Cassandra, and Peter didn't think it'd be as simple as wresting control from the woman.

"Our deal still stands, Connor," Alexander said. "Leave them. Forget these Varons, and I will let Anna live."

The deal's reverse was implied. Stay with Peter and Spencer, and Alexander would let Anna die.

"I don't desire a fight with you, son," Alexander pressed. "Every one of those people behind you will die tonight. I have no interest in killing you too."

Connor kept shifting in the snow, his feet fighting a losing battle to run to Anna. No matter what he chose, it would be the wrong choice. Stay with the Varons, and he'd lose Anna. Betray the Varons, and he'd lose her all the same, but for another reason.

A piercing *crack* reverberated through the trees to Peter's right, and somehow, he knew it had been Haley's rifle that made the shot. Just as he knew, the bullet sailed right for Lily's head. Peter's heart leaped into his throat with hope. If Lily died, the wendigo would disappear. The Druids would lose their Vessel. Their greatest problem would be solved.

He held his breath, expectant.

Then a flare of obsidian black rippled through the air, deflecting the bullet to fall into the snow.

"Nice try," Lily called into the forest. "I've got all three of us covered. And trust me, I'm not gonna let that shield drop for anything."

"I could have told them that," Silas ground out, voice low. "They've given themselves away."

As though in reaction to his statement, Alexander turned to a handful of his Druids. "Find them," he ordered.

A band of ten beasts tore into the forest, their shadowy forms speeding into the darkness. Peter's heart lurched. Though bullets *could* hurt beasts, it took too many to kill them. They'd just lost their plan B.

"Run!" Silas yelled into the woods, warning their riflemen.

Peter hoped they'd listen, praying that they'd make it back to Occasus and the vault before those beasts got them.

"This is your last chance, Connor," Alexander said furiously. "You join us now, and I'll let Anna go."

Shaking and silent, Connor stared straight at Anna.

"Don't do it," Anna told him, then gasped as the wendigo tightened its grip on her shoulder. Its razor-sharp claws dug through her coat like it was the thinnest gossamer.

Peter could practically hear the panicked gulp as Connor swallowed. "Anna, I—" He stopped, then turned to Peter. "I have to."

With absolutely zero doubt, Peter nodded. "Yeah, man," he said. "Save her!"

Connor looked frantically from Peter to Owen to Spencer, Cassandra, and Silas. "I'm sorry."

"Save her," Owen repeated.

With a single backward step, Connor whirled around to the Druids. "I'll do it."

Alexander let out a longsuffering sigh.

At his side, Lily huffed.

"Here's how this will work," Alexander said. "You come forward halfway, and we'll send Anna to meet you in the middle. Then you'll come to us, and she'll go to her friends. You will lend your power to *our* cause, or we will kill her. Understood?"

Connor gave a nod. "Understood."

"Good."

Alexander motioned for the exchange to begin.

Connor took a step forward as Alexander turned to Lily. "Release her," he ordered.

Lily smirked in Connor's direction. "No."

She said it so offhandedly that Peter hardly processed what happened before it was over.

With a bored flip of her wrist, Lily wielded her beast. Like lightning, the wendigo's clawed hands flew to Anna's head, and with a sickening *snap*, it broke her neck.

Peter couldn't exactly say what happened after Anna fell. It was as though her body hitting the cold, frosted earth released absolute chaos. A horrified cry of alarm erupted from Cassandra as a scream came from the forest. Owen began hyperventilating. Connor fell to his knees in the snow, his eyes on the body some thirty feet away.

The Druids shifted nervously as Alexander yelled at Lily, "We honor our agreements!"

Indifferently, she replied, "*I* never agreed to anything."

And Peter . . . Peter was numb.

He stood there, mouth hanging open, his brain incapable of

processing what he'd just witnessed. He thought he was trembling, but he couldn't be sure. He also thought he was crying, but that might've been the cold mist stinging his face.

Connor screamed, his deep voice tearing through the air as thick bands of charcoal surged out of him, ripping across the barren snow as he unleashed his rage.

CHAPTER THIRTY-FOUR

Spencer

The moment those charcoal arcs tore out of Connor's hunched form, screaming in fury as he knelt in the snow, Spencer knew all hell was about to break loose.

Arms around Cassandra as she shook from the shock of Anna's death, Spencer felt his body begin to thrum with anticipation. Owen stood to the side, his breathing labored as he looked ready to bolt for his sister-in-law's body. Silas watched in wide-eyed fascination and horror as the dark bands of the spirit world's essence pulsed out of Connor in wave after wave, coiling around his torso before shooting out toward the Druids.

The Druids were in chaos. Alexander looked as if he was ready to kill Lily himself, the outrage plain on his face. Spencer wondered absently if the man was purely angry because of her disobedience or if he truly felt grief over Anna.

Waiting for their Elder's orders, the rest of the Druids threw up shields of black arcs to combat Connor's attacks. They flashed and disintegrated with each arc strike. Tony MacDonald stepped forward from the group, calling Alexander's name as a handful of Connor's arcs met their target.

And all the while, Peter stood there, absolutely frozen.

With no other recourse, Spencer released Cassandra. He grabbed his brother's arm, jerking him out of his stupor. Peter blinked rapidly, gaping at him in shock.

"We have to fight!" Spencer demanded.

That seemed to snap Peter out of it. His jaw hardened as he held Spencer's stare. Then bright golden light beamed from Peter's fists, the essence of the spirit world coiling around his arms and hands. He didn't say a word but turned and strode toward the Druids.

Spencer followed, the cool tingle of the spirit world passing over his skin as he summoned its essence.

Alexander got control of his people once more, shouting at them to begin the ritual while the horde of beasts surged for their group on the hilltop.

Stepping up to either side of Connor, the brothers released their arcs at the same time. Bronze and gold light burst out, meeting with the charcoal streaks that still radiated from Connor. The arcs slammed into the rushing horde of beasts, causing an eruption of shadow and ash to filter into the fog of the lake before dissipating altogether.

Connor's shoulders began to slump with what Spencer assumed was exhaustion, so he reached down and slapped the man's arm. "Get up," he told him. "We do this together."

With little time to dwell, Spencer returned to the fight.

The beasts came at them, a stampede of shadow. Peter's broad, golden arcs took out a small grouping at the front, but more leaped forward to take their place. A trio of copper arcs flew out next, taking down three more beasts in succession.

Silas stepped up to Spencer's side. "We don't have time for this," he said, even as he summoned more arcs. "The Druids are starting the ritual."

In between sending out arcs, Spencer's gaze flew to the waterline.

Clustered by the black, glassy surface, the Druids took their places, shoulder to shoulder, hands outstretched over the water. Alexander was speaking, maybe chanting, but Spencer couldn't hear the words.

Then, as one, the Druids released their power.

Obsidian-black shadows poured out of the Druidic ranks. Shadows flowed from their hands, their arms, their torsos, all the way down to their feet. Rippling and coiling, the dark essence of the spirit world seeped from their forms and straight into the lake's surface. Some summoned arcs, while others summoned beasts. But all of them were pumping their power into the lake.

A surge of panic rose in Spencer's chest. He didn't understand their plan, but he knew he didn't like this offering of dark power. And he desperately wanted to stop it.

The lake called Spencer a step in its direction as though he could protect it. But the wall of beasts lay between him and the Druids. And the monsters were closing in.

A soft gray light like the snowy morning sky surrounded their band in a six-foot radius. Beasts slammed into its luminous forcefield, clawing and scratching and slicing to tear through.

Spencer turned to find Cassandra in the center of their group, her hand held to the sky. Ivory and that pale gray rippled around her palm, a thin thread connected to the dome above them. It was the same sort of structure that Silas had conjured in the funeral home. But instead of looking intently and desperately focused as he had, she met Spencer's gaze with a steady, unworried calm.

"Let's end this," she said, her raspy voice filling him with courage.

Charcoal arcs now subsided, Connor stood, the fury still causing his limbs to shake. "Stick to the plan," he said. "Lily *has* to die."

Though Spencer didn't doubt there was some vengeance within Connor's demand, for the sake of DeVerre, he knew it had to happen.

The beasts threw themselves against the dome of light, causing it to spark and gutter in protest. Cassandra didn't show any sign of strain. "I can hold it," she promised. "We'll make our way to the Druids, taking down beasts as we go."

Plan in place, the men did as ordered.

Bronze, gold, copper, amber, and charcoal arcs rent the night. Light met the darkness, pulling it apart into vapor.

"Don't waste your energy," Owen warned. "Small bursts. We need to save our strength for the Druids."

It took too long. Inch by inch, they moved forward, removing one beast from the forcefield for another to take its place. Five men against the beasts' slowly dwindling numbers wasn't enough. Not while the Druids were casually throwing all their power into the lake.

Spencer wondered if that was their plan. Were they overloading the Veil with power, filling it up until it couldn't contain anymore? Was that how the Veils tore? With an overwhelming power so great that they finally just burst open. If that were the case, how much power could the Veil hold?

Silas sent a large wave of copper energy, his stance staggered to support the effort. Ten beasts exploded at once. "We don't have time," he repeated his earlier warning.

"Cassandra," Silas called, "we need you to do your thing."

"Which thing?" she asked.

"The nyct," he said. "Your Patronus."

Unsure what the man was referring to, Spencer looked at Cassandra just in time to see her roll her eyes. "How is that going to help?" she asked.

"It'll protect you," he explained. "Take Spencer, Peter, and Connor and get to the Druids. Owen and I will watch your back. You have to stop them before the Veil is torn."

"You guys gonna have the energy to take on the rest of these beasts alone?" Peter asked warily.

"We'll be fine," Silas promised.

Spencer couldn't help wondering if he was just saying it to make them listen.

"I'm going to drop the barrier," Cassandra warned.

"Do it."

With a flicker, the forcefield dropped, letting the clamoring beasts swell forward, tripping over themselves and one another with the sudden release. All the men sent out another wave of arcs, taking down many of the now onrushing creatures.

Then Cassandra gasped.

Spencer whirled to find her eyes closed as radiant platinum light shimmered around her whole body. The essence rippled like an arc as it took shape with arched ears and folded leathery wings. The form looked exactly like the beasts she'd summoned to save them a week ago. Batlike, but definitely not a bat. Not given the softer, angelic features of this creature.

The rift-form hovered around Cassandra, wholly separate from her but like a second coat. When she opened her eyes and turned to look at Spencer, the light-creature's head turned with her, a soft silver gleam in her gaze. She turned with the rifts shimmering around her and sent a giant arc slicing through the ranks before them.

Connor muttered an awe-filled curse. Spencer agreed.

Cassandra reached over and grabbed Spencer's arm. The tingle of her rift-form worked through the layers of his clothes, sending gooseflesh along his skin. "Come on," she ordered, then broke into a sprint.

Amber and copper light bled into each other, keeping the path open before Cassandra. It hardly seemed necessary. As soon as any beast neared Cassandra, her form expanded, the essence lunging in all directions to defend her like a guardian angel. Nearest to Cassandra's side, Spencer gained the benefit of this defense. Peter and Connor had to protect themselves.

Spencer dropped back to help. Not far, but just enough to ensure his brother's safety.

Breaking through the final line of beasts, they came within feet of the Druids lined up along the lake's edge. Shadows writhed around their figures, power pouring into the water in undulating, smoky waves. How long had they had to infuse the Ether into the lake? How much more could the Veil hold?

Without time to question their plan of action, Spencer sent a barrier of energy toward the nearest Druids. It slammed into their backs, knocking them straight into the lake with a cracking splash. A thin, now broken, layer of ice glittered at the water's sloshing edge.

As the two Druids rose, shivering and gasping, in the shallows of the lake, several others turned to help them.

"Focus!" Alexander commanded. "You know your roles."

A handful of Druids stepped away from the line as the rest returned to their work. Spencer recognized several of the DeVerreans that now faced them. Leonard Guillaume. Joanne MacDonald. Alan Sauveterre. Dylan, the cook from The Glass Tavern. A Frossard man he couldn't put a name to and two middle-aged women he didn't know. In an instant, all seven were surrounded by newly summoned beasts.

Cassandra's rift-form swelled as she stepped to the front. Spencer stuck close, his bronze arcs melding with the ivory-gray of hers. Beasts fell as soon as they'd risen. Taking the opportunity, Spencer rushed forward to take the Druids down. He got to Alan first, the man raising his hand either to stop Spencer's approach, summon another beast, or both. Spencer twisted his arm around Alan's, gaining a solid grip to shove as he hooked his foot around the man's ankle and jerked it out from under him. Alan hit the frozen bank with a *thunk.*

Spencer sent a numbing arc into Alan's chest before spinning to face the Frossard man. It became evident to Spencer that none of these people had any self-defense training as his adept skills took the second man down in two seconds flat.

The rocky and icy terrain made it difficult for Spencer to keep his footing. He ducked as Dylan from the tavern attempted to grab him. Spencer slapped the man's arm right above the elbow, hoping to hit the nerves there. Dylan's shocked cry marked his success.

Beasts formed and dissolved around him. Arcs sailed through the air like road flares. Spencer caught a flash of movement as Connor sprinted to the far side of the Druid line. Following the man's trajectory, Spencer saw what he was headed for.

Lily.

With a fast check on Cassandra and Peter, Spencer assured himself they could handle these last few Druids and their beasts. He knocked away Dylan's next attempt to grapple, then shot his hand forward to catch the man under the chin with his fist. Dylan dropped. He probably wasn't unconscious but likely very dazed.

Dodging the others, Spencer hurried after Connor. Under normal circumstances, Spencer might have stayed at Peter and Cassandra's side, preferring to protect them over anyone. But this wasn't about Connor's protection. He needed to ensure the young Frossard didn't die before he accomplished his goal.

However callous and wrong it felt, Lily *had* to die. They couldn't let her live to receive the Spectral. They couldn't give the Druids the chance to obtain such power.

Chasing Connor across the snowy, craggy lakeside, Spencer had to draw up short as a horde of beasts formed from the shadows before him. He was faced with a trio of black-scaled monsters with ridges protruding along their spines like massive Komodo dragons. Their onyx tongues flickered out, viscous in the moonlight.

Spencer's heart pounded in his ears as he skidded to a stop. He almost lost his footing, staring at the beasts that were vaguely reminiscent of his nightmares. All beasts were bad—at least, those of the shadow variety. He'd come to that conclusion a month ago. With dull fascination, Spencer's mind told him that, yes, it had been a month ago. One month ago today, his nightmares had come to life when he and Peter ran from a hellhound.

One month and so much had changed.

The cool detachment of the thought soothed Spencer's rising fear.

He'd run a month ago because he didn't know who he was. Now, he could stand his ground, knowing exactly who he was.

Spencer Varon.

He may not be *the* Varon heir, but he was the heir of Occasus and DeVerre. He would defend his home and his family no matter what.

Summoning forth a large bronze arc, Spencer gave one glance ahead to see Connor reach Lily. He grabbed a fistful of the woman's collar, yanking her back, his other hand alight with an arc. But Lily had been prepared, and her obsidian-black arc struck first. Connor slammed onto his back, his body seizing.

Without a moment to spare, Spencer faced down the three lizardlike beasts. Huge and hulking, they towered over him. Their legs were as thick as the oldest trees in the forest, tipped with fierce talons. Dodging the snap of their horrendously large maws, Spencer shot forth arc after arc. The rifts ricocheted off their scales, drawing out smoky trails of shadow. He had to strike truer and deeper than that glossy black hide would allow.

Lily's mocking singsong reached Spencer across the distance as he fought the beasts. "It's your fault, by the way," she was telling Connor. She practically danced across the frosted ground. "I'd have let her live, but you were supposed to be *mine*." She knelt in the muddy snow, her soft lilac coat a glaring disparity in all the darkness around them.

Spencer knew what Connor fought now—he knew the paralysis of an arc. Connor was struggling to breathe. His heart had stopped, and his muscles were spasming in the demand for his body to function properly.

One of Spencer's bronze arcs hit a lizard in the sternum, causing the creature to crumble into ash.

Lily took hold of Connor's jaw with one hand. "I'm a lot of things, Connor, but I'm not good at sharing," she said, raising her free hand. Black danced around her fingertips, and Spencer knew, somehow, he *knew* that she intended to shatter Connor's soul.

With a final, determined twin burst of light, Spencer brought down the remaining beasts. He charged across the ground. His boots pounded into the hard earth, his calves near burning from the strain. If he was beginning to feel the effects of exhaustion, he feared how Peter was holding up.

Lily thrust her hand toward Connor's chest just as Spencer dove. He slammed into Lily, ripping her away from Connor's prone form. They tumbled across the rugged terrain, icy rocks digging and ripping into them, forcing Spencer to release his grip. They rolled to the lake's edge, scrambling to rise.

With unnatural speed, Lily managed to discharge an arc. The dark rift struck Spencer's shoulder, his right arm and half of his chest going entirely numb. His right lung collapsed, making it hard to catch his breath. Gritting his teeth against the awful pain that tensed all his muscles, he forced himself to his feet.

Another black arc raced for him, but Spencer summoned a bronze barrier to deflect it. Still, the force of it pushed him back a step.

So, this was what fighting a Vessel was like, Spencer thought. One with the training Cassandra would have had if she'd been raised a Druid too. Stronger, faster, and far more dangerous than even a Varon.

Lily's next arc was so powerful it forced Spencer to take a knee as he blocked it.

Lily's elegant, elfin features distorted, unnaturally ethereal under the full moon. She stood over him, black energy rolling around her, diffusing off her hands and arms. "Your girlfriend's not gonna get my Spectral," she crooned. "I've sacrificed too much for that."

Spencer's right arm tingled with the hope of returning sensation, but he knew it wouldn't be fast enough. If he wanted to survive this fight, he'd have to make every hit count. He had to be smart. He had to slow her down.

"Given the choice," he taunted, "you think the Spectral's going to pick you? Your own fiancé didn't even want you."

A nefarious gleam lit Lily's sharp green eyes as she took hold of Spencer's collar. "Such a fuss over the Varons," she said. Her hand lifted. "When you were so easy to kill."

As Lily reared her hand back, Spencer took his shot. With his off hand, he aimed as precisely as he could, hoping beyond reason that it would work. Bright, bronze light seared through the space between him and Lily, straight into those vile, green eyes.

Lily's head snapped back as though hit with an uppercut. Her eyes rolled back, and her body went limp. Her legs buckled at the knees, and she dropped, falling face-first into the frigid lake.

Gasping, Spencer's mind reeled. He'd managed to kill her so easily. Too easily. A single hit shouldn't have taken her down, not with all that power she'd displayed. His right arm still tingled, and his head screamed with shock as he stared at her body, submerged to the chest while the rest of her lay on the snowy ground.

Lily was dead. Now, they *had* to stop the Druids. If they didn't, Cassandra would take on the Spectral.

With his good hand, Spencer pushed to his feet. He turned to see Peter and Cassandra fighting side by side, her rift-form now twice its size but dimming. They fought a new host of Druids and beasts, but they weren't alone.

At the top of the hill, Haley, Aaron, and her brothers used their rifles to snipe, covering Peter and Cassandra. Their bullets weren't as impactful as an arc against the beasts, but they struck hard into the flesh and bone of Druids. Silas and Owen protected the riflemen on the hill, keeping beasts at bay. A handful of copper-tinged beasts of light worked with them, creatures of Silas's summoning.

Secure in their safety, Spencer moved to check on Connor. The arc should be wearing off, and they'd need his help to stop the Druids. Even with the members they'd lost, they had to be close to completing their ritual.

Spencer took his first step away from the lake when a shrill whining sound screeched through the air. On instinct, he dropped his head into his hands, gripping it against the piercing sound. The shrieking drone reverberated through his mind, making him sway on his feet with its force. It sounded like a boiling kettle or a whistle but grew into a trilling note that vibrated through Spencer's chest. His heart expanded as though trying to pump blood faster, and pressure built, filling his mind completely.

Grimacing through the earsplitting screech, Spencer turned. The black surface of the lake rippled, bobbing in rapid, violent undulation.

"No," he heard himself breathe as his gaze flew to the line of Druids.

They stood, hands at their sides, eyes wide in wonder as they watched the surface. It was done. The Unleashing had come.

Without warning, the whining sound cut off, and the world went still. Spencer felt the pressure settle at the base of his skull.

Silence filled the air.

Then, the lake exploded.

Like shrapnel, the water burst outward, cutting into everyone near the bank with its icy droplets. Spencer's hair was plastered to his skin, his coat drenched in the frigid water. But he didn't flinch away, his eyes too focused on the furious beam of light that tore out of the lake, ripping into the night sky.

Head tilted back, Spencer watched as the beam appeared to strike the moon. In a supernova of light, it erupted with a *thrum* that sent a blast of wind and light sailing across the expanse of the lake and into the forest, slamming into everyone in its wake.

The force of it knocked Spencer off his feet, the air rushing from his lungs. He had two seconds to question if this was what it felt like to be hit by a car before he dropped, his head colliding with something unforgivingly hard, and his grip on consciousness released.

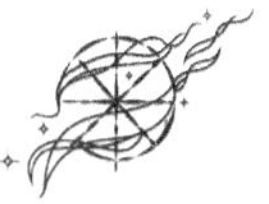

CHAPTER THIRTY-FIVE

Cassandra

Cassandra knew the exact moment the Druids tore the Veil. Even as she and Peter fought the beasts around them, she saw the immediate relaxation of Alexander Frossard's shoulders as the ritual ended. Not a second later, the high-pitched whine began.

Everyone stopped then. They all watched, the world going still.

The beasts, the Druids. Cassandra and Peter. Their friends on the slope of the hill. Spencer, far from their side.

The cry trilled higher and higher, piercing into Cassandra's body. She could have sworn she felt a pressure against her mind then. The presence of something new.

The pressure abated, and the silence came.

A beam of light ripped out of the lake, drenching them in the ice-cold water. The light erupted, and a wind careened through the clearing, barreling into all of them.

Cassandra and Peter were knocked off their feet, falling into the snow. Frozen rocks cut into her hands as she tried to catch herself. A blooming warmth spread wetly across her palms, blood beading along the jagged cuts.

"You okay?" Peter asked, grabbing her arm protectively.

Sitting up, Cassandra meant to tell him she was fine, but her jaw dropped as all sense left her.

Out of the lake, like waves on a beach, surged beast after beast. A mottled army of ashen gray creatures, their leathery skin and angular features unfinished, almost undecided. All of them bore those batlike characteristics of the nyct. Silky-skinned wings, piercing talons, and beady eyes. But they weren't terrifying like the beasts summoned by the Druids. Neither were they what Peter and Spencer had described to Cassandra when she'd summoned them.

When she'd summoned nyct of her own.

"Oh, God," Cassandra gasped out in a terrified prayer.

The Veil was torn. The Spectral was free.

Pressing a hand to her chest, Cassandra tried to focus, to determine any difference in herself. That pressure—that presence. Had that been the Spectral? Had it connected to her?

"Did you feel that?" Cassandra asked Peter, but he was too distracted watching as the water swelled, and more and more beasts rose from its waterline. Druids rose to their feet, watching with childlike wonder as the creatures spread their fibrous wings and took to the sky. The Druids began to cheer and celebrate. They'd succeeded. The Final Unleashing was complete at long last.

The ghosts of DeVerre stood in the trees. The shimmering gray host watched the celebration with a mixture of emotions. Most bore expressions of pride and elation—Druids. A few looked angry or saddened by the sight—Warden members?

Lifting a hand to her mouth, Cassandra smelled the metallic sting of blood too late. She felt the slick fluid on her chin and tasted it on her lips, making her gag as she flipped her hand around to wipe it off.

Peter was working to drag Cassandra to her feet now, his hands firm on her arms. She forced herself to help him rather than wallow in her self-pity. They'd failed. And now, the Spectral . . . had it connected to her already?

The sudden memory of Connor and Spencer rushing for Lily sprang to Cassandra's mind. What if they hadn't succeeded? What if the Spectral chose Lily?

Jerking her head to her left, she searched for Spencer or the Druid Vessel. She couldn't find either of them. Finally, she saw Connor kneeling over a body. Spencer's body.

Cassandra gasped, grabbing Peter's coat.

Peter followed her gaze, then tensed.

Several yards away, Connor looked up, meeting their waiting stares. With a single, comforting nod, he alleviated their fears. Spencer was alive. Unconscious but alive.

And they still had work to do.

In the eruption of wind and light, the beasts of the Druids had crumbled. The mist of the lake dispersed, the new nyct crowding the lakeside and the night sky. She didn't know if the Druids could control them, but she knew they had to stop this never-ending birth of beasts. They couldn't let them fill up the forests and wander into DeVerre any more than they could let the Druids win this fight.

Cassandra was tired. She was very, very tired. But torn Veil or not, she wasn't about to give up.

The initial excitement of the moment passed, and the Druids began to regain their senses. Alexander Frossard stood at the edge of the lake, surveying the landscape. Cassandra could see the moment he discovered his son standing at Spencer's side, looking out to the lake where Lily's lifeless body lay.

The Elder tensed, his expression going slack. They'd torn the Veil, but they'd lost the Vessel.

Alexander jerked his head around, his gaze landing on Cassandra. "Take her!" he commanded.

There was only a two-second delay in the Druids' obedience, during which time Peter tugged Cassandra behind him. She'd lost her holoform when she'd fallen. But she could still feel the whisper of the spirit world against her skin. The vibration of the sound beyond sound waiting for her to reach out to it once more.

Fear drew its cold fingers down Cassandra's spine. Was it a coincidence that she felt it so strongly now? Was it due to the full moon, rising higher with each passing moment? Or was it because of the connection that now linked her to the Spectral of DeVerre?

Less than twenty Druids remained. They'd brought down a handful, but Cassandra wondered if it was enough. Some of the Druids, including Alexander, began wielding arcs while the rest summoned beasts. Nine Sages, eight Clerics.

A *crack* echoed into the night, and one of the Clerics dropped as a bullet hit him square in the forehead. Cassandra jumped, wondering how many more times she'd watch someone die.

Gunshots pealed through the air, the Druid Sages throwing up shields to protect their numbers. They sent out arcs toward Peter and Cassandra, which they blocked easily. Silas and Owen were at their sides then, fighting with them. They helped bring down the beasts that charged forward, keeping the Druids back. Connor aided from the sidelines, protecting Spencer's unconscious form.

Cassandra could have let it continue with such slow, steady progress. She could have allowed them to defend against the Druids, content to kill as few of them as possible. But the nyct were still rising from the lake. They cluttered the starlit sky, their wings flapping with a dry rasp.

This had to end. And she was a Vessel. It ought to be her that did it.

Stepping around Peter, Cassandra let go of all her fear. She released the last force of control over her will and let the spirit world flood her mind, her heart, her very being. Her limbs trembled with power, ready for release.

The roar of wind filled her ears, her nerves sparking to life. And light flashed.

The last time this happened, Cassandra had gone into a strange fugue state. This time, she experienced it all. A portal of ivory-gray rippled around her, pulling back the Veil into the spirit world like tying back the curtains in her room. Half in and half out, they stood in the spiritual and natural as the portal rose higher and higher.

The Druids halted in their approach, shock written over their expressions.

When the portal hit the nyct that soared through the sky and emerged from the lake, they paused. The whole forest seemed to come to a resounding halt, silence descending in the strange in-between of spirit and physical.

The nyct landed, the lake stilled, and the world held its breath. All waited for Cassandra's command.

"No more," Cassandra said, her voice flat.

Alexander watched her with something resembling awe-filled greed. "You belong with us, Cassandra," he said. "You always have."

Without acknowledging his feeble attempt, Cassandra looked over the rest of the Druids. "I will give you one chance," she told them. "You can stand down and renounce the Druids. Or you will forfeit your life."

Her skin tingled as her mind worked to maintain its hold on the intangible essence. She had to keep her attention wholly on controlling the world beyond, controlling the ebb of beasts that wanted to walk through the now-torn portal.

The Veil had always been thin; now it felt like cobwebs, disintegrating under the touch of her will. Cassandra had to stop the Druids so that she could draw the curtain back over the spirit world. Not a permanent fix—that was impossible—but a temporary closure, one strong enough to keep the beasts from pouring out so freely.

"We will never submit," Tony MacDonald spat. "Not to unbelievers like you."

A resounding approval came from the ranks of the Druids, their loyalty unflinching.

With an internal sigh, Cassandra accepted what came next.

Without a word, the Druids sprang forward, attacking with renewed fervor. Black shadows streamed around them, racing for Cassandra, Peter, Owen, Silas, Haley, Aaron, and the Roux brothers on the hill.

Gold, amber, and copper flashed around Cassandra as gunshots rang out.

She closed her eyes, listening past the clamor of pounding feet, past the heavy breaths, past the roars, growls, hisses, clacks, bellows, and screams of beasts. She shut out all sounds, focusing on the one she wanted most: silence.

And then, she heard the almost hum that vibrated into her core—the pulse of atoms that flowed with sound.

Without opening her eyes, Cassandra felt every nyct at the lake connect with her will. Her desire became theirs. Her urging, their actions. She spoke, and they listened. And she rested in the stillness as the hundreds of ashen beasts turned to light.

~

Cassandra sat on the snow, her body still thrumming with energy. She should have been exhausted, but adrenaline didn't let her feel it. Instead, she felt a strange detachment, surveying DeVerre Lake at midnight.

Bodies littered the lakeside. All Druids. The council members. Regular citizens. Even Alexander Frossard. It had taken less than two minutes for the nyct and those from Occasus to end them.

Cassandra's throat clogged up. With Connor's help, they'd identified the bodies on the lakeside. Twenty-three DeVerreans. "It's not all of them," he said. "There are . . . there are a few kids."

"Kids?" Owen asked.

"The ones who know—the ones who became Druids themselves," Connor explained, "they're almost all in high school. But obviously, most of these people had families."

Cassandra dropped her face into her hands. They'd made orphans out of dozens of children in DeVerre. Connor and Peter tried to convince Cassandra that they hadn't had a choice.

"Druids are devout," Connor said. "And they will happily die for their cause."

"I don't think their children would happily lose them, though," Cassandra replied.

Now, she sat beside Spencer's sleeping form, her heart numb and her muscles frozen. She and Peter had rushed over to assure themselves of his safety. His pulse was low and steady, his breathing even. Other than the blood that matted the back of his hair, he was whole and well, like he was simply asleep back in the vault at Occasus.

Peter sat on his brother's other side, glassy-eyed.

Sparing a single glance to the far side of the lake, Cassandra watched as Silas managed the disaster, helping Devon and Logan Roux lay out the Druids' bodies for retrieval. Tom and Gabe had their work cut out for them. At the far side of the clearing, near the pine trees, Owen, Aaron, Haley, and Connor all wept over Anna's body.

Tears clogged Cassandra's throat. She turned back to look at the water.

"We did the right thing," Peter muttered.

Cassandra didn't answer.

He fidgeted with the golden ring on his finger. "Doesn't make it easier."

Staring over the obsidian-black glass lake, Cassandra's heart felt heavier and darker than ever before. They'd defeated the Druids, but at what cost? And what of the Spectral? She couldn't say that she felt different, but . . . would she?

The Veil was torn; Cassandra could feel that. What had once felt like a thick, velvet curtain now felt like the thinnest lace, weightless under her touch. She could clearly hear the spirit world humming through the world around them.

DeVerre might have been free of the Druids, but the danger remained.

They sat there in silence until Cassandra thought the frost had begun to spread over her body. She didn't want to walk back through the woods in the heart of the night, but they didn't have a choice. Fresh snow fell, ready to claim their bodies if they didn't leave. Peter and Silas carried Spencer's unconscious form, while Aaron and Connor carried Anna's lifeless body. Owen led the way with Haley at his side. Cassandra stayed at the back.

The DeVerrean Faction of Druids was gone, but this wasn't a victory. Not by any stretch of the imagination. And Cassandra couldn't help wondering how long it would take for the town to recover from its loss.

CHAPTER THIRTY-SIX

Owen

The hollowness of grief left Owen numb and vacant.

Waking the morning after the Unleashing, he felt no different. Somehow, he kept breathing and walking and talking. Behaving as though DeVerre hadn't lost its most wonderful and cherished resident. As though he hadn't lost his sister.

With the need to feel something beyond that aching sense of emptiness, Owen reached across the bed, looping his arm around Ava's waist to draw her closer. She didn't fight his touch but curled into his chest, more of the silent tears that neither could escape falling onto her cheeks. He pressed his nose into the braids of her hair, breathing in her scent of jasmine oil and the ever-present crisp of books.

Ava was what drove Owen's rote ability to function. Both last night when he'd been desperate to ensure her safety and this morning when he needed to ensure her comfort.

They'd returned to Occasus to find Ava unconscious. An hour after they departed for the lake, Sam realized that neither Anna nor Ava had returned to the vault. Sam and two other volunteers had chosen to leave the vault to find them in the rest of the house. They'd discovered Ava in the foyer, sprawled on the entry rug. The coat closet hung open, and Anna was gone.

Given the clear sign of a struggle, the assumption was that Anna had been taken. Whoever it'd been and however they'd knocked Ava unconscious, it had left her out cold for hours. Otherwise, she was perfectly fine.

The night stretched on for seemingly endless hours as they worked to clean up the mess. Owen did what he could to be of use during the time that Ava remained unconscious. He gave Tom his statement. Then the marshal explained what happened to their riflemen.

"We were ready, waiting for the signal," Tom said. "Then that bastard brought out Anna. I knew at that point that we didn't stand a chance. I'm not sure who sent off that first shot. I assumed it was Aaron."

Owen didn't bother telling him that it was Haley. On their walk back to Occasus, she'd admitted to firing before the signal because she knew she could make the shot. Tears stained her face as she insisted that if it hadn't been for Lily's force field, the shot would have hit its target. That had been the only reason she fired, giving away the shooters' presence.

"Once Alex sent those beasts out and Silas told us to run," Tom continued, "we did. We couldn't stay. You know that, right?"

Owen nodded to reassure him. That had always been the plan. If the Druids knew of the rifle team's location and sent out beasts, they'd have too little to defend themselves. They'd been meant to help against flesh and blood, not against supernatural creatures.

"You made the right call," he said, even as his mind screamed of their cowardice. Haley, Aaron, Devon, and Logan had stayed. They'd not been afraid of the beasts. They'd defied the agreement and stayed to help.

Tom told him about the sprint back to Occasus. The beasts had caught up to them. In the process of defending themselves, his cousin, Mitchell Garnier, fell to a hydra, while Gabe's sixteen-year-old son, Malachi, lost a leg to a bearlike beast's attack. The boy was now recovering in the vault after Silas healed what he could of the wound. He couldn't give the boy his leg back, but he could ensure there was no more danger of death.

The remaining riflemen had all sustained injuries of their own. And while Owen would typically have offered to heal them, he didn't have the heart or energy. He moved with apathy through the rest of the night.

Until Ava woke.

Silas had helped Peter get the boarders out of the vault and on their way back to their homes, leaving only Ava recovering on one of the couches in the new antechamber. With nothing else to do, Owen sat, drawing his wife's head onto his lap and waiting for her to rouse. He'd run his fingers through her thin braids, worrying about their child and her reaction to the news.

The moment she stirred, Owen prepared his already tenuous hold over his emotions. Ava's dark eyes fluttered open, and she took a long inhale as she looked up at him. Without missing a beat, she'd whispered, "Anna?" as though she'd known all through her sleep that her sister had been taken.

Owen hadn't said a word. He gave a single shake of his head.

Ava's eyes filled with tears that spilled over, but she remained silent. She didn't sob or rail as he'd expected. She simply sat up, a hand to her stomach as if to feel for the child within, and laid her head on Owen's shoulder. He'd drawn her onto his lap, holding her close as they cried together for long minutes.

Then he'd taken her down to see Anna.

Cassandra had offered her room, at which point Gabe had gone down and laid the body out properly, fixing the broken neck to appear as though she were merely sleeping. If it hadn't been for the slashes that marred her soft brown skin, she would have looked just like herself. Then the mortician left, promising to return with his hearse to recover her as soon as he saw his wife and two sons home.

When Owen led Ava into the master bedroom of Occasus, they found

Aaron and Haley sitting together on the oversized chair in the corner, crying as they clung to one another. Connor paced in front of the cold fireplace, regularly glancing at the bed with a panicked glaze over his eyes. As Ava and Owen approached, the young Frossard excused himself, barreling out of the room as he muttered, "I'm gonna fix this."

They hadn't seen Connor since.

Now, in the painful waking of a new day, Owen and Ava held one another in their bed at home. Their sleep had been fitful, the comfort of one another's presence not enough to defend against the loss of their sister. Dozing off intermittently, the morning slipped away from them, huddled as they were in their grief.

"I want to see her," Ava whispered against Owen's chest.

Owen ran his hand over her back, the cotton t-shirt she wore bunching under his touch. He kissed her temple, then murmured, "I'll call Gabe."

He left her then, rising to dress and make the call. Gabe was already at the funeral home, preparing to recover the bodies from the lake. He welcomed them to come by whenever they liked, stating that Juliet would be there to let them in and give them time with the body.

In the kitchen, Owen set about making tea for himself and his wife. They'd bonded over their mutual love of tea early in their relationship. Even when they dated, they'd begun to meet up for a morning cup and Bible study together in the university's café—Ava's way of establishing herself in his daily routine early on in their relationship. He'd found it amusing and enjoyable then. Now, twelve years later, apart from his short stint at Occasus, they maintained the routine.

While the kettle boiled, Owen prepared the loose-leaf herbal blend in the teapot. Ava was a stickler about drinking tea the "proper" way, steeping in the pot and straining over the cup. And while Owen would take tea whatever way he could get it, he didn't mind the languid process.

A sharp knock on the front door startled Owen, and he nearly dropped the glass tea jar. After carefully replacing it, he moved to answer. On the porch of their home, he found Tom and Sam, the men's heads dipped respectfully.

"Can I help you with something?" he asked after a short greeting.

His neighbors glanced at one another; then, Sam took the lead. "Gabe called and said you were awake," he explained. "We didn't want to bother you, but . . . we all spoke last night and there are some things we need to discuss."

Owen frowned, the vacancy of grief still strong. "It can't wait?"

"You know we'd wait if we could," Sam said.

Sighing, Owen motioned for them to step inside. He led them into the kitchen, offering a cup of tea. They both declined, standing around the island. Tom wore his marshal's uniform, brown trousers and tan button down under his thick brown coat, shiny silver badge glinting under the recessed lights.

So, this was an official meeting.

Owen crossed his arms loosely, wondering if he should check on Ava before beginning the conversation. He didn't want to surprise her with guests. But then, she arrived, chunky cardigan over her tee and slouchy jeans.

The marshal and reverend gave her sorrowful nods of greeting as she stepped over to Owen's side. Tom cleared his throat and deferred to Sam.

"As I said," Sam began, "we all spoke and came to some conclusions."

"Conclusions about what?" Ava asked flatly.

"About DeVerre," he said. "About its future. With—with everything that's happened, clearly, we need to make some changes. And with so many deaths, we've lost a large number of our population. While DeVerre is safer because of it . . . many of those people were the backbone of our community. They were our town council, our medical professionals, our teachers. We've lost the leadership of our town. However—"

Sam gave Tom one final look as if to ask if this was really what they wanted.

Tom nodded firmly.

Shoulders straightening, Sam looked back at Owen and Ava. "The Varons are back," he said. "Our founders, our most trusted family, have returned. And we believe that the town will rally behind them even if they were once outsiders. Especially with the additional support of the Chapelle and Garnier families."

Hearing what the reverend had left unspoken, Owen shook his head. They wanted Peter and Spencer to lead the town. They wanted those two young men, still entirely new to the spirit world and the conflicts it brought with it, to take control of an entire town. Owen trusted the brothers; he supported them, but in the short time he'd known them, he didn't see either of them taking on the role of mayor.

Upon their return to Occasus, once Peter had secured the unconscious Spencer in his room, the elder Collins brother walked around like a zombie. He'd tried to help out, working to answer questions and get people heading home. But Owen had seen how Silas had to direct the young man's every move. Peter kept zoning out, staring into space until someone gave him directions. It got so bad that, eventually, Silas just told him to get some sleep.

Owen knew it wasn't exhaustion alone that put Peter in that near-catatonic state. It was grief, fear, and shock. The night had broken him. He wasn't ready to take on the leadership of a town.

And Spencer? He let his brother dictate his every move. They were a great team, but neither Peter nor Spencer Collins could lead DeVerre out of this disaster. And Owen didn't think they'd want to.

"You don't understand," Owen said. "They're not leaders. Not like that."

Tom and Sam exchanged a look that said they'd expected this.

"Someone has to step up," Tom said.

"If it's not going to be one of them," Sam added, "we think it should be you."

Ava took a step closer to Owen as he grappled with their words. They wanted *him* to lead?

"No," Owen said without a second thought. He didn't want it any more than the Collins brothers.

"Silas told me the Warden is coming," Tom said tensely. "He made a call to his friends—to *your* friends—and they're going to send around a hundred new residents our way. We've lost a sixth of our population over the last month and a half. I've got my hands full, covering up what I can to keep out the feds. I don't have time to make sure these strangers don't screw over our town. I'm going to lose control without help."

The facts made Owen's heart constrict. A sixth of their population was dead. DeVerre was small, to begin with. That number was too high. If the state got involved, there would be dozens of investigations opened. Several of them would involve Owen.

The urge to protect himself cooled as quickly as it came. If it came to it, he'd willingly face the consequences of his actions. But he'd brought Aaron and Haley into his choices as well. Haley, the sweet, bubbly crack shot she was, had brought down many of the Druids last night. And she'd be indicted for murder because of it.

But the Warden was coming.

Owen knew firsthand how the Warden handled situations like this. They swooped in, found the mess, and cleaned it up. Their penchant for secrets made them slipperier than lawyers. And there was no doubt in his mind they would find a way to keep the state from getting involved in their affairs. But that meant they'd get involved in Tom's affairs as they worked to shape DeVerre into their town, under their control, with their rules.

Looking down at his wife, Owen worried what the town would look like when the Warden came in. DeVerre was their home. With the Druids gone, they could reclaim it. With the Warden coming in, they could lose it.

In Owen's prolonged silence, Sam took the chance to press. "You know them," he said. "They'll work with you long before they work with any of us. Fred has already agreed to step down for 'family reasons.' All we need is for you to agree to take his place as interim mayor."

"I'm grieving," Owen snapped, the first tinge of anger leaping at the responsibility they were laying at his feet. He wrapped his arm around Ava, drawing her closer. "You remember that, right? We lost our sister."

"We've all lost family, Owen," Tom returned, jaw tight.

Owen didn't want to listen. He didn't want to accept their logic. He wanted to kick them out, take his wife back to their room, and sleep away this desolation that gnawed at his heart.

Ava's gentle touch turned Owen's face to her. Her creamy brown complexion bore the purple shadows of exhaustion under her eyes and the dried tears of their grief on her cheeks. But those slanted brown eyes stared up at him with determination.

"It has to be you, Owl," she whispered in a soft tone.

Owen's heart squeezed at the nickname. She'd given it to him in college. *"Because I'm so wise?"* he'd teased.

"Because you share the first two letters of your names. And because you blink like an owl," she'd returned sarcastically. *"Slow and steady, like you're bored of every conversation before it begins."*

Here, in their kitchen, Owen held his wife closer. "I don't want it," he told her, keeping his voice low.

"I know," she said tenderly. "But you're the only one I'd trust to do it right."

Owen wanted to refuse, to pull away from Ava and walk out of the house. He always went to the lake when he needed to think, when he needed to get away. Now, the lake was tainted by the death of Anna. He didn't think he'd ever return.

With the thought of his sister-in-law in his mind, Owen turned to DeVerre's marshal and reverend. "Interim?" he repeated the term with purpose. "Meaning this isn't forever?"

Sam nodded almost hopefully. "We just need someone to help us get the town back on its feet while these newcomers make their home here."

Drawing in a quick, steadying breath, Owen accepted the job.

CHAPTER THIRTY-SEVEN

Spencer

The first thing Spencer registered was pain. A sharp, throbbing pain at the back of his head. Then he noticed the weight that pressed against his legs, trapping them as he tried to shift.

Spencer blinked drowsily at the gray light filtering through his window. He tried to lift his head to see what obstructed his legs, but it screamed in protest, and he groaned.

A gasp burst into the air, and the weight on his legs disappeared. "Peter!" Cassandra yelled.

Raising a hand to rub his eyes, Spencer finally woke fully. He found Cassandra standing over him at his bedside. Her hazel eyes were wide and her breathing rapid.

"Are you okay?" she asked.

It took a few moments for Spencer to remember what had happened. The lake. The Veil. The light. The wind. His blackout.

That explained why his head hurt so much.

Starting to push himself up in his bed, Spencer grunted against the pain. Cassandra instantly reached out to rest his pillow against the headboard and help him lean back. "I'm all right, Cassie," he said hoarsely. His vision swam, and the back of his head seared like it was on fire.

Desperate pounding erupted outside the room just before Peter exploded through the door. Hair disheveled and eyes wild, he visibly relaxed when he saw Spencer sitting up. "Oh, thank God!" he exclaimed, then looked disapprovingly at Cassandra. "I thought something bad happened."

Cassandra raised her brow. "You're the one who said to yell if he woke up."

With a dismissive wave, Peter pushed the rest of the way into the room. He rounded the bed and plopped against the headboard next to Spencer. "How you feelin', kid?" he asked.

"Not great," Spencer admitted. He brushed some hair out of his eyes. "I feel like my head's about to split open."

"That's probably because it *did* split open," Peter said.

Spencer frowned as Cassandra took a seat on the mattress next to him. "You had a *small* gash," she explained. "It was rather bloody, but I got it to close up."

"You healed it?" Spencer asked.

She nodded.

He reached out to tap her thigh. "Thanks."

A soft smile drew the corner of her mouth up, but it didn't reach her eyes.

Remembering the rest of the night before he'd lost consciousness, Spencer didn't doubt the atmosphere around DeVerre would be somber for quite some time.

"What happened?" Spencer asked, then pointed to the back of his head. "After this, I mean."

"You saw that the Veil was torn?" Peter asked.

Spencer nodded.

"Well . . ." Peter looked to Cassandra, then cleared his throat. "Things got kind of crazy. The nyct—those bat-beasts—they kept coming out of the lake. Cass managed to get them under control and put a temporary seal on the Veil."

Though Spencer was impressed, Cassandra didn't look proud of herself. "Temporary?" he asked.

Cassandra's fingers went to her right hand, then fell away when they didn't find the ring on her finger anymore. "It can't ever truly be closed again," she said. "I managed to sort of . . . tie the curtain shut to keep beasts from pouring out of it whenever they want."

"I thought beasts were only created when a Wielder summoned them," Spencer said.

"Apparently, it only happens when a Veil has been torn," she said. "The ritual is effectively summoning the essence of the Spectral, so it summons their children at the same time."

"Which is why they were all nyct," Peter added.

Spencer remembered the rift-form that had shimmered around Cassandra, the image of a batlike creature, and the beasts she'd summoned when she'd saved their lives a week ago at Occasus. They had all been nyct. All the children of the Spectral that the Druids had released last night.

Scanning her, Spencer tried to see if he could notice any difference. Her posture drooped, and her dark waves cast shadows over her face. She chewed on the inside of her cheek, drawing out that almost dimple of hers. Without a ring to twist, she tugged on the cuff of her shirt's sleeve. Aside from the worry and sorrow that haunted her like a wraith, she looked completely normal.

"The Druids are all dead," Peter said. "So, we're cult-free in DeVerre." He spoke with his usual light sarcasm, but Spencer could hear the strain in his brother's voice.

"Connor's disappeared, though," he added.

Spencer furrowed his brow. "Why? I mean, why would he leave?"

Peter shrugged. "Maybe he needed to get away from it all," he suggested. The bitter tilt to his tone made Spencer wonder if *he* wanted to get away too. "He, uh—last night, he told me that he'd been the one to kill his dad. When it all went haywire, I mean. The Druids refused to surrender, so we dealt with it, you know? And Connor—he said that he saw his dad and . . . after what happened with Anna, he said he wanted it to be him who ended it. So . . . it was."

Resting his head against the headboard, Spencer grimaced at the thought. Connor had killed his father. No wonder he wanted to get away. After everything that had happened to the young man, who wouldn't want to disappear for a while?

"What about his mom?" Spencer asked, suddenly remembering Giana Frossard.

"She wasn't there," Peter said. "Connor mentioned that too. He thinks his dad sent her away as a backup plan. Said something about a powerful aunt in California."

Spencer frowned. "But the rest of them are gone?"

"Yep," Peter said. "Aaron, Haley, and her brothers helped with that. The nyct took care of the rest."

Cassandra's head drooped.

Spencer tapped her knee. "What?"

"I was controlling the nyct," she said morosely.

Spencer raised his brow in surprise. "All of them?"

Wrapping her arms around herself, Cassandra nodded. She explained how she'd given the ultimatum, and the Druids chose to fight. She'd connected with the hundreds of nyct that had emerged from the Veil, tethering them to herself. It had taken no time at all to bring down the last of the Druids with the beasts' help.

"What now?" Spencer asked when she was through. "With the Druids gone, what's left to do?"

Cassandra turned to Peter, who sighed. "I got a call from Owen about twenty minutes ago," he said. "Tomorrow morning at church, Sam is planning to hold a bit of a dual sermon and town hall meeting. They're going to explain the situation to everyone. DeVerre will know everything. They'd . . . they'd like us to be there."

"Because we're Varons?"

Peter nodded. "They want us to lend our backing to their plans. And to Owen as the interim mayor."

Though the idea surprised Spencer at first, he cocked his head appreciatively. "I can get behind that," he said. "At least it's not you or me."

"Yeah, well, Owen said that's only because he told them we wouldn't want it."

"He was right, wasn't he?"

Peter rubbed a hand along his neck. "Yeah." He said it almost begrudgingly, like he *did* want the job but knew he shouldn't.

"Anyway," he continued, "Silas said that the Warden is in the process of sending fifty to sixty families our way. That means that DeVerre is about to have an influx of a little more than one hundred new residents. They want Owen to help facilitate the transition from being a 'normal' small town to a Warden town."

"I thought DeVerre *was* a Warden town," Spencer said.

"That was over a century ago, Spence." Peter shifted beside him. "Things have changed in the Warden since then. They've gotten more regulated and closed-minded from the sounds of it. Besides—" His eyes flashed to Cassandra. "We have a Spectral now."

With the shift in conversation, Spencer felt his chest constrict. He turned to Cassandra, raising his chin to prompt her. "Are you—do we know for sure?" he asked.

Perched on the edge of the mattress, Cassandra looked about ready to run out of the room. She tipped one shoulder up in a noncommittal shrug but said nothing.

Peter slapped Spencer on the chest. "I'll give you two a minute," he muttered. Then he got up, tromped through the room, and shut the door behind him.

Alone, Spencer turned back to Cassandra. She stared at the floor, silent.

Running a hand through his hair, Spencer did his best to lighten his tone. "Something's wrong with Peter," he said.

Cassandra's eyes flashed to his face, confused.

"He left us alone in my room without making a joke about keeping our hands to ourselves?" Spencer shook his head. "That's a sure sign of trouble."

A pained chuckle escaped Cassandra. "This isn't the time for jokes, Spencer," she said, but he could hear the gratitude in her voice. She needed to know that he wasn't afraid. She needed him to be strong and sure when she was nervous and unsteady.

Nudging her, Spencer began to shift. "Scoot," he said. "I want out from under these blankets."

It took Cassandra's help to get out of bed. Though she'd closed the wound of his head injury, it'd only healed the surface damage. His head spun as he tried to slide off the bed too quickly, and she had to hold him steady as his equilibrium caught up.

Eventually, they both sat on the edge of the mattress, their legs dangling over the side. A slight pressure remained at the base of his skull, but he took a breath, and it subsided.

Taking her hand, Spencer laced their fingers together. "Okay," he said, meeting her wary gaze. "Tell me. Have you confirmed that the Spectral chose you?"

A long, tense pause hung between them. Cassandra's eyes dropped to their hands, resting on the bed between them. Without the ring on her finger anymore, her hand looked shockingly bare. "Not yet," she whispered.

Spencer narrowed his eyes but didn't respond.

After a heavy intake of breath, Cassandra shook her head. "I don't feel any different," she admitted. "There was a moment last night when I thought . . . but it went away and now I don't know."

"Is that a good sign?" he asked, aware that she knew little more than he did about Spectrals or Vessels.

Cassandra pressed her lips together as though she didn't want to say the next part. "I spoke with Silas about it, and he told me it can take some time," she said. "The connection doesn't always . . . it doesn't always manifest right away. He said that oftentimes, the Spectral's release is so taxing for them that they go into this hibernation period."

"So, they, what? They make the connection, then they just . . . disappear?"

"Essentially."

Spencer tightened his hold on Cassandra subconsciously. He forced himself to loosen his grip when he realized his knuckles were almost white. "And how long does it take for them to . . . recover, or whatever?" he asked more calmly than he felt.

Cassandra's lips turned up in a cynical grin. "There's no definitive answer to that," she said.

"So, Silas didn't know?"

"He said they're all different. Every Spectral has its own . . . 'rebirth' after the connection. He said it happens even with the, uh—with the heirs."

Spencer's gaze shot to his bedroom door, thinking of Peter and the Varon heirs. "What heirs?" he asked.

"That's something I didn't tell you," she whispered.

He looked back at her.

"It's another reason I think I should leave," she muttered

His grip tightened again. "I thought we'd taken care of that."

Cassandra arched an eyebrow as though telling him she didn't appreciate his more possessive reaction. He loosened his hold but didn't let go of her. Her expression didn't soften. "Spencer, you need to understand that I will never be free of this," she said. "Once the Spectral makes a connection, it's with the entirety of that Vessel's bloodline."

Spencer didn't like the sound of that.

"Silas told me that . . . every child I have will be a potential Vessel," she said. "If I choose to have a family, my children will be heirs that could take on the Spectral upon my death. I know—" She cut herself off, then dropped his gaze and started over. "I know that we're not—that you and I just . . ."

Understanding, Spencer released Cassandra's hand. He slid closer to her. "You're saying that if we decide to be together, I'll have to be okay with the fact that my family will always be tied to this Spectral?" he said.

Cassandra stared at him, lips parted as she scanned his face. Their sides pressed together even though he hadn't wrapped his arm around her.

"I'm not worried about it," he promised her.

Drawing her head back as though to get a better look at him, Cassandra narrowed her gaze. A slight smirk tugged at her mouth. "Because you don't intend for this to last?" she asked.

Spencer couldn't help grinning at her backhanded question. "I've already told you once," he said. "You're never allowed to leave me."

Her head tilted in consideration. "What if *you* leave me?"

Spencer leaned in to press a kiss to her cheek, right by her ear. "Spectral or no Spectral," he whispered, "I'll be here."

Something between a sigh of relief and a sob escaped Cassandra, and suddenly, her arms were around him. Spencer followed her lead, holding her close as she buried her face against his neck. That soothing, smoky scent of vanilla and the woods enveloped him. He brushed his fingers through her hair, comforting her as she clung to him. He didn't think she was crying. Her body remained still, and her breathing was even. She just seemed to need his touch, the surety that he was there, and he would always be there.

So, Spencer held Cassandra, a promise to both of them that no matter what happened—Spectral or no Spectral—he would never leave her, and she would never leave him.

CHAPTER THIRTY-EIGHT

Peter

Without really knowing why, Peter chose to stand on the porch of Occasus. He thought maybe it had something to do with his time in the Frossard vault. Being locked up for almost five days, not seeing the sky or the sun or anything but that tiny study, made him feel stir-crazy after only seconds of standing inside any building.

Then again, it might have had more to do with the memories those walls of Occasus held that made him anxious to get outside.

Resting against the porch railing, Peter found himself breaking the promise he'd made only yesterday. He twisted the Varon ring—back and forth, back and forth—as he stared blindly at the world beyond Occasus's gates. He supposed he had reason to be mentally unstable enough to obsessively worry the ring. He'd not only killed a bunch of people over the last two weeks, but he'd also lost one of his closest friends.

Peter huffed at himself. Yeah, he had plenty of reason to worry. Plenty of reason to lose his mind.

Forcing himself to leave the ring alone, he ran his hands through his hair. It was like he couldn't stand still. He kept shifting around even as he stood in the same spot. Adjusting his coat, scrubbing a hand over his face, tapping out sporadic rhythms on the railing. He highly considered letting himself sprint from the porch, out of the gates, and into the woods just to see how far his excessive anxiety would push him.

Peter stared at his hands dangling over the rail. The gold ring mocked him. He'd been an idiot to put it on. He should have brought it back and given it to Spencer. By some miracle, his brother had become the sane one. Spencer, the boy who couldn't sleep without a nightlight until he was sixteen, no longer seemed afraid of anything.

No, now it was Peter who jumped at every sound and sudden movement.

Courage, Silas had said. This morning, when Peter had gotten his coffee, the man had told him about the call with his Warden friends. Then he reminded him of his new role as the Varon leader. He'd pointed to the ring, stating that Benedict's line bore the dagger in their crest to remind them of their undeniable courage.

Peter's eyes drifted up to the gates of Occasus, where the sigil from his ring was mirrored. The dagger, initial, and star. And all he could think was, *"I'm not ready."*

Courage.

What a joke.

The Varon ring didn't belong to him. At this point, it belonged to Spencer more than him. He was better at all of this stuff, anyway. He could fight better, he was more levelheaded, and he had that steady presence that engendered trust.

But Peter? He was a chaotic, erratic screwup.

If the Varon heir was supposed to be some grand, powerful leader, then it wasn't Peter. Not after last night.

He'd stood there.

He'd just stood there like an idiot, gaping while the Druids threatened Anna's life. If he were a real leader, he would have done something. He had the power for it, didn't he? The Varon lineage was filled with power; that's what everyone kept saying.

And Peter had just stood there, doing nothing.

He'd let Lily kill Anna while he did nothing.

Even Connor had offered himself for Anna; he'd hurried forward, demanding her life, willing to sacrifice himself in the process. And when Anna had fallen, Connor had reacted while Peter stood by and let it all happen.

Peter was worse than a failure. He was a coward.

The low rumble of an engine reached Peter's ears, startling him out of his stupor. A black SUV crested the hill and rolled through the gates of Occasus. It came to a halt next to the Jeep, and he watched apathetically as Connor jumped out.

"Where've you been?" Peter asked, his voice sounding empty to his ears.

Connor shut the Land Rover's door with a *thunk* before tromping up the porch steps. "I went to check the vault," he said flatly. "As the new owner, I thought it'd be a good idea to take stock of the place. You're the only one I'm inviting in, by the way."

"I'm flattered," Peter said, pressing his thumb against the band of his ring. "You find anything interesting?"

Coming to stand at Peter's side, Connor leaned against the rail. "Some things," he said, "but not what I was looking for."

"What were you looking for?"

"The codex."

"And it wasn't there?"

Connor shook his head.

"Do you think your dad had it at the lake?"

"I already double-checked," he said. "It's gone. Which means someone took it *before* my dad died."

"How do you know that?"

"Because when he died—when I killed him," he corrected as though reminding himself that it was the truth, "the vault instantly passed to me. Which means all previously invited guests were revoked access."

"Right." Peter tugged at his collar. "Think it was your mom?"

Connor shrugged. "Her or Danielle."

"Danielle?" Peter frowned. "Like, the chick who watched the dogs and had a huge crush on Spence?"

Connor didn't bother to confirm it. "Aside from my mom, Danielle was the only one missing at the lake last night. My best guess is that she was part of the contingency plan with Mom," he said, then added tensely, "It was her job to keep an eye on Anna."

"As leverage against you?" Peter asked.

Connor nodded. "As a Sage, she was dangerous. I knew that if I tried anything, Danielle would make Anna pay for it. Then when you two showed up, it gave her a chance to get in with you. Dad told her to see if either of you would take an interest."

Peter snarled at the thought. "You Druids aren't big on romance, are you?" he grumbled. "So, what? She was never a fan of *Wenzel & Frankly*?"

"No, she was a huge fan," Connor said. "That's part of what made her such an ideal candidate. From what I gathered, she actually had a thing for Spencer from the start."

"Not surprising, I guess," Peter said bitterly. "So, you think your dad told Danielle to deliver Anna, then grab the codex and get out of Dodge with your mom in case things didn't go their way?"

"I do."

"Great."

"The codex would have been helpful," Connor said. "But there are other things in the vault that will help us too. If—if it's all right with you and Spencer, I'd like to bring those things here. To your vault."

Peter was surprised, but he shrugged. "Sure, man, whatever works."

"And . . ." Connor picked at the porch rail. "I'm on break from classes for the next week, but I'll have to go back to Spokane for the rest of medical school after that."

Scanning the young man, Peter was somehow surprised that he seemed to *want* to go back. "I didn't realize you actually wanted to be a doctor."

"I've always liked helping people, and—I mean, I just always knew that's what I wanted to do. Plus," he shrugged, "DeVerre needs a new doctor, so it may as well be me."

"Suppose so."

Connor cleared his throat nervously. "Would you mind—when I come back, you know, for break and things, would you mind if I stayed here?"

Brow rising, Peter let out a sardonic chuckle. "Dude, you just inherited a mansion. You don't want to live there?"

Immediately, Connor shook his head, and Peter understood. Why would he want to live in his family home?

Peter gave his arm a slap. "Sure, man. You can stay in my room until Silas heads home. Then the spare's all yours."

"Thanks," Connor said, and Peter could hear the profound relief that filled that one word.

Peter was about to joke about adding another vault for all the roommates they seemed to keep accumulating when Connor spoke again.

"One more thing," he said

Looking up at the young Frossard, Peter caught the seriousness in his bright blue eyes.

Angling toward him, Peter straightened, expectant. "What's up?"

"I need your help," Connor said.

"With what?"

"I need you to help me bring Anna back."

Peter gaped at him. "What?"

"We can do it," Connor said. "That's what Dad offered that phantom, Gerard. He knew how to resurrect people."

Something between hope and disbelief crowded Peter's brain. He couldn't tell if this was the young man's plunge into insanity or if he actually believed that they could do this. "H—how?" he stuttered, desperation rising in his chest.

Connor grimaced as though disappointed that Peter had asked. "I'm—I'm not entirely sure *how*," he confessed. "But I do know, the first thing we have to do is find her ghost."

Peter's heart dropped. "You think Anna's a ghost? I dunno, man, she doesn't seem like the type to cling to this world."

"She's not," Connor confirmed despite his hopeful tone. "But that doesn't mean she's not a ghost either."

"It doesn't?"

He shook his head. "Sometimes people become ghosts simply because it wasn't their time. Not dead but sleeping."

The idea resonated with something inside of Peter even as he worked to process what they were planning to do. He scratched his forehead, working through the complications they might face. "Wh—what—what about her body?" he asked.

"I'm gonna talk to Ava," Connor said. "I think I can convince her to hold off on a burial."

Peter scoffed. "I don't think you'll have to do much convincing," he muttered wryly. He pinched the bridge of his nose. "You're sure about this? You really think we can . . . resurrect the dead?"

"I know we can," Connor insisted. "I may not have the details yet, but I've heard stories about it. And between the two of us, I know we can figure it out. You're not only a Varon, you're also a Frossard. We come from the greatest Druidic family in the past century. You and me—" He held Peter's apprehensive stare with determination. "We can do this."

The possibility was too good to be true. It was absolutely insane. They had no idea if it would actually work. For all Peter knew, Alexander could have been lying the whole time about resurrecting Franklin. Who was to say that it was possible at all?

But Peter smirked. "Hey, I'm always up for doing the impossible."

*Peter & Spencer will return
in book eight of Archives of the Warden*

If you enjoyed this book,
consider leaving a review on Amazon or Goodreads.

Amazon

Goodreads

Peter's Nicknames for Spencer

& where they come from:

J.B. — Jessica "J.B." Fletcher, mystery writer and amateur sleuth *(Murder, She Wrote; television show)*

Sherlock — Sherlock Holmes, consulting detective with Scotland Yard *(Sherlock Holmes stories by Sir Arthur Conan Doyle)*

Poirot — Hercule Poirot, private investigator *(reoccurring character in Agatha Christie's mystery novels)*

Columbo — Lieutenant Columbo, police lieutenant and homicide detective *(Columbo; television show)*

Watson — Dr. John H. Watson, assistant and confidant of Sherlock Holmes *(Sherlock Holmes stories by Sir Arthur Conan Doyle)*

Matlock — Ben Matlock, defense attorney with a knack for solving the murders himself *(Matlock; television show)*

Frankly — Dr. Charles Frankly, ex-doctor turned private investigator *(Wenzel & Frankly serial by Peter and Spencer Collins)*

Glossary of Terms & Names

Aaron Lambert — *[Lam—bert]* — Middle of the three Lambert children; boyfriend of Haley Roux; mechanic

Aimee Lambert — Mother of Ava, Aaron, and Anna; previous town librarian; descendant of Yvan Rayne

Anguis — *[An—gwis]* — German Wirehaired Pointer under the care of Peter and Spencer Collins

Alexander Frossard — *[Fros—sard]* — *aka 'Alex'* — Doctor in DeVerre; husband of Giana Frossard; father of Connor Frossard; Elder of the Druidic Faction in DeVerre

Allen Clement — *[Klem-ent]* — Father of Cassandra Clement; lives in Spokane

Anna Lambert — Youngest of the three Lambert children; bartender/waitress and artist

Arthur Wenzel — *[Wen—zuhl]* — Private investigator of the online serial *Wenzel & Frankly* written by Peter and Spencer Collins

Ava Bernard — Oldest of the three Lambert children; wife of Owen Bernard; town librarian

beast — A creature summoned from the spirit world to work on behalf of a Wielder

Benjamin Powell — *aka 'Ben'* — Stepfather of Peter and Spencer Collins; second husband of Mallory Collins-Powell

Brendan Descoteaux — *[Des—co—toe]* — High school student; boyfriend of Juliet Chapelle; third victim of the hellhound attacks

Cassandra Clement — *[Kuh—san—druh]* — *aka 'Cass' or 'Cassie'* — Best friend of Diane Larkin; Wielder

Charles Frankly — Ex-doctor and private investigator of the online serial *Wenzel & Frankly* written by Peter and Spencer Collins

Connor Frossard — Prior best friend of Anna Lambert; medical student

Danielle MacDonald — Member of Anna Lambert's Bible study; waitress at MacDonald's Diner; mega-fan of *Wenzel & Frankly*

David Collins — Late father of Peter and Spencer Collins; mechanic for the United States Navy

Debra Mercier — *aka 'Debbie'* — First cousin of Cassandra Clement's mother; descendant of the Sauveterre family; Druid

DeVerre, WA — *[Deh—Vair]* — Small town in northeastern Washington State

Diane Larkin — Late great-aunt of Peter and Spencer Collins; left the brothers her estate upon her death

Druids — *aka 'Children of Gaia'* — A cult of Wielders intent on releasing the spirit world upon the physical world

Elijah Lawrence — Son of John William Lawrence; reverend and theologian from Bushmills, Ireland, in the early 1600s

Franklin Alarie — *[Uh-lar-e]* — Older brother of Gerard Alarie; suspected murderer and Druid

Frederic Chapelle — *[Sha—pell]* — Original reverend of DeVerre; cousin of Matthias Varon

Gabriel Chapelle — *aka 'Gabe'* — Mortician; younger brother of Samuel Chapelle

Gabriel Varon — The First Varon

Gerard Alarie — Phantom from 1950s; tethered to Occasus by Cassandra Clement

ghost — The lingering spirit of a dead Wielder with unfinished business in the physical world

Giana Frossard — *[Gee—ah—nah]* — *aka 'Gia'* — Friend of Anna Lambert; wife of Alexander Frossard; mother of Connor Frossard

Haley Roux — *[Rue]* — Girlfriend of Aaron Lambert; friend and co-worker of Anna Lambert

Harmony, Saskatchewan — *[Suh—ska—chew—on]* — Original hometown of the founders of DeVerre, WA

hellhound — Wolflike beast from the spirit world

House of Occasus — *[Oh—kay—sus]* — Diane Larkin's home, left to the Collins brothers; previously built and owned by the Varon family

Hunter Durand — Deputy in DeVerre

hydra — *[hi—druh]* — Snakelike beast from the spirit world

Isaac Clement — Older brother of Cassandra Clement

Jacob Howser — *aka 'Jake'* — Best friend to Isaac Clement; ex-boyfriend of Cassandra Clement

Jessica Calderon — *[Call—der—on]* — *aka 'Jess'* — Distant relative of Thomas Garnier; second victim of the hellhound attacks

John William Lawrence — Theologian, co-founder of the Spiritualists, and founder of the Warden

Julianne Clement — Mother of Cassandra Clement; cousin of Debra Mercier; descendant of the Sauveterre family

Juliet Chapelle — High school student; daughter of Samuel Chapelle; girlfriend of Brendan Descoteaux

Lee Frossard — Town veterinarian in the early 1900s; brother of Lloyd Frossard

Lloyd Frossard — Town doctor in the early 1900s; grandfather of Alexander Frossard

Mallory Collins-Powell — Mother of Peter and Spencer Collins; remarried to Benjamin Powell; lives in Norfolk, VA

Matthew Varon — *[Vair—en]* — Previous mayor of DeVerre; father of Michael Varon

Matthias Varon — Founder of DeVerre

Michael Mercier — *aka 'Mike'* — Husband of Debbie Mercier

Michael Varon — Great-grandson of Matthais Varon; last of the Varon line

Nex — German Wirehaired Pointer under the care of Peter and Spencer Collins

Owen Bernard — Husband of Ava Bernard; ex-Warden employee; originally from Harmony, Saskatchewan; Wielder

Peter Collins-Varon — *aka 'Pete'* — Older of the two Collins brothers; writer

Phillip Collins — Grandfather of Peter and Spencer Collins; brother of Diane Larkin

phantom — A ghost that has been tethered to a specific location in the physical world

Porthaven, ME — Small, Warden-run town in the state of Maine

Rene Mercier — Daughter of Debra and Michael Mercier; second cousin of Cassandra Clement

Samuel Chapelle — *aka 'Sam'* — Reverend in DeVerre

Sandy Clement — Wife of Isaac Clement; sister-in-law of Cassandra Clement

scylla — *[sky—luh]* — Cephalopod-like beast from the spirit world

Seraphine Frossard-Varon — Illegitimate daughter of Lloyd Frossard; secret wife of Michael Varon

Spencer Collins-Varon — *aka 'Spence'* — Younger of the two Collins brothers; writer

spirit world — A parallel world that exists alongside the physical world

Taylor Ozanne — *[Oh—zawn]* — Farmer; first victim of the hellhound attacks

Thomas Garnier — *aka 'Tom'* — Marshal in DeVerre

Tony MacDonald — Owner of MacDonald's Diner; town councilman; uncle of Danielle MacDonald

Travis Mercier — Son of Debra and Michael Mercier; second cousin of Cassandra Clement

valravn — *[val-rav-en]* — Birdlike beast from the spirit world

Veil — Specific locations around the world where the boundary between the spirit world and the physical world is thin

The Warden — An organization of Wielders dedicated to protecting the spirit world from the control of the Druids

wendigo — *[when—de—go]* — Deerlike beast from the spirit world

Wenzel & Frankly — Serial historical-fantasy blog written by Peter and Spencer Collins

Wielder — A human with the ability to wield the spirit world

William Larkin — *aka 'Liam'* — Late husband of Diane Larkin; writer; researcher of history and theology

Yvan Rayne — *[Ee-vahn Rain]* — Original record keeper in DeVerre; the Lambert siblings' ancestor

Acknowledgments

After just three years of publishing, I feel so immeasurably blessed to have so many wonderful people brought into my life by this journey.

I am eternally grateful to my readers who gave my silly little (extremely complicated and wild) series a chance. It has been my dream to find such wonderful people. I will endeavor that each of my books will live up to your expectations.

Huge thanks to my husband, Josh. You're always there and always listening. Your encouragement and support has been amazing from the start, but as you've taken a more active role in my work this last year, I can safely say, I've become a better and more productive writer.

Thank you to my family and friends who are always so supportive of me.

My editor, Brittany, deserves all the thanks and applause. Britt, you have made this publication journey so special. I owe my improvement over the last three years to you!

Thank you to all my beta readers for this one: AJ, Alexandra, Anne, Lydia, Paulina, and Rachelle. All of your advice and feedback helped me make this story better, and I'm so grateful for the time you took to help ensure Peter and Spencer's story is satisfying.

And as always, thank you to God. My prayer is that these stories bring you glory and that they inspire others to deepen their faith.

About the Author

V. K. Dixon writes fantasy and romance novels filled with found family, lasting love, and unique magic. She believes that the extraordinary gives us a deeper desire for the things beyond us; for the things of God. Faith, art, and community are her guiding values as she pursues the vision on her heart.